The Devil's Playground

K. Turner

Copyright @2025 by K. Turner

ISBN: 979-8-9861997-9-5

Author website: kturnerauthor.com

For my family, who always worried that my nightmares wouldn't lead to anything good. Turns out, they were just research regarding character development.

This one's for you!

Chapter 1:

Sarah's mind wandered back to that day when she and Daniel had looked around at the office. They were shown seats, and had been asked to wait. They couldn't help but notice that it was a cold, dreary place. A place where hope went to die. Nervously, she had sat there chewing off her manicured fingers, while Daniel rocked back and forth in his chair, constantly checking his watch as he wondered what was taking so long.

"Do you think something is wrong?" Sarah had asked. Her mind wandered to dark places, the echoes of her childhood struggles.

Daniel turned to her, a hint of a smile playing on his lips. "No, I'm sure everything is fine," he said. Sarah couldn't help but notice that the smile didn't reach his eyes. She knew that he was worried too, about the possibility that things weren't going to work out.

Sarah rose from her chair, and walked to the window. *There,* she thought to herself. *That's where we first met the girls. Where we watched them play as we talked with their social worker, Erin.* Erin had been friendly, and answered all their questions as best she could. She'd been encouraging, too, despite the girls having been in their sixth home in just a year of foster care. Erin said she couldn't understand it, that the girls seemed so sweet;

however, they just seemed to have issues that the foster parents couldn't understand and deal with. But Sarah had understood, as she too had navigated this system as a child. The countless homes that welcomed her with open arms one moment, only to be turned out the next. People who only wanted a paycheck, nothing more. They offered food and a bed, and if something—or someone—better came along, she was out the door without so much as a goodbye.

The agency supervisor, Miss Grimley, finally entered the office, taking a seat and motioning for Sarah to do the same. She appeared as cold as her office, a woman with a heart turned to stone. Her voice, a grating rasp, was the complete opposite of Erin's. Sarah couldn't help but wonder why she worked with children. She wondered if Miss Grimley had ever been cheerful or if she'd always been as miserable as she seemed. She'd also noticed during their visits, that the children seemed to live in fear of her, especially the younger ones. Sarah's heart broke for them; she wished she could take them all home.

"So, your application has been approved, and we will be recommending you to the court for adoption of the two sisters, Lily and Rose Marchant," Miss Grimley stated, her expression remaining impassive. *Finally, those two troublemakers will be someone else's problem.*

Daniel and Sarah released the breaths they hadn't realized they were holding, embracing each other with smiles as their family finally began to take shape. They had tried unsuccessfully for a couple of years to have children of their own. It was only after testing that Sarah learned she would be unable to bear children. At the time, she was inconsolable, even blaming herself for things that were clearly out of her control. But in time, she saw it as an opportunity. They could still adopt. And she could provide for a child, or as it turned out, children, what had never been provided for her at an early age.

As Miss Grimley continued talking, Sarah's mind drifted back to that day when they had first met the girls. Lily was thirteen, her face already marked by a premature seriousness. Rose, five years younger, was a bundle of untamed energy, her laughter a rare burst of sunshine in their bleak existence. Despite the harsh environment which they had been dealt, their bond was as strong as the iron railings that had caged them.

"You'll of course need to appear in court in order to finalize the adoption with the judge," Miss Grimley stated, handing Daniel the paper with the date and time.

"Of course, we'll be there," Sarah heard Daniel reply, a smile spreading across her face as she remained immersed in the memories that had led them to this moment.

She'd seen the trepidation in Lily's eyes, and assumed them to be from past hardships. Little did Sarah know, however, that a cold dread had settled in Lily's heart. This was a chance to have a family again, a glimmer of hope in a world that had been painted in shades of gray. But with hope came fear. Fear of the unknown, fear of rejection, and above all, the fear of losing Rose. Lily knew children her age were often overlooked, like senior dogs at a shelter, where puppies were always the first to be chosen. Her young shoulders bore the weight of their small world, and the prospect of change was both terrifying and exhilarating.

Rose, meanwhile, was a tempest of emotions. Excitement bubbled within her, coloring her world with vibrant hues. A family, a home, perhaps even a dog—these were concepts she'd only dared to dream of. Yet, beneath the surface of her joy, Sarah's heart ached as she recognized the deep-rooted fear of abandonment lurking in Rose's young eyes.

After spending some time with the girls, Sarah smiled, her eyes softening as she had looked at them. There was a warmth in her gaze that had been foreign to them for so long. "We'd like to take both of you," she said, her voice gentle. Sarah's world had revolved around the dream of motherhood. Years of longing had tempered her optimism, but her desire to nurture a child had never waned. Her heart swelled with compassion as she looked at the two girls, their eyes mirroring a vulnerability that tugged at her soul.

"We'd like you both to be a part of our family," Daniel chimed in. Daniel was a man of quiet strength. His heart ached with every failed attempt to conceive a child of his own. He'd poured his energy into his work, building a secure life for a family that hadn't materialized. Now, as he stood there staring at these two girls, a surge of hope and trepidation washed over him. He longed to provide the love and stability for the family they had always dreamed of.

A hush fell over the room. Hope, like a fragile bird, took flight in Lily's chest. A new life, a family – it was almost too good to be true. Rose's eyes widened in disbelief, her face a mask of shock and delight. Miss Grimley's expression however, had remained impassive, as if such displays of emotion were beneath her.

The coming weeks became a flurry of activity, a mix of excited anticipation and quiet apprehension. Lily and Rose, under their foster mother's watchful gaze, emptied their small room, a space that had shifted from sanctuary to a stifling cage. Their few belongings were quickly gathered, a testament to their transient lives.

In the courtroom, a wave of bittersweet relief washed over them. The foster care system, a chapter etched with both hardship and resilience, was finally closed. With the judge's gavel, the adoption was official. After receiving several grateful embraces, they settled into the car, leaving the past behind. The world outside shimmered in a golden light, a vibrant promise against the drab backdrop of their former existence. In the backseat, Lily and Rose, their hands intertwined, moved forward into their new life.

The car eased to a halt, revealing a storybook farmhouse nestled amidst several blossoming trees. It stood there, a picture of aged grace, its porch draped in flowering vines, a gazebo style living room extending a welcoming curve. Lily and Rose exchanged tight, anxious glances. The scenic view before them was a world apart from the chaotic hum of their past foster homes. A familiar chill of dread, a constant companion of uncertain mornings, settled over them. Sarah and Daniel, their faces radiating warmth, greeted them with gentle hands, their touch a comforting presence against the rising tide of fear.

The interior of the home was a gentle explosion of color. Soft shades of green and blue painted the walls, while sunlight streamed through lace curtains, casting dancing shadows on the polished wooden floor. The air was thick with the enticing aroma of something baking, a scent utterly foreign to the institutional type foster homes they had come to know. Lily and Rose, their senses overwhelmed, clung to each other.

Their new rooms were a revelation. Large windows framed a lush green garden, promising endless hours of exploration. Toys, soft and inviting, were scattered across the floor, a stark difference from the sparse furnishings of their foster homes. Bookshelves lined one wall, filled with colorful volumes that whispered of adventure and knowledge. As they took in their surroundings, a flicker of hope ignited in their hearts, a small flame against the chill of their past.

Sarah emerged from the kitchen, carrying a towering cake adorned with swirls of creamy frosting. Its sweet scent of vanilla, strawberry, and something they couldn't quite place filled the room. Lily and Rose's eyes widened in disbelief. Food had always been a source of tension in their previous homes, where sometimes the portions had been meager and flavorless. This cake was a masterpiece, a testament to a world they could scarcely imagine. With each bite, their laughter grew louder, a joyous sound that echoed through the halls. For the first time in what felt like forever, they felt a lightness in their chests, a sense of belonging.

As night fell, the home was bathed in the soft glow of lamplight. The rhythmic patter of rain against the windowpane was a soothing lullaby. Curled up in their new beds, surrounded by the comforting weight of their blankets, Lily and Rose felt a peace they had never known. It was as if the world had finally slowed down, allowing them to simply exist. In the quiet darkness, a sense of safety enveloped them, a warmth that seeped into their souls. For the first time in their young lives, they felt loved, cherished, and truly at home.

Lily's mind drifted back to that first day, the day they met their new parents. Rose's voice, a soft whisper, echoed in her memory. "Someone's coming," she'd breathed, a faint smile playing on her lips. Lily trusted Rose's instincts implicitly; they were a silent language, a shared understanding forged in necessity. It had kept them safe on more than one occasion. "I won't let anyone separate us," She reassured her, drawing her sister into a comforting embrace. A sense of unwavering unity had filled her, the certainty of their unbreakable bond. She lay there wrapped up in her new bed smiling as sleep claimed her.

Chapter 2:

It was the beginning of summer, and Lily and Rose were enjoying the freedom that came with the school break. Their new home, a cozy farmhouse situated just outside of the town limits, was a far cry from the cold, gray walls of their previous foster homes. Daniel and Sarah, their adoptive parents, were everything they had hoped for and more. They showered the girls with affection, their hearts overflowing with a love they thought had been lost to them forever.

The sprawling backyard quickly became their favorite place, due in part to their new swingset. The rope swing, a rustic pendulum hanging from the old oak at the yard's center, offered a wilder thrill. And then there was the treehouse, a rustic fort already brimming with Rose's treasures. Up there, amidst the rustling leaves, peanut butter and jelly sandwiches became a feast, shared with the birdsong and the flutter of passing butterflies. From their lofty perch, legs swinging freely, they watched their new mother's quiet industry. Sometimes she would be tending to the vibrant flowerbeds,or at other times, hanging the laundry so that it could dance in the gentle breeze.

One sun-drenched afternoon found them in town, the promise of exploration hanging in the air. While their mother attended to the grocery shopping, Lily and Rose were granted an hour of freedom to wander the other stores in the shopping center. "Just stay together," Sarah had told them. "I won't be too long."

Walking down the sidewalk, they came across a small bookstore, a haven of literary treasures. Lily, with her quiet passion for well-worn classics, felt an immediate pull to the shelves. Rose, however, her eyes wide with wonder, was drawn to the magical worlds leaping from illustrated pages, where mermaids sang and dragons soared the skies.

As the first few weeks in their new home passed, Lily and Rose were excited to hear that their new extended family would soon be visiting. They had already met Sarah's mother, their new grandmother, who lived nearby and fell in love with her immediately; though Sarah had explained that she was actually her adoptive mother. Sarah also told them about her time spent in foster care. This seemed to bring their newly forming bond a little closer, as now they had something in common. Even if their shared experiences had not been ideal. Their grandparents on Daniel's side though, whom they had only seen in photos, were coming from across the country. They were also looking forward to meeting their cousins, whom they had only heard stories about.

"We finally have a family," Rose whispered, a single tear tracing a path down her cheek as she hugged Lily. Daniel and Sarah's hearts clenched. They gathered the girls into a warm, encompassing embrace. "And we are so lucky to have you join our family," Sarah said, her voice a little shaky, tears finally overflowing.

The day of their family's arrival finally came as a nervous excitement filled the air. Soon, the doorbell chimed, and a wave of warmth and welcoming smiles flooded the living room. Lily and Rose were thrilled to finally meet their grandparents on Daniel's side, whose gentle eyes and kind words mirrored the loving descriptions their parents had painted. Stories were shared, hands were held, and the initial awkwardness melted away like morning mist under the sun.

The arrival of their cousins unleashed a flurry of playful energy. Suddenly, the living room transformed into a playground, with giggles echoing as they built towering block castles, chased each other through the hallway, and invented fantastical games. It was a fun-filled day, a kaleidoscope of new faces, shared snacks, and a delightful whirlwind of activities that left Lily and Rose breathless with joy and a strengthening sense of belonging.

The week-long visit was filled with joy and laughter. The family went on a picnic, visited a local water park, and spent countless hours playing games and telling stories. Lily and Rose felt loved and cherished, surrounded by the warmth of their new family. And while not a day went by that they weren't grateful to finally, once again, be a part of a family. A family that was loving and supportive.

The visit from their extended family so far had been a joyous occasion. Lily and Rose had reveled in the attention, soaking up the stories and the feeling of finally belonging. However, as the week began its gentle slide towards the end, a subtle shift in the atmosphere began to cast a faint shadow over the joyous occasion.

Daniel's father, their newly acquired grandfather, who had initially been so warm and engaging, gradually retreated into a quiet solitude. His smiles became less frequent, his participation in conversations minimal. A noticeable distance grew, a subtle withdrawal that didn't go unnoticed by the observant eyes of Lily.

Adding to this growing unease was his newfound fascination with the attic. He began spending long, unexplained hours in the dusty space above, a room that, curiously, he had declared off-limits to children. This pronouncement hung in the air, a silent question mark. Daniel and Sarah had never placed any such restriction on the girls exploring their new home. The attic, with its promise of forgotten treasures and dusty secrets, had been envisioned as another space for them to discover, not a forbidden territory guarded by their grandfather's sudden silence. This unexpected behavior created a subtle undercurrent of mystery, a quiet dissonance in the otherwise harmonious rhythm of their new family life.

Lily's curiosity gnawed at her, but she held back, respecting her grandfather's unspoken boundaries. The attic held his memories, a legacy passed down through generations, and she wouldn't willingly disturb that. Still, a prickling sense of unease lingered. Rose, who was usually her intuitive barometer, hadn't voiced any warnings, which should have been reassuring. Yet, Lily thought, Rose doesn't want to go up there either. "It's probably just scary and full of spiderwebs," she'd said, but her voice had held a tremor Lily couldn't ignore.

One evening, as the family gathered in the living room, Lily overheard a low, urgent conversation between her grandparents. Her grandfather spoke of a secret, a legacy whispered through generations. "The mark in the attic... I feel something is stirring," he said, his voice strained.

"Should we tell them?" her grandmother asked, her voice barely a whisper.

He shook his head. "No," he replied, his voice firm, yet laced with doubt. "No, there's no need to frighten them. Besides, we don't even know if there's any truth to it. It may very well be nothing more than a myth, an urban legend."

Lily was intrigued. She wondered what the secret could be. She knew that her grandfather had a mysterious past, and was curious to learn more about him. Unable to shake the feeling that something was amiss, after dinner she mustered up the courage to approach her parents. "Dad, Mom," she began, her voice trembling slightly, "have you ever heard Grandpa talk about the attic?"

Daniel and Sarah exchanged an amused glance. "Oh, the attic," Daniel replied calmly. "Your grandfather loves that place. He's always going up there, rummaging through all the old stuff. He's got a great memory and he loves to go through everything and reminisce about the past."

Sarah nodded. "He's told us some fascinating stories about this house and its history. He's really attached to it."

Lily wasn't entirely convinced. "But why is it off-limits?" she asked.

"Off limits," Daniel chuckled. "Oh, that's just Grandpa being Grandpa. He used to tell me the same thing when I was little. He likes to keep his secrets. I'm sure it's nothing but an older man wishing for some privacy. After all, I've been up there many times, and I've never seen anything more than boxes, unless you're scared of a little spider," he said, giving her a wink.

"Yeah," Sarah said, swatting Daniel playfully with a dish towel. "You know that you and your sister are welcome to explore any part of this home you would like. Because now, it is your home too," she said, wrapping her arms around Lily. "Though I don't know why you would want to spend time in that drafty and dusty attic. Plus," she added, grinning, "I don't like spiders. That's why your father always has to go up there."

Lily giggled, but she still wasn't satisfied with the answers she was given. She knew her parents were trying to reassure her, but something about their grandfather's behavior just didn't sit right. Still, she decided not to press it anymore at the moment, as everything had been going so well in her new home. And she didn't want to mess that up, not only for herself, but for Rose as well.

Chapter 3:

Summer deepened, and with it, the girls' sense of belonging in their new home. The prospect of a new school still lingered on the horizon, but for now, they were content to bask in the warmth of their new life. Sarah's laughter, a cheerful melody, wove through the house, while Daniel's quiet strength provided a comforting sense of stability.

Yet, beneath the surface of their newfound happiness, an undercurrent of unease began to creep in. It started with small, almost imperceptible things. A chill that seemed to seep into the house, regardless of the fact that the air conditioner wasn't running. Shadows that danced in odd patterns across the walls, even when the sun was high. And then there were the sounds. Soft whispers, like distant echoes, seemed to emanate from the empty corners around them.

One night, as Lily lay awake, the steady tick-tock of the old grandfather clock, usually a comforting presence, suddenly amplified the silence of the house. Suddenly, a sound pierced through the stillness. A soft, almost melodic whimper drifting down from the attic. A knot of icy dread tightened in her stomach, her breath catching in her throat. Her skin prickled with an inexplicable terror, a primal instinct screaming for her to stay put, and burrow under the covers. Yet, a chilling curiosity, laced with a growing fear for the unknown source of the sound, propelled her from the safety of her bed. Her heart hammered against her ribs, a frantic drumbeat against the suffocating silence as she crept towards the door. The moment her bare feet touched the cool wood of the hallway, a sudden gust of wind snaked its way through the house, extinguishing the soft glow of her light. Darkness swallowed her whole, and in that instant, the whimper from above transformed into a distinct weight of dread, pressing down on her, stealing the air from her lungs and leaving her trembling in absolute blackness.

Her mind reeled, a chaotic whirlwind of apprehension and growing curiosity. Her grandfather's stern pronouncement about the attic, *it's off-limits to children*, echoed in the sudden silence, amplifying the sinister nature of the sound. One instinct screamed for the familiar comfort of her parents' room, a desperate urge to burrow under their protective arms, her voice a shaky whisper recounting the eerie whimper that had sliced through the night. But a growing sense of self, the stubborn pride of her teenage years, pushed back against this childlike impulse. She was older now, just a few years away from being a woman. Surely, she could confront this unsettling mystery on her own, prove her developing maturity in the face of the unknown.

Then, a flicker of memory, sharp and vivid, cut through the present fear. The sterile, impersonal walls of the foster care system flashed before her inner eye. A place where vulnerability was a constant shadow, and fear a familiar companion. Survival had meant learning to be brave, not in grand gestures, but in quiet resilience. She had learned to protect not only herself but also Rose. The lessons forged in the crucible of those difficult years – the hyper-vigilance, the silent observation, the carefully constructed walls of self-reliance – now resurfaced, rising within her like an instinctive shield against the encroaching darkness and the unsettling sounds from above. This wasn't just about a noise in the attic; it was a test, a silent echo of battles already fought and won. *Besides*, she thought to herself, *it's probably nothing more than an overactive imagination.*

The frantic pounding of her heart was a deafening drumbeat in the otherwise silent house, each thud echoing the rising tide of her anxiety. Rose's door stood as a stark, unyielding barrier, its stillness a silent confirmation that her sister remained blissfully unaware of the unsettling sounds that had roused Lily. A sharp intake of breath hitched in her throat as she hesitantly pushed open the heavy attic door, the aged wood groaning in protest, the sound amplifying the tremor in her own shaking hands. Each creaking step on the narrow, worn stairs was a deliberate act of courage, the sounds resonating in the stillness like the amplified footfalls of an intruder in her own mind. Reaching the top landing, she stretched out a hand blindly, her fingertips brushing against the cold, rough texture of the plaster wall. But it felt like a small anchor amidst the swirling vortex of her fear. Slowly, painstakingly, her eyes began to adjust to the meager light filtering through the grimy panes of the single attic window, the weak illumination doing little to dispel the oppressive shadows.

A thick, musty scent filled the air, a cloying aroma of decaying paper, forgotten fabric, and the ghosts of time. Cobwebs, delicate yet unsettling, draped from the exposed rafters like ghostly veils, swaying gently in unseen currents of air. The shadows cast by the dim light danced on the uneven floorboards, morphing familiar shapes into grotesque and menacing figures. The attic was a silent repository of echoes, a place where the present felt thin, and the weight of generations pressed down. Her parents' words about the house's age, its long history within Daniel's family, now resonated with a tangible presence in this dusty expanse. As her eyes slowly scanned the cluttered room, navigating through stacks of covered furniture and forgotten trinkets, a faint, ethereal glow emanating from a shadowed corner snagged her attention, a tiny beacon hidden within the gloom.

A sudden surge of adrenaline, a defiant spark against her fear, propelled her forward. She moved cautiously towards the light, her bare feet silent on the dusty floorboards. As she drew closer, the source of the glow became clearer: a small, intricately carved wooden chest, its surface coated in a thick layer of undisturbed dust, a testament to years of neglect. Her heart now hammered with a different rhythm, a mixture of trepidation and intense curiosity. *What secrets could be locked away inside? What forgotten stories did this old chest hold?* With a hesitant breath, she reached out, her fingers tracing the dusty contours of the lid before finally, slowly, lifting it open.

A sharp, involuntary gasp escaped her lips, her eyes wide with a mixture of shock and creeping unease. Inside the dusty chest lay a bizarre collection of objects that seemed to hum with a strange, unsettling energy. First, a tarnished silver locket, its surface intricately etched with symbols that were utterly unfamiliar, alien, and yet somehow disturbingly significant. Next, a book bound in a material that felt chillingly strange, a texture that sent a wave of revulsion through her. What her mind irrationally whispered was human skin, *but how could that be?* Its brittle pages were filled with a script that defied recognition, a series of cryptic characters that seemed to writhe and twist before her eyes. She recoiled instinctively, tossing the disturbing volume back into the chest as if even touching it would burn her skin. Then she noticed something underneath the chest. Sliding it over just enough, she was able to locate the source of the light. It was emanating from a symbol, foreign to her, yet somehow also familiar. Running her finger across it, she realized it had been carved into the wood. *But why? And was this the mark her grandfather had alluded to, the one he seemed so guarded about?* Though she didn't have the answers, a chill, deeper than the attic's cold air, snaked down her spine, raising goosebumps on her arms. With a shuddering breath, she slammed the heavy lid shut on the chest, the resounding thud echoing the frantic pounding of her own heart, before she carefully slid it back into place.

As she whirled around, desperate to escape the oppressive atmosphere of the attic, a flicker of movement in the periphery of her vision caught her attention. Her breath hitched in her throat, constricting her airway as she spun back, her eyes straining to penetrate the dim light. There, standing silently in the deepest shadows of the corner, was a figure that defied normal description. It was impossibly tall and gaunt, its form elongated and unsettlingly thin, as if stretched beyond human proportions. And then she saw its eyes. Two pinpricks of an eerie, malevolent red that seemed to pierce the gloom and fixate directly on her. A silent scream built in her chest, a trapped terror that clawed at her vocal cords, yet no sound, not even a whimper, escaped her paralyzed lips. The horrifying figure vanished as abruptly and inexplicably as it had appeared, leaving only the lingering imprint of its terrifying gaze.

Her mind reeled, a chaotic storm of disbelief and raw terror. The figure, whatever unholy thing it was, had simply dissolved back into the shadows, leaving no trace. Fear, sharp and constricting, wrapped around her like icy chains, a suffocating physical presence that stole her breath and made her limbs tremble. Her heart hammered against her ribs, a deafening drumbeat that drowned out the whispers of reason. She stumbled backwards, her outstretched hand grasping blindly for something solid, anything to anchor her to the rapidly unraveling reality.

Her hand collided with the rough edge of a large, forgotten box, sending a precarious stack of items cascading to the dusty floor with a series of muffled thuds. A fresh gasp escaped her lips as she registered what she had disturbed. A collection of old, leather-bound books lay scattered at her feet, their pages yellowed and brittle with age, their spines cracked and worn. She knelt down almost instinctively to gather them, hoping she wouldn't be in trouble if she had inadvertently woken up the whole house.

A deep shiver, unrelated to the attic's cold, ran down her spine, a warning that resonated deep within her bones. What, if any, was the inexplicable connection between these strange, unsettling objects? What did the symbol mean? And what was that terrifying, spectral figure with the glowing red eyes? A wave of nausea, sudden and intense, washed over her, threatening to buckle her knees. She had to get out of this place, this repository of forgotten secrets and unseen horrors. But as she turned to flee, her gaze was inexplicably drawn back to the grimy attic window. The cold, silvery light of the full moon was now creeping through the dusty panes, casting long, distorted, and undeniably eerie shadows that stretched and writhed across the cluttered room, turning familiar shapes into menacing specters.

Something was deeply wrong here. Very, very wrong. A sense of impending dread, heavy and suffocating, settled over her, a chilling premonition of dangers unseen and truths yet to be unearthed.

Chapter 4:

Back in the perceived safety of her room, the weight of the night's unsettling discoveries pressed down on Lily like a physical burden, each strange object and terrifying glimpse now a heavy stone added to the load. She desperately tried to rationalize what she had seen, clinging to the flimsy hope that it was merely a trick of the dim attic light, a grotesque figment conjured by an overactive imagination which had been fueled by shadows and creaking floorboards. But the vivid memory of those glowing red eyes, piercing and undeniably malevolent, burned into her mind's eye, a searing brand of raw fear that refused to be extinguished by logic. And then there was her grandfather's cryptic warning, the unspoken tension that had hung in the air around his attic excursions. Was the unsettling collection upstairs what he had been alluding to? And, more disturbingly, what else did he know? What secrets was he guarding within those dusty walls?

Sleep remained a distant and elusive prospect. She tossed and turned beneath the familiar softness of her blankets, her mind a frantic whirlwind of unanswered questions and unsettling images. What exactly had she witnessed in the dim recesses of the attic? Had it been real, or a terrifying hallucination born of fear and exhaustion? A strong impulse urged her to confide in her mother and father, to seek the comforting reassurance of their loving presence and the perceived safety of their protection. They were everything she and Rose had longed for. They were kind, patient, and unwavering in their affection, unlike anyone they had encountered in the unpredictable landscape of foster care. But another, deeply ingrained part of her, the self-protective core forged in years of uncertainty, hesitated. What if she was wrong? What if the glowing eyes were just a reflection, the gaunt figure a trick of the shadows? And what if they were disappointed, even angry, that she had disobeyed the unspoken rule and snooped where she wasn't supposed to? The lessons learned in foster care, the necessity of self-reliance and the ingrained habit of keeping her vulnerabilities and secrets closely guarded, warred against her newfound trust.

Pulling the soft covers up to her chin, she shivered, not from the cool night air, but from a deep-seated fear and a gnawing uncertainty that settled like a cold knot in her stomach. The old house itself seemed to sigh and groan around her, the settling of worn timbers taking on an almost sentient quality in the darkness. Each creak and rustle sounded like hushed whispers, like the house itself was sharing secrets in the stillness of the night, secrets that she was now, perhaps unwillingly, privy to.

The terrifying images pressed against Lily's closed eyelids, demanding her attention, but she fought them back. She needed a plan, and quickly. Not just for her own safety, but for Rose's. "Rose," she whispered, sitting bolt upright. Her feet found the floor, and she hurried to her sister's room. Relief, sharp and sweet, filled her as she saw her sister, asleep and peaceful, hugging her new teddy bear. As the house shifted, a low, ominous groan, Lily instinctively slid into bed beside Rose, seeking the warmth of her presence, a tangible connection in the face of fear.

In the immediate aftermath of her terrifying attic encounter, a fragile facade of normalcy descended upon the household, a carefully constructed veneer designed to conceal the churning unease beneath. Lily dutifully engaged in games with Rose, her laughter sounding a touch too bright, her smile feeling stiff and forced as she navigated the familiar routines of family life. But beneath this practiced exterior, a storm of paranoia was brewing, a tempest of suspicion and dread that colored her every perception. The familiar shadows in the corners of the rooms now seemed to writhe with a malevolent sentience, and every creak and groan of the old house echoed in her heightened senses as a potential harbinger of unseen danger. Rose, blessedly shielded by her innocence, remained oblivious to the undercurrent of fear, her intuitive gift, which usually hinted at subtle emotional shifts, remained strangely silent. Yet, despite the lack of external confirmation, a cold, gnawing certainty persisted in Lily's gut, a deep-seated conviction that something in their new life, in this old house, was deeply and irrevocably wrong.

As the days wore on, this unsettling feeling began to manifest in tangible, inexplicable occurrences. Objects seemed to shift positions with no discernible cause. Rose's beloved ragdoll, usually nestled beside her in bed, would suddenly appear perched on the living room sofa, despite Lily's clear recollection of having seen it on Rose's bed. Doors that had been firmly closed would creak open in the dead of night, allowing icy drafts to snake through the warm house, carrying with them a prickling sense of unease. And then there were the whispers. Faint, ethereal sounds that seemed to drift on the air, just at the edge of hearing. They seemed to emanate from nowhere and everywhere at once, their soft murmurings imbued with an otherworldly quality that sent icy shivers tracing paths down Lily's spine, raising the hairs on the back of her neck.

Sarah, ever the realistic optimist, readily dismissed these unsettling incidents as mere quirks of an old house settling, the groans of aged wood and the play of drafts. Yet, Lily, hyper-attuned to subtle shifts in emotion, couldn't ignore the faint but perceptible change in her adoptive mother's demeanor. A subtle strain had begun to etch itself into Sarah's usually serene features, a fleeting shadow occasionally darkening her bright eyes, a hint of worry where there was once only unwavering warmth. Rose, however, with the unfiltered perception of childhood, seemed more acutely aware of the growing tension. Her young mind, not yet fully bound by the constraints of logic and rational explanation, remained open to the unexplained. She would often whisper about seeing fleeting shadows darting across the periphery of her vision when she was alone in her room, or claim to hear strange, hushed noises when the house was otherwise silent. Lily noticed a growing apprehension in her sister's usually bright eyes, a growing fear that chillingly mirrored the unease that had taken root in her own heart. But the silence of Rose's intuitive gift was perhaps the most unsettling sign of all, suggesting a disturbance so profound that even her sensitive spirit was hesitant to acknowledge it.

Perched on the weathered planks of their makeshift sanctuary in the old oak tree, the afternoon sun dappling through the leaves, Lily broached the subject with delicate care. "Rose," she began, her voice soft, not wanting to alarm her younger sister, "your special feeling, your intuition... has it been telling you anything lately?" She watched Rose intently, her own heart thrumming with a nervous anticipation.

Rose tilted her head, her brow furrowed in concentration for a moment. Then, her gaze met Lily's, clear and untroubled. "No," she replied simply, a slight shake of her head accompanying the word. "I can't hear it."

"Nothing at all?" Lily pressed gently, her anxiety tightening its grip. She knew better than to push Rose too hard; her sister's gift was a fragile thing, easily silenced by pressure or fear. But the continued silence of Rose's intuition felt like an ominous sign in itself.

As Rose shook her head again, her innocent eyes reflecting no hint of the unease that had taken root in Lily's own heart, a wave of fear washed over Lily. The silence of Rose's usually perceptive inner voice felt like a confirmation of the growing darkness she sensed around them. Yet, looking at Rose's trusting face, Lily knew she couldn't burden her sister with her growing paranoia. She had to be the strong one, the protector. With a conscious effort, she forced down the rising tide of her anxiety, shoving it deep within until she could find a moment of solitude to confront the chilling certainty that something was deeply wrong in their new home. For now, she would keep her fears veiled, a silent sentinel guarding Rose's youthful innocence.

With Sarah's casual nod of permission, a silent understanding passing between them that Lily needed some space, Lily slipped into the familiar embrace of the woods nestled behind their house. Usually, Rose, her small hand eagerly seeking Lily's, would plead to tag along, her bright curiosity a constant companion on their woodland explorations. But today, a heavy cloak of unease clung to her, and she craved the quiet solitude of the trees, hoping the rustling leaves and dappled sunlight could somehow banish the haunting shadows that danced at the edges of her thoughts. She deliberately strayed from their well-worn paths, venturing deeper into the tangled undergrowth, the familiar scents of pine and damp earth a small comfort. It was then, at the end of a barely discernible, overgrown path, that she stumbled upon it: an old, abandoned house. It stood silent and skeletal against the backdrop of the dense trees, its windows like vacant eyes staring out at a forgotten world. A pronounced sense of foreboding washed over her, a cold premonition that prickled her skin, yet a mysterious curiosity, a morbid fascination, drew her forward, like a moth irresistibly drawn to a flickering flame.

As she cautiously approached the dilapidated structure, a figure emerged from the deep shadows of the porch, coalescing from the gloom like a phantom. It was an elderly woman, her face a roadmap of wrinkles etched by the relentless passage of time, each line seeming to tell a silent story. But it was her eyes that truly captivated Lily. They were a startlingly clear and piercing blue that held a depth of ancient wisdom, a knowing that somehow defied her frail, aged appearance. There was something strangely familiar about her, a fleeting flicker of recognition that danced just beyond the grasp of her memory, a sense of having seen her before, perhaps in a dream or a half-forgotten image. This uncanny familiarity causing Lily to shudder. The prickling sensation made her hesitate, causing her steps to falter on the overgrown path.

The old woman remained motionless on the porch, her slender figure framed by the decaying doorway, a silhouette against the deeper shadows within. Her piercing blue eyes, unwavering in their intensity, seemed to possess an uncanny ability to see beyond Lily's surface, to peer directly into the turmoil churning within her. An aura of an almost otherworldly tranquility emanated from her, a stillness that contrasted sharply with the disquiet she was feeling. It was as if the woman existed outside the normal flow of time, radiating a sense of timelessness that both drew Lily closer with a strange magnetism and repelled her with an instinctive sense of the unknown.

"You shouldn't be here, child," the woman's voice was a soft, breathy whisper, so gentle it seemed to be carried by the very breeze that rustled the leaves in the nearby trees. Yet, despite its delicate quality, her words were laced with an undeniable, almost ancient authority, a quiet command that resonated deep within Lily.

Wrapping her arms around herself and ignoring the subtle but firm warning, drawn by an unseen force she couldn't comprehend, Lily took another hesitant step closer. The woman's piercing blue gaze remained fixed on hers, and in that moment, an inexplicable connection sparked between them. It was a strange, unsettling sensation, as if the threads of their very souls had become momentarily entwined, a silent recognition passing between two strangers across the chasm of age and experience.

A sense of disorientation washed over Lily, the weight of the encounter making her breath catch in her throat. "I...I don't know why I'm here," she stammered, the words feeling inadequate to explain the pull that had led her to this forgotten place and this puzzling woman.

A slow, mysterious smile spread across the old woman's wrinkled face, her eyes crinkling at the corners. "Some things are meant to be found, child," she said, her voice regaining a touch more strength, "not sought." The words hung in the air, heavy with an unspoken meaning that Lily couldn't quite grasp.

Before Lily could formulate a response, could press for clarification on the cryptic pronouncement, the woman turned with a fluid grace that belied her age and disappeared back into the shadowed depths of the dilapidated house. One moment she was there, a tangible presence on the porch, the next she was gone, swallowed by the darkness within, leaving Lily standing alone in the unsettling silence of the deserted path. Lily wrapped her arms around herself once more as a chill ran down the length of her spine. There was something undeniably strange, almost otherworldly, about this woman and her sudden appearance and disappearance, something that hinted at a hidden world, a reality that lay just beyond the veil of the ordinary, and left Lily with a growing unease settling in her heart.

Driven by a curiosity that felt both compelling and perilous, she hesitated only for a fleeting moment. The old woman's cryptic warning, her soft voice carrying an unsettling weight, echoed in the recesses of her mind, a haunting melody that both intrigued and unnerved her. Taking a deep, steadying breath, she pushed against the heavy, protesting door, the rusty hinges groaning in a long-forgotten language as it reluctantly swung inward, granting her passage into the silent depths of the abandoned house.

The interior was cloaked in a dim, ethereal light, the weak rays of the afternoon sun filtering through grimy, cracked windowpanes, illuminating a swirling ballet of dust motes suspended in the stagnant air. These tiny particles danced like ghostly apparitions, casting long, distorted, and undeniably eerie shadows that stretched and writhed across the decaying floorboards. The house felt like a time capsule, a place where the march of years had abruptly halted, leaving everything frozen in a moment decades past. A thick, undisturbed layer of dust blanketed every surface, a silent, gray testament to the years of neglect and the stories the house had silently witnessed. The air hung heavy with the scent of decay and forgotten things, a poignant reminder of lives once lived within these crumbling walls.

As Lily cautiously ventured deeper into the house's silent embrace, a peculiar and unsettling sense of familiarity began to wash over her, a disorienting wave of *déjà vu*. It wasn't just a vague feeling; it was a visceral conviction, a strange certainty that she had walked these dusty floors before, had perhaps even touched these decaying walls. It was as if fragments of a forgotten dream, or echoes of a past life, were stirring within her. But how could that be? She had never seen this house before, had never even known of its existence until today. The house seemed to hum with unspoken secrets, to resonate with the faint whispers of a past that stubbornly refused to be entirely erased, a history clinging to the very fabric of its being.

Drawn by an unseen pull, Lily found herself in the heart of the house, where she discovered a hidden room, its entrance cleverly concealed beneath a loose and warped floorboard. A dark, narrow opening beckoned. She paused, a moment of apprehension tightening her chest, her gaze sweeping over the silent, dust-filled room around her before making the snap decision to descend the creaky, uneven steps. The small, underground room was surprisingly dry, its air thick with the musty scent of old paper and dried ink. The walls were lined floor to ceiling with tightly packed bookshelves, their wooden surfaces coated in a thick layer of grime. A single, small, grimy window, barely visible above ground level, offered a sliver of weak, diffused light, casting long, distorted shadows within the confined space. Hundreds of dust-covered books filled the shelves, their leather spines cracked and faded, many embossed with strange, unfamiliar symbols that seemed to writhe and twist in the dim light. In the very center of the room, a large, ornately carved wooden desk stood silently, its surface cluttered with scattered papers, strange and unidentifiable artifacts, and the remnants of a long-forgotten occupant's work. The air in the hidden room felt thick with secrets, a strong sense of a past waiting to be unearthed.

A chill, deeper than the dampness of the basement room, seeped into Lily's bones, and she could feel her blood curdling, a visceral reaction to the oppressive atmosphere and the unsettling discoveries. This was no ordinary, forgotten house; it was a repository of secrets, a silent keeper of a past that felt both compelling and perilous. It was a place where the veil between the mundane and the extraordinary seemed to fray and thin, allowing glimpses into something ancient and unknown. Hesitantly, her fingers trembling with a mixture of fear and morbid curiosity, she reached out to touch the spine of one of the dust-laden books, its leather strangely textured beneath her fingertips. But before full contact could be made, a sudden, violent gust of wind shrieked through the small window, a malevolent sigh that extinguished the feeble sliver of light, plunging the hidden room into absolute, suffocating darkness. The sudden void enveloped her, stealing her sight and amplifying her sense of dread, a feeling that was both chillingly familiar from her recent attic encounter and yet somehow magnified, more terrifying in this confined, and unknown space.

As the darkness swallowed her whole, her heart hammered against her ribs. A clammy cold sweat slicked her forehead and the back of her neck as she instinctively groped around her, her outstretched hands flailing in the inky blackness, seeking something, anything solid to cling to in this disorienting void. The silence that followed the extinguishing of the light was deafening, a heavy, oppressive stillness that seemed to press in on her from all sides, punctuated only by the frantic, erratic thumping of her own terrified heart, a frantic drumbeat against the suffocating silence.

Then, a touch. Cold. Unnatural. It brushed against her arm, sending a jolt of pure, unadulterated terror through her entire being. A strangled scream built in her throat, a silent shriek of raw fear that clawed at her vocal cords but remained trapped, unable to escape her paralyzed lips. Her mind raced, conjuring vivid, horrifying images of the gaunt, shadowy figure from the attic, its glowing red eyes burned into her memory. With trembling hands that felt numb and unresponsive, she instinctively reached out towards the source of the chilling touch, her fingers closing around something cold and hard.

A small, cardboard matchbox. Where did it come from? Her fingers, still trembling violently, fumbled with the rough surface, her mind racing to understand its sudden appearance in the oppressive darkness. With a desperate surge of hope, she managed to strike a match against the abrasive strip. The tiny flame sputtered to life, a fragile lifeline in the overwhelming blackness, casting wild, dancing shadows that writhed and stretched across the dusty walls, momentarily transforming the earlier shapes of the room into grotesque and unsettling figures. As the weak, flickering light illuminated the space, her breath hitched in her throat. Standing silently in the far corner, partially obscured by the shadows, was a figure. It was a woman, her form slender and still, her face pale and gaunt, as if drained of all color and life. Her eyes, large and dark, were fixed on Lily, filled with a profound and haunting sadness that seemed to emanate from the very depths of her soul.

The woman's gaze met Lily's, causing an inexplicable shiver to run down her spine. There was something achingly familiar about her spectral presence, a deep, resonant connection that transcended the boundaries of time and space. Then, as quickly and silently as she had materialized from the shadows, the woman vanished, seeming to dissolve back into the darkness, leaving Lily once again utterly alone in the suffocating silence of the hidden room, the lingering image of her sorrowful eyes now imprinted on Lily's mind.

The small match in her trembling hand flickered and died, plunging her back into darkness. But this time, her fingers, guided by an instinct she couldn't explain, brushed against something smooth and cylindrical on the cluttered surface of the nearby desk. A candle. Relief washed over her in a small wave. With another strike of the match from the box, the fragile flame caught the wick. A soft, golden glow gradually filled the small room, pushing back the oppressive darkness and casting a more stable light on the dust-covered surroundings. In the steady illumination, the space took on a less menacing air, though the lingering image of the vanished woman and the profound sadness in her eyes would forever remain etched in her memory. The only sound now was the soft crackling of the candle flame, a small, comforting sound in the otherwise silent room, a stark contrast to the pounding of her heart.

Drawn back to the cluttered desk, Lily's fingers, still trembling slightly from the encounter with the spectral woman, hesitantly reached out to explore the strange artifacts scattered across its dusty surface. Her gaze fell upon a small, circular object crafted from a dark, unfamiliar metal. Intricately etched into its surface was a peculiar symbol, a series of swirling lines and sharp angles that immediately sparked a flicker of recognition. It was identical, undeniably so, to the unsettling mark she had seen earlier on the tarnished silver locket tucked away in the attic chest. As her fingertips brushed against the cool, smooth metal of the object, a sudden, unexpected surge of energy coursed through her, a vibrant tingling sensation that began in her hand and rapidly spread throughout her entire body, leaving her momentarily breathless with a strange mix of shock and exhilaration.

Compelled by a newfound sense of urgency, a feeling that time was somehow slipping away, she turned her attention to the towering bookshelves that lined the walls of the hidden room. The spines of the ancient tomes were embossed with the same strange symbols she had seen on the locket and the circular object, and the titles were inscribed in an unfamiliar, elegant script that seemed both alien and strangely familiar. Her fingers trailed along the worn leather of the bindings until she selected a book, its cover surprisingly soft and pliable beneath her touch. As she carefully pulled it from the shelf, a cloud of musty, age-old dust billowed forth, carrying with it the faint, evocative scent of decaying paper and forgotten secrets.

The pages within revealed intricate celestial drawings, depicting constellations and planetary alignments in ways she had never seen before, alongside dense blocks of cryptic writing interspersed with complex diagrams and unsettling symbols. As her eyes scanned the text, a cold dread began to creep into her heart, a chilling realization that she was delving into something far more ancient and sinister than she could have ever imagined. The book spoke of dark forces that lurked beyond the veil of human perception, of forgotten gods and ancient rituals steeped in a power that defied human understanding and threatened to unravel the very fabric of reality. But it was the language itself that truly terrified her. Though archaic and unlike any she had ever encountered, the script seemed to bypass her conscious mind, the meaning of the words and symbols flooding her understanding with an unnerving urgency. It was as if she wasn't just reading these forbidden texts; she was remembering them, the knowledge of these dark practices sinking deep into her soul, stirring something dormant and unsettling within her.

As the chilling tendrils of fear tightened their grip around her heart, a terrifying clarity began to dawn in Lily's mind. The intricate script and unsettling diagrams weren't just abstract curiosities; they were not mere stories whispered down through the ages, or fantastical legends meant to frighten children. They were instructions, precise and detailed, a guidebook to a hidden world that existed just beyond the edges of their everyday reality, a world she had been blissfully unaware of until this moment. The more she deciphered the archaic language, the more the solid, familiar lines between the tangible world she knew and the shadowy realm of the supernatural began to dissolve and blur, the impossible suddenly feeling terrifyingly real.

A chilling realization struck her with the force of a physical blow. She was not simply a passive observer, an accidental discoverer of forgotten lore. She was a part of something much larger, something intricate and terrifyingly interconnected. The strange occurrences that had plagued their arrival into their new home. The unsettling whispers that seemed to dance on the wind, the fleeting glimpses of a gaunt, shadowy figure in the attic, the inexplicable movements of objects within the house. They were not random, isolated events. They were all threads in a dark tapestry, and this ancient book, filled with its forbidden knowledge, held the key to understanding the terrifying pattern woven within it. But with every brittle page she carefully turned, with every cryptic symbol she deciphered, she felt herself being drawn deeper into a darkness that felt ancient and inescapable, a vortex of secrets threatening to consume her.

Compelled by a morbid fascination that warred with her growing dread, she sank onto the dusty floor, the weight of the ancient text heavy in her lap. She continued to delve deeper into its forbidden wisdom, the flickering candlelight casting long, dancing shadows that mirrored the turmoil within her. The knowledge she was uncovering was both profoundly terrifying and strangely, dangerously alluring, a siren song whispering promises of understanding and power. She felt an undeniable pull, an almost magnetic force emanating from the book itself, drawing her further and further into the heart of a darkness that felt both old and intimately connected to her own growing fear. The whispers of the past were becoming a roar in her mind, and the shadows in the corners of her vision seemed to deepen, as if the very house was responding to the awakening of its long-dormant secrets.

But as Lily became increasingly absorbed in her clandestine studies, poring over the cryptic text and deciphering its unsettling secrets, the atmosphere within the house began to subtly, then dramatically, shift. Objects that had been left undisturbed for years were inexplicably moving on their own, sliding across surfaces or toppling over with no apparent cause, as if responding to the silent command of an unseen force that now permeated the very structure of the old dwelling. The familiar shadows that played in the corners of her vision began to deepen and writhe, no longer innocent tricks of the light but contorting themselves into grotesque and menacing shapes that were watching her with malevolent intent. And the whispers, which had initially been faint and distant murmurs on the edge of hearing, grew steadily louder, more insistent, as if the house itself was trying to communicate, its hushed tones now carrying an undercurrent of anxious urgency and something akin to hungry anticipation.

Trembling uncontrollably, her heart a rapid drumbeat against her ribs, Lily snatched up the heavy, leather-bound book and fled the suffocating confines of the hidden room. As she scrambled up the creaking steps and burst back into the main part of the house, the whispers intensified, swirling around her like a rising tide of pure malice, their hushed tones now laced with an undeniable hostility. She didn't dare to look back until she had put a significant distance between herself and the ominous stillness of the abandoned house, finally turning to witness a sight that froze the blood in her veins. With a sudden, violent groan that tore through the afternoon air, the old house abruptly and terrifyingly collapsed in upon itself, a chaotic cascade of splintered wood and crumbling stone collapsing into a heap of dust and debris. The laughter of the whispers, no longer faint but a deafening, triumphant roar, echoed in her ears, a chilling and unmistakable testament to the power she had unknowingly disturbed, a force now unleashed upon their unsuspecting world.

That night, back in the relative sanctuary of her own room, Lily sat alone, the weight of the ancient book heavy in her lap as she continued her perilous journey through its forbidden pages. Suddenly, a bone-chilling draft swept through the room, extinguishing the warm glow of her bedside lamp, plunging her once more into the oppressive embrace of darkness. But this time, the darkness felt different, heavier, more sentient. An ominous presence filled the room, an unseen entity that seemed to emanate from the deepest shadows, a malevolent force that prickled her skin and stole the air from her lungs, whispering promises of terror and the chilling certainty that she was no longer alone.

Chapter 5:

A low, guttural growl, primal and menacing, echoed through the suffocating darkness, vibrating in the very air around Lily. "You have awakened a great power," the voice hissed, a chilling whisper that seemed to slither from the shadows themselves.

Terror, sharp and absolute, seized her, constricting her chest and stealing her breath as the voice, cold and utterly devoid of warmth, filled the confines of her room. It was a voice that seemed to emanate not from any living being, but from the very depths of the earth, resonating with an ancient, primordial evil that had slumbered for centuries. Her body froze, every muscle locking tight, transforming her into a rigid statue of fear, paralyzed in the face of this unseen, unimaginable horror. Her heart hammered against her ribs, a desperate drumbeat that seemed to echo in the oppressive darkness, a frantic plea for escape that her body couldn't obey. She opened her mouth to scream, to unleash the terror that clawed at her throat, to fight back against the unseen assailant, but her vocal cords refused to cooperate, her limbs heavy and unresponsive, completely and utterly paralyzed by the sheer, overwhelming dread.

Then, a darkness greater than the physical night descended upon her, a suffocating void, a terrifying nothingness that seemed to open up and swallow her whole, extinguishing the flickering remnants of her awareness. Time ceased to exist, the frantic beating of her heart fading into an echoing silence. There was only the all-encompassing darkness and the lingering echo of the terrifying whisper, a chilling imprint on the void of her consciousness.

When consciousness finally flickered back to life, like a fragile flame rekindling in the dark, she found herself lying on her bed, bathed in the soft, ethereal glow of the moonlight filtering through her window. Her body ached in every muscle, as if she had endured a great and brutal physical ordeal, though she couldn't recall any actual struggle. A clammy cold sweat drenched her skin, clinging to her like a second, icy layer, and her breaths came in ragged, shallow gasps, as if she had just emerged from a deep and terrifying nightmare. The familiar comfort of her room seemed subtly altered, the very essence of the space feeling somehow different, tainted by the unseen presence of the night before. Or perhaps, the change wasn't in the room at all, but within her, a deep and unsettling shift in her perception, a mark left by the darkness and the ancient whisper.

Fear was a relentless beast gnawing at her insides, its sharp teeth tearing at her peace, a sheer terror that refused to be quelled by the return of daylight. She had plunged into the abyss of darkness and somehow been pulled back, but the experience had marked her, leaving an invisible scar on her soul. A new awareness was stirring within her, an understanding of a world hidden from ordinary eyes, a sense of power and dread inextricably intertwined, like two serpents coiled around a single truth.

As the first pale light of dawn painted the eastern sky, a cold, hard resolve settled over Lily, solidifying within her like ice. She couldn't pretend it hadn't happened, couldn't bury the terror and hope it would fade. She had to confront the darkness once more, to delve into its secrets, to understand its nature, and, if there was even a sliver of possibility, to find a way to defeat it before it consumed everything she held dear. The ancient book, with its terrifying promise of both profound knowledge and unimaginable peril, was now her only weapon, a dangerous key to a door she may wish had remained locked.

The morning air was crisp and clean, carrying the invigorating scent of pine needles and damp earth. Lily once again sought refuge in the familiar embrace of the woods behind their house, a place where the natural world seemed simpler, quieter, a balm to the chaos that was swirling within the turbulent landscape of her mind. The rhythmic crunch of twigs and fallen leaves beneath her sneakers provided a soothing counterpoint to the echoes of the growling voice and the chilling whispers that still lingered in her memory. Wandering deeper into the trees, the dappled sunlight filtering through the canopy, a fragile sense of peace began to tentatively wash over her, a momentary reprieve from the oppressive weight of her fear.

Then, her eyes found him. Standing at the edge of a sunlit clearing, his tall figure almost seamlessly blending into the dappled shadows of the surrounding trees, was a man unlike any she had ever seen. His eyes, a deep, captivating blue that seemed to hold the wisdom of ages, met hers across the clearing. There was a quality about him, a stillness and a grace that suggested he belonged to a different time, perhaps even a different realm entirely. A jolt of recognition, sharp and unexpected, shot through her. Her mind raced back to the day she had first found the book, to the older woman she had encountered at the abandoned house, her piercing blue eyes also filled with an ancient knowledge. The house that was now gone. Vanished without a trace, as if it had never existed, swallowed back into the earth, leaving behind only an unsettling emptiness. The connection, though intangible, felt undeniable, a thread weaving through the strange tapestry of events that had begun to unravel her new life.

An invisible thread, taut and compelling, seemed to snake out from the man and wrap itself around her, drawing her forward with a strange, irresistible pull, an inexplicable magnetic force that defied logic and reason. Her heart hammered against her ribs, a drumbeat echoing the tumultuous mix of apprehension and an almost desperate anticipation that churned within her chest. Cautiously, her senses on high alert, she took a hesitant step, then another, the soft earth yielding beneath her feet as her mind raced, desperately trying to categorize this unexpected encounter, to place this ethereal figure within the familiar framework of her new reality.

"Who are you?" she finally managed to ask, her voice trembling, betraying the fear that still clung to her despite the undeniable pull she felt. The question hung in the still morning air, a fragile thread connecting her uncertainty to his serene presence.

The man's lips curved into a gentle smile, a mysterious expression that hinted at knowledge far beyond her own. "Call me Elias," he replied, his voice as soft and soothing as a summer breeze rustling through the leaves, yet carrying an undercurrent of profound resonance. His next words sent a fresh wave of unease washing over her. "I've been watching you, Lily."

A tremor ran through her, a chilling sensation that prickled her skin and snaked its way down her spine. The way he spoke her name, with such familiarity, as if he had been observing her for an eternity, filled her with a deep sense of disquiet. He knew her name, a simple fact that spoke volumes about his unseen surveillance. Yet, amidst the apprehension, a strange, unsettling sense of familiarity also tugged at her, a whisper of recognition, as if she had known him her entire life, a connection that defied the logical reality of never having seen him before. How could that be? He was a complete stranger, an anomaly in the quiet woods.

"Watching me?" she repeated, her voice barely a whisper, the question laced with a mixture of fear and a dawning sense of inevitability.

Elias nodded slowly, his deep blue gaze unwavering, holding hers with an intensity that felt both unnerving and strangely comforting. "You are in danger, Lily. A darkness is gathering, its tendrils reaching, and you are caught directly in its path."

His words echoed the chilling warnings she had heard in the disembodied whispers that haunted the old house, and resonated with the deep, intuitive sense of dread that had taken root in the very depths of her soul. Fear and a strange, almost fateful anticipation warred within her, a confusing battle between instinctual caution and a desperate yearning for understanding. This strange man, with his otherworldly aura and his unsettling knowledge, seemed to hold the key to unraveling the terrifying mystery that now consumed her. But could she truly trust him? Was he a guide sent by the heavens, or another player in the unfolding darkness? The question hung heavy in the air, unanswered, a silent plea for clarity in the face of the encroaching shadows.

As the strange man began to speak, the fragile tranquility of the woods was abruptly and violently shattered. A low, guttural growl, a sound that resonated with pure menace, echoed through the trees, followed by the sharp, brutal crack of thick branches snapping under immense pressure. A cold wave of terror seized Lily, constricting her chest and stealing her breath as a colossal shadow, impossibly large and grotesque, lumbered and crashed its way out of the dense undergrowth. The creature's form was distorted and nightmarish in the dim light filtering through the forest canopy, its hulking silhouette a terrifying amalgamation of shadow and brute force. Its eyes, twin orbs of an eerie, malevolent luminescence, burned through the dimness, fixing on both Lily and Elias with a predatory intensity that sent shivers down her spine and made her blood run cold.

Elias, who had been a picture of serene calm moments before, now moved with a swift, decisive grace, his expression hardening into a mask of grim determination as he instinctively positioned himself protectively in front of Lily, a human shield against the monstrous onslaught. An unmistakable primal energy emanated from him now, a raw, untamed power that belied his gentle human appearance, a silent promise of protection that flickered in his intense blue eyes. Lily instinctively clasped her hands over her ears as the creature unleashed a deafening roar, a sound that was not merely loud but physically vibrated through her very core, shaking the air and rattling her bones. Its massive, shadowy body lunged forward with surprising speed, its enormous claws, sharp and wickedly curved, extended in a deadly, sweeping arc aimed directly at them. The peaceful woods had become a battleground, and Lily knew, with a chilling certainty, that their lives hung precariously in the balance.

With a speed that transcended the limits of human perception, a blur of motion that seemed to defy the very laws of physics, Elias intercepted the creature's deadly lunge. Their bodies collided with a thunderous impact, a force so immense that it sent a visible shockwave rippling through the surrounding trees, causing leaves to flutter and the very ground beneath Lily's feet to tremble. She stumbled backward, her breath caught in a strangled gasp in her throat, her eyes wide with disbelief and terror. The world seemed to warp and distort, the rapid action unfolding before her as if viewed through a thick, viscous liquid, a horrifying ballet of life and death played out in agonizing slow motion.

As she frantically scrambled to regain her footing, her senses reeling from the shock, she continued to watch in frozen horror as Elias and the monstrous creature engaged in a brutal battle, a savage dance of claws and teeth against an almost supernatural focus of agility and strength. The forest itself seemed to shudder and groan under the sheer ferocity of their struggle, the air thick with the scent of torn bark and disturbed earth. Towering trees groaned and snapped like brittle twigs under the weight of their colliding bodies, the sounds echoing through the once-peaceful woods like the thunder of an approaching storm. Lily could feel the icy grip of fear and the burning rush of adrenaline coursing through her veins, an overwhelming mix of paralyzing terror and a desperate defiance. Her mind screamed at her to do something, anything to help the man who had stepped between her and death, but her limbs felt like lead, heavy and unresponsive, rooting her to the spot in a terrifying paralysis of inaction.

The sight of Elias locked in a desperate struggle against the monstrous entity, a whirlwind of impossible speed and brutal force, had finally shattered the icy grip of fear that had held her captive. It wasn't a sudden burst of valiant bravery that propelled her forward, but rather an instinct, a fierce, unyielding refusal to remain a helpless spectator to the life-and-death battle unfolding before her. A raw, unadulterated desperation, fueled by the terrifying realization of her own vulnerability and a growing sense of protectiveness towards Elias, surged through her. Her legs, which had felt like lead weights moments before, now moved with a jerky, uncontrolled urgency, each step a testament to the sheer force of her will overcoming her paralyzed fear.

Her gaze frantically scanned the immediate surroundings, her eyes latching onto a thick, fallen branch lying discarded near the base of a towering oak. Its rough bark had been scraped bare in its fall, revealing the pale wood beneath. With a guttural cry that echoed the savage roars of the monstrous creature, a sound born of pure adrenaline and terror-fueled determination, she snatched it up. Her hands trembled violently, the wood slick with sweat, her knuckles turning stark white as she gripped it with every ounce of strength she could muster. Focusing all her fear and desperation into a single, desperate act, she aimed the crude, makeshift weapon and hurled it through the air with every fiber of her being. The heavy wooden missile, a desperate projectile launched in the face of unimaginable terror, spun end over end, a fleeting brown arc against the green and shadow of the forest, and found its mark with a sickening thud, striking the monstrous creature squarely in one of its eerie, luminescent eyes. A deafening howl of pure, agonizing pain erupted from its monstrous throat, an unearthly sound that echoed through the trees, momentarily eclipsing the sounds of the ongoing, brutal struggle and causing the very air to vibrate with its agony.

Seizing the fleeting opportunity created by Lily's desperate strike, Elias unleashed a blinding burst of energy, a radiant torrent of pure power that erupted from him as if he had somehow summoned the incandescent might of a thousand suns. The monstrous creature, caught completely off guard and fully exposed in the sudden, searing light, thrashed wildly in unimaginable agony, its shadowy form contorting and writhing as if consumed by an internal fire. A deafening scream, an unearthly shriek that seemed to tear through the very fabric of reality, echoed through the stunned silence of the woods. When the blinding light finally faded, dissipating into the dappled sunlight, the creature was gone, vanished without a trace as if it had never existed, leaving behind an eerie, unsettling silence that pressed down on the forest, broken only by the frantic, rapid thumping of Lily's heart.

Completely drained, her limbs trembling uncontrollably, her knees buckled as she collapsed to the damp earth, her body weak and spent from the terrifying ordeal. Elias turned towards her, his usually serene face now etched with deep lines of concern, his intense blue eyes filled with a worry that mirrored her own exhaustion. "Are you alright?" he asked, his voice, though still gentle and soothing, now held a deeper note, a resonance of shared experience, a connection forged and intensified in the crucible of their desperate battle against the unseen darkness.

Lily managed a weak nod, her voice barely a shaky whisper. "Yes... I think so." She was physically safe, for now, shielded by Elias's power. But the brief respite offered no true comfort. The battle was far from over; she could feel it in the lingering chill in the air, in the unnerving silence of the woods. The darkness she had glimpsed in the abandoned house, the malevolent presence that had filled her room, was undeniably real, and it was growing stronger, its tendrils reaching further into their world. And a chilling certainty settled deep within her soul. She was not just a witness to this unfolding terror; she was somehow, inexplicably, at the very center of it all.

As the immediate threat subsided and the adrenaline began to recede, leaving them both shaken and breathless, a strange, ethereal energy began to emanate from Lily. A soft, inner glow bloomed around her, a gentle luminescence that seemed to radiate from her very skin, bathing her in a faint, otherworldly light. The air around her shimmered and distorted, carrying with it a subtle, almost musical hum. Elias watched this astonishing transformation unfold, his intense blue eyes widening in surprise and a dawning sense of wonder, tinged with a flicker of something similar to awe and perhaps even a touch of fear.

"What's happening to you, Lily?" he asked, his voice filled with a mixture of stunned surprise and a hesitant apprehension, as if witnessing something both miraculous and potentially dangerous.

Lily was as bewildered as he was. She had no answers, no understanding of the strange power that was now surging through her veins, a potent force that was both terrifying in its unfamiliarity and exhilarating in its raw energy. It felt ancient and primal, a deep reservoir of something extraordinary awakening within her. It was as if the darkness she had confronted had not only threatened to consume her but had also somehow struck a hidden chord within her soul, unleashing a dormant strength that was now surging to the surface, demanding to be recognized.

A look of profound wonder spread across Elias's face as he gazed at the radiant aura surrounding her. "How marvelous," he murmured, his voice hushed with reverence. "What type of magic do you possess, Lily?"

"Magic?" she repeated, the word feeling foreign and impossible on her tongue. "I... I'm not magical. I don't understand what's happening." The idea was ludicrous, something out of fairy tales, not her ordinary life.

"Well, of course you are, my dear. Just look at you!" he exclaimed, holding his hands out in a gesture that encompassed her glowing form. His initial apprehension seemed to have been replaced by an almost childlike fascination. "Try to do something," he urged her anxiously, his eyes bright with anticipation. "Focus on it. What do you feel like you can do?"

"Like what?" she asked, her brow furrowed in confusion, still trying to reconcile the impossible sensations coursing through her with the mundane reality she knew. The power felt formless, undirected, a raw potential waiting to be shaped.

Elias's gaze, sharp and focused, scanned their surroundings until it settled on a small, brown bird perched precariously on a slender branch of a nearby oak. "There," he said, pointing a steady finger towards the unassuming creature. "That bird. See if you can…I don't know, change it." His voice held a quiet intensity, a blend of instruction and eager anticipation.

"What do you mean, change it?" Lily asked, her brow furrowed with a mixture of concern for the innocent creature and a hesitant curiosity about the strange energy that now enveloped her. The idea of altering something so natural felt both daunting and strangely compelling.

"See if you can transform it into something else," Elias elaborated, his eyes fixed on the bird. "Or perhaps try to move it to another branch, or... I don't know, just try anything that comes to mind. Focus on the shimmering, on the feeling inside you. Just try, Lily, and see what happens." His voice was gentle but insistent, urging her to explore the boundaries of this newfound, bewildering power.

"I don't want to hurt it," Lily protested, a wave of protective empathy washing over her for the small, vulnerable bird. "Besides," she added, her voice laced with disbelief, "I still don't understand what this shimmering is, this feeling inside me. I'm not magical. People don't just... change things." The concept felt utterly foreign, a leap of faith she wasn't yet ready to take.

Elias's gaze softened, a knowing smile gracing his lips. "But indeed you are, Lily," he said, his voice filled with a quiet certainty that seemed to resonate with an ancient truth. "And I think, deep down, beneath the layers of your disbelief, you know it too. You can feel the power. Now, try to guide it."

Chapter 6:

The glow emanating from within Lily intensified, bathing the forest floor in an ethereal light. It wasn't just a visual phenomenon. It was a tangible presence, a vibrant hum that resonated deep within her bones. And it wasn't some external force acting upon her. It was *her*, a part of her she never knew existed, now rushing to the surface. The connection she felt wasn't a gentle observation but an intimate understanding, as if the rustling leaves whispered secrets directly into her mind, the roots of the trees pulsed in rhythm with her own heartbeat, and the vast expanse of the sky breathed in unison with her lungs. Every blade of grass, every scurrying insect, throbbed with a life force that mirrored her own expanding power.

Closing her eyes, she surrendered to the sensation, no longer a passive recipient but rather an active one in this symphony of existence. The surge of power wasn't just an emotional feeling. She could feel it physically within her, like liquid fire flowing through her veins, making her skin tingle and her senses sharpen to an almost painful degree. It was exhilarating and terrifying all at once, a wild, untamed current threatening to overwhelm her yet somehow feeling intrinsically right.

With a concentration born not of conscious thought but of instinct, she reached out with her mind. It wasn't a deliberate act of will, but more like extending an invisible limb into the world around her. The air responded instantly, gathering itself into a swirling vortex. The gentle breeze transformed into a powerful gust that tore through the canopy, sending a cascade of leaves spiraling into the air like a thousand startled birds. Thick branches groaned and swayed violently, and the dense undergrowth bowed in unison, as if acknowledging an unseen command. A gasp escaped from her lips, a mixture of pure astonishment and an overwhelming fear at the sheer force she had unwittingly unleashed. This was her? This raw, untamed power resided within her?

Elias, who had been observing her with a mixture of curiosity and apprehension, now stood frozen, his eyes wide with undisguised awe. He had witnessed many strange occurrences in his life, but this… this was different. It wasn't an external magic being wielded; it was as if the very essence of the forest was responding to Lily's inner being. A tremor of reverence ran through him. "You are something truly extraordinary, Lily," he finally managed, his voice hushed, almost a whisper against the howling wind. The ancient wisdom in his eyes now held a deep concern. "But with great power comes great responsibility." The words hung in the air, heavy with unspoken warnings and the weight of experience.

Lily nodded slowly, her breath catching in her throat. The exhilaration of the moment was quickly being overshadowed by the profound implications of her newfound abilities. She was no longer just Lily, the girl who wandered through the woods. Something fundamental had shifted within her. She was a conduit, a focal point for a force that could shape the world around her, for better or for worse. The possibilities stretched before her, vast and unknown, filled with both dazzling light and terrifying shadows. A thrill of excitement mingled with a deep sense of trepidation. The path ahead, she instinctively knew, would be fraught with challenges, with difficult choices and unforeseen dangers. But looking at the swaying trees and feeling the residual energy thrumming within her, a flicker of determination ignited in her eyes. She wouldn't shy away from this. She would learn to control this power, to understand it, and she would use it for good, whatever the cost.

As the initial tremor of astonishment subsided, replaced by an increased sense of self-awareness, a fledgling purpose began to crystallize within her. The ingrained helplessness, a shadow cast by her years navigating the often indifferent landscape of the foster care system, started to recede. She was no longer the vulnerable child shuffled between homes; something profound had shifted. The raw power that coursed through her veins declared her something more, something formidable. The realization settled within her: she wasn't just a girl with strange abilities; she was a warrior, unexpectedly thrust onto a grand, cosmic stage, caught in an age-old, invisible conflict between the radiant forces of light and the encroaching shadows of darkness.

Her gaze drifted to Elias, who stood beside her, an enigmatic presence whose true origins and allegiances remained veiled in a captivating mystery. His quiet strength was a comfort, yet an air of ancient secrets clung to him like the scent of old parchment. In this precarious moment, bound by the shared experience of the impossible, she instinctively reached for the fragile tendril of hope that he was an ally, a steadfast protector in this bewildering new reality. His very presence seemed to emanate a quiet competence that offered a sliver of reassurance amidst the swirling uncertainty.

Her thoughts then turned to the ancient book, rescued from oblivion, its leather worn smooth by the countless unseen hands that had come before her. The cryptic symbols etched onto its pages seemed to pulse with a hidden energy, and the faint whispers that sometimes emanated from it hinted at forgotten lore and potent magic. She understood, with a certainty that resonated deep within her soul, that this book held the key. The key to this extraordinary and perilous world that had abruptly unfurled before her eyes. A realm where breathtaking wonder danced with unmistakable terror, and where the delicate threads of magic were inextricably woven with the sinister strands of darkness. Deciphering its secrets was no longer a matter of curiosity; it was a necessity, the only path to understanding the forces at play and ultimately, to defeating the malevolent evil that had been lurking in the periphery, now emboldened and threatening to engulf them all.

A fresh wave of hopeful determination bloomed within her, a warm, protective light chasing away the last whispers of fear. This newfound power wasn't a burden, but a promise, a chance to safeguard not only Rose, the precious light in her life, but also the family she was building, the connections she cherished. With a hopeful heart, she knew she would embrace this extraordinary ability, eager to learn its delicate intricacies and guide its formidable strength. Her spirit lifted at the thought of wielding this force, not with grim resolve, but with a loving intention, a shield to guard her family and anyone caught in the encroaching darkness. The shadows might have stirred this power awake, but they wouldn't claim her. Instead, she would rise, not as a figure of stark defiance, but as a hopeful beacon against the coming storm, ready to protect all those she held dear.

As the morning matured, the sun climbed higher, drawing back the long shadows that had clung to the forest floor. A subtle shift occurred in the air, the initial coolness giving way to a gentle warmth that hinted at the approaching heat of midday. Yet, beneath this surface tranquility, a prickle of unease remained with her. She sensed that the receding darkness of night wasn't truly vanquished, but merely biding its time, regrouping its shadowy tendrils in unseen places. It felt less like a full retreat and more like a strategic pause, a deceptive lull before a renewed assault. She could almost feel the unseen forces subtly shifting, preparing to lash out once the sun reached its zenith. A chilling premonition gripped her; she could almost feel the unseen energies coalescing, gathering their shadowy legions, preparing for a violent counterattack that threatened to tear them apart, leaving nothing but fragments in its wake.

A sudden, sharp pang of fear constricted her chest, stealing her breath. "I think… I need to go," she stammered to Elias, her voice barely a whisper, her eyes wide and reflecting the growing dread that clawed at her insides. The vibrant energy she had felt earlier now seemed to be draining away, replaced by a cold, hollow emptiness.

Before Elias could offer a word of reassurance, the ground beneath their feet lurched violently, a deep, guttural rumble emanating from the earth's very core, echoing through the ancient trees like the growl of some colossal beast. A shared, terrified glance flashed between them both, a silent acknowledgment of the great and immediate danger. The earth itself seemed to be alive, not in the vibrant, connected way she had sensed before, but as a monstrous entity, writhing with an unseen, malevolent power that threatened to erupt.

With each passing moment, the tremors intensified, escalating from a subtle shaking to a violent undulation that made it difficult to keep their balance. Jagged cracks began to spiderweb across the forest floor, dark fissures opening in the earth like gaping wounds, revealing an abyss of unknown depth. A suffocating sense of impending doom washed over them, heavy and absolute. They were no longer simply facing an external darkness; something far more primal and terrifying was awakening. They were not alone in this forest. Something very old and unspeakably evil was stirring deep beneath the surface, and its awakening promised nothing but destruction.

Just as the fractured earth groaned, threatening to widen into an inescapable maw and swallow them whole, a grotesque figure clawed its way from the inky blackness of the chasm's depths. It was a towering monstrosity, its skin a sickly, jaundiced green stretched taut over sharp, angular bones. Its eyes burned with an inner, malevolent fire, an otherworldly intensity that spoke of pure hatred and hunger. Its form was a nightmarish amalgamation, a twisted mockery of human anatomy, limbs contorted at unnatural angles, and razor-sharp claws dripping with an unseen, viscous fluid. A guttural roar ripped from its throat, a sound that vibrated through the very air, shaking the remaining leaves on the trees and sending a fresh wave of terror through them. With terrifying speed, it lunged forward, its intent unmistakable, etched in its burning gaze and the outstretched talons…to kill.

Elias reacted in a heartbeat, a blur of motion as he positioned himself swiftly between Lily and the monstrous creature, his lithe body coiled and tense, every muscle screaming readiness for the inevitable attack. The creature's elongated claws, like obsidian daggers, aimed directly for his chest, but he moved with a speed that defied human perception, a fleeting shadow against the backdrop of the fractured earth. He dodged the brutal assault with impossible grace, his form momentarily blurring as if he had vanished from sight, leaving only the lingering impression of movement in the air.

Before the lumbering creature could register its missed attack and recover its footing, Elias reappeared behind it, as if conjured from the very shadows. His hands now pulsed with an ethereal, silver light, casting an eerie glow on the creature's repulsive form. With a swift, decisive motion, like the strike of a viper, he slammed his glowing hands into the creature's back. A shockwave of pure energy erupted upon contact, sending the monstrous being hurtling forward with unnatural force, crashing back into the gaping chasm from whence it came. The impact reverberated through the forest, causing the earth to tremble once more as the creature disappeared with a sickening thud and a strangled shriek.

Lily stood frozen for a breath, her mind reeling at the impossible display of Elias's power. He was more than just a man, more than just someone who had offered her guidance. He was a guardian, a silent sentinel standing against the encroaching forces of darkness, a stronghold against the nightmares that clawed at the edges of reality. But the deep, resonant rumbling beneath their feet was a stark reminder that the battle was far from over. The chasm, though it had momentarily swallowed their attacker, continued to widen, its dark gullet promising further horrors. It was a wound in the world, and something sinister was clearly stirring within its depths.

A sudden, unexpected surge of energy coursed through Lily's veins, a potent force that felt both alien and intrinsically hers. Her eyes flickered, and a faint, ethereal blue light began to emanate from within them, casting a soft glow on her determined face. As the energy intensified, a shimmering, translucent shield of pure light materialized around her, a protective barrier against the unseen threats. With a newfound confidence that bloomed in the face of terror, she stepped forward, her voice ringing with a strength and conviction she hadn't known she possessed. "I won't let you harm us," she declared, her voice echoing through the disturbed forest, a challenge thrown into the abyss.

With a furious roar that echoed from the depths, the grotesque creature reappeared from the chasm, its burning eyes fixed with unwavering hatred on her. Ignoring Elias for now, it charged towards her, its razor claws outstretched, driven by a primal need to destroy. Though her limbs still trembled slightly from the initial shock, she stood her ground, raising her hands, instinctively channeling the energy that pulsed within her. A brilliant beam of pure, focused light erupted from her palms, streaking through the air and striking the creature squarely in its chest. The impact was like a physical blow, sending the monstrosity reeling backward with a strangled howl of pain. Its sickly green form flickered and wavered as the intense light began to consume it from within.

With a final, agonizing shriek and a blinding flash of light, the creature vanished completely, leaving behind only a small pile of smoking, black ashes on the fractured earth. The violent shaking of the ground abruptly ceased, and the jagged chasm began to slowly, grudgingly, close itself as if the earth itself was healing. Lily stood breathless, her heart pounding against her ribs, her body trembling with the aftershocks of fear and adrenaline. She had done it. Somehow, impossibly, she had faced the nightmare and emerged victorious.

Chapter 7:

Every muscle in Lily's body screamed in protest as she finally reached the familiar silhouette of her home. Exhaustion clung to her like a heavy shroud, each step up the porch steps a monumental effort. Her mind was a frantic whirlwind, replaying the terrifying events of the morning, the raw power she had unleashed, the monstrous creature, and Elias's impossible abilities. A morning that felt like it had compressed a lifetime of experience into a few harrowing hours. Just as suddenly as he had materialized, a guardian angel against the encroaching darkness, Elias was gone, leaving her adrift in the unsettling quiet that followed the storm.

The farmhouse emanated an almost eerie stillness, a stark and unsettling contrast to the life-and-death struggle she had just endured in the heart of the woods. Inside, the normalcy was almost jarring. She found her mother in the kitchen, humming softly as she expertly chopped vegetables, the rhythmic clatter of the knife against the cutting board a mundane counterpoint to the earth-shattering roars she had so recently heard. Rose sat at the kitchen table, her brow furrowed in concentration as she diligently flipped through the pages of her animal encyclopedia, her small foot tapping a steady beat against the linoleum floor. The scene felt like a tableau from a different reality, a world untouched by the horrors she had just faced.

"Lily, you're back! You look like you've seen a ghost," Sarah exclaimed, her warm, familiar voice laced with genuine concern as she turned from the counter. Her eyes scanned Lily's pale face and disheveled appearance.

Lily could only manage a weak nod, the enormity of what she had witnessed was a suffocating weight in her chest. The words caught in her throat, a jumbled mess of monstrous forms, glowing hands, and earth-shattering rumbles. How could she possibly articulate the sheer impossibility of it all? Would her mother look at her with pity, or worse, with disbelief? The truth felt too bizarre, too terrifying to share, a secret that threatened to shatter the fragile peace of their ordinary lives. Instead, she forced a weak, unconvincing smile, desperately trying to plaster over the raw fear and confusion that churned within her. "Just a long walk," she lied, the tremor in her voice betraying the inadequacy of her words.

Rose, ever observant when it came to her big sister, raised a curious eyebrow, her gaze lingering on Lily's pale face for a moment longer than usual. But with a childlike understanding of unspoken distress, she didn't press the subject, returning her attention to the fascinating world of the animal kingdom.

"Well, lunch is almost ready. You look like you could use something to eat," Sarah said, her sweet smile radiating a comforting warmth that Lily desperately needed. The simple offer of food, the familiar routine of a midday meal, was a small anchor in the sea of chaos that threatened to engulf her. For now, she clung to that normalcy, a fragile shield against the terrifying reality she now knew existed just beyond the walls of their ordinary world.

As they sat around the table, the plate of food was doing little to soothe Lily's frayed nerves, but she made a concerted effort to engage in the normalcy of lunchtime conversation. She listened to Rose excitedly recount a fascinating fact about the migratory patterns of arctic terns and offered polite responses to her mother's inquiries about her "long walk." But beneath the veneer of casual interaction, her mind was a relentless projector, constantly replaying the terrifying images of the sickly green creature, its burning eyes, and the gaping chasm that had scarred the forest floor. A deep sense of isolation began to settle within her, a cold knot in her stomach. While she knew her mother and Rose had occasionally noticed strange sounds or unsettling feelings within the old house, those instances had largely been dismissed and attributed instead to the settling timbers, the wind whistling through cracks, the overactive imaginations of children. Now, however, Lily felt a terrifying certainty that she was the sole witness, the only one who truly understood the encroaching darkness, the evil presence that lurked just beyond their oblivious comfort.

A sudden, involuntary shiver traced a path down the length of her spine, causing her to shudder. A heavy sense of dread, far more potent than the lingering fear from the forest, washed over her, a chilling premonition of something imminent and terrible. Just then, the grandfather clock in the corner of the living room, a familiar and comforting presence that usually marked the passage of time with a stately chime, began to stir. But instead of the usual resonant hourly melody, a discordant, haunting tune echoed through the house, a series of jarring notes that scraped against the silence like fingernails on glass. Simultaneously, the clock's ornate hands began to spin wildly, blurring into an incomprehensible frenzy, as if time itself was fracturing and unraveling within the aged mechanism. Sarah and Rose froze mid-bite, their eyes widening in alarm, the fine hairs on their arms standing on end in instinctive fear.

The jarring melody hung in the air, a strong wave of chilling dissonance that seemed to seep into the very foundations of the house, vibrating in their teeth and resonating deep within their bones. Sarah's face, moments before filled with maternal warmth, now paled to a ghostly white, her eyes wide with a terror that Lily had never witnessed before. Rose, her small body visibly trembling, instinctively reached out and clung to her mother's arm, her knuckles white against Sarah's sleeve. Lily, her own heart pounding frantically, felt a familiar yet still startling surge of energy coursing through her veins, a visceral response to the strange magic that now saturated the air. This was no ordinary malfunction of the old timepiece, no simple mechanical failure. Something deeply sinister, something connected to the darkness she had encountered in the woods, was at play within the very walls of their home.

The grandfather clock continued its eerie performance, the frantic spinning of its hands accelerating into a dizzying, hypnotic swirl. A low, ominous hum filled the room, a deep, resonant vibration that grew louder with each passing, distorted second, pressing against their eardrums and creating a suffocating tension. The air itself seemed to thicken, becoming heavy, as if an unseen presence had entered the room, a cold and malevolent entity that exuded an aura of dread.

Sarah, her voice barely a trembling whisper, her eyes darting nervously towards the violently spinning hands of the clock, finally broke the petrified silence. "We need to leave this room. Now!"

Without a word of protest, Lily and Rose instinctively followed their mother, their footsteps a soft, almost hesitant echo in the suddenly charged and tense silence of the hallway. They huddled together in the relatively open space of the foyer, only steps to the door. Their gazes drawn, as if by an invisible cord, towards the living room and the grandfather clock within. A once-familiar object now transformed into a monstrous entity, its silent ticking in the adjacent room feeling like the measured countdown to some unseen doom.

The icy grip of dread tightened around them, a suffocating presence that seemed to steal the very air from their lungs, silencing even the smallest of breaths. The comforting familiarity of their home had been shattered, replaced by an unsettling awareness. They were no longer alone within these walls. Something dark and undeniably powerful had breached their sanctuary, an unseen intruder that had announced its presence with a chilling symphony. And with each passing, silent moment, the oppressive atmosphere suggested that this unwelcome presence was growing stronger, its influence spreading like a creeping shadow.

Then, just as abruptly and inexplicably as it had begun, the haunting, discordant melody ceased. The unsettling silence that followed was almost more unnerving than the cacophony had been. From their vantage point in the foyer, they could see the grandfather clock standing unnervingly still, its ornate hands frozen in a bizarre, unnatural position, as if time itself had been forcibly altered. Slowly, almost imperceptibly, the oppressive atmosphere that had filled the house like a suffocating blanket began to dissipate, replaced by a heavy, expectant silence that crackled with unspoken fear.

Sarah let out a shaky, uneven breath, her hand instinctively finding its way to clasp both Lily's and Rose's, her touch offering a small measure of fragile comfort. "Oh, girls," she said, her voice trembling ever so slightly, a forced attempt at normalcy battling the fear in her eyes, "This is an old house, you know. Filled with old antiques. And old things... they make strange noises sometimes." She pulled them close, enveloping them in a tight hug, a desperate embrace that felt as much about reassuring herself as it was about comforting her daughters, a silent plea to believe in the safety of their familiar world even as the evidence to the contrary hung heavy in the air. "Perhaps it's time to replace a few things, starting with that clock."

Lily and Rose clung to their mother's side, their small bodies still trembling from the raw fear that had gripped them. They knew, with an unsettling certainty that transcended their mother's reassuring words, that this was no ordinary old house, no mere creaking of ancient timbers. Something sinister was indeed lurking in the shadows, something that had just given them a chilling, undeniable taste of its dark power. And Lily, her mind racing, couldn't help but wonder: how far was this malevolent force willing to go? What horrifying acts might it commit, and what did it truly want?

But for now, in the comforting circle of their mother's arms, they allowed themselves to be lulled by her warmth, succumbing to the desperate need to believe her fragile fiction. For a few precious moments, they could pretend that the terrifying spectacle of the clock, the oppressive atmosphere, and the noticeable dread were nothing more than a shared nightmare, a figment of their overactive imaginations.

Once the immediate tension had diffused, and the pretense of normalcy had somewhat settled back into the house, Lily retreated to the sanctuary of her room. She craved solitude, desperate for a moment to process the overwhelming weight of the day's events that pressed down upon her, threatening to crush her very soul. With a deep, shuddering breath, she reached for the ancient book, its worn leather cover feeling cool against her trembling hands. She knew, with a quiet conviction, that answers lay hidden within its cryptic pages. Perhaps there were clues, warnings, or even a forgotten method to combat the growing evil that now seemed to permeate their world. She had to find something, anything. Not just for herself, but for Rose, her little sister whom she had sworn to protect, who was too young to understand the dark forces now closing in. The thought of Rose, oblivious but vulnerable, fueled her courage. She had to do something.

The book lay open on her desk, its aged pages filled with a dizzying array of strange symbols, intricate diagrams, and what looked like constellations of stars. Perhaps within its mysterious depths lay the very answers she was so desperately searching for. A way to truly understand the growing darkness that menaced their home and the monstrous creature that had violently emerged from the fractured earth. She immersed herself in the dense, cryptic text, her mind a whirlwind of confusion yet propelled by an unshakeable determination. The language, though undeniably archaic and alien to her conscious mind, resonated with a strange, almost unsettling familiarity, as if a long-dormant part of her recognized its patterns. The symbols seemed to dance and shift before her eyes, revealing hidden meanings and connections with each passing, focused moment. Though she couldn't articulate *why* or *how* this was happening, a sense of urgency was surging through her, a desperate need to unlock the book's secrets before the opportunity vanished, before it was truly too late.

As the hours slipped away, Lily felt a growing exhaustion begin to creep in, a weariness deep in her bones, though her mind stubbornly refused to rest. She was on the cusp of something monumental, a breakthrough that felt like it could unravel everything she thought she knew about their world. A sudden, involuntary shiver traced a path down the length of her spine, causing her to shudder as the chilling implications of what she was about to discover slammed into her. The knowledge she sought held a terrifying duality: it possessed the potential to either vanquish the insidious darkness or, conversely, to unknowingly empower it further. The weight of this realization pressed down on her, leaving her feeling heavy and cold.

Just as the answer to all of it felt within her grasp, her eyes flickered upwards, noticing a stark shadow suddenly fall across the open pages of the book. Startled, her head snapped up, her gaze drawn to the doorway. Standing there, filling the entrance to her room, was a man. His form was tall and imposing, radiating an unnerving darkness that seemed to suck the very light from the air around him. His eyes, two fathomless pools of chilling black, met hers, and from them, a wave of pure evil emanated, washing through the room and making her blood run cold.

The man's face remained shrouded in the deep shadows of the doorway, yet she could feel the piercing intensity of his gaze, as if it stripped away her very defenses. He stepped into the room, his movements slow, deliberate, each footfall a soft thud that echoed the chilling purpose of a predator stalking its chosen prey. She remained frozen in her chair, a silent gasp caught in her throat, unable to move, unable to breathe.

"You've awakened something my child," his voice rumbled, a low, menacing growl that seemed to vibrate the very air in the room, carrying with it the cold weight of ancient power.

A fresh wave of fear washed over her, rooting her to her chair. But beneath it, something else stirred. Once more, there was a strange, unsettling sense of familiarity. The timbre of his voice, the oppressive aura of darkness that clung to him, it was as if she had encountered this man before, not in the physical world, but in a realm beyond her waking comprehension. How could that be? Her mind raced, trying to grasp the impossible connection.

Before she could even begin to process the implications, a small, desperate gasp filled the silence. Rose rushed into the room, her breath catching in her throat, her eyes widening in alarm as she took in the tall, dark stranger. "Who is he, Lily? Why is he here?" she asked, her voice a thin, trembling whisper, instantly shattering the precarious bubble of terror and strange recognition that had enveloped her.

The man's head slowly swiveled, his chilling black eyes now locking onto Rose. A sinister light seemed to glint in their depths, and a fresh shiver of dread ran through Lily. The knot in her chest tightened into a cold, hard stone as she realized the true, horrifying scope of their danger. This man wasn't just a threat to her newfound abilities which she still didn't understand; but he was a very real, existential threat to Rose, to her parents, to their very home, and perhaps even to the entire world they knew.

With a surge of protective instinct, she lunged forward, placing herself squarely in front of Rose, shielding her younger sister with her own body. Her voice, though it held a tremor, was firm and defiant as she looked up at the towering figure. "Who are you? What do you want?"

The man's lips curled into a slow, cruel smile, and a low, rasping chuckle, devoid of any warmth, filled the room. The sound was like gravel scraping over stone, causing both girls to tremble. Without hesitation, Lily instinctively grabbed hold of Rose, pushing her farther away from him. "I'm here to claim what is rightfully mine," he finally said, his voice dripping with menace, each word a venomous drop.

Her mind raced, a frantic kaleidoscope of terror and desperate calculation. She had to protect Rose, but a terrifying truth resonated deep within her: they were utterly outmatched. This man was not of this world, and whatever he wanted, it could only mean unimaginable destruction.

The tension in the room stretched, thin and brittle, threatening to snap. Just as the silence became unbearable, a sudden, jarring *slam* echoed through the house. The bedroom door thrust against the wall, revealing their mother standing there, her face a portrait of fear and concern, her eyes wide with alarm. "How did you get in here?" she asked, her voice trembling, her gaze instantly falling upon the stranger. The man's black eyes narrowed, a predatory gleam sharpening in their depths as he turned his attention to Sarah. A suffocating dread, heavier and colder than anything before, settled over the room. With a surge of fierce, maternal protectiveness, Sarah snatched both Rose and Lily close, her grip firm and unwavering, pulling them into the shaky, desperate safety of her embrace.

Sarah's sudden, terrified presence seemed to momentarily disrupt the intruder's chilling focus, but his eyes, though momentarily diverted, held a sinister promise of retribution. The air in the room crackled with a volatile tension, thick and suffocating. Sarah's mind reeled, desperately searching for a viable solution. Her thoughts, typically a whirlwind of plans and protective strategies, were now a blank slate that rendered her immobile. Every fiber of her being screamed for action, yet she remained rooted to the spot, her body refusing to obey, utterly unsure of what to do.

Meanwhile, Lily's mind was conjuring its own paths to safety. With a surge of fierce determination, she recalled the way she had reacted that morning in the forest, the power she had unleashed. A wave of raw energy pulsed through her, warm and powerful, and a soft, ethereal glow emanated from her body as she instinctively slipped free from her mother's protective grasp.

The intruder's eyes widened, a flicker of genuine surprise momentarily eclipsing the malevolence within them. His hand instinctively tightened on a previously unseen, wickedly sharp weapon that now seemed to materialize from the shadows at his side. "What sorcery is this?" he hissed, his voice a low, echoing snarl that filled the room.

Before he could so much as flinch, Lily unleashed a torrent of concentrated wind, a powerful, invisible force that slammed into the intruder with brutal intensity. He was hurled backward, his tall, imposing body crashing against the opposite wall with a thunderous boom that vibrated through the floorboards. Plaster dust billowed from the ceiling, raining down like ghostly snow.

Seizing the precious moment of the intruder's disorientation, Sarah looked around her for something, anything that could be a weapon. Her eyes darted around, landing on a nearby ceramic vase, its delicate porcelain surface gleaming faintly in the dim light. With a fierce grunt, she snatched it up and hurled it with all her might at the intruder. "Stay away from us!" she shouted. The vase shattered against him with a sharp, explosive crack, scattering shards across the floor. Yet, he remained strangely unmoved, as if the blow were nothing more than a passing breeze, his dark form already beginning to coalesce from the cloud of dust.

A guttural roar, filled with unbridled fury, ripped from his throat, a sound that promised violent retribution. He surged forward, his chilling black eyes burning with a renewed, deadly intensity.

Lily knew, with a sudden, chilling certainty, that this was not a foe they could defeat with brute force or shattered vases. Her earlier victory in the forest had taught her that. She had to use her newfound powers to their full potential, just as she had against the monstrous creature, harnessing the earth itself. Channeling her entire focus, she reached out with her mind, connecting to the raw, ancient energy pulsating beneath their feet. The very floorboards beneath the intruder began to groan, then crack and splinter, crumbling inward as if dissolving into nothingness. With a strangled cry of surprise and fury, the dark figure plunged into the rapidly widening abyss, the earth swallowing him whole. As the ground convulsed and then slowly, silently, closed over the void, a wave of shaky relief washed over them.

But even as they gasped for breath, clinging to that fleeting sense of victory, a cold truth settled in their hearts: this was only a temporary reprieve. The darkness was far from defeated. A strange, throbbing energy pulsed through the very foundations of the house. The walls vibrated, a low, ominous hum resonating in the air, deepening with each passing second. Something was coming, something terrible, its presence growing stronger, more intense with every agonizing creak of the old house. They had to prepare, for whatever it was, it was coming for them.

Agonized creaks echoed through the house, the sounds like tortured screams of wood and plaster, as if the very structure were in torment. The ominous hum deepened, rising in pitch and intensity, a resonant tide of sound that vibrated the very glass in the windows, making them rattle in their frames. An icy dread, colder and more pervasive than anything they had felt before, crept through them, a chilling whisper of the true horror about to unfold.

Then, with a cataclysmic roar that seemed to rip the fabric of reality, the closet door splintered inward, tearing from its hinges with explosive force. A wave of suffocating darkness surged from the gaping hole of the ruined doorway, instantly engulfing the room in a chilling void. It was as if a portal to hell had opened, and its denizens were pouring through. A terrifying horde of shadowy creatures, their forms indistinct and writhing within the abyssal blackness, flooded into the house. Their eyes, malevolent pinpricks of unnatural light, glowed with an unholy intensity, and their cries were not roars or growls, but the screech of tortured souls, a sound that promised unimaginable suffering.

Sarah, her maternal instincts blazing like a wildfire, instinctively pulled Lily and Rose even tighter against her, her body forming a desperate, trembling shield. Her eyes, wide with sheer terror, darted frantically as the monstrous, shadowy creatures poured through the splintered doorway, their forms indistinct yet menacing in the encroaching darkness. Lily and Rose pressed back against their mother, their hearts hammering a frantic, desperate rhythm against their ribs. The horrifying truth was undeniable: they were hopelessly outnumbered, completely outmatched, and utterly trapped. Any flickering thought of escape was instantly crushed by the sheer, overwhelming tide of creatures that now blocked every conceivable path.

Lily's mind had been racing, however, and had come up with a plan. She drew in a sharp, steadying breath, then unleashed the earth's raw might. The very floorboards beneath the grotesque invaders groaned and then violently quaked, splintering cracks spreading like lightning bolts across the worn wooden planks. Rose, without a moment's hesitation, instantly mirrored what her sister was doing. Her mind telling her it was nothing more than a futile attempt at being brave. But instead, her own energy flaring outward, amplified the tremor until the ground beneath the creatures bucked and heaved. Sarah, though momentarily stunned by the otherworldly display of her daughters' supernatural abilities, surged forward with a fierce, primal protectiveness. A raw courage she never knew she possessed flared in her eyes. With a defiant cry that defied her trembling voice, she launched herself into the grasping, shadowy forms, a mother determined to shield her family against impossible odds.

Together, the three of them, a desperate triad, fought against the overwhelming darkness. Though razor-sharp claws scraped against the air where their skin had been moments before and unseen teeth gnashed menacingly, threatening to devour them whole, they refused to submit. The house, once their cherished home filled with the echoes of laughter and ordinary life, was now irrevocably transformed into a brutal, terrifying battleground. The familiar walls, which had once held warmth and comfort, now reverberated only with the chilling sounds of chaos, cries of desperation, and relentless destruction.

Just when it seemed as if the shadowy horde would finally overwhelm them, when their strength was ebbing and the sheer numbers of the creatures threatened to engulf them, another figure emerged from the deeper shadows of the ruined doorway. His presence was unlike anything Lily had encountered before; his eyes glowed with an ancient power that surpassed even Elias's abilities. With a single, effortless gesture of his hand, he unleashed a silent wave of incandescent energy that swept through the house. The shadowy creatures, caught in its devastating wake, shrieked in unison, their indistinct forms dissolving into nothingness in an instant.

The house fell into an unnerving silence, the only sounds now being the heavy, ragged breathing of Sarah, Lily, and Rose. The air, moments before thick with malevolence, now felt strangely purified. The figure turned his attention towards them, his glowing eyes holding a mixture of profound admiration and deep concern. "You are stronger than you know," he said, his voice low, resonant, and strangely reassuring, a calm in the heart of the storm. "But the battle is far from over."

A cold dread settled over them all as the stranger simply melted back into thin air, vanishing as quickly and mysteriously as he had appeared. They knew, with a certainty that chilled them to the bone, that this was just the beginning. The darkness which had invaded their home was undeniably growing, a malevolent force expanding its reach, and for some unknown, terrifying reason, their family was now inexplicably at the very center of it all.

Chapter 8:

The kitchen was a stark, almost unsettling contrast to the chaos they had just endured on the upper floor. The familiar warmth that usually clung to the space, born of countless meals shared together, had utterly vanished, leaving it feeling cold and sterile. Sunlight, now streaming through the window, no longer brought cheer but instead created long, eerie shadows that danced like phantom figures across the walls, mirroring the unsettling images burned into their minds. Lily and Rose, their faces drained of all color, remained unnaturally still and silent, their shock an intense presence between them. Sarah, moving with a deliberate, almost ritualistic slowness, retrieved the first aid kit. Her touch was gentle as she cleaned the superficial scrapes and bruises on their skin, a deep, shuddering wave of relief washing over her that she, as both the adult and their mother, had borne the brunt of the more severe assault.

The events of the day had shattered their sense of security. The house, once a safe haven, a sanctuary from the outside world, now felt like a haunted, hostile place. Every creak of the old timbers, every groan of the pipes, sent fresh shivers down their spines, making them jumpy and hyper-aware. A wave of nausea washed over Sarah as the terrifying reality of what had transpired truly sank in. Her gaze drifted towards the front door, a silent, beckoning exit. For a fleeting, desperate moment, she contemplated leaving it all behind. She could grab the girls, and simply go, find refuge in a sterile hotel room, or her mother's house, anywhere that felt safe. But then, the image of her husband, Daniel, flashed in her mind. He would be home in minutes, and she couldn't bear the thought of trying to explain the unimaginable, the otherworldly horrors, to him over the phone. The fear of the unknown, of what lay outside and what their departure might provoke, was almost as paralyzing as the terrifying fear of staying within the now-breached walls of their home.

Sarah shook her head, as if to physically dislodge the terrifying thoughts. She moved to the kettle, the trembling in her hands a stark reminder of the recent terror they had endured. Pouring herself a cup of tea, the steam curled upwards, creating a mist that seemed to waft around her like a ghostly veil. "I can't believe that just happened," she whispered, her voice barely audible, thick with disbelief. "I just can't believe it. None of this makes any sense."

Lily nodded slowly, her eyes fixed on the kitchen window. The world outside, bathed in the innocent light of the evening sun, seemed utterly unreal, a distorted, peaceful reflection of the nightmare they had just experienced within their own walls. "It feels like something out of a horror movie," she said, her voice filled with a disquieting mix of lingering fear and utter disbelief.

Rose, the youngest, remained unnaturally quiet, her eyes wide and dark with lingering terror. She clung to her mother's hand, her small body shaking intermittently. Sarah pulled her daughter closer, offering silent comfort, stroking her hair. The immense weight of protecting her children, of being their sole shield against an unimaginable darkness, settled heavily on her shoulders. She knew, with a certainty that both terrified and strengthened her, that these two girls needed her now more than ever before.

Sarah's unspoken question hung in the air, heavy with a fresh wave of dread. She recalled how the girls had moved through several foster homes before being adopted by her and Daniel. Was this the reason? Her gaze, hesitant at first, then firm, moved from Rose to Lily, her eyes searching. "Girls, the magic you used... how long have you known about it?"

Lily's denial was immediate, a sharp, almost frantic sound laced with genuine shock. "I didn't know, Mom. Not until today, I swear." The words tumbled out, desperate to convince. After the unimaginable horror that had just unfolded within their home, the last thing Lily felt she could reveal was the monster in the forest, Elias, or the old, cryptic book she had found. That truth felt too fantastic, too dangerous to burden her mother with right now. Not to mention the thoughts of being sent back to the foster care system.

Rose, her voice barely a whisper, echoed her sister's sentiment. "Me neither. I was just trying to do what Lily was doing. I just wanted to help." Her small hands, still trembling slightly, clutched to her mother's shirt.

Their answers, though sincere, only deepened the unsettling mystery surrounding the day's events. Sarah desperately wanted answers, needed them now, this very minute. The rational part of her mind screamed for an explanation, for clarity in the face of the impossible. But the raw, unadulterated fear in her daughters' wide eyes, the lingering tremors in their small bodies, stopped her. This baffling puzzle, this terrifying secret, would have to wait. It was a question for another time, when the immediate danger had truly passed.

The rhythmic, unnerving ticking of the grandfather clock in the living room now only amplified the suffocating silence in the kitchen. Sarah and the girls waited, each of them straining their ears, listening intently for any sound, any indication that the nightmare was not truly over, that the evil had not fully receded. The faint creak of the front door opening, followed by familiar footsteps in the hallway, brought a wave of relief that washed over them all. Daniel stepped into the kitchen, his presence a sudden anchor in their fractured reality.

His face, usually etched with the familiar lines of a tired but content smile, was now drawn and alarmingly pale. The usual crinkles around his eyes, signs of laughter and a lifetime of worries, deepened into an expression of deep concern as he took in the sight of his family. They were huddled together, an almost feral instinct to protect one another evident in their tight embrace, their faces bearing the unmistakable weight of a haunting fear. Daniel's briefcase slipped from his fingers, the worn leather hitting the tiled floor with a dull thud that echoed ominously in the tense silence. "What happened?" he asked, his voice hoarse, a stark contrast to his usual calm and reassuring demeanor.

Sarah and the girls exchanged quick, wide-eyed glances, a silent conversation filled with unspoken terror passing between them. The full weight of the day's events pressed down on them like a physical force, suffocating any attempt at immediate explanation. Finally, Sarah found her voice, though it came out in a trembling whisper, barely audible. "We... we had visitors," she began, her words fragile and uncertain.

Daniel's eyes widened in alarm, his brow furrowing in confusion. "Visitors? What do you mean?" he pressed, his voice rising slightly, the question sharpening as his gaze fell upon the angry red scratches marring his wife's arms. The horrifying truth of what she was implying was beginning to dawn on him. "Where are they? Did you call the police?" he asked, his eyes scanning all around for signs of the intruders.

Sarah shook her head, a raw, trembling sigh escaping her lips. "No, Daniel. They're... gone. And the police wouldn't understand." Her voice was barely a whisper, laden with a despair that spoke volumes about the unexplainable nature of what they had just faced.

Lily, though traces of the fear still clung to her voice like a shroud, pushed through it, desperate to make her father understand. "It was... it was like something out of a nightmare, Dad. Creatures, dark things... they came into the house." Her voice caught in her throat, a fragile whisper, as she struggled to articulate the incomprehensible horror they had witnessed, the sounds and images flashing behind her eyes.

Daniel's face blanched, the color draining from his cheeks, leaving him stark white. His gaze darted frantically from Sarah to Lily, then to Rose, whose small body was still trembling violently, tucked into her mother's side. Disbelief warred fiercely with a growing, cold dread in his eyes. "Creatures? What are you talking about?" he demanded, his voice now edged with a desperate, bewildered fear. He knew his wife; she wasn't prone to exaggeration or fanciful tales.

Sarah nodded, her lips quivering, tears welling in her eyes. "It's true, Daniel. We saw them. They were horrible. We're lucky to be alive." She couldn't bring herself to elaborate further, the memory of those terrifying, shadowy forms, their glowing eyes and the chilling screeches, still fresh and searing in her mind. Her silence, however, only amplified the terrifying weight of their words.

A long, heavy silence descended upon the kitchen. Daniel looked at his family, his mind racing, grappling with a concept that shattered his every rational belief. He desperately wanted to believe them, to offer comfort, but the sheer impossibility of their words made it hard to comprehend. "Creatures? You mean like, animals?" he asked, his voice betraying his confusion, trying to force their horrific account into a framework his mind could process.

"No, Daniel," Sarah replied, a shudder running through her. "Creatures, as in shadowy figures with glowing eyes. I don't know. Demons, I guess," she added, shaking her head slowly as though she couldn't even believe the words escaping her own lips. The absurdity of it all, juxtaposed with the stark terror etched on her daughters' faces, was overwhelming.

Daniel had always been the steady, rational one, the unwavering rock of their family, the one who fixed things and solved problems with logic and reason. But now, faced with something utterly inexplicable, something that defied every law of nature he understood, he could feel a wave of fear washing over him, stealing the breath from his lungs. He loved Sarah more than anything, and he knew, with absolute certainty, that she wasn't the type of person to fabricate such a monstrous tale. Plus, he could visibly see the trauma etched onto their faces. The lingering tremors in their bodies, evidence that no lie could produce. His gaze swept over the messy kitchen, the disturbed antique clock in the other room, the scratches on Sarah's arm. It was all too real. "Okay. We need to leave," he said finally, his voice firm, the decision solidifying in his mind. "We can't stay here. I won't have any of you in harm's way."

Daniel's demand to leave hung in the air, a heavy, unspoken weight in the room. The idea of abandoning their home, the very foundation of their family life, was painful, yet the terrifying thought of what might happen if they stayed was even more paralyzing.

Sarah looked at her daughters, their eyes wide with fear and confusion, reflecting the turmoil she felt inside. She yearned to protect them, to shield them from the incomprehensible horrors they had witnessed, to wrap them in an impenetrable bubble of safety. But a stark realization solidified within her: staying put was no longer an option. The house, once their sanctuary, their haven, had irrevocably transformed into a chilling battlefield, its familiar corners now harboring unspeakable threats. "Okay," she replied. "If that's what you think is best."

Lily, her mind racing at a dizzying speed, tried to process the whirlwind of everything that had happened: the monstrous creatures, the suffocating fear, and the astonishing, terrifying power she had discovered within herself. She felt utterly overwhelmed, a churning maelstrom of emotions swirling inside her. "What if they follow us?" she asked, her voice barely a whisper, voicing the chilling fear that had just solidified in her own mind as she recalled the creature from the forest.

Daniel and Sarah exchanged deeply worried glances, a silent, grim acknowledgment passing between them. The question hung in the air, echoing Lily's deepest fear: what if the monsters, these *things* that defied explanation, could simply follow them, rendering any escape futile?

Rose, still clinging desperately to her mother's hand, looked around the kitchen with wide, frightened eyes. The once familiar surroundings now seemed alien and threatening. The shadows on the walls, previously benign, now appeared to writhe and dance, taking on grotesque, menacing shapes in her terrified imagination, a visual testament to the terror that had invaded their home.

A new dread settled over the family, chilling them to the bone. The horrifying truth was undeniable: they were no longer safe in their own home. The creatures they had faced were not ordinary trespassers; they were something born of nightmares, something sinister that had marked this place as its own. And what if leaving didn't stop it, or even made it worse.

"Okay," Daniel conceded, his voice tight with a newfound, grim resolve. The words were difficult, but the alternative was unthinkable. "We'll stay. But," he added, his gaze sweeping over their pale, shaken faces, "We're having a campout in the living room tonight. All of us. We're sticking together until we know what we're dealing with. And if anything out of the ordinary happens, and I mean anything, then we get in the car and we leave. No arguments, no questions asked." There were no arguments, no protests from anyone. The thought of being alone, even in their own familiar rooms, was now a terrifying prospect.

"Dad," Lily spoke up, her voice tinged with a fresh layer of uncertainty. She hesitated, glancing at the floor. "Remember when Grandpa was here, and he said kids weren't allowed in the attic?"

"Yeah," Daniel said, a flicker of curiosity crossing his worried expression as he noticed her hesitation. "What about it?"

"Well," Lily admitted, her eyes still cast downwards as if she'd confessed to a grave transgression. "I went to the attic."

"That's okay, sweetie," Daniel reassured her, his voice softer now, sensing the underlying distress. He reached out and gently squeezed her shoulder. "This is your home now, and we gave you permission to explore. We told you that Grandpa just likes to be alone when he's going through memories up there." He was trying to bring a comforting normalcy to the situation, though his eyes were still filled with an unspoken tension.

"But," she replied, the word catching in her throat as tears began to well in her eyes, blurring the edges of the room. "I went to the attic. And I saw something."

"When did you go up there, Lily?" Sarah asked, her voice a little sharper, a flicker of concern about her daughter's solitary venture now overriding the immediate terror.

"A few nights ago, while everyone was sleeping," Lily admitted, her voice barely a whisper. "I thought I heard something."

"Why didn't you wake us up?" Daniel asked, his tone taking on a mix of concern and bewilderment. The idea of her venturing alone into the dark attic at night was unsettling enough without the added layer of her current fear.

"I thought you might get mad if it turned out to be nothing," Lily confessed, her voice barely a whisper, the old fear of judgment resurfacing. "Like they did in the foster homes." The lingering memory of past dismissals, of being told her concerns were overreactions, were a heavy weight on her small shoulders.

"Oh, honey," Sarah said, her voice filled with heartache, reaching for Lily and pulling her into a fierce, comforting hug. "You don't ever have to worry about that here. Not with us. Do you understand?" Her gaze met Lily's, direct and unwavering, filled with a promise that transcended the chaos of the day.

"Yes," Lily murmured, hugging her back tightly, letting herself be enveloped in the warmth of her mother's unconditional love.

"Okay, but now… what did you see?" Sarah pressed gently, her voice now a hushed urgency.

"I was looking around, and I found something with a strange symbol," she began, recounting the events of that night. "But then I noticed something in the corner. A shadow, and it had glowing eyes. So I ran out of there as quickly as I could," she replied, shivering from the memory.

"Why didn't you tell us about this sooner?" Daniel asked, his voice softer now, but still laced with a desperate need for answers. The pieces of the terrifying puzzle were beginning to fall into place, though he still didn't understand what it all meant. But the forming picture in his mind was more horrific than anything he could have ever imagined.

"I was afraid you would be mad at me for going up there, and I didn't know if you would believe me," she said, the tears that had been welling now freely rolling down her face. The confession, finally spoken, seemed to unburden her slightly.

Daniel and Sarah, despite the gnawing terror in their own hearts, did their best to reassure both girls, pulling them close again. "No matter what, you can always talk to us about anything," Sarah murmured, stroking Lily's hair. "Anything at all." Daniel added, his voice firm, "No matter how crazy it may sound." It was a desperate promise, spoken in the face of the impossible, meant to mend the fragile trust that had been strained by their past experiences.

As night finally fell upon the old farmhouse, casting deep shadows that seemed to hold their breath, Lily and Rose, exhausted by the day's unimaginable events, managed to find a fitful sleep. They lay side by side in the sleeping bags Daniel had retrieved from the garage, their small forms huddled together for comfort. Daniel and

Sarah, however, found very little rest. They slept only in brief, anxious shifts, each of them listening intently to every creak and groan of the old house, their senses alert for any sign that the nightmare might return.

When Sarah finally drifted off to sleep, Daniel quietly dialed his father's number. He knew it was the middle of the night, and that he would undoubtedly wake him. But he couldn't help himself. A gnawing suspicion, fueled by the day's horrors and Lily's confession about the attic, had taken root. He had to know what, if anything, his father knew about this house. Was there truly something more in the attic besides the dust-laden memories of years past? Something his father had known about all along?

The phone rang only twice before a gruff, familiar voice answered, thick with sleep but immediately alert. "Daniel?" his father asked, his voice already laced with concern, a stark contrast to his usual jovial tone. "It's the middle of the night, son. Is anything wrong?"

"Dad, I'm sorry to wake you," Daniel began, his voice strained, the weight of the day pressing down on him. "But I've got to know something. Something important."

"What is it?" his father replied, the sleepiness now entirely gone from his voice. A subtle hardening entered his tone, a shift that suggested he knew, or at least suspected, what question was about to come.

"Dad, is there anything strange about this house?" Daniel asked, the words tumbling out in a rush, a mix of desperation and a desperate plea for sanity.

"What do you mean strange, son? Like creaking floorboards?" the old man chuckled, a sound that, under any other circumstance, would have been comforting. But now, it only grated on Daniel's frayed nerves.

"No, Dad, like symbols in the attic that you always said kids weren't allowed in. Or shadow creatures, or a portal to hell. I don't know, Dad, anything," he said, his voice rising with barely suppressed frustration.

"Ah," the old man simply stated, the single syllable heavy with unspoken meaning. "I wondered when this would come up."

"What?!" Daniel gasped, the word ripped from him. His blood ran cold. "You mean you knew!"

"Calm down, son. Yeah, your mother and I knew." The old man's voice was weary now, stripped of its earlier pretense, leaving only a heavy admission.

"Why didn't you bother to tell me this before I moved my family here?!" Daniel's voice cracked, raw with disbelief and a surge of furious betrayal. He gripped the phone tighter, as if it were the only thing grounding him. "I can't believe what I'm hearing right now."

"We hoped it wouldn't matter," his father replied, a deep sigh rustling through the phone line. "That nothing would happen, and you would never have to find out. We thought the house was quiet now. After all, it has been for years. We hoped that whatever was there, if it ever was anything, that it was dormant."

"Find out what, Dad?" Daniel asked, the anger that had been simmering now swelling inside him, hot and bitter. "What was dormant? What is in this house?"

"Son, that house has been in my family for generations. You knew that, of course." His father's voice took on a grave, almost resigned tone. "But what you didn't know is that my great-grandfather was part of a secret society."

"You mean a cult?" Daniel scoffed, even as a fresh wave of dread washed over him. The word tasted metallic on his tongue, dragging this horrifying reality into an even darker, more sinister territory.

"No, nothing like that," his father patiently clarified, though a tremor was evident in his voice. "This wasn't some wild-eyed group chanting in robes. This was a secret society of just a few members, chosen with extreme care. They were charged with protecting a secret, some ancient prophecy."

"What prophecy?" Daniel demanded, his voice tight with a mixture of fear, frustration, and an unwilling fascination. The word "prophecy" felt absurd, yet in the face of the inexplicable events of the day, he couldn't dismiss it. He could hear Sarah's sharp intake of breath beside him, and the faint rustle as she likely held the girls even closer. The silence on the other end of the line was heavy, filled with a history Daniel was just beginning to unravel. Though a part of him wasn't certain he wanted to.

"I don't know, son. He did his job well. I never did find out," his father confessed, his voice heavy with regret and something akin to a long-held burden. "But, what I can tell you is that those symbols are part of it. He's the one who built the home, and those are his things inside the trunk up there in the attic. I could sometimes feel some strange, I don't know, energy I guess, whenever I was around it. And I never moved the trunk out of that spot. But I never saw anything, nor were there ever any disturbances. But that's why I always said the attic was off limits to you, and kids in general. I didn't know if somehow messing with that stuff would wake whatever the hell it was."

"Oh my god, oh my god," Daniel muttered, running his hands roughly through his hair, the horror of the situation finally crashing over him with full force. His voice was raw with a growing panic. "So what you're telling me is that some prophecy, which we know nothing about, has just unleashed hell on my family?"

"It's open," the old man gasped, the realization hitting him with force. His voice, now sharp with a rising sense of urgency and alarm, barely a whisper through the phone, questioned, "How? Why?"

"I don't know why, Dad," Daniel said curtly, his own frustration and fear bubbling to the surface. He didn't have the luxury of philosophical questions right now. "But something came after my family while I was gone to work today. Something…evil."

A heavy pause hung in the air before his father spoke again, his voice filled with regret. "I'm so sorry, son. Look, if you want to come stay with us for a while, you're more than welcome. We'll make room, no questions asked."

"Yeah, leave my job and drag my family across the country, uproot my girls, just so demons can take over my house and then God only knows what. No thanks, Dad," he said, the sarcasm sharp and bitter in his voice. His disbelief quickly morphed into a sense of outrage. "But what I really want to know is, how are you okay with anyone living in this house? How could you live here so long with mom? With me, and my brothers and sisters? How could you let me move my family into a place like this?"

"The house has to stay in the Monroe family, son. That's the way it's always been," his father replied, his voice taking on an unyielding, almost preachy tone. "And you remember me and your mother lived there for years, and nothing happened. And you and your siblings all had a good childhood."

"Oh, I had a good childhood," Daniel scoffed, the words dripping with incredulity. "That's just supposed to make everything okay? That makes all this right?"

"Look, son, you have to understand," his father began, his voice laced with a weary authority.

"No," Daniel interrupted, his voice cutting through his father's attempt at explanation, raw and filled with a desperate finality. "What you have to understand is that I'm done. I'm taking my family, and we are moving somewhere else. Away from this home, away from all of this."

"No, you can't do that, son. Someone has to stay there and watch over it," his father said firmly, the tone unyielding, almost a command. The line crackled with the unspoken weight of generations.

"Are you serious right now?" Daniel asked, his voice now a low, dangerous rage. He couldn't believe what he was hearing. "You really think I'm going to keep my wife and our two daughters in this house after what happened today? And then what, I'm just going to pass it on to them when the time comes so that they have to continue dealing with this problem? This… curse?"

"No, son. I don't expect you to leave it to the girls," the old man said, his voice flat, matter-of-fact, a chilling pronouncement.

"But you just said that it has to stay in the family," Daniel replied, his voice laced with confusion and a growing sense of dread. The inconsistency in his father's words was glaring.

"Yes, it does. But you can't leave it to the girls," he hesitated, a strange tension entering his voice. "They are very sweet girls, Daniel, and I know that Sarah has always wanted to be a mother, but—"

Daniel's tone shifted, becoming sharp and edged with a dangerous warning. "But what, Dad?" he asked, his voice low, simmering with a sudden, icy premonition.

"But they're not family. They're not Monroe blood. They were adopted," his father stated, his voice flat, matter-of-fact, as if he were stating a simple truth.

"Oh my god!" Daniel yelled, the words ripping from his throat, infused with disbelief and a fresh wave of incandescent fury. "Are you kidding me right now?!" The cold, objective declaration felt like a cruel, calculated insult.

"Look, son, I know you're upset, but our family made a promise that this house would stay in our family. And like it or not, Daniel, they are not blood related." His father continued, his voice unwavering, when all he heard was silence from the other end of the line, a silence heavy with Daniel's shock and fury. "I'm really sorry, son. Maybe a priest can help you cleanse the house or something. I wish I knew more that could help you. Perhaps something in the trunk will be of use."

"I'm sorry you feel that way, Dad." Daniel's voice was flat, devoid of emotion, the anger now replaced by a chilling detachment. He didn't wait for a reply, simply ending the call, the sound of the phone being dropped echoing hollowly through the room.

Sarah, having been roused by the agitated tone of Daniel's voice, had woken and was now standing by his side. She walked over and wrapped her arms around him, offering a silent embrace. "Did he know anything?" she asked, her voice soft, already knowing the answer from the tense silence that had filled Daniel's end of the conversation.

"No," Daniel lied, his voice flat. "Just something about a prophecy and that our family is somehow like the guardian of it or something. But he didn't know what it was. And nothing he said made any sense." He couldn't bring himself to reveal the cruel, cutting truth—that his own father considered their daughters, the very light of their lives, to be outsiders, not truly family. The words would shatter her, and he couldn't bear to inflict that pain on top of everything else.

"I'm sorry, Daniel," she replied, her voice trembling, unsure of how to console him. Their home, once a sanctuary, was now under siege by otherworldly creatures, and his father had kept a monumental secret from him his entire life. From both of them. The weight of it all was suffocating.

As the first pale light of dawn crept into the home, casting long, eerie shadows that seemed to stretch and twist with a life of their own, a sense of hopelessness washed over them all. They were trapped, surrounded by a darkness they couldn't comprehend, tethered to a house that had somehow overnight become their prison. Daniel had called into work, his voice tight with a fabricated excuse. "I won't leave you all here alone," he had insisted, a silent agreement settling among them that today would be a day of uneasy togetherness.

But as the morning wore on, a suffocating sense of unease settled over the house. The unspoken weight of what had happened the night before, despite their collective silence on the subject, was beginning to crush them. The incessant drumming of rain against the windows didn't help, mirroring the relentless anxiety within. The girls were unnaturally quiet, their minds no doubt replaying the terrifying events in an endless loop. Sarah moved through the house with a grim determination, methodically cleaning up the remnants of yesterday's chaos. Her hands trembling with every sweep and wipe of the shattered plaster and stray debris. Daniel sat hunched at the kitchen table, staring blankly out the window, lost in thought. He had already ventured up to the attic, searched the old trunk, but found nothing that foretold what this supposed prophecy was, or how to combat the insidious evil it had unleashed.

As the morning came and went, Sarah was getting ready to call everyone for lunch. The thought of even a mundane meal was a small comfort. But when a sharp, insistent knock echoed through the house, they all froze, their hearts immediately pounding. Who could possibly be visiting them at such a time, after a night filled with such unimaginable horrors?

With trembling hands, Sarah watched Daniel move cautiously towards the front door. Through the peephole, he saw a lone figure standing on the porch. It was a man, dressed in a long, dark coat, his face completely obscured by the deep shadow cast by the brim of his hat. Daniel hesitated, his hand hovering over the doorknob, every instinct screaming at him to keep the door shut after everything that had happened.

The man knocked again, more insistently this time, the sound a jarring intrusion into the house's tense quiet. Sarah exchanged a worried glance with Daniel, her eyes silently asking if this was another threat. "It's probably just a salesperson," Daniel murmured, his voice lacking conviction, a desperate attempt to normalize the situation.

They knew they couldn't hide forever, but the fear of the unknown, of what lay beyond that door, was paralyzing. Taking a deep, fortifying breath, Daniel slowly unlatched the lock and opened the door.

The man on the porch was taller than average, his frame imposing even beneath the long, dark coat. Daniel, bracing himself, was about to launch into a practiced dismissal, something about not needing any services, but then he noticed the subtle shift in the man's demeanor. There was a gentle kindness in his posture, a quiet composure that softened his otherwise formidable stature. His face, though partially shadowed by the brim of his hat, was lined with the marks of experience, deep creases around his eyes and mouth suggesting a life well-lived. Yet, those same eyes held a profound warmth, an immediate reassurance that seemed to cut through Daniel's apprehension.

Daniel instinctively opened the door wider, his initial apprehension slowly fading, replaced by a cautious curiosity. "Can I help you?" he asked, his voice still tinged with the caution born of the recent events.

The man smiled, a genuine and comforting expression that reached his warm eyes. "I believe I can help *you*," he replied. His voice was deep but gentle, carrying a soothing quality that seemed to calm even the agitated air in the house.

Daniel, sensing the undeniable shift in atmosphere, felt his shoulders drop slightly, a subtle release of tension. "Who are you?" he asked, his voice still guarded, but the edge of fear had visibly softened.

"My name is Silas," the man introduced himself. "I've lived around here for many years." Hesitating a moment, he finally continued, "I don't know how else to say this, so I'll just come out with it. I couldn't help but notice the commotion coming from your home yesterday."

Sarah and Daniel exchanged a glance, their curiosity piqued. "Commotion?" Sarah questioned, puzzled.

Silas nodded understandingly. "I heard the sounds of distress. I hope everything is alright." His concern was genuine, and it began to ease their worries. "I was worried about whoever was living here."

"Well, it's a long story," Daniel began, hesitant to share the details of his family's terrifying ordeal. "But as you can see, we're fine."

Silas's expression turned serious. "I understand. We can talk inside, if you're willing." His voice held a quiet promise of support. "This isn't the first time I've encountered... situations like this," he said, drawing invisible quotation marks in the air. Sarah and Daniel, though unsure if they could trust him, felt a fragile hope beginning to bloom. Has someone else experienced what they are now going through? Could this stranger be of help?

Sarah clutched Daniel's arm, a silent question in her eyes. The memory of the previous day playing on a loop in her mind. The strange noises, the chilling whispers, and the feeling of being watched still sent shivers down her spine. They had tried to rationalize it, to convince themselves it was just the wind, or an old house settling, but deep down, they knew it was something more.

Daniel, sensing Sarah's apprehension but also a glimmer of hope, finally spoke. "What do you mean, like this? What kind of situations?" He was torn between a desperate need for answers and a growing unease about what those answers might reveal.

Silas looked from one to the other, between Daniel and Sarah, his gaze steady and kind. "Let's just say I've learned a few things about the unseen, about forces that can sometimes cross into our world." He didn't sound like a lunatic, but rather a man who had simply witnessed too much. "I don't have all the answers, but I might be able to help you understand, or at least feel less alone."

Chapter 9:

The family spoke only with hushed whispers, their curiosity piqued by Silas's directness. They had no idea how this stranger could possibly help, or how he even knew about their ordeal. Yet, their desperation for answers and a way to protect themselves outweighed their skepticism.

Silas's words hung in the air, a promise of hope amidst the despair that had consumed them. The family exchanged uncertain glances. They were desperate for help, yet wary of trusting a stranger with such a terrifying secret. The weight of their situation pressed down on them, a heavy burden that seemed almost unbearable.

"How can you help us?" Daniel asked, his voice laced with skepticism. He wanted to believe this stranger, but he couldn't shake the feeling that this was some kind of elaborate hoax, a cruel twist of fate to add to their mounting fears.

Silas didn't flinch at Daniel's challenge. His gaze was steady, and calm. "I can help you because I've seen things like this before, more times than I care to count," he said, his voice quiet but firm. "This isn't your average creaking house or a rodent in the walls. What you're experiencing, the commotion I heard, has a specific signature."

He paused, letting his words sink in. "I'm not a priest, or a ghost hunter from a TV show. I'm just a man who's learned to recognize patterns, to understand certain things... energies. I've helped others in similar situations find peace, or at least understanding. Sometimes it's about making sense of what's happening. Other times, it's about knowing how to make it stop."

Sarah, who had been clutching her husband's arm, found her voice. "But *how* did you know? We haven't told anyone what happened." The memory of the oppressive presence, the cold spots, the whispers that seemed to claw at their sanity, was still fresh and raw.

A faint, almost sad smile touched Silas's lips. "Some things are felt, not just seen or heard. This neighborhood... It has a history. And certain disturbances leave a mark, a kind of echo that someone attuned to it can pick up on." He gestured vaguely toward their house. "The distress from your home yesterday, it was strong. It resonated."

Daniel, still hesitant, looked from Silas to Sarah, then back to the older man. The air around Silas seemed to be humming with a quiet authority, a sense that he truly did understand the unexplainable. The logical part of Daniel's brain screamed caution, but the fear in his gut urged him to listen. What did they have to lose that they hadn't already lost to the terror of the unknown?

"What kind of signature?" Daniel pressed, a flicker of desperate hope mixing with his lingering skepticism. "What are we dealing with?"

Silas stepped into the house, his movements deliberate and purposeful. There was a sense of authority about him, a quiet confidence that hinted at a lifetime of experience. "What you have been encountering is not of this world," he began, his voice low and measured. The words hung heavy in the air, confirming their worst fears.

The family exchanged nervous glances. They had sensed an otherworldly quality to the creatures, a darkness that transcended human comprehension. But to hear it confirmed filled them with a sense of impending doom. A cold dread crept into their hearts as they realized the full extent of the danger they faced.

"I have studied these beings for many years," Silas continued, his voice taking on a more authoritative tone. "Learning their weaknesses, their origins. And I believe I can help you protect yourselves." A glimmer of hope ignited in their hearts. If anyone could help them, perhaps it was this mysterious stranger who seemed to possess knowledge beyond their comprehension. But there was also a sense of unease, a fear of the unknown. They were about to embark on a journey into the darkness, and they had no idea what horrors awaited them.

Silas walked further into the living room, his eyes scanning the space with an almost exceptional focus. He seemed to be seeing things they couldn't. "These aren't ghosts in the traditional sense, nor are they simply malevolent spirits. They are... predators from another dimension." He turned to face them, his expression grim. "They are drawn to our world, for what reason I do not know, but they seek to establish a foothold here on earth."

Sarah gasped, clutching Daniel's hand. The realization hit them like a physical blow: their home was being invaded by something truly alien and terrifying.

"How do we fight something that isn't even truly here?" Daniel asked, his voice raw with frustration and a growing sense of helplessness. "What are their weaknesses if they don't abide by our rules?"

Silas nodded slowly, his gaze distant for a moment, as if remembering something painful. "That's the key. They *don't* abide by our rules, but they have their own. And those rules, their weaknesses, are what I've spent my life uncovering." He moved toward a bookshelf, running a hand over their spines before turning back to them. "They are drawn to certain emotional frequencies, certain lines of energy. This house, this land, it has a history that makes it a beacon for them. I... I know the kind of devastation they can wreak. I've seen it firsthand." His voice dropped, heavy with an unspoken sorrow.

He looked directly at Daniel and Sarah, his gaze unwavering. "My help won't be easy, and it won't be without risk. You'll have to face truths you might not want to acknowledge, and you'll have to be brave in ways you never imagined. But if you're willing to trust me, I can teach you what to look for, how to understand their nature, and how to drive them back to where they came from."

The silence in the room was heavy, broken only by the rapid beating of their hearts. The idea of confronting such unimaginable horrors was terrifying, but the alternative was even worse. They couldn't go on living in perpetual fear, consumed by an unseen enemy.

"How can we trust you?" Lily asked, her voice small but determined.

The room was thick with tension, the silence punctuated only by the soft ticking of the clock. Lily's question hung in the air, a challenge, a demand for reassurance. Silas, his face etched with a mixture of determination and weariness, met her gaze.

"Trust is indeed earned," he replied, his voice low and measured. "But consider the fact that I've walked a path similar to yours, a path darkened by the same shadows. I've seen the fear, the helplessness, the despair. It's a heavy burden to bear alone." His eyes swept over the family, searching their faces for understanding.

His gaze locked with Daniel's, then Sarah's. "I lost someone I loved very much to these very same forces. My wife... she endured what you're enduring now, and I was too late to fully understand, too late to truly help her." A sadness deepened the lines around his eyes, a grief that was still raw despite the passage of time. "I learned through bitter experience. I have dedicated my life to learning what they are, what they want, and how to fight them. I wouldn't wish that kind of loss on anyone, which is why I'm here. To offer you the knowledge I wish I'd had."

As the weight of his words hung in the air, he continued, "I have no reason to deceive you. My only aim is to prevent another tragedy. What I offer isn't a quick fix, or a magic spell. It's understanding, guidance, and a shared fight against something truly out of this world and evil." He paused, allowing his words to settle. "The alternative is to face this alone, and I promise you, that is a path you do not wish to take."

A furrow creased Daniel's brow. "You heard the commotion yesterday? Then why wait until now to offer your assistance?" Rage brewing inside of him as he thought of his wife and his daughters having dealt with that all alone.

Silas's voice, soft and regretful, filled the silence. He turned his hat slowly in his hands, his gaze shifting between Daniel and the others. "I desperately wanted to help. The sounds...they froze me in my tracks." A shimmer of tears threatened to spill, but he blinked them back. "I ran to your steps the moment I understood. But the noise had vanished. I stood there, hand raised to knock, unsure of myself. Then I saw the girls through the window." He nodded towards them with a gentle gesture. "Knowing they were physically safe, I couldn't risk frightening them further by seeing a stranger at the door. I hoped that, by today, you'd all had time to process the event."

Sarah's lips tightened. "How can we be sure you're not just another threat?" Her voice was steady, but her eyes betrayed her fear.

Silas nodded, as if expecting her doubt. "I understand your skepticism. But I assure you, my intentions are pure. I've spent years studying these creatures, these... demons if you will. Learning their weaknesses, their tactics. I believe I can help you. Otherwise, I would not have come."

He reached into his pocket, producing a small, metallic device. "This EMF transmitter has detected demonic energy fluctuations around this house for weeks. I've been monitoring the situation from a distance."

The family exchanged alarmed glances. The implications were chilling. Demonic entities had invaded their home, their sanctuary. And on top of that, a stranger was monitoring them from afar. Their safe haven had been breached long before yesterday's attack.

Lily, her curiosity momentarily overpowering her fear, asked, "What kind of demons are we talking about? Succubus? Incubus? Something worse?"

Lily's parents exchanged confused glances, wondering how their daughter could be so knowledgeable about such dark matters. Despite this, they awaited an answer as to what they were up against.

Silas hesitated, his expression grim. "I cannot say for certain. But they are not beings of light. They are malevolent, manipulative, and undeniably dangerous."

Silas held up the EMF device, its small screen displaying a fluctuating series of numbers and an erratic graph. "This isn't just about presence; it's about intensity. The readings from your home have been steadily climbing, especially in the last few days. That's why I finally decided to approach you." He put the device away, his gaze serious. "My monitoring wasn't an invasion of privacy, but a necessary precaution. When these entities become active, they have the ability to affect more than just one household. They can spread."

He turned to Lily, a flicker of something unreadable in his eyes. "Lily, your questions are astute. Most people wouldn't even know those terms." He paused, choosing his words carefully. "While specific classifications like succubi or incubi are often associated with particular folkloric manifestations, what you're dealing with here is less about a singular type and more about a class of entity. They are interdimensional parasites, drawn to places where the veil between worlds is thin, and where they can create turmoil."

"They don't have physical forms in the way we understand," Silas continued, gesturing vaguely around the room. "But they can influence, manipulate, and even materialize to a degree, depending on their strength and the energy they've accumulated." He looked at Daniel and Sarah. "What's important now isn't naming them, but understanding their behavior, their patterns. They learn, they adapt, and they will push boundaries until they are actively resisted. And then," he spoke with a somber tone, "they'll just keep pushing."

The air in the room seemed to grow heavier with his words. The family exchanged wide-eyed glances, the terror they had felt now mixed with a chilling sense of validation. This wasn't their imagination, or a faulty old house. This was real. And Silas, a stranger full of strange knowledge, seemed to be their only hope.

A heavy, oppressive silence descended upon the room. The crushing weight of Silas's pronouncement brought with it the horrifying realization that their torment was not random, but part of a calculated, malevolent design. A terrifying game was being played, they were told, and their family, their very existence, were nothing more than pawns in a horrifying unknown. They weren't just victims; they were pieces on a board, moved by unseen, malevolent hands, their lives mere fodder in a conflict they couldn't begin to comprehend. The dread deepened with the mention of some prophecy connected to this house that they knew nothing about. It was as if their fate had been sealed long before they ever crossed the threshold, their present agony merely the inevitable unfolding of an ancient, preordained curse. They were caught in a story where the ending was already written, and they hadn't even been allowed to read the first page.

The family remained rooted to the spot, stunned into silence, their collective breath catching in their throats. Though their bodies were still, their minds raced with a frantic, desperate energy, scrambling to process the unthinkable. Demons? Prophecy? It was the stuff of nightmares, yet it was their horrifying reality. Silas, however, continued to shatter their world, even as he offered a sliver of clarity. He claimed to have been watching them, studying the creatures that had invaded their home. This thought, the idea of a silent, unseen observer privy to their most vulnerable moments of fear was terrifying, but it also sparked a glorious and desperate glimpse of hope.

If he had been watching, if he had been studying, then he possessed knowledge. He wasn't just a messenger of doom; he was a witness, an analyst, perhaps even an expert. He had seen the horrors they had only felt, confirming their sanity in the face of the impossible. This terrifying knowledge, however chilling, offered the first real potential for understanding, for strategy, for a chance, however slim, to fight back against the horrifying unknown that had swallowed their lives whole.

The chilling silence that followed Silas's terrifying revelation was eventually broken by the shifting dynamics within the family. Sarah, the family matriarch and the most cautious of the group, felt an unbearable tension coil in her stomach. Her maternal instincts screamed at her to protect her family, to shield her daughters from this unimaginable horror, yet every fiber of her being recoiled from the idea of placing their fragile hope in a stranger. Trusting Silas felt like a desperate gamble, a leap into an even darker unknown. Her gaze flickered to her daughters, their faces etched with fear, their young eyes wide with a terror that mirrored her own. They were clearly at their breaking point; they needed help, desperately, even if that help came from a source as unsettling as Silas.

Lily, always the curious one, found herself caught in a whirlwind of conflicting emotions. The unsettling idea of someone having watched over them in secret, observing their escalating torment, sent shivers down her spine. It felt like a huge violation of their privacy, a testament to how truly exposed they had really been. Yet, the tantalizing promise of protection that Silas subtly offered was a powerful allure amidst their deepening despair. A part of her, the rational, skeptical part, warned her to be wary, to question his motives. But another, more desperate part, yearned to believe, to cling to the hope that this mysterious man held the key to their survival.

Rose remained silent, clinging to her mother's side, her small hand gripping Sarah's skirt as if her life depended on it. Her wide, innocent eyes reflected the fear that permeated the air, though she understood little of the complex, terrifying words exchanged between the others. A thick, suffocating tension filled the room, a heavy weight that even her young mind could register. Her world had been irrevocably shaken, and her only compass was the unwavering trust she placed in her family. Whatever her mother and father decided, whatever perilous path they chose, she would follow, her small, trembling heart beating in sync with theirs. More so, she trusted Lily's decision, for it was Lily who had always managed to keep them safe.

Finally, the uneasy quiet was shattered by Daniel, the steady rock of the family. His voice, usually a soothing anchor of calm and reassurance, was now frayed, edged with doubt and a protective instinct. He stepped forward, his gaze locking onto Silas's eyes, a direct challenge in his own. "How can we be sure you're not one of them?" he demanded, the question hanging heavy in the air, echoing the unvoiced fear shared by every member of his besieged family. It was the crucial question, the gateway to either a fragile alliance or a terrifying new threat.

Silas's expression remained impassive, a perfect mask of calm in the face of Daniel's raw accusation. "That is a fair question," he replied, his voice unnervingly steady in the charged atmosphere. "Doubt is a natural human response to the unknown, especially when confronted with something as unbelievable as what you're experiencing. I understand your skepticism." He paused, allowing his words to settle, then continued, "But I assure you, my intentions are pure. I've walked a long and arduous path, one that has brought me face-to-face with the very darkness you now fear, a darkness that has consumed those I loved."

A fleeting flicker of something close to vulnerability, perhaps some deep sorrow, crossed Silas's face, a momentary crack in his otherwise impenetrable demeanor, before he quickly regained his composure. "I have faced these creatures, these demons before, and lived to tell the tale. I know their methods, their tactics, their insidious whispers that seek to break the human spirit. I can help you... help you protect yourselves." His voice, though still calm, now carried a weight of conviction, a promise that hung heavy in the air, offering a lifeline in their desperate situation. It was a promise that begged to be believed, even as their minds screamed for caution.

Daniel's eyes, however, remained narrowed, his skepticism seemingly undiminished by Silas's earnest pronouncements. He was the protector, and he wouldn't easily yield to a stranger's assurances. "And what do you hope to gain from this?" he pressed, his voice low and challenging, cutting through the tension. "People don't just *help* without a motive, especially not when dealing with something like this."

Silas paused, his gaze seeming to drift inward as if considering his answer carefully, weighing every word. The silence stretched, amplifying the unspoken fears in the room. "Nothing," he said finally, his voice soft but clear. "I seek no reward, no recognition, no personal gain. My path is not one of profit or glory. I simply want to help. I wish to make sure that what happened to my family doesn't happen to anyone else." A hint of melancholy now touched his voice, a deep, resonant sadness that spoke of past tragedies, of a personal experience with loss that perhaps mirrored their own burdening nightmare. It was a raw, unvarnished admission that, for the first time, revealed a glimpse of the man behind the impassive mask.

A long, agonizing silence stretched between them, thick with unspoken questions and the terrifying gravity of their situation. The family found themselves ensnared in a brutal dilemma. On one side stood Silas, a man who had appeared from nowhere, claiming to possess the answers to their nightmares, a key to understanding the monstrous forces assailing them. On the other lay the chilling prospect of continuing to face the horrifying unknown alone, their every desperate defense crumbling under the relentless demonic siege.

The weight of this decision pressed down on them, a crushing burden that threatened to suffocate what little hope remained. Trusting a stranger, a man whose past was a mystery and whose sudden appearance bordered on the supernatural, was an immense gamble. It was like crossing a precarious tightrope above a bottomless void. Yet, the alternative, to confront the ever-darkening abyss entirely on their own, with no knowledge, no guide, and no apparent means of defense, seemed an even more terrifying descent into despair.

In the suffocating grip of their terror, a fragile flicker of hope stubbornly ignited in their hearts. It was a faint, almost imperceptible spark, born from Silas's claims of understanding the creatures and his solemn vow to protect them. It was a hope that whispered of a possible salvation, a chance to reclaim their lives from the clutches of unimaginable evil, even if it meant placing their faith in the hands of a man as mysterious as the darkness they faced.

A heavy silence descended once more, punctuated only by the ragged breaths of the terrified family. Then, with a visible effort, Sarah took a deep, shuddering breath, as if steeling herself for an unimaginable plunge. "We have no other choice," she stated, her voice not forceful, but laced with a bone-deep resignation. It was the sound of a desperate parent confronting the last, terrifying option. Her eyes, filled with a maternal fear, met Silas's. "We want to trust you, Silas. God help us, we need to." Her gaze hardened, the unspoken threat a tangible presence in the tense air. "But if you betray us..." Her voice trailed off, leaving the dark, chilling consequence hanging in the heavy silence, a stark promise of retribution if their fragile faith in him was shattered.

"Or if any harm comes to my family," Daniel continued, his voice a low, dangerous rumble that underscored

Sarah's unfinished sentence. His eyes, usually steady, were now narrowed, fixed on Silas with an intensity that promised dire consequences should their trust be misplaced. It was a united front, a desperate gamble laid bare, with the lives of their children as the ultimate stake.

Silas nodded, his gaze steady, understanding the weight of their words. "Your trust is not taken lightly," he replied, his voice resonating with quiet conviction. "I will do my best to prove my worth, not with empty promises, but through guidance and my own unwavering actions."

A fragile sense of relief began to unfurl within the family, yet it was stubbornly tempered by a cold, lingering unease that clung to the air like a damp shroud. They had, collectively, made a huge decision, a terrifying leap of faith into the unknown. The winding road ahead was undeniably uncertain, shadowed by the looming specters of both desperate hope and paralyzing fear. But for this fleeting moment, they had chosen a path, a singular, difficult path that, they prayed, led towards the light.

Silas turned to fully face the family, his expression now etched with a deep gravity that silenced any lingering whispers. "The absolute first step," he began, his voice dropping to a low, serious tone, "is to thoroughly cleanse this house." He swept his hand in a slow, deliberate arc, encompassing the living room, the silent witnesses to their recent terror. "The creatures, in their vile presence, have left their insidious mark, a deep, pervasive taint that will, without a doubt, continue to draw them back, just as a lighthouse beckons ships in the night."

He paused, allowing the unsettling truth of his words to fully sink into their already frayed nerves. The family exchanged wide, worried glances, their faces paling further. The very notion of their cherished home, their sanctuary, being so thoroughly contaminated by an unseen evil was, quite simply, terrifying. Rose instinctively clung even tighter to her mother, burying her face slightly into her side. Her wide, innocent eyes, now swimming with fear, darted around the room as she envisioned those grotesque creatures, with their razor claws and soulless eyes, coming back. She couldn't imagine their chilling presence once more defiling the fragile peace they so desperately craved. The thought of them returning, drawn by an invisible pull, was a fresh wave of horror that threatened to overwhelm them all.

The family watched with a mix of fascination and anticipation as Silas moved purposefully about their home, his presence filling the space with a quiet intensity. "With the cleansing complete," Silas said upon finishing up, his voice firm but now carrying a note of determined purpose, "the next critical step is to fortify this home. We must now create an impenetrable barrier, a powerful ward to protect this place from any further intrusion."

Lily, ever the inquisitive one, tilted her head, her curiosity overcoming her lingering fear. "What kind of barrier?" she asked, her voice a little softer than usual.

A faint, almost imperceptible smile touched Silas's lips. "A magical one," he replied, his eyes gleaming with a quiet confidence. "A seamless combination of age-old knowledge and modern science, woven together to create a formidable defense." He then proceeded to explain, in meticulous detail, that he would require a specific array of natural elements: rare herbs, carefully selected stones that have been charged with elemental energy, and various other unique materials to meticulously craft the ward. The family, their faces now reflecting a renewed sense of hope mixed with unwavering resolve, nodded in unison, their silent agreement echoing their absolute willingness to do whatever it took to safeguard their home.

"While I dedicate myself to preparing and imbuing the ward with its protective energies," Silas continued, his gaze sweeping over each of their faces, his expression serious once more, "you, in turn, must learn to protect yourselves. Remember, the creatures are inherently drawn to fear and weakness. They are predators who sense vulnerability. Therefore, it is paramount that you begin to strengthen your minds, as well as your bodies."

He paused, allowing his words time to settle in the quiet room. "I will teach you to harness your inner strength through Taoism, a philosophy and practice that will enable you to tap into an enormous wellspring of power you didn't even realize you possessed. This isn't about physical combat, but about cultivating a resilience that will make you less susceptible to their influence and more capable of facing any challenge that comes your way."

Daniel, his jaw set with a newfound determination, stepped forward, his voice firm. "Silas, we'll do whatever it takes. Whatever you need us to learn, we'll learn it. Whatever you need us to do, we'll do it. Our daughters... their safety is all that matters."

Sarah, her hand instinctively going to Rose's shoulder, echoed his resolve. "Absolutely. We won't hesitate. But you said they're drawn to fear and weakness... are those the only things? Is there anything else about us, or this house, that draws them in?" Her gaze swept around the still-somber room, a faint shiver running down her spine despite the recent cleansing.

Silas listened patiently, his gaze unwavering as Daniel and Sarah spoke. When Sarah finished, he nodded slowly. "Your commitment is admirable, and necessary. As for your question, Sarah, fear and weakness are indeed powerful draws for them. Think of it like an animal who uses scent to locate an easy meal, a vulnerable target."

He paused, a shadow of genuine regret crossing his features. "I'm truly sorry, but I cannot be absolutely certain that fear and weakness are the *only* things that might attract them. The supernatural world is vast and often defies simple categorization. There are forces we don't fully understand, connections we may not perceive. Sometimes an entity may even become attracted to an individual or a place. It's often difficult to say what is the driving force behind these creatures." He looked from Sarah to Daniel, his gaze softening slightly. "However, what I *can* assure you is this: the wards I am putting in place, combined with the strength you will cultivate within yourselves, will provide a formidable layer of protection. They will make this house, and everyone in it, far less appealing and significantly more difficult for these creatures to reach."

With Daniel's nod of approval, Silas made his way through the house with an almost ritualistic air of purpose. His keen eyes examining every corner, every shadow, every space that had felt the chill of the recent intrusion. He paused in various spots such as the thresholds of doorways, the centers of rooms, and the hearth of the fireplace, muttering low words under his breath, chants that seemed to hum with an unseen energy. The family watched him, their faces a complex mosaic of curiosity about his methods and a lingering apprehension about the invisible forces he was manipulating.

From a worn, leather bag, he carefully pulled out an assortment of intriguing items: bundles of dried herbs that released a faint, earthy scent, smooth, peculiar stones that seemed to absorb the ambient light, and a small, intricately carved wooden box whose contents remained a mystery. With deliberate precision, he placed these items in strategic locations around the house, not haphazardly, but as if following an invisible blueprint. In the corners of each room, and along the window frames, he drew intricate, swirling symbols with a chalk-like substance that settled into a soft white.

As Silas worked, a transformation began to settle over the house. The oppressive weight that had lingered since the creatures' visit slowly began to lift. A sense of calm began to replace the lingering fear that had permeated every room. The shadows, which had seemed to cling to the corners and walls, now appeared to retreat, as if afraid of the growing, benevolent energy that Silas was weaving into the very fabric of their home. It was a subtle shift, yet undeniably present, offering the family their first true breath of peace in days.

Hours melted away as Silas meticulously crafted his protective wards, his movements precise and unhurried. When he finally stepped back, he regarded his work with a quiet satisfaction, a faint sheen of perspiration on his brow. "These wards," he announced, his voice filled with a quiet but firm confidence, "will now help to protect you from the creatures, creating a strong shield around this home." He paused, his gaze sweeping over their hopeful faces. "But remember, it is not impenetrable. Like any defense, it requires vigilance. It will weaken over time and, to remain effective, will need to be reinforced."

The family nodded, their eyes wide with a mixture of relief and silent awe. They had just witnessed something truly extraordinary, a glimpse into a world that was utterly new and bewildering to them. A world of ancient forces and unseen energies that stretched far beyond their previous comprehension. Yet, beneath the wonder, an undeniable wave of relief washed over them, deep and comforting. Their home, which had so recently been full of sheer terror, now felt protected, encased in an invisible shield. They stood for a moment longer in the center of the living room, surrounded by the intricate, chalk-white symbols that Silas had meticulously drawn throughout their home onto their well-worn, cherrywood floors, each one a silent promise of safety.

With the immediate tension dissipated, a crushing wave of exhaustion swept over them all. The harrowing events of the past two days, the sudden intrusion of the supernatural, the terrifying ordeal, and the subsequent intense ritual, had taken a monumental toll on their minds and bodies. Their adrenaline, which had been running high for so long, finally plummeted, leaving them utterly drained. With a shared glance, Daniel gestured towards the sofa. "Please, Silas, have a seat," he offered, his voice raspy with fatigue. One by one, they collapsed onto the cushions, their bodies aching from the weight of the world that now seemed to rest squarely on their shoulders. Rose, too tired to even fidget, leaned heavily against her mother, her eyes already drooping. It was a physical weariness, but it was also a sign that, at least for now, they were safe.

As the sense of relaxation was settling over them, the shrill, unexpected ring of the phone shattered the quiet, startling them all. Sarah jumped, a jolt of adrenaline cutting through her exhaustion, and rushed to answer it. Her voice, when she spoke into the receiver, was tight and strained, laced with an immediate anxiety that sent a fresh wave of unease through the room. The rest of the family exchanged worried glances, their brief reprieve from fear evaporating with every hushed word Sarah uttered.

"It's my mother," Sarah finally choked out, her face paling to an ashen white, her hand trembling slightly as she lowered the phone. "She's... she's being taken to the hospital. We need to leave now."

As if the supernatural ordeal they had just endured wasn't enough, a brutal new wave of panic washed over them. They had just found a semblance of safety, a sense of security within the protective embrace of the wards Silas had so painstakingly created, only to be torn away from it by the harsh realities of their ordinary lives. Daniel stood up, his face grim, a battle between deep worry for his mother-in-law and a steely determination to face whatever came next warring in his eyes. "Let's go," he said, his voice flat with urgency.

He turned to Silas, a difficult request forming on his lips. "Silas," Daniel uttered, his gaze pleading, "I hate to ask, especially after everything you've done, but would you be willing to stay here and keep an eye on things? To ensure the wards hold? Of course, I would completely understand if you wanted to run out the door and head back to your own home; you've already helped us more than we could ever ask."

Silas didn't hesitate. He stepped forward, his expression grave, but with an unwavering resolve. "Of course, Daniel. I will be glad to stay and ensure that the wards don't let anything in, that your home remains a sanctuary. I'll also do some research on the home, see if there's anything unique about it. But please, be careful," he warned, his voice dropping to a low, serious tone. "The darkness is always watching. No matter where you are, no matter how far you travel from these wards, its influence can stretch. Best wishes for your mother," he said, turning to Sarah. "And remain vigilant."

The family nodded, their hearts heavy with a mixture of gratitude, fear, and urgency. Gathering what they needed in a hurry, they cast one last, longing glance at their suddenly quiet home, the intricate symbols on the floor now their only visible comfort. Then, with heavy steps, they descended the porch steps and climbed into their car, the hum of the engine a stark contrast to the magical energies they had just witnessed, driving away into the uncertain night.

Chapter 10:

The house fell into an immediate, heavy silence as the car's engine faded into the distance, leaving Silas utterly alone with his solemn task. With the family gone, a strong sense of urgency settled over him, sharpening his senses. The powerful ward he had just meticulously crafted was, he knew, merely a temporary measure, a crucial stopgap designed to hold back the encroaching darkness until a more permanent, unyielding solution could be found. He felt the weight of that responsibility intensely.

He moved through the house with deliberate, measured steps, his eyes no longer just scanning, but truly seeing every corner, every shadowed recess. There was an undeniable darkness to this place, a clinging, pervasive residue of the creatures that had so violently invaded it. He could feel it, a subtle chill beneath the recently established warmth of the wards, a persistent whisper of lurking evil. And more overtly, the lingering, foul stench that had permeated the air, a sickeningly sweet and metallic odor, still clung stubbornly to the walls, the furniture, and the very fibers of the rugs, a constant, visceral reminder of the recent terror. The cleansing had helped, but it had not eradicated every trace.

Silas paused in Lily's bedroom, his gaze fixed on a particular section of the cherrywood floor where the scuff marks of the struggle were still faintly visible. From his pocket, he pulled out a small, leather-bound book, its worn pages filled with intricate, strange symbols and complex diagrams. He opened it to a specific page, his finger tracing the intricate patterns before him with a reverence born of deep knowledge. As his eyes absorbed the text, a low, resonant murmur escaped his lips, a continuous, undulating chant that echoed softly through the silent home, weaving itself into the fabric of the newly created ward. It was a sound that seemed to pull at something deeper, a prelude to the true work yet to begin. He needed to understand the source of the lingering taint, the particular nature of the malevolence that had been drawn to this specific place.

As Silas's chant deepened, the very house began to respond. The air grew incredibly still, thick with an unseen energy, as if it were holding its breath in anticipation. Looking around him, the lamp light was casting dancing, almost playful shadows onto the walls and ceiling. Silas stared down at the ward he had created, its power now amplified, humming with a newfound potency under the influence of his incantations.

For what felt like an eternity, but was likely only a few hours, Silas worked, his concentration unwavering. With each passing moment, the house seemed to actively cleanse itself, shedding the lingering darkness and residual despair that had clung to it like a shroud. The foul stench, which had been a nagging, nauseating presence, finally began to dissipate, replaced by a subtle, clean scent, like ozone after a distant storm. When, at last, he stepped back, utterly satisfied with his work, the house felt different, remarkably lighter. It was as if a crushing weight, unseen but deeply felt, had been lifted from its very foundations.

But Silas knew that this was just the beginning, and the larger battle was far from over. The demonic creatures that had invaded this home were not isolated incidents; they were part of something far grander, a pervasive, insidious force that threatened to unravel the very fabric of the world as the home's inhabitants knew it. While he still didn't fully understand the what or how of it all, he knew with chilling certainty that this family, the one he had just helped, was inextricably caught in the crossfire. And he had walked willingly into this terrifying battle, unafraid to do what was needed. His mind kept wandering back to the girls, Rose and Lily. He could still hear the echoes of their terrified screams reverberating from this home as he walked by yesterday, a sound that had pierced him to the bone. He could vividly see the raw fear in their faces, especially the little one, Rose, who had clung so tightly to her mother that her tiny knuckles had turned stark white. The memory twisted something painful inside him. With a tear threatening to spill over his eyelid, a rare crack in his usually stoic demeanor, he shoved a fist into the air, raw anguish tearing from his throat. "Damnit!" he roared, his gaze searching the vast, indifferent sky for any sign, any explanation. "Why? They're just little girls!" His voice cracked with a desperate plea directed at the heavens, or perhaps, at the unseen darkness itself.

With his raw outburst echoing in the suddenly heavy silence, he took a long, shuddering breath, forcing his emotions back down. He looked around the now quiet home, the faint outline of the ward a comforting, if subtle, presence. The ward would hold, for now. It had to.

Pushing the harrowing images of the girls' fear aside, Silas moved towards the kitchen, his practical nature reasserting itself. He needed to eat, to ground himself. He quickly made a simple sandwich, the mundane act a stark contrast to the arcane rituals he had just performed. He was halfway through it when the phone's sharp ring suddenly cut through the silence, making him jump despite himself. It was Daniel, with news of Sarah's mother, and it didn't sound good. "Take as long as you need, just be careful," Silas had said, the concern for these people he barely knew evident in his voice before he hung up. After cleaning up his few dishes, the quiet efficiency of the task a welcome distraction, he decided to begin a more thorough exploration of the house. After all, there had to be a reason those creatures had been able to infiltrate it in the first place. And why this family and this house, specifically, as opposed to all the others in this quiet, unassuming neighborhood? The question gnawed at him, a puzzle he felt compelled to solve.

His investigation began methodically, moving from room to room, his senses attuned to anything amiss. The ground floor revealed little beyond the typical signs of a family home, albeit one recently steeped in terror. It was the attic, however, that truly called to him. A room shrouded in thick dust and deeper shadows, it felt heavy with neglected memories and stagnant air. Silas made his way around, his flashlight cutting through the gloom, looking for anything out of the ordinary, anything that didn't belong or seemed to hum with an unnatural energy.

He meticulously sifted through several boxes of forgotten Christmas decorations, then a box filled with faded, old photo albums, each holding a silent narrative of the family's past. It was tucked away in a dark corner, half-hidden beneath a moth-eaten blanket, that he noticed an old, battered wooden trunk. Taking a closer look, his breath hitched. He gasped, a sharp intake of air, as a peculiar, unsettling symbol came into view, carved deeply into the aged wood of the floor. His heart pounded with a chilling certainty; it was identical to one he had seen in his ancient, leather-bound book of demonic lore. This wasn't just some random carving; it was a mark of immense dark power, a malevolent sigil that resonated with an evil he had encountered only once before, a time he rarely spoke of. "This must be what Lily saw," he whispered to himself, the realization a cold wave washing over him. The connection was clear, terrifying, and now, deeply personal.

With his heart pounding, Silas knelt to examine the chilling symbol that lay before him. It wasn't merely carved *into* the flooring; it was a deep, almost three-dimensional impression, as if burned into the very fibers of the aged wood. Tracing its contours with a hesitant finger, a sudden, violent wave of nausea washed over him, bile rising in his throat. This was more than just a symbol; it was undeniably a gateway, a direct portal to something clearly sinister. He could feel the malevolent energy emanating from it, a cold, hungry hum that seemed to vibrate through the wood itself. With a guttural gasp, he quickly yanked his hand away, as if it had burned him.

A fierce internal battle raged within him, fear and determination both warring for dominance. He knew, with an absolute certainty that settled deep in his bones, that he had to destroy this mark, to somehow sever the terrifying connection it forged with whatever darkness lay beyond. But as he stared at the grim sigil, a horrifying realization hit him with the force of a physical blow: this was just the beginning. What if the grotesque creatures they had faced were not rogue anomalies, but rather they were part of a larger, seemingly more organized, and far more powerful force? And this house, this unassuming family home, had been targeted for a reason. He just had to find out what that reason was, before the darkness returned to claim its due. The trunk, the symbol, even the lingering stench were all connected, hinting at a far deeper and more insidious plot than any of them realized.

Frozen in place by the grim discovery, he was brutally reminded of the past. Emma's death had not been just a simple tragedy, a cruel twist of fate. No, there had been whispers at the time, hushed rumors that circulated like a chilling draft on the night of the accident. There were unexplained shadows dancing at the periphery of people's vision, an eerie, unnatural silence that had descended over the area, and a pervasive sense of impending doom that had enveloped anyone nearby. These whispers had been swiftly dismissed as mass hysteria in the frantic, grief-stricken aftermath, but they had never wavered from the sharp edges of his thoughts, gnawing at him for the past two decades.

Silas, a man now in his early fifties, was a mere shadow of the vibrant author he once was. The once-sharp mind that effortlessly crafted intricate worlds and compelling narratives now struggled to form a coherent sentence, often losing itself in the labyrinth of corridors filled with both memory and grief. The sudden, unexplained death of his beloved wife twenty years ago, had been a cataclysmic event that shattered his world into a million irreparable pieces. He had been a promising novelist on the very brink of literary stardom, poised for greatness, before being suddenly plunged into an abyss of unimaginable grief and despair. He had turned his back on the flashy world of writing, abandoning his growing career and lifelong dream to plunge headfirst into the study of the afterlife's deepest mysteries, the chilling secrets of demonology, and the forbidden lore of the occult. He knew, with a desperate, all-consuming conviction, that it was there, within those shadowed texts and whispered legends, that he would finally find the answer he was seeking. The true, terrifying reason behind Emma's death. And now, seeing this symbol, he felt a cold dread, and a flicker of dangerous hope that he was growing ever closer to an answer.

As his gaze lingered over the symbol before him, the chilling realization solidified: the same darkness that claimed Emma was indeed lurking within these walls, a malevolent force seeking to extend its reach. To tear apart another family. Or worse. Shaking the thought from his mind, he refused to allow himself to go down another fruitless rabbit hole, as he had done so many times before.

The night Emma died, a suffocating blanket of terror had descended upon the small town. An unexpected thick fog had rolled in, twisting familiar streets into spectral, ethereal pathways. An unnerving quiet fell over the community, a stillness so deep it was broken only by the mournful sighs of the wind. Yet, amid this eerie calm, something far more sinister had unfolded.

Witnesses, their memories forever scarred by the horror, recounted an unnatural phenomenon. As the fog coiled ever tighter, the sky above the ill-fated stretch of highway where Emma met her end began to pulse with an unearthly glow. A sickly crimson hue spread across the heavens, painting the world below in an unsettling, blood-red light. It was a fleeting, otherworldly spectacle, a stain of scarlet on the night's canvas, a haunting imprint burned into the minds of all who saw it.

Through this treacherous, crimson-tinged gloom, cars crept along. Then, in a sickening flash, the horrific scene unfolded. Emma's car, swallowed by the fog's blinding embrace and disoriented by the bizarre crimson light, swerved across the center line. A sudden, thunderous roar ripped through the air as an enormous tractor-trailer materialized from the swirling mist. The massive vehicle bore down on Emma's car with unstoppable force. In a brutal instant, metal shrieked and glass exploded, snuffing out Emma's vibrant life without a whisper of warning. Her spirit, once so full of promise, was extinguished, leaving behind a shattered family and a community haunted by the tragedy that had claimed her.

The truck driver, a family man with children waiting anxiously at home, was shaken but miraculously unharmed. He struggled to piece together the collision for the authorities, his voice raspy with shock. He spoke of the near-impenetrable fog and the bizarre red light that had utterly clouded his vision. He swore he never saw Emma's car, only a sudden, phantom shadow that seemed to rise from the very road itself, a dark specter in the blood-red haze.

In the bewildering aftermath, hushed whispers of the strange light and mysterious shadow spread like wildfire. Some theorized it was a meteor, a celestial traveler streaking across the night sky, while others dismissed it as a bizarre weather anomaly, a trick of the fog and the failing light. There was also talk of government conspiracies and failed science experiments. But a handful of people in town believed as Silas did, that it was something far more sinister. A malevolent force that had breached their world, seeking lives to claim for its own dark purposes.

Meanwhile, Emma's memory, for the wider world, had already faded. She became a whisper lost in the wind, her name uttered with a shrug and a dismissive, "wrong place, wrong time." For most, her life was quickly forgotten, a tragedy swiftly filed away. But for Silas, there would be no forgetting.

Consumed by an unshakeable certainty that something unnatural had transpired that night, he had returned to the site of the crash. He retraced Emma's last moments, the chilling crimson glow still vivid in his mind. Then, amidst the scorched earth, he saw it: the same unsettling symbol which lay before him now, was subtly etched into the cracked asphalt as if branded by an invisible hand. Its presence there, at the very nexus of Emma's demise, solidified his growing dread. Her death had been no accident. And this home, this family, were all connected to it somehow.

As Silas reached out once more, his fingers hovering just above the strange symbol, a sharp, insistent knocking suddenly echoed from another part of the house. It was a sound utterly out of place, a jarring, violent interruption to the otherwise oppressive silence that had settled around him. His heart beat in his chest as he froze, his hand suspended in mid-air above the ominous etching. The knocking was swiftly followed by a heavy, resonant thud, as if something substantial had toppled or been thrown with considerable force.

A cold fear began clawing its way up Silas's spine, a terror that tightened its grip with each passing second. He was aware he was alone in the sprawling house; he knew the family hadn't returned, their absence a chilling void in the suddenly hostile space. He strained to listen, every nerve ending taut, the silence that followed the thud was now a suffocating weight in the air. The house, usually a symphony of subtle creaks and groans, was eerily and unnaturally quiet. The jarring thud had left behind an emptiness that amplified the frantic, deafening rhythm of his own pulse. His hand, still trembling visibly, continued to hover over the symbol, in spite of his escalating dread.

The gears of his mind, though sluggish with fear, began to turn, desperately trying to force logic into the unraveling situation. The rational part of him screamed for escape, urging him to flee this place, to call for help, to sever all ties with the growing madness. But a perverse, almost obsessive curiosity held him rooted to the spot, an invisible tether he couldn't break. The symbol, radiating an undeniable pull; the house, steeped in its dark, unfolding mystery; and the haunting, unyielding memory of Emma. All of it conspired to pull at him, urging him to delve deeper into the encroaching darkness, to uncover the terrifying truths that lay concealed.

Slowly, deliberately, he pulled back his hand from the symbol, taking a cautious step backward. The solid floor beneath his feet offered a small, fleeting comfort, a stark contrast to the swirling chaos in his mind, but it did little to calm his still-racing heart. His hand, now steadying slightly, fumbled for his phone, its sudden beam of light a stark, almost blinding intrusion into the oppressive gloom, illuminating his pale, anxious face. He grimaced at the sight of the screen: a single, flickering bar of signal, stubbornly fading in and out. There was no way he'd be able to make a call, not with this pathetic connection.

Besides, he mused, a bitter laugh catching in his throat, who would he even call? The family was already dealing with a crisis at the hospital, and he couldn't possibly ask them to return home because he'd heard a strange sound. After all, he was supposed to be helping them, not becoming more of a burden to them. The thought solidified his resolve, albeit a reluctant one, to face whatever lurked in the shadows.

As he stood there, attempting to muster what little courage he had left, a new sound began to echo through the expansive home, causing him to visibly cringe. It was a low, guttural growl, deep and resonant, and he couldn't for the life of him pinpoint its origin. The sound seemed to crawl beneath his skin, a primal, ancient threat that sent a shiver of icy dread straight to his bones, chilling him to the core.

The growl deepened, a growing rumble that vibrated through the floorboards and directly into his chest, getting louder, more menacing with each terrifying second. It was no longer a distant, unsettling echo but a real, predatory presence, closing in, suffocating him. Fear consumed him entirely, stripping away any pretense of composure. He raised his phone again, his fingers trembling uncontrollably, the dim screen his only tether to sanity. He had to call for help, to escape this waking nightmare before it devoured him whole. But before he could even begin to dial, his gaze snagged on the battery icon. One percent.

"Shit," he whispered, the expletive laced with self-loathing. How could he have been so careless? So stupid? The fury at his own oversight warred with the paralyzing terror that was gripping him.

As he silently chastised himself, a flicker of movement caught his peripheral vision. A deeper shadow was detaching itself from the oppressive darkness in the far corner of the attic. His heart hammered in his ears, a frantic drumbeat that drowned out all other sounds, even the persistent growl. Slowly, agonizingly, he turned, his eyes wide with a terror that stretched them to their limits. In the meager, failing light of the lone bulb, a pair of glowing red eyes emerged from the inky blackness. They were enormous, inhuman, burning with a cold, predatory intent that promised only annihilation.

Another low growl, a rumble that seemed to emanate from the very fabric of the darkness, erupted from the monstrous shape as it began to fuse together, to take form. Just as the creature's horrifying outline became agonizingly clear, the lone bulb in the attic flickered once, twice, then extinguished with a soft pop, plunging him into an absolute, suffocating pitch-black. He was utterly vulnerable, blind, and at the mercy of the unseen horror.

With desperation clawing at his throat, a surge of pure survival instinct overriding his fear, he frantically rummaged through his pockets. His trembling fingers finally closed around his lighter. With a desperate flick of his thumb, a single, defiant spark erupted, momentarily pushing back the oppressive darkness. In that sudden, fleeting illumination, the monstrous shape, the glowing red eyes, the very essence of the creature, dissolved into nothingness, as if it had been merely a construct of shadow and fear.

Adrenaline, sharp and potent, coursed through his veins, replacing the terror with a fierce, burning resolve. He lunged towards the door, his exit from this hellish chamber now his singular focus. His mind raced, a single, overriding purpose consuming him: he had to find out how to destroy the symbol. Whatever unholy connection existed between that etching and the horrors in this house, it had to be severed.

Chapter 11:

The sudden onset of Sarah's mother's illness had blindsided them all. It had been her neighbor, Mr. Henderson, who had discovered her. He'd gone over to check in after not seeing her lights on that evening, only to find her unconscious on the living room floor. It was him who had made the frantic call to 911, and then, with a trembling voice, to Sarah. Now, she lay in the hospital, a fragile figure hooked to an array of machines. The doctors, their faces grim and perplexed, were still running tests, baffled by her sudden, unexplained collapse. They had no answers, only more questions.

The hospital was a sterile, impersonal place, a stark contrast to the usual warm, familiar chaos of home. The fluorescent lights hummed overhead, casting an unnatural glow on the pale faces of the visitors. Sarah sat by her mother's bedside, her hand clasped tightly in the older woman's. Memories flooded her mind, thoughts of how happy she had been when she found her forever family, though she had never really got along with her new brother, Philip. He had tormented her from the beginning, constantly reminding her that she was not their biological child as he was. Her parents had done their best to shield her from him, but it took her standing up for herself to finally get him to back down. At least all those years alone in the foster care system had taught her one thing, to stand up for herself because no one else would. Between these memories, bits of fear and doubt crept into her mind, as she fought with her newfound worries and wondered how she was going to protect her family.

Lily and Rose huddled together in the corner of the room, their young eyes darting nervously between their grandmother's still form in her bed and the flickering television screen. Though the muffled drone of the evening news offered a distracting hum, the constant stream of grim headlines provided little comfort. Their hearts ached with sorrow for their new mother whose distress was intense, and a growing worry for a grandmother they'd only just begun to know. The recent, supernatural events that had spiraled out of control back home had left them perpetually on edge, their momentary sense of safety shattered.

Outside the door, Daniel, a restless shadow of his usual self, paced with a frantic energy. His mind was a tempest of a million uninvited thoughts, each one a fresh stab of anxiety he couldn't push away. Yesterday had taken a brutal, unexpected turn, and they were all caught in its relentless undertow. His daughters... the thought hitting him like a physical blow. These two girls, whom he had come to love as fiercely as if they were his own in such a painfully short time, were now in so much danger. And now his wife's mother was in the hospital, her life possibly hanging by a thread. What more, he wondered with a bitter despair, could possibly happen? Though he wasn't what you would call a religious man, he found himself silently, desperately praying for a sign, any glimmer of help, to guide them all through this deepening nightmare.

The collective weight of their troubles seemed to be pressing down on all of them, a heavy, suffocating burden each of them carried. The strange occurrences at the house, with its unsettling atmosphere, and the puzzling stranger they had left behind, Silas, lingered fresh and disturbing in their minds. But for now, their main, agonizing focus remained solely on Sarah's mother, whose health seemed to be teetering precariously on the brink, a silent testament to the encroaching darkness that now shadowed their lives.

Hours passed, each tick of the clock seeming to stretch into an eternity. Lily and Rose, their initial distraction from the television long gone, grew increasingly restless, their young minds inevitably drifting back to the unspeakable horrors of the day before. They yearned for the familiar safety of their home, the comforting routine it offered before the monstrous creatures had shattered their peace. And, surprisingly, they found themselves missing the strange, quiet comfort of Silas's presence, a guardian angel who had showed up in the midst of chaos.

As dusk deepened and the hospital lights took on a colder, harsher glow, a sense of isolation began to creep over the girls. The sterile, unwelcoming environment of the hospital stirred up unsettling memories, echoing the countless foster homes they had endured. Places where they had never truly belonged and never wanted to return. They instinctively huddled closer on the rigid sofa, seeking solace in the shared warmth of a thin, scratchy blanket, finding what little comfort they could in each other's presence.

The night stretched long and heavy, laden with unspoken worry. Eventually, exhaustion claimed the girls, and they drifted off into a fitful sleep, their heads resting on each other's shoulders. Sarah, however, remained vigilant by her mother's bedside, her heart a crushing weight in her chest, heavy with concern for the woman whose life now hung precariously in the balance. Meanwhile, Daniel continued his relentless pacing in the hallway, his mind a never-ending churn of anxieties: his mother-in-law's condition, the demon infested house; the mysterious man named Silas with his unsettling knowledge; and the unknown, lurking dangers that might still be waiting for them back home. The silence of the hospital, broken only by the beeping of machines and the hushed whispers of staff, offered no respite from the storm that was brewing within him.

Sarah's mind, a whirlwind of present anxieties, kept wandering back to the cherished memories of her mother. She recalled with bittersweet clarity the day she first met her adoptive parents, George and Martha Taylor. Both had been so kind, their smiles gentle and welcoming, but it had taken her a long, cautious while to truly learn to trust them. Years spent in the system, always dealing with uncertainty, had taught her to guard her heart, to doubt that anyone would truly mean the comforting words they spoke, to fear that they would inevitably leave when someone better or younger came along.

But George and Martha had been steadfast, unwavering in their love and commitment. Six months after the adoption had officially gone through, a significant milestone in her young life, Sarah had finally found the courage to call Martha "Mom" for the very first time. A single, solitary tear slipped down Sarah's cheek now as she recalled the overwhelming joy that had flooded Martha's face that day, the tears of pure happiness that had streamed down her mother's cheeks. It was a memory etched deeply into Sarah's soul, a testament to the love she had finally found. And now, all she could do was sit by this sterile hospital bed, holding that same beloved hand, watching it lie helpless and fragile, a stark reminder of the preciousness of life and the terrifying fragility of it all. The unfairness of it all gnawing at her insides.

The relentless rays of the morning sun shone through the hospital window, ushering in a new day but little, if any, hope. Sarah's mother lay tragically still. Her shallow, irregular breathing the only proof of her fragile state. Even in her brief moments of wakefulness, her gaze had been distant, lost in a silent, agitated world of her own, a world no one else could access. Across the room, Lily and Rose, their youthful energy slowly draining, were growing increasingly restless, their unease a noticeable presence in the quiet room. Daniel, his exhaustion etched deeply into his bloodshot eyes and slumped shoulders, finally took the girls to the cafeteria, promising to bring something back for his wife. The hospital, once a place of healing, seemed overnight to have transformed into a cold, clinical prison, its sterile walls trapping their spirits in an agonizing cycle of worry and exhaustion.

As the morning dragged on, marked by the hushed movements of nurses coming and going, there was still no sign of the doctor, no shred of news about Martha's elusive condition. Sarah's eyes, red-rimmed and puffy from a night spent crying and devoid of sleep, never left her mother's side. She hadn't moved, hadn't rested, a silent protector in the face of overwhelming fear. Daniel, returning with a tray of untouched food, was a mere shadow of his former self, his once vibrant features now hollowed with worry, every line on his face showing his exhaustion. Lily and Rose, usually a source of lively chatter, had grown eerily quiet, their silence a somber reflection of the heavy atmosphere that surrounded the room. The air was thick with unspoken fears and the lingering question of what unknown forces had brought them here.

Shortly after the untouched lunch trays were removed, the doctor finally emerged from Martha's room, his expression grave, a stark contrast to the sterile white of his coat. "We're doing everything we can," he said, his voice soft, almost apologetic, yet devoid of any true reassurance. "Unfortunately, her condition isn't improving. I've ordered some more tests to be done later today, comprehensive scans and specialized blood work. But until we know what's specifically causing this sudden decline, I'm afraid our hands are tied in terms of targeted treatment. Rest assured, though, we're going to great lengths to ensure she is at least comfortable." His words, carefully chosen, hung in the air like a thick, suffocating fog, heavy with unspoken fears and the chilling implication that comfort was all that could be offered.

The devastating news hit Sarah like a physical blow. Her knees buckled beneath her, and Daniel, ever watchful, swiftly reached out, his arms wrapping around her in a desperate attempt to steady her. The girls, their young faces already pale with worry, clung to each other on the sofa, their eyes wide with a dawning comprehension of the doctor's somber pronouncement. The world around them seemed to shrink, the bright hospital lights dimming, as their entire focus narrowed to this single, crushing reality: the terrifying possibility that their grandmother, the kind, loving woman who had so recently welcomed them into her life, might never leave this hospital room. The hope they had clung to, however fragile, seemed to evaporate, replaced by a cold dread that settled deep in their bones.

The overwhelming weight of Martha's failing health eclipsed everything else. The bizarre occurrences at the house, the unsettling presence of Silas, and even the terrifying creatures that had invaded their home. All of it now seemed strangely insignificant compared to the desperate fight for their loved one's life. Yet, a nagging sense of agitation lingered, a dark, unsettling undercurrent to their overwhelming grief. The house was still out there, a looming, silent presence in the back of their minds, a place of unsettling secrets. And Silas, wherever he was, was undoubtedly caught up in a perilous battle of his own, a battle that for the moment they knew nothing about.

As they sat in the sterile, white room, bathed in the harsh fluorescent glow, they were no longer just individuals. They were now a family under siege, their world violently turned upside down, every familiar comfort stripped away. The shadows of their fear and uncertainty were growing, clawing and gnawing at their resolve, threatening to consume them entirely. It was in this crucible of despair that Daniel, with a quiet strength, stepped forward to lead. Taking Sarah's trembling hand, he looked deeply into her red-rimmed eyes, his voice steady despite the chaos within him. "We don't give up," he vowed, his grip firm. "I will be by your side through this. Through all of this." Then, turning to the girls, his gaze softened but his resolve remained ironclad, "And I will never let anything happen to you. We are a family now, and we fight together." In that desolate hospital room, surrounded by the unknown, they forged a silent pact. As a unified family, they would face whatever challenges lay ahead, their collective strength their only shield against the threatening darkness.

As they were grappling with the agonizing reality of Martha's condition, a new and unsettling element entered their lives, shattering the sterile quiet of the hospital waiting room. A stranger, a man with piercingly intelligent blue eyes and an air of quiet determination, appeared seemingly out of nowhere. His presence, while calm, was undeniably unexpected.

"Hello," he began, his voice a gentle, steadying presence in the tense atmosphere. "Silas has sent me to check on you. And to offer my assistance."

Daniel, his guard immediately raised, eyed the newcomer cautiously. "Silas didn't mention anything to me about you," he stated, his voice laced with suspicion. The last thing they needed was another unknown variable.

The stranger offered a slight, reassuring nod. "I just spoke with him on the phone," he explained, his gaze briefly flicking to Sarah, a flicker of genuine empathy in his eyes. "He told me where I could find you. I am truly sorry for your situation." He then added, with a gentle, disarming smile, "I'll gladly wait while you phone him yourself if you'd like to confirm. I understand this is... a lot to take in." His calm demeanor and the offer to verify his story, even as their world felt like it was crumbling, added another layer to the vicious puzzle that now surrounded their lives.

However, Lily, her mind remarkably sharp despite the recent ordeal, instantly recognized the man. He was undeniably the same mysterious figure she had encountered in the depths of the woods, the one who had, with startling efficiency, helped her repel a monstrous entity before its sudden, terrifying disappearance. A storm of fear and confusion now swirled within her, battling for dominance as she observed him interacting with her unsuspecting family. A silent plea echoed in her thoughts: *Could he truly be trusted? Was his story genuine, or was there a far more sinister agenda at play?*

The man, who introduced himself as Elias, spoke with a practiced ease, claiming to have had a prior discussion with Silas regarding the unsettling situation at the house and the delicate family matter at hand. Lily's gaze remained fixed on him as he smoothly expressed his condolences for Sarah's mother and offered his unconditional assistance. Yet, an almost imperceptible undercurrent rippled beneath his composed demeanor. A sense of unnatural urgency and a depth of knowledge that continued to further Lily's suspicion. She could practically feel her father's similar apprehension radiating from his stiff shoulders and intensely watchful eyes.

Elias, with a subtle yet impactful shift in his tone, began to hint at a deep connection to the house itself, a bond far more intricate and ancient than anyone present could possibly conceive. He spoke in hushed, reverent tones of ancient forces, of an age-old battle between light and darkness, and of a cryptic prophecy that inextricably linked the family to this cosmic struggle.

Lily's mind raced, becoming a whirlwind of doubt and rising panic. The question gnawed at her: *Was this man a savior or an evil entity in disguise?* The initial terror that had gripped her in the house surged anew, amplified by the stark vulnerability of her loved ones. She knew, with a chilling certainty, that she had to exercise extreme caution, to shield her family from whatever unseen peril lurked just beyond the veil of their understanding. Elias, with his mysterious aura, his unsettlingly practiced sympathy, was a complex puzzle with far too many crucial pieces missing. She recalled the unsettling intensity of his gaze, how his eyes had seemed to pierce directly into her very soul during their fleeting encounter in the forest.

Now, here he stood, offering both help and condolences, his carefully chosen words resonating with a hollow echo in the unsettling quiet of the room. Lily couldn't shake the glaring omission from his narrative: he hadn't breathed a word to her parents about the terrifying encounter in the forest, the one where he had, against all odds, saved her life when this whole nightmare began. Yet, a strange reluctance held her back from revealing it herself. She recoiled from the thought of them seeing her as some eccentric oddball, prone to seeking out bizarre encounters. Still, the uncanny timing of his sudden appearance gnawed at her, an insistent sensation of uneasiness. And then there was the unsettling memory of the bird, the one he'd urged her to use her newfound powers on, utterly oblivious to the potentially devastating consequences.

Her already frayed trust, stretched thin by the relentless events of the past few days, finally snapped under the immense strain. She perceived his arrival not as a much-needed lifeline, but as a deeply unsettling intrusion, a potential threat disguised as an ally. She quickly sought out her sister, Rose, her eyes mirroring the deep skepticism that now clouded Lily's own features.

As Daniel continued to engage Elias in conversation, Sarah discreetly stepped away, pulling out her phone to call Silas. After a brief but meaningful exchange, she rejoined the others, her expression softening slightly. "Silas spoke highly of you," she announced, her voice a careful blend of caution and possible hope. "He vouched for your intentions." Given their current state of vulnerability, any offer of assistance, however suspicious, felt like a desperate lifeline. She suggested they extend a tentative chance to Elias, at least for the moment. Daniel, after a moment of heavy consideration, finally conceded. "Fine," he replied, his voice gruff. "But I'll be watching him like a hawk."

"As will I," Sarah replied, her voice firm despite the slight tremor in her hands, before she turned and made her way back to her mother's bedside.

But Lily remained utterly unconvinced. A persistent, icy tendril of dread snaked around her heart, whispering that this man, Elias, was irrevocably tied to the insidious darkness that had so suddenly consumed their lives. *I'll be watching as well,* she vowed silently, her gaze hardening with resolve.

As night draped its heavy cloak over the town once more, a hush settled upon the hospital room. The only sound was the soft, rhythmic beep of the heart monitor, a stark counterpoint to the deafening silence that often accompanies grief. Sarah sat vigil by her mother's bedside, her hand clasped tightly around her mother's frail one, a silent testament to both her enduring love and her fear. Daniel sat in a chair nearby, his face etched with worry lines that seemed deeper than ever before. In the corner, huddled together on a small couch, Lily and Rose were curled up, seeking the elusive embrace of sleep, their exhaustion unmistakable even in the dim light.

Hours bled into one another, each tick of the clock amplifying the oppressive atmosphere. The hospital, usually a hive of activity, seemed to hold its breath alongside them. Lily, despite her best efforts, found sleep an impossible luxury. Every creak of the door, every distant cough from the hallway, made her tense. Her mind replayed Elias's unsettling words, the way he had spoken of ancient forces and prophecies as if they were as tangible as the monitors surrounding her grandmother's bed. She couldn't shake the image of him, standing there with his unsettling calm, his eyes that seemed to hold too much knowledge. Was he a predator patiently waiting for his moment, or a guardian angel burdened by secrets? The uncertainty was torturous. She shifted on the couch, pulling her blanket tighter, wishing for the uncomplicated safety of yesterday, a world where monsters were only found in stories and prophecies were merely fables.

Suddenly, the fragile peace of the hospital room shattered as Rose's peaceful, rhythmic breathing abruptly morphed into a series of ragged gasps and guttural whimpers. Her eyes, previously closed in the innocence of sleep, snapped open, wide with an unholy terror, reflecting the faint, clinical glow of the monitors. She bolted upright, her small body trembling uncontrollably. "Mommy! Mommy!" she shrieked, her voice thin and high-pitched, laced with a desperate fear that pierced the quiet like a knife. It wasn't just a cry; it was a pure, unadulterated wail of terror that seemed to tear from her very core.

Lily, startled from her own troubled half-sleep, reacted instantly. She lunged forward on the couch, grabbing hold of Rose and wrapping her arms around her sister's shaking form, her own eyes wide with a mixture of confusion and dawning horror. She squeezed Rose tightly, as if her embrace alone could banish the unseen dread that had so violently awakened her little sister.

Sarah, her heart instantly catapulting into a frantic rhythm against her ribs, rushed to her daughter's side, Daniel right behind her, his usually composed demeanor replaced by a look of wide-eyed alarm. "Rose, what's wrong? Are you okay?" Sarah pleaded, her voice trembling with barely suppressed panic as she knelt, trying to meet her daughter's terrified gaze.

Rose didn't answer immediately. Instead, she slowly, agonizingly, lifted a small, trembling finger and pointed towards the far corner of the dimly lit room. Her eyes, still enormous and swimming with unshed tears, were fixed on something only she could perceive. "There's something there," she whispered, her voice barely audible, a fragile thread of sound that was almost swallowed by the sterile quiet. Her breath hitched, and a fresh wave of tremors wracked her small frame, shaking her from head to toe. She squeezed her eyes shut for a moment, as if to make the image disappear, but then they snapped open again, still glued to whatever she was seeing. A soft, guttural sob escaped her lips, and she pressed herself deeper into Lily's arms, burying her face against her sister's shoulder as if to hide from the terrifying vision.

Daniel and Lily instinctively followed her gaze, scanning the empty corner, their eyes searching for any anomaly in the muted shadows. They saw nothing other than the plain hospital wall, a trash can, and a faint reflection from the window. "It's okay, Rose," Daniel said, his voice softer than usual, trying desperately to inject a calming reassurance into the strained air. "It's just a bad dream. There's nothing there, sweetie." He reached out a hand, intending to gently stroke her hair, but Rose flinched away, a quick, involuntary reaction that sent a fresh wave of concern through them all.

But Rose's fear only intensified. With a sudden, explosive burst of adrenaline, she tore herself from Lily's embrace, her small body thrashing violently, consumed by the unseen horror. Her screams, raw and piercing, filled the room, each one tearing at the hearts of her family. Her limbs were responding in frantic, desperate movements that were both frightening to witness and heartbreakingly pathetic. She kicked, flailed, and writhed, as if battling an invisible assailant, her face a mask of pure, unadulterated terror, though her eyes still held that vacant, unseeing stare of someone deeply asleep.

Daniel, his own face ashen, didn't hesitate. He practically roared for assistance. "Nurse! We need help!" he bellowed, his voice laced with a desperate urgency. Almost immediately, the door burst open and a nurse, a woman with kind but harried eyes, rushed into the room, her expression instantly shifting from concern to alarm as she took in Rose's violent struggle.

"We need to get her to the pediatric unit," she said, her voice calm but firm, already moving towards the distressed child. "She needs to be examined right away." Her gaze swept over the family, offering a quick, reassuring nod, a silent promise that they would handle this. She immediately spoke into the call button, her words hushed but rapid-fire. "Code White, Room 312. Pediatric consult needed stat. Possible severe night terror."

Mere minutes later, though it felt like an eternity, the room filled with the quiet efficiency of two more nurses and a pediatric resident, their movements precise and practiced. They spoke in low, soothing tones, even as Rose's screams continued to echo. The medical team approached Rose carefully, assessing her state while reassuring the family. One nurse gently but firmly held Rose's flailing arms, while another checked her pulse and breathing. The resident quickly confirmed the rapid heart rate and dilated pupils, all consistent with a severe night terror. The family watched, helpless and horrified, as the medical team carefully but swiftly lifted Rose onto a gurney, her small body still writhing, her frantic cries still filling the air, a devastating soundtrack to their escalating nightmare. One nurse quickly secured soft restraints around her wrists and ankles, not to harm, but to prevent Rose from injuring herself in her terror.

Lily, tears streaming down her face, clung to her mother, burying her face into her side as if seeking refuge from the unbearable sight. Sarah, equally distraught, held her daughter close, her own tears mingling with Lily's. "What's wrong with her?" Lily sobbed, her voice muffled against her mother's shoulder.

"I don't know, honey," Sarah whispered back, her voice thick with dread and exhaustion. She looked at Daniel, her eyes pleading for answers he couldn't give.

Daniel, despite his own anguish, forced himself to be the pillar of strength. He gently pulled Lily from Sarah's embrace, his hand firm on Lily's shoulder. "I'll stay with her," he assured Sarah, his voice steady despite the tremor in his hands. "You stay with your mother. I'll take Lily with me, and I promise we will let you know as soon as we hear something." He gave Sarah's shoulder a reassuring squeeze, a silent promise to protect both of their daughters. The pediatric resident gave a confirming nod, indicating they would keep Daniel updated. As the gurney was wheeled out, accompanied by the medical staff and Daniel, Rose's fading screams were replaced by an unsettling silence, leaving Sarah and her mother alone in the sudden, echoing emptiness of the hospital room.

Daniel and Lily stayed by Rose's side, their figures hurrying alongside the medical staff. Elias, whom the family had momentarily forgotten in the chaos, appeared as if from nowhere, stepping from the waiting area just outside the room and following silently behind them, his face etched with a newfound worry. The only thing Sarah could do was remain by her mother's bedside, her hand clasped tightly around her mother's, tears rolling silently down her face as she offered a desperate, wordless prayer.

In the pediatric unit, the atmosphere was slightly different. It was still clinical, but with a softer edge, decorated with cheerful murals on the walls. Rose, though calmer now, was still trembling, her little body exhausted from the terrifying night terror. Daniel sat by her bedside, his hand gently stroking her hair, willing his own tears not to fall. He had to remain strong for his family. Lily sat on the other side, still holding Rose's small hand, her own eyes bloodshot and swollen from the continuous flow of tears.

Elias remained in the corner of the room, a silent, watchful presence. His facial expression was one of deep concern, his brow furrowed. Yet, even in his apparent distress, his eyes maintained their vigilant intensity, cautiously sweeping their surroundings as if searching for something unseen. He then began to murmur to himself, a low, rhythmic cadence of words that were indecipherable to Daniel and Lily, a strange sounding recitation that seemed to hum beneath the sterile quiet of their room.

"How is she, Doctor?" Daniel asked, his voice tight with anxiety as Dr. Evans finally re-entered the examination room. The minutes since Rose's sudden episode had stretched into an agonizing eternity, each tick of the clock amplifying his fear.

Dr. Evans offered a small, reassuring smile, though a hint of concern lingered in his eyes. "She's stable, Mr. Monroe. Her vital signs are good, and she's resting comfortably now." He paused, his expression growing more serious. "Based on what you described, and after my examination, I strongly believe Rose experienced a night terror. It's a fairly common parasomnia, particularly in children."

He leaned forward slightly. "Has anything like this ever happened to her before? Any similar episodes of screaming, thrashing, or extreme distress during sleep?"

Daniel shook his head slowly, running a hand through his hair. "I don't think so, Doctor. I mean, we just adopted Rose and her sister, Lily," he said, gesturing to his other daughter seated directly across from him. "They've only been with us for a couple of months."

Dr. Evans nodded, his gaze softening as he turned to Lily. "Hi, Lily. We really want to help your sister, so tell me, do you remember if she has ever had one of these… scary dreams before you came to live with the Monroe's?"

"No," Lily whispered, her voice barely audible, her gaze fixed on her sister's pale face. A shiver ran through her, despite Daniel's comforting presence.

Dr. Evans's voice remained a gentle murmur, doing his best to ease the family's worry. "Any trouble she might have mentioned with sleeping, or with nightmares perhaps?" he pressed, his eyes kind and understanding.

Lily chewed on her bottom lip, a flicker of something unreadable crossing her face. Fear? Shame? "She never mentioned nightmares," she finally said, her words a hesitant trickle. "She did have some trouble sleeping in a couple of our foster homes, but…" She trailed off, her eyes darting to Daniel, then quickly away.

Daniel rose up and moved swiftly around the bed so that he was standing next to his oldest daughter. He gently squeezed her shoulder. "Lily," he coaxed, his voice laced with warmth, "It's okay. What is it?" He could feel her trembling slightly beneath his embrace.

A deep, shuddering breath escaped her lips. Her shoulders slumped, and she finally met her father's eyes, a raw vulnerability exposed. "We both had trouble from time to time," she confessed, her voice barely above a whisper, filled with a maturity far beyond her years. She looked down at Rose, a silent understanding passing between the sisters even in Rose's unconscious state. "Some foster parents, they aren't what they claim to be." The words hung in the air, heavy with unspoken pain and betrayal.

Daniel felt a pang in his chest, a fierce surge of protectiveness washing over him. He pulled Lily closer, wrapping her in a tight hug, pressing a kiss to the top of her head. "It's okay," he murmured, his voice thick with emotion, his own eyes welling up. He held her close, stroking her hair. "You're safe now. Both of you. I promise I'll do whatever it takes to keep you safe."

"We'll certainly let her sleep here for the night to ensure she's fully recovered and stable," Dr. Evans said, offering Lily a warm, understanding smile. He then turned back to Daniel, his expression shifting to a more clinical, yet still empathetic, demeanor.

"Night terrors, or night tremors as they're sometimes called, are relatively common in children, particularly between the ages of three and eight. However, given Rose's age, and the fact that this appears to be her first documented episode, it suggests there might be an underlying trigger. Often, these episodes are linked to some form of anxiety or stress. It could be something significant, or even a subtle shift in their routine. Perhaps the adjustment to a new home, even a loving one, can sometimes be a significant transition for a child."

Daniel immediately shook his head, another wave of protectiveness washing over him, tinged with a familiar, unwelcome guilt. "No, Doctor, I don't believe it's that. Both girls, they're adjusting remarkably well to our home. My wife and I… we truly love them, and they seem to be thriving." He paused, his gaze flickering away for a moment. How could he explain the invisible weight, the creeping dread that had settled over their house since *that* night, without sounding utterly insane? The image of his mother-in-law in her own room upstairs, flashed in his mind. He couldn't burden this doctor with the full, terrifying truth. Instead, he opted for a more palatable explanation, one that felt like a flimsy shield against the doctor's perceived scrutiny.

"My wife, her mother, is actually a patient here at the hospital," Daniel continued, his voice a little strained. "We stayed overnight last night... it's been a very difficult and stressful time for all of us, especially with her condition." He omitted the feeling of living in a home which had become a magnet for darkness. He felt a prickle of resentment, imagining the doctor was judging him, dissecting his every word for signs of inadequate parenting, as if *he* was the source of all their troubles.

Dr. Evans listened patiently, his expression unreadable for a moment before a flicker of insight crossed his face. "Ah, I see. That certainly adds a layer of significant stress to the household. Given that, it may very well be the change of scenery, so to speak, coupled with the heightened anxiety of the situation here at the hospital. Perhaps if she were in her own bed, in the familiar and comforting environment of her own room, she might rest more peacefully. A change in sleep environment, even a temporary one, can sometimes be enough to disrupt a child's sleep cycles and trigger such an episode."

Daniel nodded, a polite, almost desperate gesture. "Of course. Thank you so much, Doctor, for taking care of her."

"I'll stop by and check on her again in the morning, first thing. As long as she's back to her usual self, I'll release her then," Dr. Evans said, offering one last reassuring nod before turning and exiting the room, his footsteps fading down the hallway.

The moment the door clicked shut, the fragile composure Daniel had maintained began to crack. Lily, who had been sitting rigidly beside him, finally looked up, her eyes wide and glistening with unshed tears. Her voice was a bare whisper, trembling with a fear that echoed the gnawing dread in Daniel's own heart. "Dad," she breathed,

"I'm scared. What if the darkness followed us here? What if it's not just at our house anymore?"

Daniel's breath hitched. He wrapped his arms around her, pulling her close, burying his face in her hair. "We'll figure something out," he murmured, his voice rough with emotion, hoping to convince himself just as much as he hoped to calm her. The walls of the hospital room, meant to be a sanctuary, suddenly felt paper-thin against the insidious dread that seemed to cling to them. *How could he protect them from something he couldn't even see?*

From the corner of the room, where he had been a silent, watchful presence, Elias stepped forward. "I can help protect you," he said, his voice firm and unwavering. "I have already placed wards around the hospital to help deter these things and to hopefully, the good lord willing, keep them out." His gaze swept over them both, a silent promise in his eyes.

As the next couple of days unfolded in the sterile, quiet rhythm of the hospital, Rose's condition completely stabilized. The terrifying night terrors had vanished as suddenly as they appeared, leaving no lingering shadow on her bright, energetic demeanor. She was back to her usual playful self, her laughter once again echoing softly in the room, a soothing potion to Daniel and Sarah's frayed nerves.

Elias, with his unsettlingly calm presence, often sat near Rose. He'd watch her with a strange, unblinking intensity. Rose, perhaps sensing his unusual nature, seemed to find a unique comfort in his proximity. This dynamic, however, did not go unnoticed by Lily. She watched Elias with an almost unnerving focus, her young mind meticulously sifting through his every subtle gesture, every carefully chosen word. There was a quiet suspicion in her eyes, a deep-seated instinct that whispered of something amiss.

Despite his reassurances and the perceived protection he offered, something about him simply did not sit right with her. She was searching for any sign of deception, any crack in the carefully constructed facade which he presented.

Meanwhile, Daniel and Sarah were trapped in a desperate limbo, their hearts aching with a fierce need to protect and nurture their daughters. Yet, they were confined to the stark reality of a cold, impersonal hospital room, the harsh fluorescent lights a constant reminder of their predicament. They knew, logically, that the girls shouldn't be spending so much time in such an environment. It wasn't healthy, emotionally or physically. But the terrifying events that had unfolded in their seemingly idyllic home had instilled a paralyzing fear. The thought of letting the girls out of their sight, even to the care of a trusted sitter, felt like an unthinkable risk. The creeping dread that something truly malevolent had attached itself to their home, and perhaps to their family, bound them to the hospital, a self-imposed prison in the desperate hope of keeping their children safe from an unseen enemy. They were utterly exhausted, their minds a whirlwind of worry and unanswered questions, yet every instinct screamed that they had to remain vigilant.

Chapter 12:

Lily's suspicion of Elias gnawed away at her with each passing day. His presence, initially a supposed source of comfort amidst their turmoil, had begun to cast a long, unsettling shadow. She saw a man with a carefully constructed facade, a man hiding something. And though she wasn't sure what that something was yet, a chilling certainty settled in her gut that it was sinister. She couldn't shake the feeling that he was playing a part, a subtle performance for their benefit, and that his true intentions lay buried beneath layers of calm reassurance.

Daniel and Sarah, were greatly aware of the dangers lurking both within and outside the hospital walls. With the unsettling events back home, and the continued strain of Sarah's mother's condition, their protective instincts were on high alert. The thought of either Lily or Rose wandering off alone, even within the seemingly safe confines of the hospital, sent shivers down their spines. Every shadow seemed to hold a potential threat, every unfamiliar face a possible danger. They had instilled a strict *buddy system* rule: no one went anywhere alone. This unspoken pact was a constant, tense hum beneath the surface of their everyday interactions.

One morning, while Daniel and Sarah were deeply preoccupied with a consultation regarding her grandmother's condition, Lily saw her chance. Rose was still asleep, nestled in her makeshift bed on the couch, and her parents' attention was entirely consumed by the hushed medical discussions. "I'm just going to get Rose a blueberry muffin," she announced, her voice as innocent as she could make it. "Those are her favorite. I won't be long. I promise." Her parents, their faces etched with exhaustion, hesitated for only a moment. They knew Elias was downstairs in the cafeteria, and the thought that he would be nearby, even inadvertently watching over her, was just enough to sway them.

Lily moved with purpose, her heart thumping in her chest. She located Elias easily in the hospital cafeteria, a solitary figure at a corner table, sipping coffee and staring into space. She positioned herself carefully behind a large, decorative column, observing him. He was utterly still, almost unnaturally so. "What are you up to?" she whispered to herself, the words barely audible. Just as the thought formed, his eyes, dark and piercing, met hers. For a startling moment, there was a flicker of recognition in their depths, as if he had been expecting her all along. But how could that be? How could he have known?

Shaken but resolute, Lily stepped out from behind the column and approached his table, her gaze fixed on him, refusing to waver. "We need to talk," she stated, her voice steady despite the furious churning in her stomach.

Elias slowly lowered his coffee cup, a faint, almost imperceptible hint of amusement dancing in his eyes. He leaned back in his chair, a picture of unnerving calm. "Of course," he replied, his tone smooth as polished stone, "Please, sit."

Lily pulled the chair out and sat, her gaze fixed on him, refusing to waver. She took a deep, bolstering breath. "I don't trust you," she said bluntly, the words cutting through the quiet hum of the cafeteria.

Elias's expression remained utterly peaceful, unperturbed by her direct accusation. "Why is that, Lily?" he asked, his voice even, as if they were simply discussing the weather.

"You know too much," she retorted, leaning slightly forward, her youthful face etched with suspicion. "You knew about the creatures, you knew about the house. It's like you've been watching us our whole lives. You just… appeared when we needed you most, almost as if you were waiting."

Elias's calm demeanor shifted subtly. He leaned forward, his eyes suddenly intense, captivating hers. "I have been watching you," he admitted, his voice dropping to a near whisper, yet carrying an undeniable weight. "I told you as much that day in the forest, didn't I?" He paused, allowing her memory to catch up. Seeing the shock blooming in her eyes, he continued, "But not in the way you think. I've been observing your family for generations. There's a lineage in your blood, Lily, a power that has been dormant for centuries, waiting to be reawakened."

Lily's eyes widened in disbelief, her mind struggling to reconcile his words with anything she understood. "What are you talking about?" she whispered, the question escaping her lips almost involuntarily. She sat frozen, waiting for an explanation that felt both fantastical and chillingly plausible given all they'd experienced. Elias simply smiled at her, a strange, cold amusement playing on his lips, as if her bewilderment was merely a quaint spectacle. It was a smile that didn't reach his eyes, a smile that made the hairs on her arms stand on end.

He noticed her body visibly shiver, her eyes growing wider, more wary, like a cornered animal. He took a slow sip from his cup, his gaze never leaving hers, before placing it back down with a soft click. "The creatures, the house, the darkness that surrounds you... it's all connected," he finally replied, his voice a low, resonant hum that seemed to vibrate in the air between them. "Lily, your family is the key to unlocking something far greater than you can imagine. Something that has been stirring, waiting for the right moment."

Though another undeniable chill traced its way down her spine, Lily refused to yield. She straightened her posture, deliberately projecting a boldness she didn't entirely feel, her chin lifting defiantly. "What do you want?" she asked, willing her voice to remain steady, to betray none of the fear coiling in her stomach.

"I want to help you," he replied, his voice suddenly laced with an unsettling sincerity, a warmth that seemed almost out of place. "I want to help you harness your power. The power that is your birthright. Together, we can end this nightmare, and perhaps, prevent an even greater one from unfolding."

A long, heavy pause filled the air, punctuated only by the distant hum of the hospital and the clinking of cutlery from other tables. Her mind raced, trying to process his astonishing words, to sort through the tangle of fear, disbelief, and a strange, growing curiosity. "Why would you help us?" she asked, her voice still thick with suspicion, her brow furrowed in a deep frown. "What do you get out of this?"

His eyes held a mysterious depth, a knowledge that seemed both ancient and vast. He held her gaze, a faint, mysterious smile touching his lips. "Because your destiny is intertwined with mine, Lily. More closely than you can possibly comprehend right now."

Her blood curdled at his words, a cold dread washing over her. The implications of such a statement were terrifying. "What do you mean?" she whispered, the question a desperate plea for clarity in the face of his bewildering pronouncements.

"You and your family are special, Lily," Elias said, his voice dropping to a low, almost hypnotic tone that seemed to cut through the cafeteria's ambient noise. "I mean, you can't truly think it's a mere coincidence that you were adopted by this particular family, can you? Especially given all the prospective parents you witnessed come and go, jumping from foster home to foster home. Why then, out of all the couples, would Daniel and Sarah Monroe be the ones to give you and your sister a chance, seemingly against all odds?" He paused, his gaze fixed on her, subtly gauging her reaction, watching for any flicker of understanding or denial before continuing. "You and your sister, Rose, possess a power that is both incredibly rare and inherently dangerous. A power that they, your adoptive parents, are destined to protect."

Her mind reeled, a whirlwind of fragmented memories and chilling possibilities. She thought of the morning in the dark woods, the surge of raw energy that had coursed through her, the primal force that had seemed to emanate from her very core. Was that what he was talking about? The uncontrollable tremor that had seized her hands, the almost physical push she felt emanating from her being? She had used it again in their home that same day, but it was a sensation she'd tried to forget, to rationalize away as fear or adrenaline. But now, under Elias's piercing gaze, it felt terrifyingly real.

"What do you want with us?" she asked, her voice trembling slightly, as she used the back of her hand to brush away a lone tear that had escaped and traced a cold path down her cheek. The words were a desperate plea for clarity, for an end to the unsettling riddles.

Elias hesitated for a moment, his eyes seeming to weigh his words carefully, as if selecting them from an infinite library of knowledge. "I want to help you," he said finally, his voice resonating with an unshakeable conviction. "To guide you. To protect you."

Despite his seemingly benevolent words, her skepticism deepened, a cold knot forming in her stomach. His answers were always tantalizingly vague, hinting at profound truths without ever fully revealing them. "From what?" she pressed, her voice laced with growing frustration. "Protect us from what, exactly?"

Elias looked at her for a long, silent moment, his gaze unwavering. Then, with a chilling certainty that sent a fresh shiver down her spine, he said, "From that which seeks to destroy you."

Lily literally halted, his words a physical blow that locked her in place. Her breath hitched, a sharp, painful gasp, and the violent thrumming of her heart threatened to tear through her chest. Her vision blurred at the edges, narrowing until all she could register was the encroaching darkness. It was the same oppressive shadow she had faced in the house, the terrifying blackness from the forest, the same insidious void that now seemed to be closing in on them from all sides, even within the sterile confines of the hospital. A cold dread seeped into her bones, tightening its grip.

Finally, after what felt like an agonizing eternity, stretching minutes into an unbearable silence, she found the courage once more to speak. Her voice was barely a whisper, raw with a mix of fear and defiance. "How can we be sure you're not part of it?"

He exhaled slowly, a soft, almost weary sigh. "You have every right to be cautious, Lily. I'm a stranger to you. To all of you, really. And you've been dealing with so much, for so long already, far more than any child should." His gaze softened, a hint of genuine empathy in his deep eyes as he leaned in closer, his voice dropping to a confidential tone. "But I assure you, with every fiber of my being, I am on your side."

She desperately wanted to believe him. The sheer exhaustion of living under this constant cloud of terror made the thought of an ally, any ally, incredibly appealing. But the years of navigating the treacherous waters of the foster care system had honed her instincts to a razor's edge. She had become an expert at reading people, at spotting the subtle tells of deceit, at discerning true intentions from false promises. It had been a vital skill, one she had relied on heavily to protect herself and, more importantly, to protect Rose. Elias might be telling the truth, but she couldn't afford to take any chances, not now. Not when she and Rose had finally found what they had yearned for their entire lives: a family. A home. A sanctuary that was now, terrifyingly, compromised.

As she made her way away from Elias and out of the cafeteria, the muted sounds of hospital life echoing around her, she couldn't shake the growing sense of unease. The encounter had left her with far more questions than answers, each one swirling in her mind like an unsettling vortex. His words about power and destiny, about generations and intertwined fates, resonated with a chilling ring of truth, yet his cryptic nature still sparked distrust. She knew, with a certainty that settled deep in her soul, that she had to find a way to uncover the truth about him, to determine whether he was truly a friend, or, as her gut instinct stubbornly insisted, most likely a very dangerous foe. The safety of her newfound family depended on it.

Meanwhile Silas, despite still grappling with the terrifying memory of his monstrous encounter in the attic, had thrown himself into a relentless search of the sprawling home. He was desperate to find anything: a clue, a hidden passage, a forgotten artifact. Anything that would explain the sudden appearance of these grotesque creatures, or why this particular house had become their chosen portal. He ran a hand through his already disheveled hair, shaking his head as he dug through a stack of books on a shelf. He forced himself to push away the chilling thought that there might be more portals elsewhere, that the threat wasn't confined to these walls. He had, after all, already gone around the entire perimeter of the home, more than once, meticulously checking that the intricate runes of protection he had drawn were still firmly in place, shimmering faintly with an invisible, reassuring energy.

Driven by a strange, almost obsessive compulsion, he had been exploring the house with renewed scrutiny. But each creak of the floorboards, each gust of wind through a loose pane, only amplified the unsettling silence. He'd begun his search upstairs in the bedrooms, focusing most of his attention on Lily's room. That was where they had fought the creatures the day before his arrival, where the remnants of their struggle were still visible. But aside from the lingering chill that seemed to cling to the air, the only truly strange thing he'd found was the book of archaic text the family had told him about. He ran his fingers over its worn leather cover, the pages filled with symbols and script utterly alien to him. He spent a long time looking through it, his brow furrowed in concentration, trying to comprehend not only how Lily had understood any of it, but also how she had come by it in the first place. He sank into the plush armchair in the corner of the room, his memory recalling the conversation they had all had just days earlier.

Sarah's voice, usually so steady, had held a perceptible tremor, her words hesitant as she addressed Lily. "Lily, about yesterday... when we were fighting those creatures..." Worry creased her forehead, deepening the lines of exhaustion around her eyes as she struggled to articulate the unbelievable situation they had faced. "How were you and Rose able to...?" The question hung unfinished, laden with awe and bewilderment.

Panic flickered in Lily's wide eyes as she registered the intense, questioning looks from both Silas and her parents. Her body stiffened, and her hands instinctively clenched into small fists. "I don't know," she insisted, the words tumbling out in a rush, desperate to deflect their scrutiny. "It's never happened before, I swear!" Her gaze darted between their faces, a plea for understanding in her desperate denial.

Daniel approached cautiously, his brow furrowed with concern. "Has anything else like that ever happened to you before?" he asked, his voice gentle, trying not to push too hard.

The denial on Lily's face was stark, a desperate attempt to shield herself. Her youthful features, usually so expressive, were suddenly burdened by a familiar fear. It was the fear Sarah recognized immediately. The ingrained terror of being judged, rejected, or abandoned once more by the very people who were supposed to care for her. The chilling legacy of the foster care system, a system that had taught her to hide anything that might make her "too much trouble."

Sarah, tears welling in her eyes, didn't hesitate. She quickly gathered both girls into a tight, protective embrace, pulling them close against her chest. Her voice was thick with emotion, a fierce declaration of unwavering love. "Lily, Rose, listen to me very carefully. You never, ever have to hide anything from us. Not your fears, not your worries, not anything strange that happens. We love you. Both of you, fiercely and unconditionally. We're a family now, and that means we stand together, we support each other, we face everything together, no matter what."

Rose, sensing the deep sincerity in her mother's words, clung to her, burying her face in her shoulder. Lily, however, remained stiff for a moment, fighting back a torrent of tears. The raw emotion in her mother's voice, the genuine warmth of the hug, was breaking down walls she had built around herself for years. A long, agonizing moment of silence stretched across the room, filled only by the subtle sounds of birds chirping somewhere in the distance. Then, finally, Lily's resistance crumbled. Her small body began to shake, and when she spoke, her voice was thick with unshed tears, barely above a whisper. "Ever since I found a book... a really strange book... strange things have been happening. Things that weren't happening before."

Daniel's confusion was clear, etched on his face as he exchanged a quick, bewildered glance with Sarah. "What book, Lily? What are you talking about?"

"One day," Lily began, her voice a little hesitant, "I went for a walk in the woods. It was after I had discovered the symbol in the attic. Mom said it was okay."

"Yes," Sarah affirmed gently, her expression encouraging Lily to continue.

"I walked for a while," Lily continued, her gaze drifting as if reliving the moment. "Just looking at the trees, listening to the birds singing. I just wanted to clear my head. But then... I must have walked further than I thought, because I came to the edge of the woods, and there was a house. An older lady was standing on the porch, watching me."

Daniel's skepticism was immediate. "Wait a minute, Lily. That's not possible. These woods are huge. You'd have to walk for nearly a whole day, if not more, to get to the other side. And there's never been a house in the middle of them. Not that I've ever heard of, and I've lived here my whole life."

"But it was there!" Lily insisted, her voice cracking as tears welled in her eyes. "I swear it was!"

Daniel and Sarah exchanged uneasy looks, while Silas watched Lily with a sharp, assessing gaze. "It's okay, Lily," Sarah reassured her gently. "Just tell us about the house and the woman you saw. Tell us what happened."

"It was an old house," Lily began, her voice hushed. "Like it was about to fall apart. But the woman... she was just standing there on the porch. When she saw me walking closer, she went back inside, but the door didn't close completely. I know I shouldn't have gone up there," she admitted quickly, "but I couldn't help it. It was like something was pulling me in. I stopped at the bottom of the steps and called out to her. But she didn't answer. I called again from the doorway, but still nothing. I was worried something had happened to her." Before her parents could interject, she rushed on, "I know it was dangerous and really stupid, okay? I know. I'll never do anything like that again, I promise."

Seeing their concerned expressions, she continued, her voice gaining a strange, distant quality. "The house... it felt wrong, somehow. Out of place. And it was so dusty, like no one had lived there in ages, but all the furniture was still there. And all of the things for the home, like I noticed a lamp, and there was even a throw blanket situated over the couch. There were dishes in the kitchen, and even potted plants. Well pots anyway, the plants were all dead. But I kept looking. I looked all around but I couldn't find the woman anywhere. Then I noticed a doorway leading down to the cellar," she said, a shiver tracing her spine at the memory. "I was scared to go down, but... it was that same feeling. Like I had to. I just couldn't stop myself."

"And what did you find in the cellar?" Daniel asked, his voice low with anticipation.

"It was incredible," Lily breathed, her eyes wide with the memory. "Completely unexpected for that old house. There was a desk, and the walls... they were lined with shelves. Floor-to-ceiling bookshelves."

"And that's where the book was?" Sarah prompted gently.

"Yes," Lily confirmed. "And I don't know why that one, out of all of them, felt important. There was just this feeling..." She trailed off, unable to explain it fully. "I opened it, but then I heard something, so I left." She chose to keep the unsettling details of the ghostly woman and the house's ultimate demise to herself.

Silas pushed his chair back under the desk, the scrape of its legs against the wooden floor echoing in the silence. The fleeting memory of how Lily came to possess the book, dissolved as he rose. With the strange book tucked firmly under his arm, his mind already racing with thoughts of further research into its unfamiliar contents, he descended the steps. The first floor beckoned, a maze of unanswered questions, and he resumed his thorough exploration. He opened every creaking cabinet, pulled open every stubborn drawer, and even tapped along the solid walls as if hoping for some hidden secrets to jump out at him. He peered behind framed photographs, convinced that a hidden safe or a secret passage lay concealed within the old home.

Despite his exhaustive search, the first floor seemed to mock his lack of discovery. And the surrounding silence only helped to amplify his growing frustration. With a weary sigh, he retreated to the kitchen table. The strange book which Lily had found lay before him, its very presence generating more questions than answers. He ran a finger over its aged, textured cover, a ripple of nervousness mingled with his curiosity as he slowly turned its pages. "So utterly strange," he murmured, his brow furrowed in concentration as he gazed at the unfamiliar script and unsettling, almost grotesque, illustrations. He reached into his worn leather bag, pulling out a thick encyclopedia. It was his trusted manual of arcane symbols and forgotten languages. This, he had hoped, would be the key to unlocking the mysteries held within the found book. But as he painstakingly compared the cryptic text, a knot of frustration tightened in his chest. The answers he sought remained elusive, just out of reach. With a sigh that carried the weight of defeat, he returned both books to his bag, the unsolved secrets feeling heavy on his shoulders. His gaze then fell upon the dark, unexplored entrance to the basement. It was his last, and perhaps most desperate hope.

Inhaling deeply, he braced himself for the descent into the basement. Even as a child, a tremor of anxiety had always accompanied basement steps, a feeling amplified by his older brothers' tales of a monster lurking beneath. He could still hear their taunting laughter echoing in his memory as they locked him inside, the sting of their cruelty sharp even now. His father's dismissive words, *Be a man*," had offered no comfort. It was his mother's quiet compassion, a gentle hand on his shoulder, a hushed word of understanding, that had offered the only solace against the creeping dread.

He flicked the light switch. The sudden illumination did little to alleviate the anxiety thumping in his chest as he slowly made his way down. "There are no monsters down here," he repeated to himself, a fragile shield against the lingering dread. But the words withered on his tongue. *The family just battled some upstairs!* That meant they were real. *Not to mention that thing in the attic.* The terrifying truth consumed him, his hand trembling against the railing.

Reaching the cold concrete floor, his gaze swept across the small space. A washer and dryer stood guard beneath the window, surrounded by the scattered clothing. No doubt, remnants of their hasty departure. Shelves lined one wall, bearing the mundane necessities of household life: various cleaning supplies, empty flower pots, and jugs of laundry detergent. Another set of shelves held stacked boxes, likely more collections of forgotten memories and family treasures. "Okay, it's just a basement," he whispered, irritated at his brothers for instilling this irrational fear in him. "Let's do this," he murmured, his voice a low affirmation against the silence, as he moved toward the boxes.

After searching meticulously through every box, he could find nothing. He knew his best chance of finding anything was going to be back in the attic. The weight of the family's lives depended upon him, and he had promised them that he would do all he could to help. Yet a familiar dread, a relic of his last venture into that shadowy space, held him captive. It was a confrontation he wasn't ready for, not today. The memories of the creature he had seen there, still too vivid in his mind.

With a sigh, he dragged over a large plastic tote and sank onto it, his head dropping heavily into his hands. What else was there to do? He had exhausted every other avenue. Frustration gnawed at him, helping to keep his creeping fatigue at bay. But he couldn't stop, not now, not ever. He had to keep searching, keep fighting against the encroaching darkness. Not just for this family, who looked to him for answers and protection, but for his own sake. He had to prove to himself that he could overcome these terrifying obstacles. And above all, he had to keep going for Emma. He needed to know why she had died and to know that her death had not been in vain.

He drew in one more steadying breath, preparing to return upstairs. *Perhaps one more attempt at deciphering Lily's text will turn up something new,* he thought to himself. As he nudged the tote back against the wall, a faint clicking sound resonated through the quiet basement. Curious, he leaned down to investigate. A subtle shift in the wall caught his eye, a barely perceptible difference that, for some reason, heightened his awareness.

He activated the flashlight feature on his phone, its beam illuminating the section more closely. "I wonder..." he murmured, his fingers tracing over the surface before finally encountering a small lever cleverly disguised nearby. "Clever, very clever," he breathed, recognizing how its design blended in seamlessly with the surrounding wall. With a flick of his finger, the lever moved its position, creating a soft clicking sound. He watched in amazed silence as a section of the wall slowly, silently, swung inward, revealing a secret passageway shrouded in darkness.

Though he didn't know what to expect, he stepped inside. Like the basement, this room was also small. But in contrast to the mundane space he had just been in, this was a world that seemed to belong to a horror story. The air felt heavy and damp, clinging to his clothes, and the very walls seemed to sweat. His flashlight beam danced across their surface, revealing a chilling picture. They were adorned with strange, otherworldly symbols, etched directly into the stone. An unsettling array of peculiar artifacts were scattered about the floor. A stark, black pentagram had been inlaid directly into the concrete, its points ominous and sharp. A rickety shelf against one wall groaned under the weight of thick, leather-bound books, their titles obscured by age and shadow, no doubt promising forgotten rituals and forbidden knowledge.

Every instinct screamed at him to retreat, to slam the hidden door shut and pretend this room, with its unsettling vibe, never existed. Yet, a stubborn flicker of resolve ignited in his chest, battling back the fear. This was it. This felt like the true heart of the mystery, the very source of the darkness that was plaguing this family. He knew, with an undeniable certainty, that the answers they desperately sought, the key to understanding the shadow creatures and their haunting presence, lay hidden within this secret chamber. Despite the goosebumps prickling his skin and the rapid beat of his heart, he took another shaky breath. He had to search. He had to push past the terror, because the fate of this family, and possibly himself, depended on what he found here.

As he got busy examining the room, an unshakeable chill snaked down his spine, settling deep in his bones. Every creak of the old house above, every shift of dust in the stagnant air, made him flinch and glance over his shoulder, half-expecting a shadow to coalesce in the periphery of his vision. This wasn't merely a collection of bizarre objects; it was unmistakably a shrine, a place consecrated to dark rituals and unspeakable acts. The air itself seemed to hum with a malevolent energy, each strange symbol on the walls and every tarnished artifact whispering of sinister intentions. The creatures they had encountered, the shadow beings that had terrorized this family, were more than just random threats or unfortunate anomalies; they were clearly part of a larger, more insidious plan. A plan that, he now realized with dawning horror, had been in motion for far longer than anyone could possibly imagine.

His flashlight beam, a shaky beacon of light in the darkness, danced from the chilling pentagram on the floor to the tarnished silver artifacts. His gaze lingered on an aged, leather-bound book, thicker and more ominous than the others. As he reached for it, his fingers brushed against a faded inscription on the spine, a sequence of symbols that mirrored a small, almost imperceptible drawing on a loose stone near the far wall. A flicker of intuition, cold and precise, guided him. He moved, his heart thudding a frantic rhythm, towards the etched stone. Behind it, nestled in a hidden alcove, he found a small, rusted iron box. Its clasp yielded with a groan, revealing not gold or jewels, but a series of cryptic, blood-stained parchments.

The realization hit him, like a physical blow, a cold, crushing wave that stole his breath and sent a wave of nausea through him. The creatures they had encountered, the shadow beings that had terrorized this family, were more than just random threats. These gruesome artifacts, this hidden shrine, and this ritualistic space were all pieces of a much larger, more insidious plan. The monstrous figures the family had bravely faced were nothing but mere pawns in a much larger, more terrifying scheme, a cosmic chess game involving powerful forces utterly beyond human comprehension. This wasn't just some random house they had chosen; it was a focal point, a crucible for something truly evil.

"Oh my god," he uttered, the words barely a whisper, his hands trembling uncontrollably as he stared from the grisly contents of the box to the pentagram on the floor. This home was the nexus, the very portal through which all manner of unspeakable creatures would come. Creatures he couldn't at that moment allow himself to fully contemplate, their potential forms too horrifying for his mind to grasp. Overwhelmed by the enormity of his discovery, and a survival instinct to flee, he backed slowly out of the room. He reached for the hidden lever, pulling the secret door shut with a soft click that seemed deafening in the sudden silence. His heart pounding as he made his way back upstairs, each step heavy. His mind wrestled furiously with this newfound, terrifying revelation, struggling to process the impossible truth he had just uncovered. The world, as he knew it, had just been shattered.

Chapter 13:

Sarah continued sitting by her mother's side who remained unresponsive, her life hanging by a thread. Daniel, burdened by the weight of his responsibilities, was becoming a shadow of his former self. His normally vibrant spirit dimmed by exhaustion and despair. Both of them felt even more horrible as the girls were both exhausted and frightened, often clinging to each other for comfort. But the heartbreaking reality was that there were no nearby relatives to call for help, they had no safe haven in which to send them. And given the fact that something dark and evil seemed to be pursuing them, they wanted to keep them close in order to protect them. And though Silas had put a protective barrier around the home, they knew it was still far from inpenetrable.

Amidst their growing despair and the constant dread, new threats were emerging, insidious and unsettling. Strange occurrences had begun to plague the very halls of the hospital, a subtle but sinister shift in the atmosphere. Medical equipment sputtered and died without explanation, vital machines were flatlining with an unnerving frequency. Unsettling shadows flickered at the edges of vision, seen only in hurried glances, hinting at presences that shouldn't be there. An oppressive, almost suffocating silence frequently blanketed the halls, a heavy stillness that seemed to absorb all sound, as if the very air itself held its breath in anticipation of something awful.

The hospital staff, already overwhelmed by the relentless influx of patients and the immense emotional toll of their demanding jobs, largely attributed these strange occurrences to collective stress, exhaustion, and overwork. The flickering lights and sputtering equipment were dismissed as aging infrastructure, the unsettling shadows as tricks of tired eyes, and the oppressive silence as merely a sign of the late hour. But the family knew, their minds having been sharpened and altered by the terrifying ordeal they had endured, recognized the sinister patterns with chilling clarity. They knew, with a certainty that settled deep in their bones, that the pervasive darkness which had haunted their home was now busily spreading its tendrils into this new environment. It had followed them, just as Silas had warned, and they could feel its chilling presence growing with every passing hour.

Elias, their mysterious ally, had assured them that he had erected barriers to protect them all. Yet, as the strange occurrences at the hospital multiplied with unnerving frequency, a cold dread began to set in. Their initial faith in his promises, once a fragile comfort, started to waver, eroding with each flicker of lights and every unsettling shadow. "We're dealing with the unknown," he would often insist, his voice a carefully modulated blend of concern and unwavering determination. But despite his outward composure, Lily could detect a growing tension beneath his calm exterior, a subtle tremor in his reassurances that spoke volumes.

Her growing suspicions, a constant whisper in her mind, became too heavy for her to bear alone. She sought out her parents, her young face a mask of serious apprehension. "I don't trust Elias," she began, her voice barely above a whisper, the words a stark contrast to her usual tone. Her eyes, wide and earnest, scanned their faces, searching for any glimmer of understanding, any sign that they too might share her growing doubts about their mysterious ally.

They listened intently as she briefed them on her suspicions, recounting Elias's sometimes evasive answers, the subtle discrepancies in his explanations, and the unsettling feeling he sometimes evoked. Their faces, already etched with the deep lines of concern from their current ordeal, grew even more troubled. Daniel remained cautious, his mind grappling with the notion of distrusting one of their only known allies. Raising an eyebrow, a familiar gesture of his critical thought, he asked, his tone carefully measured, "What makes you say that, Lily?" Despite the caution in his voice, his eyes, dark and searching, held a distinct flicker of concern, an acknowledgment that her words, however unsettling, carried weight.

Before Lily could speak more of her concerns, Sarah spoke up. Her maternal instincts on high alert, and her voice laced with an undeniable tremor of fear. "I've been feeling uneasy around him too," she admitted, her gaze meeting Lily's, a silent understanding passing between them. "I thought it was just the stress, the exhaustion of everything we've been through, but there's something *off* about him. I can't explain it either, but it's like there's something lurking beneath his calm exterior, a darkness he tries to hide." The admission hung heavy in the air, confirming Lily's unspoken fears.

Daniel sighed, running a weary hand over his face. He wanted to believe Elias, wanted to believe in the help he offered. "All of us are tired and stressed out," he stated, trying his best to reassure his aching family, to cling to some semblance of normalcy. "Silas said he was a good man, that he could be trusted." He paused, the weight of his responsibilities pressing down on him. "So, for now, I'll keep an eye on him. We'll be careful. But it's not like we have a lot of options in regard to assistance right now, so we can't afford to alienate the only resource we have." The words were meant to calm, but even Daniel knew they rang hollow, a desperate attempt to maintain control in a world that was spiraling further into the unknown.

Silas, driven by an urgency to unravel the mysteries of the house, worked tirelessly, his mind a whirlwind of theories and desperate hopes. It was during one of his exhaustive re-examinations of the basement room that he made a truly startling discovery. The symbols etched into the damp, cold walls, which he had initially dismissed as mere decoration, were far more than that. They were a map, a meticulously detailed blueprint for a ritual. Silas leaned in, his fingers tracing the intricate lines and unfamiliar glyphs, his brow furrowed in intense concentration. He studied them over and over, cross-referencing with the few texts he possessed, but the full meaning remained maddeningly out of reach. The one terrifying truth he could decipher, however, was that this was a ritual designed, if completed, to open a gateway to a realm of unimaginable horror.

A chilling fear gripped him, seizing his breath as he realized the full, catastrophic implications of his findings. The shadow creatures they had encountered, the entities that had terrorized the family, were not the true threat. They were merely precursors, insignificant heralds of something far, far more sinister. The house itself was not just a target; it was the epicenter of a vast, ancient plan, a cosmic design that, if brought to fruition, could plunge the entire world into an eternal, inescapable darkness. The weight of this revelation pressed down on him, a suffocating burden.

With a newfound, desperate resolve, he delved deeper into the forbidden knowledge. He poured over the books he had brought with him, his own precious collection of arcane lore, and cross-referenced them with the dusty, leather-bound books he had discovered within the hidden room itself. The day blurred into night as he sifted through cryptic passages and unsettling illustrations. Then, buried within the brittle pages of several ancient journals, he discovered a name, mentioned repeatedly, always with a chilling blend of reverence and dread: Morpheus. The name resonated with an unholy power. Morpheus, he soon understood, was no mere participant. He was the architect of the darkness, the elusive mastermind behind the monstrous plan that was now rapidly unfolding. The realization brought with it a fresh wave of terror, for it meant their enemy was not some random evil, but an intelligent force of malevolence with a name and a terrifying purpose.

With this chilling new information, the terrifying realization of Morpheus and his grand design, Silas knew he had to act with desperate speed. Time was no longer a luxury they possessed. The immediate danger to this family, already so close to the brink, was now amplified a thousandfold. But it wasn't just them. The entire world was on the brink of catastrophe, teetering on the edge of an unimaginable darkness. He fumbled for his phone, his hands still trembling uncontrollably from the shock of his discovery, and punched in Daniel's number. His voice, when it finally emerged, was raw with urgency, stripped bare of anything but the stark truth.

"We all need to leave," he said, the words tumbling out in a rush, desperate to convey the gravity of the situation. "Now. The house... the house is a trap, a portal."

"What?" Daniel's voice on the other end of the line was laced with disbelief, unable to fully comprehend the frantic urgency, the sheer impossibility of what he was hearing. "Silas, slow down. What are you talking about?"

Silas took a shaky breath, forcing himself to put into words the unbelievable. He quickly explained everything he had found, the words spilling out in a torrent of terrifying revelation. The secret room in the basement, a hidden chamber the family had never known existed, a place steeped in evil. He spoke of the house's true, horrifying history, its dark purpose laid bare. He described the chilling symbols on the walls, not mere markings, but a blueprint for a ritual, a gateway. He spoke of the pervasive darkness, its true nature and its creator, Morpheus. He left nothing out, every horrifying detail, every piece of the puzzle that now painted a grim picture of their impending doom.

Daniel involuntarily slouched down into the nearest chair of the lobby, the worn fabric doing little to cushion the sudden weight of Silas's terrifying revelations. He was incredibly thankful for the fact that he had instinctively sought out the solitude in the waiting area, away from his family's prying eyes and ears. His hand raked through his hair, a gesture of disbelief and growing anger. "Oh my god," he uttered, the words a guttural whisper that quickly escalated. "How the hell did I not know any of this? What the fuck did my father hide from me?" he nearly shouted, the question aimed at no one, a desperate cry of betrayal and overwhelming confusion. The silence of the lobby, broken only by the distant murmur of hospital activity, seemed to mock his sudden, violent outburst.

"Daniel," Silas said slowly, his voice calm but firm, cutting through Daniel's rapidly escalating panic. "I understand your anger and frustration. Believe me, I really do. I've been wrestling with similar questions myself." He paused, letting the emotion in Daniel's voice subside slightly before continuing, his tone becoming more urgent. "But right now, I need you to focus. I need you to get your family and get back here. We all need to leave. Immediately." The emphasis on "immediately" was stark. "I know a place not far from here, a cabin. It's a place where we should be secure for now, and from there, away from this escalating danger, we can try to come up with a plan to stop it."

"But Sarah's mother, what about her?" Daniel interjected, the question tinged with desperation and conflict. "I mean, we can't just leave her here while she's helpless. Besides, there's been strange things happening all over the hospital as well, not just the house. Equipment failing, shadows, lights flickering... it's like the darkness is spreading. And Elias, no matter what he does, he can't seem to stop it." The admission of the strange occurrences added another layer of panic to his voice.

"What? Wait a minute. Daniel, who's Elias?" Silas cut in, a new edge of concern sharpening his tone. The name was unfamiliar to him, and in his current state of high alert, any unknown factor was considered a potential threat.

"You know, your colleague," Daniel retorted, his voice rising with exasperation, "The guy you sent over here to help us. Sarah spoke to you about him just the other day. Remember?" Daniel's mind raced, recalling Lily's urgent plea about Elias, Sarah's instinctive distrust, and his own vague sense that something was amiss. The puzzle pieces, once scattered, were now snapping into place with a chilling precision.

"Daniel," Silas said slowly, his voice now holding a detached quality, utterly devoid of its previous urgency. For a terrifying moment, he couldn't even be certain if any air was moving in his lungs. His blood ran cold, a wave of dread washing over him. "We've only spoken once since you left for the hospital. And I've never spoken with Sarah. Daniel, I'm telling you, I do not, nor have I ever, known anyone named Elias, and I certainly didn't send him." The unspoken implication hung heavy in the air between them. If Silas hadn't sent him, who was Elias, and what was his true purpose? And who exactly had his wife spoken with that day on the phone?

"I gotta go," Daniel said urgently, the words forced past his suddenly constricted throat. The realization hitting him like a physical blow. The man they had trusted, the one Silas supposedly sent, was an impostor. A chill far deeper than the hospital's air conditioning seeped into his bones. "We'll meet you in front of the house in twenty minutes. Be ready to go." He didn't wait for a reply, disconnecting the call with a trembling finger, his mind already racing with the grim necessity of protecting his family from yet another, perhaps even more, insidious threat.

He knew he had to act quickly. His eyes, now scanning every face with suspicion, hurried to locate the man who called himself Elias. He finally found him in the hospital cafeteria, casually finishing a meal. Not betraying his sudden, grim discovery, Daniel simply nodded curtly and then spun on his heel, returning to the third floor with not a moment to waste. Lily and Rose were still thankfully oblivious, their faces illuminated by the television, lost in the vibrant world of animated characters. He leaned close to Sarah, his voice dropping to a low, urgent whisper as he shared the new, terrifying details. Confusion flickered across her face, quickly followed by an intense wave of fear. "He was here... around Lily and Rose," she breathed, the realization dawning on her. "This whole time?"

"The girls are okay for now, that's all that matters," he said, trying to infuse his voice with a calm he didn't feel, desperate to offer her any kind of comfort amidst this never ending nightmare. His gaze swept over their daughters, their innocent laughter a stark contrast to the chilling deception they had just uncovered.

Sarah's eyes widened in disbelief. "How could we have been so blind?" she asked, her voice filled with a desperate anguish. "I questioned him, I really did, about his presence, but..."

Daniel cut her off gently, his hand touching her arm. "Don't go there now, Sarah. There's no time for that. The girls are safe, we're all safe, for the moment at least. But we have to focus on what's next." His mind was already racing, plotting their escape, their desperate dash towards a safe haven.

A sudden, even more unsettling thought clearly struck Sarah. Her eyes narrowed, a different kind of fear entering them. "Wait a minute," she asked, her voice hushed, "If I didn't speak to Silas when Elias first showed up…if he never sent Elias, then who was I on the phone with, Daniel? Because it sure sounded like Silas." The question hung in the air, as they both sat in silence.

"I don't know, Sarah," he finally managed, his voice strained. "But what I do know is that it wasn't Silas. And unlike Elias, I do trust Silas. He has been helping us. He has been at our home, looking for anything that could help. And I think he's found something," he said, shaking his head. "I don't know what yet, but I don't believe he has any reason whatsoever to lie to us." He glanced towards the door, then back at Sarah, a desperate plea in his eyes. "Now, I hate leaving your mother here all alone, truly I do, but we have to go. We need to leave *now* before Elias gets back from the cafeteria and realizes we're onto him. Who knows what he's really after." *Or worse, what he'll do.*

Sarah shook her head, tears already streaming down her face, her shoulders trembling with quiet sobs. The new fear about Elias warred within her against a deeper agony. "Daniel, I can't go," she whispered, her voice cracking. "Mom, she... she might not make it through the night." Her gaze drifted to her mother's still form, the frail rise and fall of the blanket almost imperceptible. "That's what the doctor said when he came in just a few minutes ago. They still don't know what's causing her condition, but they don't expect her to hold out much longer." A fresh wave of tears choked her words. "I can't leave her alone, Daniel. Not now. Not when she might be..." Her voice trailed off, unable to speak of her mother's fate.

"Then we stay," Daniel affirmed, drawing in a sharp, resolute breath. The words felt heavy with consequence, but also right. There was no way he could force his wife, the woman he loves, to abandon her mother in what might be her final hours. He nodded, pulling her into a tight, comforting embrace, his own fear momentarily eclipsed by the overwhelming protectiveness he felt for his family. "I'll call Silas and let him know to leave without us. We'll figure something else out for ourselves, for your mom." He held her close, feeling the tremble in her body, silently vowing to protect them all, no matter the cost.

Sarah pulled away from his embrace, her movements surprisingly firm despite the lingering tears that still streaked her face. She wiped them away with the back of her hand, her expression hardening with a quiet determination he hadn't seen in days. "No," she said matter-of-factly, her voice clearer now, though still hoarse. "You go. Take the girls somewhere safe. I'll sit with Mom until my brother arrives." Her gaze was unwavering, reflecting a resolve that stunned him.

"Philip is on his way?" Daniel asked, the question laced with a sudden worry that creased his brow. The name brought with it a different kind of tension, a familiar, deep-seated skepticism. "Philip never does anything that doesn't directly benefit him, Sarah. What makes you think he'll show up now, for this?"

"Daniel," Sarah said, cutting him off with a look that plainly told him to be quiet and respect her decision. Her eyes, though tear-stained, were unyielding. "He called this morning, right after the doctor made his morning rounds, and said he was coming. I didn't tell you immediately because I know he's not your favorite person. To be honest, he's not mine either. You know that. But right now, none of that matters." Her gaze softened as it drifted back to her mother's still form. "I just don't want to leave her alone. When he gets here, when he takes over by her bedside, then I will be okay to leave. So, when you pick up Silas, get my car and park it in the garage across the street. I have a set of keys in my purse." Her voice gained a firmer, more practical tone. "Text me your exact location, where you are or where you're going, and I will meet you as soon as I possibly can."

"No!" Daniel's voice was sharp, laced with a mix of both fear and indignation. He shook his head. "I don't like any of this, Sarah. Not one bit. I won't leave you here to fend for yourself, especially not when we don't even know who Elias really is or what he's capable of. We would all be worried about you. I would be worried sick about you, unable to focus on anything else." He stepped closer, attempting to take her hand. "We can all stay. We'll wait here, together, until Philip arrives. And then, we'll leave as a family. All of us."

"No, Daniel," Sarah said, shaking her head again, more forcefully this time. She took a deliberate step back, composing herself. "I'll be okay." She put on her best face of determination, her chin tilted defiantly, despite her insides trembling with every word. "I'm the one who needs to stay with my mother. This is my place right now. And I need you right now to be a father to our children, not my protector." Her voice pleaded, raw with urgency. "Take our girls and get them out of here. Please. Promise me that you will keep them safe, no matter what happens here."

Daniel had seen that look on her face many times, always in triumph. And as gut wrenching as the situation was, a fear clawing out his insides, he knew with certainty that she wouldn't back down. Her determination, even amidst her grief and terror, was unwavering. He also knew, with a chilling clarity, that the girls weren't safe around Elias, or whoever the hell that impostor really was. But neither, he realized with a fresh surge of dread, was his wife.

"Okay," he finally conceded, the word leaving a bitter taste on his tongue. It went against every protective instinct, every fiber of his being, to leave her there all alone. "But promise me you'll stay safe. Don't go anywhere alone with him. Stay in here with your mother, right here in her room where the nurses can see you, where there's at least some foot traffic. Got it?" His voice was hoarse with suppressed anxiety, his eyes pleading with her to truly understand the danger.

"Of course," she said, nodding firmly, and quickly wiped a fresh tear from her cheek with the back of her hand, her resolve momentarily eclipsing her sorrow.

"I'm going on the record though as saying that I think this is a really bad idea," he reiterated, the protest still strong in his throat, even as he reached out to gently wipe another tear from her face. The mere idea of separating, of leaving her in this unknown danger, gnawed at him. "And keep your phone turned on. Don't let the battery die so that I can reach you, and answer immediately if I call. And whatever you do Sarah, don't take any chances."

"I promise," she replied, her gaze meeting his, a flicker of genuine fear returning to her eyes. "But do you have any idea of what I should tell Elias? He'll want to know where you all are, won't he? He's bound to come back in here sooner or later."

Daniel's gaze flicked nervously towards the door, his eyes scanning the hallway to ensure Elias wasn't yet returning. His mind raced to concoct any plausible excuse, something Elias might swallow without suspicion. "Just tell him the girls were getting restless," he began, his voice dropping to a low, urgent murmur. "Say they've been cooped up in this room too long and needed to get some fresh air. So, I took them out for a bit, maybe to get some ice cream to cheer them up." He paused, imagining Elias's likely response. "Then, when you're finally ready to leave, tell him Silas has requested his immediate assistance back at the house. Make it sound urgent, like there's a new development he needs to be there for." Daniel's face was etched with a deep, grim concern. "And hope he takes the bait. As soon as you're absolutely sure he's gone, that he's truly left the hospital, you run to the car. Don't walk, run. Get out of here as fast as you can."

"Okay, yeah," Sarah said, the words coming out as a whisper. She nodded, her eyes wide as she processed the risky plan. The sheer audacity of the lie, coupled with the chilling necessity of it, made her stomach clench, but she understood the stakes. The urgency in Daniel's voice, the genuine fear in his eyes, solidified her resolve. She had to play her part perfectly.

Giving the girls and Daniel one final hug, Sarah clung to them for a moment longer than usual. "I love you," she whispered, her voice thick with unshed tears, imprinting their warmth on her memory. As they stepped into the elevator, its doors beginning to slide shut, her eyes locked with Daniel's. "Be careful," she mouthed, the silent plea carrying the full weight of her fear and her love, watching them until they vanished from sight. The metallic clang of the doors closing echoed the sudden void in her chest. Turning, she walked slowly back to her mother's room.

As Daniel pulled the car away from the hospital, merging into the afternoon rush hour traffic, a heavy, suffocating silence settled over the vehicle. It was a silence filled with unspoken anxieties and the chilling specter of what they had just left behind. Leaving Sarah, the woman who was the very bedrock of their family, was a decision born of sheer desperation, a painful gamble against the encroaching darkness. Each turn of the tires felt like a betrayal, a deepening severance from the fragile hope she represented. They were escaping one prison – the hospital, now tainted by Elias's sinister presence and the spreading malevolence – with the possibility of entering another: a world full of uncertainty and fear, a future where every shadow held a potential threat. And they were doing so, temporarily, without the matriarch of the family, the woman who effortlessly held them all together, whose quiet strength was their anchor in any storm. The thought gnawed at Daniel, a bitter counterpoint to the relief of having the girls beside him, safely away from both the horrors of their home and the stranger known as Elias.

Their destination was uncertain. Silas had suggested a remote cabin in the woods, a place he claimed would be safe from the reach of the darkness. Though that same darkness had already proven its terrifying ability to follow them, seeping into the seemingly sterile and secure environment of the hospital. So, absolute certainty of their safety was a luxury they couldn't afford. Still, for the desperate moment, it was their only hope.

The quiet of the car, now shared with Silas, was punctuated by Rose's persistent questions, each one a painful reminder of the deception they were now living. "But why can't Mommy and Elias come too?" she kept asking, her small voice tinged with genuine confusion and a hint of longing. "He said he would protect us too." The simple trust in her tone felt like a knife twisting in Daniel's gut, highlighting the layers of betrayal and the perilous game they were forced to play. He glanced at Lily in the rearview mirror, whose solemn expression revealed she knew far more than her younger sister, sharing his burden of this grim secret. Silas, seated beside him, remained silent, his gaze fixed on the road ahead, his brow furrowed with the weight of the discoveries he had just shared. He had heard Rose's question, and Daniel could feel the tension radiating from him, the unspoken dread that Elias was indeed no protector at all.

"Rose, Mommy will join us as soon as Uncle Philip shows up to sit with your grandmother. And Elias is not who he said he was," Daniel replied, doing his best to stay calm for the girls. "Now, we will protect you. Your mom and I, and Silas, will keep you safe. So just forget about Elias." He tried to make his words sound definitive, hoping to close off that line of questioning entirely.

"Dad's right," Lily added, her voice surprisingly steady. She put her arm protectively around her little sister, pulling her closer for comfort. "I sensed something was off about him. I've been watching him closely, ever since he arrived. And you trust me, don't you, Rose?" Her gaze was firm, a silent plea for her younger sister to accept the difficult truth and move past the confusing betrayal. Rose, still puzzled but reassured by Lily's certainty and her father's unwavering presence, finally nodded, burying her face into Lily's side.

"Yes, Lily," Rose said, her voice small, the word catching in her throat as fresh tears welled in her eyes. "But I liked Elias. He was nice." The simple statement, laden with innocent disappointment and confusion, tugged at Daniel's heart. He glanced at Silas, who shifted uncomfortably in his seat, the gravity of the situation weighing on them both.

"I know you did," Lily replied softly, her own voice betraying a hint of sadness for her sister's broken trust. She tightened her arm around her, pulling her even closer. "But I think he's a bad man, no matter how nice he seemed." She then leaned in, her voice dropping conspiratorially, appealing to a shared past only they fully understood. "I kept us safe in the foster homes, didn't I?" Her gaze was earnest, seeking confirmation of their bond and her protective role. "And I promise, I'll keep us safe now."

Rose sniffled, slowly shaking her head in reluctant agreement, then nodded, wiping her nose with the sleeve of her shirt. The painful memories of past betrayals, though different in nature, served as a grim reminder of Lily's uncanny ability to stand firm against any danger.

"Okay, then let's forget about him," Lily said, her voice firm. She gave her sister another squeeze. "We always keep each other safe. That's all that matters." It was a simple promise, a shared mantra that had carried them through countless difficult times.

With Rose's questions having stopped, a heavy silence cloaked the car, broken only by the hum of the engine and the soft murmur of the girls' conversation in the back. Though the afternoon sun still filtered through the trees, bathing the road in light, the emotional atmosphere inside the vehicle mirrored that of an intense storm. They were a family on the run, hunted by forces beyond their comprehension, each member lost in their own maze of fear and uncertainty, their minds racing to outrun the shadows closing in from behind.

Daniel, in particular, was consumed by a gnawing guilt. The image of Sarah's tear-streaked face, her resolute stance as he left her behind, burned in his mind. "I shouldn't have left her," he mumbled, the words raw with sorrow, barely audible even to himself.

Silas, seated beside him, glanced back, his eyes searching to see if the girls had heard Daniel's anguished confession. Thankfully, they seemed to be lost in their own little world. He only hoped, for their sake, that their internal world wasn't as frightening as the one running through his own head. "It wasn't safe to stay," Silas whispered, his voice low and firm, placing a reassuring hand on Daniel's shoulder and giving it a squeeze. "Sarah knew that. That's why she wanted you, their father, to get them to safety. She'll be here with all of you soon. You'll see," he added, though a subtle worry line creased his brow. He prayed he was telling Daniel the truth, that Sarah would indeed make it out of the hospital unscathed. And without Elias knowing what they were up to.

As they drove deeper into the country, the landscape around them began changing. The familiar sights of suburbia with its manicured lawns and orderly houses, gave way to rolling hills and dense forests. The road became narrower, winding its way through a seemingly endless expanse of towering trees. The air grew cooler, carrying the damp scent of pine and damp earth, a stark contrast to the hospital's sterile atmosphere.

Finally, after what felt like an eternity, though the clock confirmed it had only been an hour's drive, they reached their destination. The car slowly bumped down a barely visible pathway, emerging into a secluded clearing soaked in the evening sunlight. There, nestled amidst a protective circle of towering pines, stood the cabin. It was small and undeniably rustic, built of dark, weathered logs, with a simple stone chimney. Its windows, dark and unassuming, seemed to watch them as they approached. The sheer isolation of the place was both comforting and deeply unsettling at the same time, emphasizing their complete removal from the world they all knew.

As they stepped out of the car, the air felt warm on their skin. And the scent of pine and rich earth was pleasing to their nostrils after having spent the last week in the hospital. The sunlight filtered through the trees, painting the clearing in hues of amber and gold. The cabin, nestled peacefully amidst the pines, seemed to glow in the soft light, yet a deep sense of foreboding crept over them. A chilling intuition that despite their isolation, they were not alone. There was a feeling that they were being watched, even from the silent depths of the forest.

For Silas, stepping onto the familiar, weathered porch was a bittersweet ache. This wasn't just *a* cabin; it was their cabin. He remembered countless summer afternoons here with Emma, their private sanctuary from the demands of the world. He could almost see her now, stretched out on the very porch swing he was passing, her face turned to the lingering sun, basking in its warmth, smiling up at him.

She'd always brought a book to read. But mostly she would just be there, radiating a serene calm while he hunched over a laptop at the small wooden table inside, wrestling with his latest novel. This was their getaway, a place where time slowed, where the only sounds were the wind in the trees and the gentle murmur of their contentment. The vivid contrast between those cherished, sun-drenched memories and the grim reality of their present escape was a sharp, painful jolt.

"We should be safe in here," Silas offered, his voice attempting a lightness that didn't quite reach his eyes. The words sounded more like a desperate hope than a solid certainty, a fragile assurance against the darkness. He managed a strained smile for the girls, but it failed to mask the deep worry etched onto his face as he ushered them towards the heavy wooden door, eager to put the solid walls between them and the unsettling silence of the woods.

Inside, the cabin was warm and inviting. Silas got to work on a fire, which soon cast dancing shadows on the walls, creating a sense of comfort. The girls, their bodies stiff and aching, slowly began to explore. Their eyes, wide with a mixture of apprehension and curiosity, darted around the rustic living area, taking in the rough-hewn furniture and the sparse, utilitarian decor. Daniel, meanwhile, had already started moving towards the small, functional kitchen, his mind shifting from escape to the immediate need for sustenance. He began to put away the few groceries Silas had managed to grab, his thoughts turning to how he could prepare a comforting meal for them all. For this precious moment, amidst the flickering light and the scent of pine, they were safe. But the knowledge that the darkness which had relentlessly pursued them was still out there, waiting for an opportunity to strike, was a silent, chilling presence in the room.

"I'll be right back," Silas assured them, his voice a low rumble, before heading back outside. A quiet anxiety settled in the cabin, the crackling fire doing little to fully dispel the apprehension his departure created. Fifteen minutes later, the door creaked open, and Silas re-entered, a new sense of grim satisfaction etched on his face. "This place is protected," he said, his voice low but firm. "For now, at least. I've walked all around the perimeter, placing every ward I know of on it, reinforcing the natural defenses of this place." He wiped his hands on his pants, a faint scent of herbs and something metallic clinging to him, a testament no doubt to his tireless efforts.

Daniel and the girls exchanged relieved glances, a collective sigh of tension escaping them at Silas's assurance. "Thank you," Daniel replied, the simple words full of gratitude. The thought of being safe, even for a short time, was a powerful comfort. Yet, a shared understanding hung in the air: this battle was far from over.

As they sat down at the table to have their meal, a bowl of beef stew paired with a few saltine crackers, the wind outside began to howl. Its presence seemed to press against the very cabin walls around them. The darkness, now absolute beyond the small, lit windows, felt like a chilling reminder of the evil that lurked just beyond their fragile circle of light.

"I miss mommy," Rose finally mumbled, her voice small and trembling, as she swirled her spoon around mindlessly in her bowl. Her food untouched, her appetite lost in the overwhelming anxieties of the recent events.

"I know, baby," Daniel replied, his own voice thick with emotion, as he gently stroked her hair, trying to soothe her. "I do too. But she'll be here as soon as she can. We just have to be patient." He pressed a kiss to her forehead. "Now, try to eat something, okay? You need your strength. Then you can lay down and get some sleep." He did his best to project a calm he didn't feel, his own mind still churning with the deafening noise of the past week's horrifying events. A cold dread settled over him. He knew the road ahead would be filled with unimaginable dangers, and he worried, a deep, persistent ache in his chest, that they were not prepared to fight it.

Chapter 14:

The following morning, a thick fog had descended upon the isolated cabin, wrapping it in a chilling embrace. It was unlike any mist they had witnessed before; so dense that it swallowed the familiar landscape, reducing visibility to mere yards. The towering pines around their dwelling were now ghostly silhouettes, barely discernible from their front window. The usual sounds of a summer forest, like the chirping of birds, were now absent, as if the world beyond their immediate surroundings had ceased to exist.

Inside, Daniel and the girls gathered by the flickering warmth of the fireplace, its cheerful crackle a small comfort against the oppressive stillness outside. Their eyes, wide with a mixture of apprehension and fascination, were repeatedly drawn to the window. They watched as the fog rolled in thicker, a ghostly tide of white that seemed to press against the glass, threatening to seep into the very corners of their refuge.

Across the room, Silas remained oblivious to the unsettling spectacle outside. His face was a mask of intense concentration, etched with a deep furrow between his brows. He was entirely absorbed in the textbooks spread before him. His long, calloused fingers meticulously traced intricate, arcane symbols, following lines of script that seemed to writhe with their own hidden meanings. His lips moved silently, forming words that only he could hear, as if engaged in a hushed conversation with the very essence of the pages. There was an undeniable sense of urgency about him, and the air which surrounded him was permeated with tension. The weight of his singular focus was so strong that none of them dared to disturb him, sensing that whatever he sought within those books held the key to their present predicament, or perhaps, their very future.

"Where's Mommy?" Rose's small voice asked as she clung tightly to her sister, her eyes still full of fear. The question, barely a whisper, cut through the tense silence of the room, a stark reminder of their mounting anxiety.

"She'll be here soon," Daniel said, his voice a little strained as he tried to keep it from catching in his throat. He forced a reassuring smile, hoping it would mask the gnawing worry he felt. "She's on her way." He turned then to look out the window in order to hide the flicker of concern that he knew would betray his words. He didn't want the girls to see the deepening lines on his forehead or the slight tremor in his hands.

Earlier, Sarah had called, her voice tight with a frustration Daniel rarely heard. Her brother's flight, the one she'd been waiting on before she could leave the hospital, was unexpectedly delayed. Sarah was only supposed to be a few hours behind them, yet here it was the following day, and the agonizing wait was killing him. A horrifying reel of "what ifs" played in his mind: *What if something happened to her mother? What if she's pushing too hard, driving too fast to get to them, and something happens to her on the road? Or worse, what if she stopped by the house to retrieve some things and the shadow creatures attacked her? What if Elias hadn't bought her story and had already done something to her?*

Moments later, he watched as the thick fog that had enveloped the cabin was finally beginning to lift, peeling back its ghostly layers as the morning wore on. Yet, with its retreat came a different kind of tension, a restless energy that permeated the small space. Daniel paced, his gaze constantly flicking towards the window, then to the winding path that led back to the main road. The girls, usually full of boundless energy, were subdued, their quiet play interrupted by anxious glances towards their father. Silas, though still immersed in his books, occasionally looked up, his brows furrowed with a worry that had nothing to do with the answers he was searching for. Sarah's continued absence weighed heavily on them all, a silent, growing dread that no amount of lifting fog could dissipate. Each passing minute without her arrival tightened the knot of apprehension in Daniel's stomach.

To break the monotony and stretch their legs, Lily and Rose were tasked with gathering some wood from the surrounding area, a small chore meant to provide a semblance of normalcy. The cabin's dwindling supply of firewood was a practical concern, but the true purpose was to occupy their minds, to give them something to focus on beyond the growing anxiety. Simultaneously, Daniel fetched water for them from the shallow creek, which gurgled just a few yards south of the cabin, its gentle sounds now audible as the fog thinned.

"Stay in sight, girls," Daniel reminded them, his voice firm but gentle as he shouldered the empty water buckets. He watched them for a moment, a familiar ache in his chest. The woods, though now less shrouded, still held an air of mystery, and he couldn't shake the feeling that they were never truly safe.

"We will," Lily replied, her voice steady despite the slight tremor in her hand as she took Rose's smaller one.

Equipped with a sturdy firewood sling draped over her shoulder and a sense of trepidation that clung to them both, they ventured cautiously towards the edge of the still misty woods. The trees, though more defined than before, still loomed, their branches dripping with condensed moisture, and the silence within their depths felt almost watchful.

Inside the woods, the lingering tendrils of fog, though thinning, still clung to the undergrowth and the lower branches of the pines, creating an unsettling sense of isolation. It was like a ghostly veil, obscuring their vision beyond a few yards, muting colors, and dampening all sound. Every shadow seemed deeper, every rustle of leaves more significant.

"Rose!" Lily's voice, sharp with a mixture of fear and exasperation, cut through the quiet. She gripped her sister's arm, her fingers tightening instinctively. "You know we're supposed to stay within sight of the cabin." The rule was meant to keep them safe in this new world they were learning to navigate.

"But Lily, just look at the flowers!" Rose pleaded, her lower lip beginning to tremble. She pointed with her free hand towards a vibrant, almost luminescent patch of wildflowers blooming amidst the trees. They were a riot of purples, yellows, and deep blues, a burst of defiant color in the otherwise muted landscape. "We can pick some for Mommy! She'll be so happy when she sees them."

Seeing the disappointment on her sister's face, and the earnest desire to bring a bit of cheer to their mother who was dealing with a lot, Lily softened her grip. She knew how much her mother loved flowers. "Okay," she conceded, her voice gentler now as she took Rose's hand firmly in her own. "But we go no further than that patch. Understand? We pick them and then we go straight back.

Remember, we're supposed to stay where Dad can see us."

Rose nodded eagerly, her small hand already tugging Lily towards the colorful patch of wildflowers. Her face was alight with pure joy, completely absorbed in the task of gathering a bouquet for their mother. Lily, despite her growing anxiety, found herself momentarily distracted by her sister's innocent delight.

It wasn't long, however, before a strong sense of disorientation washed over Lily. The thin veil of fog, which had seemed to be lifting, now appeared to be swirling around them, becoming thicker with each step they took away from the clearing. The path they had just followed, once clear, was now indistinguishable. Rose, humming softly to herself, remained blissfully unaware, lost in the delicate beauty of her small, but growing bouquet. With each soft crunch of leaves underfoot as they continued deeper into the silent forest, an unsettling tranquility settled over the air. It was a silence that felt less like peace and more like a held breath. The trees, which moments before had been familiar and comforting, now loomed over them, their branches dripping with moisture, their forms distorted by the swirling mist. A prickle of cold fear, sharp and sudden, ran down Lily's spine as she glanced back. The comforting silhouette of the cabin had vanished, swallowed whole by the encroaching, hungry mist.

When Rose finally had enough flowers, she looked up, her smile wide. Suddenly, a splash of vibrant red caught her eye deeper within the shadows of the trees. "Look, Lily! Berries!" she exclaimed, her eyes sparkling with unadulterated delight. The morning's tension, coupled with the long wait for their mother, had left Lily's stomach gnawing with hunger, and the temptation of sweet, ripe berries was a powerful lure. Her earlier resolve, the strict promise to stay within sight of the cabin, wavered and then dissolved completely. Before she could truly stop herself, or even rationalize the decision, she found herself drawn deeper into the hushed, almost spectral woods, Rose eagerly by her side, their vital promise forgotten in the irresistible allure of the wild.

As they moved further into the dense thicket, their fingers stained with berry juice, they began to notice a faint but persistent sound. It was more than just the rustle of leaves; it was like a whisper, a soft, almost rhythmic disturbance, as if someone or something was moving deliberately through the dense undergrowth just out of sight. Lily's heart began to pound a frantic rhythm against her ribs. An unwelcome memory surfaced. Elias's strange behavior from the day before, the unsettling, almost predatory aura he had exuded. A terrifying thought solidified in her mind. Could he be out here, watching them, perhaps even following them? The possibility sent a violent shiver down her spine, chilling her far more than the damp air.

"Did you hear that?" Lily whispered, her voice barely a breath, though it felt deafeningly loud in the oppressive stillness. She clutched Rose's hand tighter, her fingers digging into her sister's soft skin.

"I think it's just a rabbit," Rose replied, her own voice surprisingly steady, though the slight tremble in her lower lip betrayed her attempt to sound brave. Her little hands, stained purple from the berries, continued to pick at the vibrant clusters before her.

But Lily wasn't convinced. The faint rustling and whispering sound persisted, closer now, a rhythmic disturbance in the otherwise silent forest. A sense of unease, cold and unwelcome, washed over her, a chilling certainty that they were no longer alone. It wasn't just an animal; it felt like they were being watched, their presence noted, perhaps even hunted. And then, through a fleeting break in the swirling mist, she saw it. A shadowy figure seemed to move, its shape indistinct. But it was too tall, too deliberate, to be a rabbit or even a deer.

Lily froze, every muscle in her body locked in place, her breath catching in her throat. The vibrant berries and colorful flowers faded from her perception, replaced by an overwhelming sense of terror. They were deep in the woods, far from the cabin, and all alone, terrifyingly vulnerable. And something was out there, in the formless depths of the fog, something that felt sinister and cold, and it was getting closer. The silence around them was no longer tranquil but heavy, as if the forest itself held its breath.

With trembling hands, Lily reached for her sister, her fear mutating into a fierce, protective instinct. Her fingers clamped onto her sister's arm, pulling her close. Just as her grip tightened, Rose looked up, her innocent gaze following Lily's terrified stare into the swirling mist. Her breath hitched, a small, choked sound, as she too saw it. She pressed herself against Lily, a tiny, trembling weight, seeking refuge in her sister's embrace.

They stood motionless, two small figures dwarfed by the looming trees and oppressive fog, their breath held captive in their chests. Every fiber of their being was focused on the faint, unsettling sounds that had now intensified. The rustle grew louder, more distinct, closer than before, accompanied by the snapping of twigs under an unseen weight. And then, a low, guttural growl, deep and chilling, echoed through the damp woods, vibrating through the very ground beneath their feet. Their hearts hammered in their chests, a frantic drumbeat against the silence. This was no ordinary animal. This was something else, something dark, a presence that radiated malevolence and hunger.

As the creature emerged, their fear transformed into horror. A massive, shadowy figure stood before them, its form indistinct yet undeniably menacing, its contours distorted and exaggerated by the swirling fog. Its eyes, twin points of unnatural, malevolent light, glowed with an eerie luminescence that seemed to pierce through the gloom and fix upon them. It was larger than any animal they had ever seen, its bulk immense and unsettling, yet it moved with a silent, predatory grace that belied its size. A low, guttural sound rumbled from its unseen throat, a sound of anticipation that promised nothing but sheer terror. The air around it seemed to grow colder, heavy with a suffocating dread that threatened to swallow them whole.

A scream built in Lily's throat, desperate to break free, yet no sound escaped her lips. Beside her, Rose was trembling, her small hands fisted into the back of Lily's shirt, her entire body vibrating with a frantic energy that spoke volumes of her petrified state. The creature remained an unmoving silhouette against the swirling grey, its presence a pronounced weight in the already heavy air. Its eyes held the girls captive in their gaze, a silent, predatory assessment that seemed to stretch into an eternity. The world shrank to the space between those eyes and their own. Then, with a suddenness that made Lily's head spin, the creature was gone. One moment it was there, a terrifying reality, and the next, only the swirling, indifferent mist remained, swallowing the space it had occupied as if it had never been. The silence that descended was thick and absolute, pressing against their eardrums, a void more terrifying than the growl that had preceded it. For a fleeting instant in the aftermath, as her vision swam with lingering fear, Lily could almost swear she saw him. Not the monstrous shape that had just vanished, but Elias. He stood just at the edge of the mist, his familiar form momentarily solid before the fog seemed to claim him once more. And on his lips, a smile played. A soft, knowing curve that sent a fresh wave of icy dread washing over her, a dread far more personal and insidious than the fear of the unknown creature. Was it real? A trick of the light and her terror-addled mind? Or something far more sinister? The question hung heavy in the silent air, unanswered and deeply unsettling.

Lily's breath hitched, a strangled gasp escaping her lips, as her fingers clamped around Rose's hand like a vise. The image of the creature, its glowing eyes burned into her memory, spurred her into action. "Rose, hurry!" she gasped, pulling her sister along, not caring about the dropped bouquet or the discarded berries. Their legs felt like jelly, each step a wobbly, uncoordinated effort over the uneven forest floor. What they had just witnessed played on repeat in their minds, a terrifying, silent loop of the impossible, each detail more vivid and horrifying with every frantic heartbeat. The silence of the woods, once merely unsettling, now felt actively predatory, as if the very air was holding its breath, waiting for them to falter.

Just as the comforting, familiar shape of the cabin came into view through the thinning mist, they saw their father running towards them, his brow furrowed with worry, a mixture of impatience and relief on his face. But the moment his eyes landed on their ashen faces, their wide, terror-stricken eyes, and their trembling bodies, the concern vanished, replaced by stark, undeniable fear. "Lily! Rose! What is it?" he exclaimed, his voice sharp with alarm, his arms instinctively reaching for them. He pulled them close, a powerful, protective embrace, his body shielding them as he practically swept them towards the cabin. The heavy wooden door slammed shut behind them with a resounding thud that echoed through the suddenly quiet interior. Without a moment's hesitation, he shoved the heavy bolt across the door frame, the metallic clunk slicing through the sudden, heavy silence that had fallen over the cabin, a silence now permeated not just by the lingering dampness of the fog, but by the chilling residue of pure terror.

Silas stood, his research momentarily forgotten. His eyes, usually deep with scholarly concentration, were now sharp with unspoken questions, darting between Daniel's grim face and the two trembling girls.

Lily, still catching her breath, her small chest heaving, could only manage a shaky, choked sound. "Out there... another one." She pressed a trembling hand to her chest, her heart hammering against her ribs as if trying to escape. Her gaze, wide with residual terror, was fixed on the heavy wooden door. "Another monster."

Rose stood beside her, frozen still, her small hand fisted so tightly in Lily's shirt that her knuckles were white. Silent tears tracked glistening paths down her pale cheeks, her eyes, usually so bright, now dull with shock and fear.

A visible tremor ran through Daniel, a ripple of dread that started at his shoulders and worked its way down his arms. "Another one?" he repeated, his voice barely a whisper, the question hanging heavy in the air. The familiar scent of woodsmoke and pine in the small cabin now seemed thin, overpowered by an undeniable undercurrent of fear. The woods, which was meant to be their sanctuary, a place of peace and relative safety, had suddenly turned hostile, a vast, untamed expanse teeming with unseen horrors. Even within the sturdy walls of their cabin, the illusion of safety had shattered into a thousand irreparable pieces.

Silas's jaw tightened, a muscle twitching in his cheek, his gaze hardening as the full weight of Lily's words settled upon him. "This confirms it," he said, his voice low and grim, devoid of its usual academic calm. "They're not just out there, at the house, even the hospital; they're lurking in the shadows, they're hunting. They're seeking us out." He ran a hand through his sparse hair, his eyes scanning the sturdy, familiar walls of the cabin, no longer seeing them as a comforting shelter but assessing their defenses with a grim, practiced eye. "This cabin... it's not a safe haven any longer. Or maybe it never was. It's a fortress under siege." The words hung in the air, a chilling reminder of the battle they now faced.

"So all that... leaving everything behind... running away…leaving my wife behind…it was for nothing?" Daniel asked, his voice raw, a bitter note creeping into its edges. He gestured vaguely around the cramped cabin, at the hastily packed bags they had brought with them. The sacrifices they had made, the life they had abandoned, the constant gnawing fear. Was it all for nothing? The thought was a crushing weight.

Silas's gaze was steady, unwavering, but filled with a deep well of concern and understanding. He knew the despair that gnawed at Daniel. "It might appear that way, Daniel. It might feel as though every step we've taken has only led us closer to the brink. But the truth is... we're in the most precarious situation imaginable." His eyes flickered to the heavy wooden door, then back to Daniel's tormented face. "And your home... it's not just a house. It's the gateway, the portal. The very fabric of reality there is thin, compromised, a constant tear in the veil between worlds." He paused, choosing his words carefully, the gravity of them settling in the quiet room. "Therefore, it's safe to say that the farther away from there we are, the better off we are. Every mile we put between ourselves and that place buys us time, buys us a fighting chance. It's not for nothing, Daniel. It's for survival."

Daniel's mind was still reeling from Silas's grim pronouncement, the word *siege* echoing ominously in his thoughts, when a distant, familiar rumble sliced through the stillness. It was the low thrum of an engine, a sound he had been desperate to hear for what felt like an eternity. He leaped to his feet, a sudden surge of adrenaline mixed with an overwhelming sense of hope coursing through him. "Oh, thank God," he breathed, the words a silent prayer of overwhelming relief, his heart pounding with hopeful anticipation.

He darted to the window, peering through the still-present, though thinning, fog. And there it was. A wave of pure, unadulterated relief washed over him, so potent it almost brought him to his knees. Sarah's car was pulling up to the cabin, its headlights cutting through the swirling mist like powerful beacons, dispelling the gloom. With a joyous cry that was more a choked sob of gratitude, he scooped up the girls, one in each arm, and rushed outside, their mingled laughter and excited squeals echoing with the crunch of gravel beneath their feet. The crushing tension of the long, anxious night and the harrowing morning seemed to melt away in the sheer warmth of their reunion, replaced by an intoxicating sense of wholeness and safety.

He hugged Sarah fiercely, the girls still clinging to them both, a family reunited against the world. As they finally pulled apart, Daniel's relief was quickly tempered by his lingering anxieties. His eyes, still wary, scanned the remaining tendrils of fog, searching for any lingering shadows, any sign that their fragile peace was about to be shattered. "Any trouble with Elias?" he asked, his voice low, the question laced with a protective urgency.

Sarah hugged her girls even tighter, burying her face in their hair for a moment before looking up at Daniel. A tired smile touched her lips, but her eyes held a lingering shadow of the cunning she'd had to employ. "No, he took the bait," she replied, her voice soft but firm. "At least I think he did." Her gaze met his, a shared understanding passing between them of the dangerous game she had just played.

"And Grandma?" Lily asked, her small voice cutting through the lingering relief of the reunion, a look of concern masking her young face.

"She's holding her own," Sarah replied, doing her best to make her face match her reassuring words. Her smile felt fragile, a thin veil over the exhaustion and anxiety she truly felt. "Don't you worry, sweetie." Meanwhile, the inner turmoil from all the stress was eating her alive, a gnawing ache in her stomach and a constant thrum behind her eyes.

Daniel's arms tightened around her for a moment before he pulled back, his brow furrowed once more. His eyes, though filled with relief at her presence, now held a question. "Why did it take you so long?" he asked, his voice softer, but the underlying anxiety was clear. "We've been worried sick. You were expected last night."

Sarah sighed, running a weary hand through her hair. "I know, I know. I'm so sorry." She quickly explained, "Philip's flight was severely delayed. By the time he finally landed and got to the hospital, it was almost time for the doctor to do his rounds and see Mom." She knew Daniel would understand the unspoken implication: leaving before Philip had a chance to speak with the doctor would have been suspicious, especially given Elias's watchful presence. "So,

I waited with him, to see if there was any news, any change in her condition." The hours had crawled by, each minute feeling like an eternity of forced calm. "And then," she added, trying to lighten the mood slightly, "I made a quick stop at the store on the way. Figured we'd need some proper provisions. I grabbed some things to do for a few days, you know like bottled water, and some fresh fruit." She hoped the practical concerns would distract him, if only for a moment, from the deeper worries that still shadowed them all.

With the whole family finally back together, a semblance of their former unit restored, they settled onto the worn-out sofa inside the cabin. The girls instinctively curled into their mother's side, drawing comfort from her presence, while Daniel wrapped an arm around her. It was time to catch Sarah up on the morning's harrowing events. Lily, still pale but resolute, recounted the unsettling sounds in the woods, the growing dread, and then, the terrifying emergence of the creature. Rose, sniffling softly, chimed in with breathless fragments.

As Lily described the shadowy figure and the subsequent gut-wrenching realization that it was no animal, a tremor ran through Sarah's voice. "Elias was here?" she asked, her eyes wide with disbelief and a fresh surge of fear. The thought that this stranger, twisted by whatever dark forces consumed him, might have figured out their plan and been so close was a chilling prospect.

"We think so," Daniel replied, his voice carefully neutral, even as his own agitation mirrored hers. He quickly added, trying to soften the blow and quell her rising panic, "but we're not certain. It could have been just the stress of seeing the monster, an overactive imagination, a lack of sleep, anything. Please don't worry about this," he said, tightening his arm around her, pulling her closer into his embrace. He desperately wanted to shield her from this new layer of terror, to convince her that it was a possibility, not a certainty.

Lily and Rose listened intently, their small faces betraying little of the intense thoughts swirling within them. *I'm certain it was him,* Lily thought to herself, the memory of the shape, and the familiar, cold dread it had evoked, burning clear in her mind. It had even felt like *him*. But not wishing to add more distress to an already overwhelmed situation, or to see the fragile relief on her mother's face shatter, she wisely decided on keeping her mouth shut, guarding her conviction in the silence of her own mind. The family was reunited, but the dangers outside, and the questions within, still remained.

"Well," Silas remarked, his voice cutting through the thick, anxious air that had settled over the cabin. He stood up, stretching his back, a deliberate movement meant to ease the tension he could feel so heavily around them from the conversation regarding the possible sighting of Elias and the creature which the girls had encountered in the woods. His gaze swept over the worried faces of Daniel and Sarah, then to the pale, shaken girls. "I think we need to fortify this cabin, make every effort to ensure that these creatures don't get in here." His tone was firm, shifting the focus from fear to action.

"Yes," Daniel replied, already on his feet, his mind racing with practical concerns. "And no one goes outside alone. Understood?" he asked, his gaze firm as he looked towards Lily and Rose, who were still huddled on the sofa. He waited, making eye contact with each of them until they both gave solemn, shaky nods. Satisfied with their understanding, they immediately got to work.

They worked through the remainder of the day tirelessly, driven by an instinctive need for security. The initial relief of Sarah's return and the lifting fog had given way to a grim determination. The cabin was transformed from a rustic refuge into a makeshift fortress. Windows were systematically boarded up, the splintering wood and hammering echoing through the small space, each nail driven became a small act of defiance against the unseen threats. Makeshift barricades were erected around the doors, furniture dragged and stacked, creating formidable obstacles designed to deter any unwelcome intruders.

Silas, with his extensive knowledge of the occult, moved with a quiet intensity, his fingers tracing intricate patterns in the air, murmuring ancient words as he created additional wards. He daubed strange symbols above entryways and along the window frames with a chalky substance, infusing them with protective energies drawn from ancient lore. Each of them, united by a common, desperate purpose, worked in harmony, their movements efficient and synchronized. Their fear was no longer paralyzing, but a potent fuel, channeled into a desperate need to survive, to protect not only themselves, but their family against the growing darkness that now truly felt as if it was laying siege to their very existence. As twilight began to paint the sky outside, casting long, purple shadows, the cabin stood grim and defiant, a stronghold against the encroaching night and whatever horrors it might hold.

That night, following their frantic preparations, it was unusually calm. The stillness, rather than bringing solace, felt almost unsettling after the day's terror. No growls echoed from the darkened woods, no shadowy figures pressed against their barricaded windows. Yet, sleep was a fragile thing. Silas and Daniel took turns in shifts, their senses heightened, keeping a vigilant guard. Every creak of the old cabin, every rustle of leaves outside, sent a jolt of adrenaline through them. Sarah slept very little, her mind replaying the day's horrors and the grim reality of Elias's proximity. She lay awake, listening to the soft breathing of her daughters, a fierce protectiveness overriding her exhaustion. They had made it through the night, but the quiet offered no true peace, only a temporary reprieve.

The following day, with the sun a muted glow through the still-present, though dissipated, mist, the entire family began a rigorous training regimen under Silas's guidance. The calm of the night, while a relief, had only underscored the urgency of their situation, as they knew it would only be a matter of time before the next attack came. There would be no more waiting, no more passive defense. They plunged into lessons about the nature of their enemies, their weaknesses, and their tactics. Or at least, the ones they knew of from Silas's studies. He spoke of creatures that fed on fear, of methods to confuse and deter them, and the critical importance of understanding their patterns. "Physical training, along with mental conditioning, will help us all prepare for the battles to come," he stated, his voice resonating with authority. "We must forge both our bodies and our minds, for one cannot truly protect the other without both being equally strong."

Following a quick, almost silent lunch of the provisions Sarah had brought, they moved to the open expanse of their front yard. Daniel first conducted a careful, comprehensive survey of their familiar surroundings, his eyes sweeping the tree line and checking the integrity of their newly installed defenses. Finding no immediate cause for alarm, their physical conditioning commenced. They started with basic calisthenics, push-ups and sit-ups pushing their untrained muscles. Daniel demonstrated proper form, while Silas offered quiet encouragement. For pull-ups, they utilized the robust limb of a low-hanging oak tree, its rough bark digging into their palms as they struggled to hoist themselves up. Silas, ever resourceful, quickly fashioned an impromptu obstacle course from discarded barrels and old tires he had located in a shed on the property, transforming everyday objects into tools for endurance and agility training. They crawled through tires, leaped over barrels, and sprinted between markers, their muscles screaming in protest. By late afternoon, a bone-deep exhaustion had settled upon each of them, a heavy cloak of weariness that promised a deep, dreamless sleep. Yet, despite the aches and pains, there was also a quiet satisfaction, a sense of having taken the first real steps towards reclaiming some control over their new perilous reality.

As the week continued, the rigorous training under Silas's watchful eye persisted, pushing them physically and mentally. Yet, despite their growing strength and resolve, the tension within the cabin thickened, a noticeable presence that settled into every crevice. Outside, the woods seemed to breathe with an unseen, malevolent presence. Faint, disembodied whisperings carried on the wind, like secrets hissed through unseen lips, and the shadows themselves appeared to lengthen and writhe with a sinister, almost intelligent intent. Silas meticulously made certain the cabin's runes and wards held their power, his fingers tracing the protective symbols daily; yet, every rustle and every subtle shift in the outside world kept their senses razor-sharp, leaving them in a constant state of alert.

A storm was brewing, a tempestuous beast gathering strength beyond the forest's edge. The air grew heavy, charged with an almost electric anticipation. As the first cold raindrops began to splatter against the cabin's stout wooden walls, a sense of foreboding washed over them, chilling them more than the plummeting temperature. The wind began to howl like a wounded animal, its mournful, escalating cries a chilling counterpoint to the rhythmic drumming of rain on the roof and windows. A sudden, violent gust rattled the cabin, and then, with a pop and a flicker, the old oil lamp, their sole source of light, sputtered and died, plunging the cabin into an inky, suffocating blackness.

Rose whimpered, a small, trembling sound, trying her best not to scream as she clung desperately to both her sister and her mother. The sudden darkness was overwhelming as they could feel it pressing in on them. Daniel, his own heart thudding, instinctively made his way towards the kitchen, his hands fumbling in the familiar gloom for the flashlight he had left in one of the drawers. Across the room, Silas fought a losing battle against his lighter, its tiny flint sparking uselessly against the pervasive dampness.

Fear, cold and sharp, filled the room, replacing the air itself. They each stood frozen, rooted to the spot, their eyes straining to adjust to the oppressive gloom. Their hearts pounded in their chests, a frantic, shared rhythm. And then, at the periphery of their vision, a shape materialized, a dark, imposing figure that seemed to glide rather than walk, its presence filling the room with an almost physical dread. Terror seized them, an icy grip that paralyzed their limbs, rendering them helpless.

Clutching both girls tightly, Sarah began backing away slowly, inch by agonizing inch, her movements deliberate, being careful not to alarm the creature or provoke it further. Daniel's hands trembled violently as he frantically searched for the elusive flashlight, his fingers brushing against cold metal, then smooth wood, but never the familiar contours of the torch. Silas, meanwhile, continued his desperate, insistent flicking of his lighter, the tiny clicks sounding impossibly loud in the overwhelming silence.

The figure loomed larger, its form increasingly menacing as it seemed to glide closer with each passing second, its presence suffocating. *Come on,* Silas willed the lighter, his plea echoing in his own mind. Finally, miraculously, after what felt like an eternity, he coaxed a flickering flame from the lighter. The brief, dancing light, though feeble, pierced the impenetrable darkness. It revealed the shadowy figure in the act of dissolving, its indistinct form melting away as suddenly as it had materialized, gone as if it had been merely a figment of their collective, terrified imagination. The cabin remained dark, save for the tiny, defiant flame in Silas's hand, leaving them with the chilling knowledge that they had just faced something truly monstrous, and barely escaped.

Chapter 15:

"Daniel, I need to go see my mom again," Sarah said, her voice filled with a desperate mix of worry and unshakeable determination. The words hung in the air, heavy with unspoken fears. "Philip was only going to be in town for a couple of days, and I need to make sure she's okay. He was leaving this morning, and I can't bear the thought of no one being by her side. Last I checked with him, she's still holding on, but," she began, her eyes welling with tears as she struggled for the words to complete the sentence, the raw emotion catching in her throat. She swallowed hard, shaking away the tears, and continued, changing the subject, "Plus, we desperately need to restock on supplies. We're running dangerously low, especially on food."

Daniel nodded slowly, his face etched with concern that mirrored her own. He knew the risks, but the thought of her facing it alone was unbearable. "We can go together," he offered immediately, his hand reaching for hers.

Sarah squeezed his hand, her gaze firm. "No, it isn't safe to take the girls away from the cabin. We've spent days fortifying this place, and at least Silas is able to keep it somewhat protected with his wards. We have no idea what will happen if we take them out there, if we expose them to whatever is lurking in those woods, or worse, if we encounter Elias. And as much as I want you with me, as much as I hate the thought of you being alone, I don't feel right with both of us leaving them defenseless, even with Silas here. Besides, she's my mother, Daniel. I'm the one who needs to go." Her voice was quiet but resolute, leaving no room for argument. The weight of responsibility, both for her ailing mother and for their daughters, settled heavily on her shoulders.

A heavy sigh escaped Daniel's lips, a sound weighted down with weariness and deep exasperation. He ran a hand through his hair, his frustration undeniable as he began pacing the worn floorboards of the cabin. "What are we going to do?" he asked, his voice rising slightly in pitch, the question echoing the crushing weight of their impossible situation. "I can't go to work, Sarah. My boss probably thinks I've vanished off the face of the earth. We're on the run like criminals, hiding out from things that shouldn't even exist, trying to avoid being swallowed by some twisted version of the supernatural world. I mean, this is insane. We can't live like this forever."

Sarah stepped forward, reaching out and gently squeezing his hand, trying her best to comfort him. "I know," she murmured, her own voice thick with the strain of their predicament. "We're all stressed out, Daniel. Every single one of us." Her gaze softened, filled with a brutal honesty. "I don't know how to keep my family safe, and my mother…" she began, her voice trailing off as the thought of her ailing mother, alone in the hospital, brought a fresh wave of heartache. She squeezed his hand again, a silent promise. "I know, and it's terrifying. I have no idea what's going to happen. None of us do. But I do know that we're in this together, no matter what."

Daniel stopped pacing, his eyes sweeping over the barricaded windows, the worn-out sofa where their daughters sat huddled together. His initial instinct was to argue, to demand that he go with her, to confront the impossible dangers head-on. But then his gaze fell on the dwindling stack of canned goods on the kitchen counter. He remembered the desperate look on Lily's face earlier, the sheer terror in Rose's eyes. The image of that monstrous figure in the mist, coupled with Silas's grim assessment of their cabin as a *fortress under siege*, solidified a terrible realization. Their supplies were indeed dangerously low, and the risk of taking the girls out of their only protected space, however fragile that protection might be, was simply too great. A shudder ran through him. "You're right," he said, the words heavy with resignation, "the girls... they're too vulnerable. We can't risk their lives." He looked at Sarah, a silent apology in his eyes for his earlier resistance, replaced by a grim acceptance of their horrifying reality.

Before Sarah could even move towards the door, Silas stepped forward, his expression grave. He held out a small, intricately woven leather pouch. "Here," he said, his voice low and earnest. "It contains some protective stones and herbs that may help you. Believe in their power, especially against... well, against what's out there. Stay safe, Sarah." He clasped her hands firmly around the pouch, his gaze steady and filled with a rare, genuine smile that held both encouragement and deep concern.

Daniel then pulled her into a tight embrace, his voice hoarse with suppressed anxiety. "Sarah, please be careful," he implored, his words a desperate whisper against her hair. "Don't take any chances. If anything feels off, if you even think you see something, turn around. Come back. The supplies can wait. Your mother... I know you need to see her, but your safety has to come first. Promise me you won't be a hero."

"I promise," she replied, leaning into his embrace, giving him a tender kiss.

As she pulled away, the girls clung to her waist, their small faces crumpled with fear. "Please don't go, Mommy!" Rose whimpered, her voice muffled against Sarah's jeans, tiny hands fisted in the fabric of her shirt. Lily, ever the more outwardly passive, merely looked up, her wide, tear-filled eyes silently pleading, mirroring her sister's desperate plea.

Sarah knelt, wrapping her arms around them, the goodbye kisses accompanied by a painful lump in her throat, a desperate effort to memorize their warmth. The morning air, though now clear and crisp with the fog having completely retreated, offered no solace. Instead, the earlier anxiety now surged back, insistent and strong, twisting in her gut. With the clarity of the sunlight came a chilling sense of exposure. Something felt inherently wrong about leaving them, about venturing back into a world that was clearly no longer their own. Taking one final, lingering look at her family as she headed out the door, she noticed Daniel's grim face, Silas's watchful eyes, and her daughters' trembling forms. With all her strength, she got in her car and pulled out of the driveway, a whispered promise escaping her lips, "Dear God, I've never been religious, definitely not one for praying, but please, please, keep my family safe."

The four of them stood on the porch watching Sarah's car disappear down the winding, gravel road. The crunch of tires on stone faded, then the hum of the engine, until only the quiet rustle of the woods remained. Daniel remained rooted to the spot, his gaze fixed on the empty space where her car had been, his jaw tight, clearly needing a moment to process the gnawing fear that now settled heavily upon him. Sensing this, Silas gently placed a hand on his shoulder. "Girls," he said, his voice calm and steady, drawing their attention. "Your mother has shown us how brave she is. Now, we need to be brave too. How about you help me check the wards I placed around the cabin? We'll make sure they're strong enough to keep everything out until she gets back." It was a clear attempt to restore some order, to give them a task, and to allow Daniel the space he needed to compose himself.

***

A growing sense of unease settled over Sarah as she drove through the familiar streets towards town. The usual vibrant energy of the place was notably absent, replaced by an unsettling stillness that made the hairs on her arms stand. Even the sky, which should have been a bright July blue, was now bruised with darkening hues, a canvas of dark purples and grays. A cold wind, starkly out of season, whipped through the streets, carrying an inexplicable chill that seeped into her bones, hinting at a change that went far deeper than simply the weather.

A knot of apprehension tightened in her stomach as the imposing structure of the hospital came into view. The afternoon sun, usually a source of warmth and comfort, seemed to cast long, distorted shadows across the manicured lawn, lending the familiar building a distinctly ominous air. A strange sensation, cold and inescapable, washed over her. An innate certainty that something was amiss, something terribly, irrevocably wrong. It wasn't a logical thought, no reasoned deduction, but a deep-seated instinct that prickled her skin and sent a shiver down her spine, a silent scream of warning from the very core of her being. The air itself felt heavy, charged with an invisible dread.

Her anxiety level increased as the multi-story parking garage came into view, its Brutalist architecture looking particularly menacing against the darkening sky. The concrete structure, usually a mundane transitional space she navigated without a second thought, felt extremely ominous under the diffused, grimy afternoon light filtering through its upper levels. She shivered again, as a strange, icy sensation chilled her to the bones, bringing with it a deep-seated certainty that something was wrong. It was an alarm bell ringing in her very core, a knowing premonition of the dread which was awaiting her.

Her senses, already frayed from the mounting terror, were on high alert as she navigated the echoing ramps. The tires crunched loudly on the scattered gravel and debris, each turn deeper into the concrete maze intensifying her growing apprehension. Her eyes darted frantically between the parked cars, each dark window a potential hiding place, searching for any flicker of the encroaching darkness, any unsettling silhouette that might betray the presence of Elias, or worse, one of the monstrous creatures. The mundane sounds of a distant car starting, the sharp clang of a closing door from a higher level, seemed amplified in the enclosed space, imbued with a potential for threat that made her muscles tense. Every shadow felt alive, every creak of the aging structure a whisper of hidden malevolence. The air itself, usually stagnant, felt heavy and oppressive, as if it too held its breath in anticipation of something horrific.

Finding an empty spot on the third level, she pulled in and cut the engine. The sudden, oppressive silence that followed amplified the rapid thumping of her heart, a frantic drumbeat in her ears. The hum of the idling engine had masked the eerie quiet, but now it was all-encompassing, broken only by the occasional groan of the concrete structure itself. Gathering her resolve, a disquieting thought flickered through her mind. Were the hurried, almost cautious glances of the few other people in the garage just her own heightened paranoia, a reflection of the dread churning within her? Or could they sense it too? Was there an almost imperceptible shift in the atmosphere, a shared awareness of something being greatly amiss that left them all feeling uneasy, quickening their steps and avoiding eye contact?

She got out of the car quickly, the usual click of the seatbelt release sounding unnervingly loud in the stillness. Her gaze immediately swept across the faces of a couple walking purposefully towards the exit, their footsteps echoing. Their expressions seemed neutral, perhaps a little preoccupied with their own thoughts, but Sarah couldn't shake the feeling that there was something else there, a flicker of anxiety in their eyes that subtly mirrored her own. It was a fleeting, almost imperceptible hesitation in their hurried movements, a subtle tightening around their mouths. Or was it just her imagination, her own pervasive fear projecting onto innocent strangers, warping her perception of their everyday concerns into something more sinister? The paranoia coiled tighter in her stomach, making every shadow seem deeper, every distant sound a potential threat.

With a shaky breath, she locked her car. The click of the key fob, a tiny, sharp sound in the vast quiet of the garage. She then hurried towards the stairwell, the hollow echo of her footsteps amplifying her growing tension. Each passing person, even those she barely glimpsed, became a source of intense scrutiny. Her eyes darted, searching for subtle cues. Did that woman's tightly pressed lips betray a hidden tension, a secret fear she shared? Was the quickening pace of that man's stride a sign of shared urgency, a desperate attempt to escape an unseen threat? Or was she merely spiraling, her own escalating fear twisting ordinary observations into ominous, exaggerated signs? The unsettling question lingered, a persistent, chilling hum in the back of her mind, as she reached the hospital entrance. The automatic doors slid open with a hushed *swoosh*, revealing an interior that felt both familiar and strangely alien, bathed in an unnerving, and sterile silence.

Despite the handful of people she had seen outside in the parking garage, the hospital was unusually quiet. The normal hum of activity – the chatter of visitors, the distant murmur of announcements, the rhythmic beep of medical equipment – was replaced by an eerie, almost suffocating silence. A gnawing sense of wrongness prickled at her skin. Nurses and doctors seemed to be moving at a frantic, hurried pace, their faces etched not with routine exhaustion, but with overt worry and a sense of urgency. Their hushed conversations, normally comforting, now sounded clipped and tense. A cold dread, heavier than any she'd felt in the parking garage, crept into her heart. The unsettling feeling intensified with every quiet step she took, solidifying into a stark, undeniable realization that it wasn't just her imagination. It wasn't paranoia. Something is truly happening here, and it feels deeply, and dangerously wrong. Every instinct screamed at her to turn back, to run, but the image of her mother's frail form, alone and vulnerable, propelled her forward into the deepening silence.

She navigated the sterile, now eerily quiet hospital corridors, each footfall echoing the frantic rhythm in her chest. The fluorescent lights hummed with a detached indifference, casting a harsh, unforgiving glow on the polished linoleum. The numbers on the room doors blurred as she scanned them, her vision tunneling, her breath catching in ragged gasps until she finally found the familiar digits. Her mother's room. It seemed to loom larger than the others, as though it were a silent guardian of an unknown truth.

With a trembling hand, she reached for the cool metal of the door handle. A wave of enormous apprehension washed over her, a chilling premonition that mirrored the icy dread she'd felt in the parking garage, now intensified by the hospital's oppressive stillness. Part of her, the logical part she was desperately clinging to, tried to reason with the fear. Elias wouldn't be here, in her mother's hospital room, a place of order and light, a place where people were supposed to be safe. It defied all reason. But another, more primal instinct screamed an intuitive warning, painting a vivid, terrifying picture of his menacing figure lurking in the shadows just beyond the threshold, waiting. Every muscle in her body tensed, bracing for whatever horror lay beyond that door.

Pushing it open slowly, her senses on high alert, she took a hesitant step into the room. It was cloaked in a dim, unsettling darkness, a stark contrast to the sterile brightness of the hallway. The only illumination emanated from the rhythmic green pulses and digital readouts of the medical monitor beside her mother's bed, casting a sickly glow that danced across the room. The familiar scent of antiseptic hung heavy in the air, now tinged with a sense of wrongness, a cloying sweetness beneath the sterile cleanliness that made her stomach churn.

Her eyes, already straining in the gloom, were drawn instantly to the still form in the bed. Her mother lay motionless, her face pale and drawn, almost translucent against the white pillow. The vibrant life Sarah knew so well, the warmth, the laughter, the stubborn strength, was now muted and fragile, clinging precariously to a thread. The rise and fall of her chest was shallow, barely perceptible, each breath a whisper against the overwhelming silence. A choked sob escaped her lips, a sound of raw anguish torn from deep within her, and a wave of despair, heavy and suffocating, crashed over her, threatening to pull her under. Tears welled in her eyes, blurring her vision as they spilled down her cheeks, hot trails on her suddenly cold skin. In that moment, the adrenaline that had fueled her journey drained out of her, leaving her hollow and helpless, the weight of the world pressing down with an unbearable force. All the training and frantic preparations back at the cabin seemed utterly meaningless in the face of this personal helplessness.

Just as the despair threatened to consume her entirely, a soft click broke the pervasive silence of the room. The door eased open further, and a nurse entered, her presence a gentle intrusion into Sarah's private grief. The soft padding of her rubber-soled shoes hitting the floor barely disturbed the stillness. It was Nurse Jenkins, a kind-faced woman Sarah recognized immediately, who had taken such loving care of her mother during Sarah's previous visit.

"Hello, Mrs. Monroe," Nurse Jenkins said, her voice a low, comforting murmur that somehow managed to cut through the oppressive atmosphere without shattering it. Her eyes, sweet and understanding, held a gentle inquiry, but also a subtle flicker of something else. Perhaps a hidden concern that wasn't solely for Sarah. "We haven't seen you in a few days. How are you holding up?"

Sarah struggled to find her voice, her throat tight with unshed tears. "Not so well," she finally managed, her voice thick with emotion as she wiped at the wetness on her face with the back of her hand, the coldness of her skin still lingering. She looked down at her mother, her gaze filled with a desperate plea that spoke volumes more than words ever could. "How's she doing? Has there been any change since I was here last?"

Nurse Jenkins approached the bed, her movements practiced and gentle, checking the monitor. She paused for a moment, then turned back to Sarah, a small, troubled frown creasing her brow. "She's stable, holding on as best she can," the nurse replied, her voice soft but with an undertone of strain. Her gaze, though still kind, seemed to drift towards the window for a fleeting moment, as if she were listening for something beyond the room. "It's been... an unusual day here at the hospital, and around town, for that matter." She then confided, her voice dropping a little, "We've just had news come in about some issues with the electric grid. It hasn't gone out completely, not yet, but there's definitely something wrong with it. They've been reporting it on the news all afternoon, saying there's widespread disruption, flickers, power surges. We're on generator power for some of the non-essential systems just in case. It's got everyone on edge." A fresh ripple of foreboding traced its way down Sarah's spine. The world outside was indeed spiraling, and the whole town was now caught in its unsettling grip.

"Do you think... do you think it's a terrorist attack?" Sarah asked, the question a desperate, almost automatic reflex. Even as the words left her lips, a cold, undeniable certainty settled in her gut. She knew the answer. This wasn't human. This was something far darker, far more insidious than any earthly threat. The darkness was spreading, and she could feel its chill seeping into the very space all around her.

Nurse Jenkins leaned in closer so as to be heard, her expression softening with genuine sympathy as she met Sarah's terrified gaze. "I'll be honest with you," she replied, pausing, her gaze flickering nervously around the dimly lit room, as if hesitant to speak further, to give voice to the unspoken fears that haunted them all. Then her voice dropped to a conspiratorial whisper, barely audible above the rhythmic pulse of the monitor. "That's what some people are saying, but I don't think so. Strange things have been happening around here lately. Beyond the power grid issues. Equipment malfunctioning for no reason, patients acting... different. Agitated, confused... almost like they're seeing things we can't. But the thing is, even some of the staff have reported sightings as well. Like shadows moving around when they shouldn't be, things like that. It's like there's an unseen force at work in this place, an evil presence that's just... settling in." The confession hung in the air, a chilling confirmation of Sarah's deepest fears.

A cold dread seized Sarah as she heard about all the strange occurrences. Her mind raced, feverishly connecting the unsettling atmosphere in the parking garage, the subtle unease she'd sensed in others, and the nurse's hushed confession about malfunctioning equipment and agitated patients. It all clicked into place, forming a terrifying mosaic that pointed to one horrifying truth. Morpheus's plan to invade Earth, which Silas had warned them about, wasn't a distant threat. It was already underway, and spreading like a plague. Nor was the darkness simply tethered to her or her family. It was infecting the very fabric of this place, turning the familiar into the frightening. This wasn't just personal danger. It was pervasive, and insidious. The thought sent a fresh wave of icy fear through her veins.

"Nurse Jenkins," Sarah said, her voice barely a whisper, filled with an urgency that transcended her grief. She reached out, clasping the nurse's arm. "Please, be careful. Truly. I just have a feeling that things are...they're much worse than anyone realizes. Watch your back, watch your patients. Trust your instincts."

Nurse Jenkins looked at Sarah, her eyes wide with a mixture of confusion and a shared, unspoken fear. "Of course, Sarah," she replied, her voice soft but firm, a strained smile touching her lips. "Always. You take care of yourself too." With a final, worried glance at Sarah's mother, she turned and slipped out of the room, leaving Sarah alone again with the chilling reality that the world outside was unraveling faster than she could have ever imagined.

As she sat vigil by her mother's bedside, the sterile quiet of the room was suddenly broken by an unexplainable chill. A cold draft, like an icy finger, traced its way across her skin, raising goosebumps on her arms and making the fine hairs stand on end. She glanced around the small space, her eyes desperately searching for an open window, a vent, any logical source for the sudden drop in temperature. But the window was sealed shut, its heavy drapes unmoving, and the air vents remained still. A shiver ran down her spine, a primal warning that resonated with the unease she'd felt since the moment she arrived at the hospital. This was no ordinary draft or drop in temperature.

The unsettling feeling of being watched intensified, a prickling sensation at the back of her neck as if unseen eyes were boring into her, scrutinizing her every breath. The air grew heavy, thick with an unseen presence. Slowly, reluctantly, she turned her gaze towards the window, the dim, harsh light from the hallway reflecting on the glass, momentarily obscuring the view outside. What she saw beyond the pane, however, sent a jolt of pure terror through her veins, freezing her blood in its tracks and stealing the air from her lungs.

The familiar overcast sky had vanished entirely. In its place, a swirling vortex of unnatural crimson pulsed ominously, like a gaping, festering wound in the heavens. A sinister, malevolent glow emanated from above, bathing the entire town in an eerie, blood-red light that twisted familiar shapes into grotesque, dancing shadows. The trees outside appeared like skeletal hands clawing at the stained sky, and distant buildings looked like ruined husks. Then, a low, guttural, menacing growl, ripped through the unnerving silence, echoing in the distance and vibrating through the very walls of the hospital. It was a sound that spoke of something ancient and evil, something that had absolutely no place in the natural world, and it chilled her to the very core of her being, confirming her deepest, most terrifying fears. The invasion had truly begun.

In that instant, all thoughts of the strange happenings within the hospital, the nurse's cryptic words, the power grid issues, faded into insignificance. The monstrous crimson sky outside eclipsed every other concern. She knew, with a certainty that transcended logic, that she had to get back to the cabin. To her husband, to her children. They were in danger, a danger she could now vividly see, and she needed to be there to protect them, or at least face whatever unspeakable horror was unfolding together. Something truly terrible was happening, something far beyond her comprehension, and she had a terrifying, gut-wrenching feeling that it was intrinsically connected to her, and to her family. A dark thread pulled from the house's past.

A fierce protectiveness surged through her terror, overriding the paralysis that had momentarily gripped her. With a desperate urgency, she leaned down and pressed a soft, lingering kiss to her mother's pale cheek, a silent promise to return, a fleeting moment of tenderness amidst the encroaching nightmare. Then, with a sudden, decisive movement, she turned and fled.

Rushing out of the hospital room and into the dimly lit corridor, her mind raced with terrifying possibilities, each one more horrifying than the last. The quiet order of the hospital had completely shattered. The corridors that moments ago had seemed eerily subdued were now alive with a frantic, desperate energy. People were everywhere, no longer just moving quickly but openly panicking. Nurses and doctors, their faces stark with fear, were herding patients, trying to maintain some semblance of control, but their voices were strained, their movements jerky. Some visitors openly wept, clutching their loved ones, while others simply stood frozen, staring blankly ahead, their faces reflecting the blood-red glow that seeped through every window.

Sarah dodged a gurney being pushed too fast, and swerved around a cluster of sobbing individuals, her eyes darting all around. She saw people frantically trying to push open emergency exits that seemed stuck, others huddled in corners, attempting to hide from the unseen horror, their whispers sharp with terror. The pretense of normalcy was gone. The hospital was no longer a place of healing but a scene of impending chaos. The world outside was indeed changing, twisting into something nightmarish, and she was no longer just an observer. She was at the heart of it, running headlong into the crimson-stained night, a desperate race against an apocalypse that had just begun.

Bursting through the automatic doors of the hospital, the cool night air hit her face like a physical blow. It carried a metallic tang Sarah couldn't quite place, like ozone mixed with something coppery and vile. The unnatural red glow in the sky had intensified, no longer just a distant vortex but a vast, pulsating ceiling of unholy light that painted the familiar buildings in stark, terrifying shades of blood and shadow. Every tree, every lamppost, every parked car was transformed into a grotesque silhouette against the lurid backdrop. A sense of impending doom, a cold, heavy weight, settled on her heart, crushing her with its immensity. The distant, guttural growls now seemed closer, more numerous, a horrifying symphony building around her. Her family needed her. There was no time for fear, only for action, for a desperate need to bridge the distance between them. She had to get back to them, before this terrifying, crimson-soaked night swallowed everything she held dear, before it was truly, and irrevocably too late.

Speeding away from the hospital, the terrifying scene outside her window unfolded with dizzying speed. Sirens, initially a distant wail, now erupted into a deafening chorus, converging from every direction. The piercing shrieks of police cars, the roar of fire engines, and the desperate bleats of ambulances sliced through the air, each adding another layer to the cacophony of impending doom. It wasn't the orderly, reassuring sound of emergency services responding to a singular incident. No, this was the chaotic clamor of an entire city in freefall, a soundtrack to the end of the world.

The familiar landscape outside her car windows began to warp into something alien and terrifying. It wasn't just the unnatural crimson light that painted everything in shades of blood and fear. The very fabric of reality seemed to be fraying at the edges. Trees, usually green and vibrant, now appeared as skeletal silhouettes against the lurid sky, their branches clawing at the unnatural glow. Houses, once symbols of comfort and normalcy, stood as hollowed-out husks, their windows reflecting the unholy light like vacant, burning eyes. The few people she encountered were either gripped by a frantic, uncoordinated panic, sprinting down sidewalks and across lawns with wide, terror-stricken eyes, their screams swallowed by the sirens. Or they stood frozen in place, faces upturned towards the ominous, swirling vortex above, their expressions a chilling mixture of disbelief and utter dread, as if witnessing the impossible become horrifyingly real. Each frantic siren blare, each desperate figure, confirmed Sarah's deepest fears: the invasion was here, and it was preparing to consume everything.

The low, guttural growl she had heard near the hospital was growing louder, closer, a monstrous sound that vibrated through the chassis of her car, sending shivers of fear down her spine. Panic, sharp and icy as a shard of glass, surged through her, threatening to overwhelm her resolve. She fought it back, focusing on the road ahead, her foot pressing down harder on the accelerator, the engine roaring in response. Her mind raced, a chaotic jumble of fear and determination, a desperate, silent prayer for her family's safety echoing in the frantic rhythm of her heart.

Reaching the outskirts of town, the familiar streets were now eerily deserted. The red glow in the sky had intensified, blooming into a terrifying spectacle that illuminated the landscape with the stark, unforgiving light of a raging inferno. The darkness at the edges of her vision seemed to dance with movement. Strange, distorted shapes flickered in her peripheral vision, their outlines indistinct and shifting, yet undeniably menacing. They seemed to writhe and coalesce just beyond the reach of the unnatural light, hinting at horrors yet unseen. She gripped the steering wheel tighter, her knuckles bone-white against the worn leather, her gaze fixed on the empty road ahead, a single thought pounding in her brain. *I have to get to my family.*

A particularly grotesque shape lumbered out of the inky blackness that had clung to the edges of the red light, its sheer size eclipsing the already distorted landscape. It planted itself squarely in the middle of the road, an insurmountable obstacle blocking her desperate flight. It was a monstrous creature, a grotesque amalgamation of twisted limbs and sharp angles, its form defying any natural order under the sinister glow. Fear, cold and sharp piercing her heart, seized her, paralyzing her for a fraction of a terrifying second. Her foot instinctively slammed down on the brake pedal, the tires screaming in protest as the car skidded violently, throwing her forward against the seatbelt before shuddering to a jarring halt mere feet from the unholy entity.

She froze, her breath caught in her throat, as the creature unleashed a blood-curdling roar that seemed to tear through the very air. It was a sound of pure agony and rage, like grinding metal and tearing flesh amplified to an unbearable volume. Without warning, it lunged, its massive, distorted form eclipsing her headlights, plunging the immediate area into shadow even amidst the red-tinged night. A sickening thud reverberated through the car as it collided with the front fender, the metal groaning under the impact. The windshield erupted in a spiderweb of cracks, obscuring her already limited vision. Adrenaline surged through her veins, a potent cocktail of paralyzing fear and desperate survival instinct.

Her mind screamed for help. She fumbled frantically for her phone in the center console, her hands shaking so violently she could barely grasp the smooth metal. Finally, her fingers closed around it, but the screen remained stubbornly blank. No signal. She was utterly alone. The creature was getting closer, its rabid, guttural growls filling the night air, punctuated by wet, tearing sounds that sent bile rising up in her throat. Desperation, a raw and potent fuel, overrode her terror. Her gaze fell on the red cylinder in the back seat. The fire extinguisher. With a surge of adrenaline-fueled strength, she twisted in her seat, grabbed the heavy canister, and swung it around, aiming the nozzle blindly at the monstrous shape looming outside her shattered windshield.

Taking a shaky breath, a sliver of courage igniting within the overwhelming fear, she squeezed the handle. A deafening hiss filled the car as a blinding cloud of white foam erupted from the nozzle, engulfing the creature in a disorienting spray. The monstrous roar turned into a pained bellow as the creature recoiled, its movements visibly slowed and hampered by the slippery substance. Seizing the precious opportunity, Sarah slammed the gearshift into reverse, her foot pressing down on the accelerator just enough to gain some distance. The tires spun briefly on the foam-slicked road, the car lurching backward a short way. Without taking her eyes off the creature, she shifted into drive, maneuvering the car in a wide arc around its still-struggling form, her heart racing. The creature's enraged roars grew fainter as she put distance between them, speeding onward towards her family.

But the icy grip of fear that had seized her would not release its hold. She had come face-to-face with the darkness, and its monstrous features were now seared into her memory. It had touched her, threatened her, and she knew, with a chilling certainty, that it had marked her, marked her family. As she sped towards the cabin, her mind raced with terrifying questions. What awaited her at the cabin? Were her husband and her daughters safe from this nightmare? And what about Silas, the only one who had offered to help them? Did he have the knowledge to fight this? The questions were endless, each one bringing with it a fresh wave of anxiety. But one terrifying truth remained. The battle for their survival had just escalated to a horrifying new level.

Chapter 16:

Sarah arrived back at the cabin, her face pale and streaked with dried tears, her breathing labored from a combination of fear and the desperate rush back to her family. The events of the past few hours had left her shaken to the core, each horrifying image replaying in her mind. Her voice, when she finally found it, was trembling as she recounted her terrifying encounter with the monstrous creature she'd glimpsed, the unnaturally crimson sky, and the chaos erupting in town. The family listened in horror, huddled close, their hearts pounding in their chests, the grim reality of her words painting a vivid picture of the world unraveling outside their walls. They too had noticed the strange red sky, but thankfully, had not encountered any creatures.

"Well, did you hear anything on the radio while you were gone? Are they reporting anything on the news?" Daniel asked, his voice tight with a mixture of concern and an urgent need for information.

"No, I didn't stop long enough to watch the news, Daniel," Sarah said, frustration lacing her tone, though it was directed more at the situation than at him. She ran a hand through her disheveled hair, taking a shaky breath before continuing. "And I'm not even sure if I had the radio on. I was so focused on getting back here, to my family, to make sure you were all safe." She paused, then added, a flicker of memory returning, "Though, the nurse at the hospital did tell me about some issues with the electric grid. She said it hasn't gone out completely, but there's widespread disruption, flickers, and power surges. They were apparently reporting it on the news all afternoon, and the hospital was even running some non-essential systems on generator power. It's not just us, Daniel. It's everywhere." The last words hung heavy in the air, confirming their worst fears.

Daniel reached for his cell phone, pulling it from his pocket, his thumb already hovering over the power button. Just as he pulled it out, the screen flickered to life, displaying not his usual apps, but a stark, unwelcome low battery warning. A frustrated sigh escaped his lips. "Great," he muttered, running a hand through his hair, "That figures. Just when we really need to know what's going on in the rest of the world." He shoved the phone back into his pocket, the dead weight of it now a symbol of their escalating isolation.

"It'll be okay, Daniel," Sarah said, her voice surprisingly steady, even as her own heart was pounding. She pulled her phone from her own pocket, the familiar device feeling like a lifeline. "I have mine, and one extra battery pack." Her fingers quickly began inputting her passcode, intent on retrieving the latest news, on finding out just how widespread this terrifying invasion truly was.

Daniel, however, reached out, his hand closing gently but firmly over hers, stopping her mid-swipe. "No. Don't use it for that," he insisted, his gaze intense. "We don't know how long this will last, or when we'll get power back. You'll need that to stay in touch with your mom, to check on her when you can. That's more important than the news right now." His words, while difficult, hit home. "Besides, we already have a pretty good idea of what's happening out there."

Sarah paused, her thumb hovering over the screen, the weight of his logic settling over her. He was right. That phone, that precious remaining battery, was her only potential link to her mother, her only way to fulfill the promise she'd made just hours ago. With a reluctant sigh, she put the phone away, the glow of the screen fading as quickly as her brief hope for outside information. The silence that followed was even heavier than before, punctuated only by the frantic beat of her own heart.

The realization that the darkness was no longer confined to the ominous woods surrounding them, or even to their family as a targeted affliction, but had insidiously spread into the very heart of the town, sent a fresh, chilling wave of panic through them. They were surrounded, trapped in a nightmare from which there seemed to be no discernible escape. And to make matters worse, with Daniel's phone dead and Sarah's saved for emergencies, they had no way to communicate with the outside world or find out what was truly happening beyond the walls of their little shack. The isolation which was once meant to be their refuge, now felt like a suffocating blanket.

Silas, his face grim and etched with newfound lines of worry, hurried to a cabinet tucked in the corner of the room. He rummaged inside, his fingers brushing past forgotten odds and ends before seizing a small, outdated handheld radio. It was clearly a relic from a bygone era, the kind used for emergency broadcasts, its worn casing speaking of a time before the sleek screens of modern communication. "I keep this on hand for dire situations," he murmured, his fingers deftly adjusting the dial. "I never thought I would actually need it. It runs on regular batteries. Perhaps we can find something." He fiddled with the tuner, and static filled the cabin for a tense moment before a voice, distorted and frantic, momentarily broke through. It was a local news report, riddled with interference, speaking of "unprecedented power fluctuations," "mass hysteria," and then, chillingly, "unconfirmed reports of... aggressors." The word hung in the air, followed by a guttural scream that was abruptly cut off by a burst of static. Silas quickly clicked the radio off, the sudden silence even more deafening than the terrified broadcast.

His face now even more grim, he began hurriedly flipping through one of his worn out leather-bound journals. His eyes scanned the archaic script he had written down at the farmhouse, as well as his notes and translation, confirming their worst fears. "It's as I suspected," he finally murmured, his voice low and heavy. "The creatures are multiplying. Their influence is spreading far beyond the localized confines of the house. This isn't just an attack; it's an invasion." The world they knew was changing, twisting into something monstrous and unrecognizable, and they, huddled together in their fragile haven, were at the epicenter of this cataclysmic, terrifying shift. It was true...the apocalypse had begun.

Despair had settled like a heavy fog in the cabin, chilling them far more deeply than the rising apprehension of the encroaching night. Daniel paced like a caged animal, his restless energy a stark contrast to the oppressive stillness that had fallen over them. His eyes darted incessantly between the barricaded windows, searching with a desperate futility for any sign of normalcy in the chaotic, blood-red world outside, a world that seemed to be tearing itself apart. Each silent revolution around the small room only seemed to amplify the crushing weight of their helplessness.

Sarah huddled on the sofa, her arms wrapped tightly around Rose, who was valiantly fighting back tears, her small body trembling against her mother's. Sarah whispered reassurances she barely believed herself, her gaze constantly flickering towards the door, then to the windows, a silent prayer forming on her lips for her own absent mother. Lily sat motionless beside them, her vacant gaze fixed on a distant point only she could see, her small hand clutching a throw pillow. Her mind, usually so bright and lively, was now a tumultuous sea, battered by relentless waves of darkness, despair, and an instinctual, terrifying fight for survival.

Silas, normally the embodiment of unwavering resolve, the eternal optimist who always had a solution or a comforting word, was now a mere shadow of himself. He was buried deep within his books and journals, their pages filled with forgotten lore and terrifying prophecies. His brow was furrowed in a permanent frown, his fingers tracing lines of script that spoke of unimaginable horrors. "I have to find something," he muttered, his voice barely audible, swallowed by the cabin's heavy silence. His hope was visibly dwindling with each passing hour, leaving them all teetering on the edge of utter desolation.

As the evening dwindled on, the crimson glow outside deepened to a murky purple as true night descended. Inside the cabin, the flickering oil lamp cast long, dancing shadows that seemed to magnify their silent dread. Sarah, clinging to the last vestiges of normalcy, moved to the small kitchen area. She fixed what she could with their meager supplies for their dinner. A simple meal of vegetable soup and crackers, warmed over their small propane burner. She set out bowls for everyone, but the oppressive atmosphere had stolen their appetites. Daniel merely pushed his food around with a spoon, his gaze distant. Rose took only a few tiny bites, while Lily, utterly withdrawn, didn't touch hers at all. Even Silas, usually one for hearty meals, picked at his portion mechanically, his mind clearly miles away, still wrestling with the notes scattered around him. The untouched food was a vivid reminder of how thoroughly their world had been upended, and how deeply the fear had settled in within them all.

As Sarah gathered the untouched dishes, the clatter of bowls hitting one another was a jarring sound in the oppressive silence as everyone else instinctively left the table. Just as she placed them in the sink to begin washing, a strange, almost suffocating energy began to emanate from the cabin itself. It seeped through the walls, making the very hairs on their arms stand on end. The air grew thick with a tension, heavy and charged, and the old wooden floorboards beneath their feet began to tremble with a low, rhythmic vibration. It was a tremor that resonated not from the earth, but from something massive and powerful approaching.

Then, from the inky blackness of the surrounding woods, a low, guttural growl echoed, vibrating through the cabin's very foundations. It wasn't the distant sound of a wild animal. It was deeper, more resonant, and filled with malevolence. And it wasn't fading. Instead, it grew louder with each passing second, morphing into a chorus of hungry, rasping roars that seemed to encircle them, closing in from all sides.

Eyes wide with dawning horror, they all stared at each other. Fear, cold and absolute, gripped them as the terrifying realization slammed home that they were being hunted. The creatures, those unspeakable horrors from the encroaching darkness, were closing in, their presence no longer just an unseen threat but a strong, terrifying force pressing against the cabin's fragile defenses. There was no time to waste, no time for debate or despair. With a unified, desperate surge of adrenaline, they grabbed whatever they could use to defend themselves. A heavy poker from the fireplace, a sturdy wrench, anything that could offer even a sliver of resistance against the nightmare just beyond their walls.

The first creature hit the cabin like a battering ram, a sickening thud that vibrated through the floorboards and sent a shower of dust motes dancing in the dim light. It was enormous, a hulking mass of twisted limbs, and its grotesque head crowned with a jagged rack of antlers. Its eyes, glowing with malevolent red light, fixed on the cabin, and a guttural roar tore through the night, a sound that promised nothing but agonizing death.

Then another slammed into the opposite wall, and another, and soon the cabin was surrounded. Horrific screeches and snarls tore through the night as the creatures clawed at the walls, their immense weight groaning against the timbers. Splinters flew inward as jagged claws desperately ripped through the wood.

"The windows!" Sarah shrieked, pointing to the largest pane, which was already spiderwebbed with cracks. A monstrous face, all snarling teeth and dripping maw, pressed against the glass, distorting it into a nightmare caricature.

Daniel, axe raised, lunged for the window. The creature let out a high-pitched whine, recoiling slightly from the glinting steel. It wasn't much, but it was a flicker of hope. He swung, the axe biting into the thick frame, sending a jolt up his arms. "They don't like the light!" he yelled, the realization sparking in his eyes.

Across the room, Rose, clutching a heavy flashlight, aimed its beam at a shadow writhing just outside the other window. The shadow recoiled, hissing, and a wave of relief, however fleeting, washed over the family. The light, even this weak, artificial glow, seemed to offer some small reprieve.

Lilly, her small face contorted with fierce concentration, extended her hands towards the wall where a particularly large creature was tearing at the wood. A shimmering, invisible force pulsed from her fingertips, and with a guttural roar of pain, the creature was thrown backward, its massive body crashing into the trees.

Silas grabbed a broom handle, thrusting it into the roaring fire of the fireplace. The dry wood caught quickly, bursting into a makeshift torch. He yanked it out, flames dancing wildly, and thrust it towards the shattered window. The creatures outside the immediate area shrieked, backing away from the sudden glare. It was chaos, a desperate, frantic dance between survival and certain doom. The air was thick with the scent of fear, dust, and something else. It was a foul, sulfuric odor that seemed to emanate from the creatures themselves.

The cabin groaned under the relentless assault, each impact shaking them to their core. A section of the roof threatening to buckle inward. "Keep the lights on them!" Sarah screamed, her voice hoarse with terror but clear with newfound resolve. "Any light!" The fight for their lives had just begun, and the only weapon they had, aside from their desperate will to survive, was something they'd always taken for granted: light.

The battle raged. Each minute stretched into an eternity, the cabin groaning and shuddering under the relentless assault. It felt like hours, a never-ending nightmare of roars and crashes. Daniel swung the axe with grim determination, dropping creatures that dared to breach the weakening walls. Sarah, her face streaked with dirt and tears, helped Rose keep the flashlight beams fixed on any grotesque face that appeared in a shattered window, the harsh light sending the creatures recoiling with guttural shrieks.

Silas, his improvised broom-torch held aloft, became a whirling vortex of fire and fury. Each swing of the flaming wood was a defiant act against the encroaching terror. The flickering light from his torch cast grotesque shadows, making the creatures outside writhe and hiss. The flames, though pitifully small against the vast, oppressive darkness that swirled beyond the cabin, were surprisingly effective. They drove back the monstrous forms that tried to claw their way through the door. Silas grunted with the effort, the acrid smell of burnt wood and something far more foul filling his nostrils, but he couldn't stop.

But it was Lily who had truly turned the tide. Her small body trembled visibly with the immense effort, a testament to the power she was channeling. Yet, despite her physical strain, her eyes blazed with an intensity that belied her young age, reflecting a fierce, unyielding resolve. With every surge of her unseen power, a wave of force erupted from her, and another hulking beast was flung backward. They crashed through the trees with sickening thuds, leaving trails of broken branches and startled squawks in their wake. She was a pure force of resistance, pushing back against the overwhelming darkness that threatened to consume them all. Her powers, though still new and untamed, created invaluable pockets of momentary reprieve, allowing the family precious seconds to brace themselves for the next terrifying wave of attacks. It was in these fleeting moments of calm that they could take a ragged breath, readjust their makeshift defenses, and prepare for the endless onslaught.

As the first, faint hint of grey bled into the eastern sky, a new desperation pulsed through the cabin. The family was bone-weary, their muscles aching, their throats raw from shouting. Every swing of Daniel's axe was slower, every flash of Sarah and Rose's lights were less steady. Silas's torch had burned down to a charred stick, its flame now a mere ember. They had fought through endless hours, powered by pure terror and a primal need to survive, but exhaustion threatened to smother their last reserves of strength.

Yet, with the coming dawn, something shifted. The creatures, though still a formidable force, seemed to falter. Their roars, once so full of menace, now carried a strange, desperate edge. The red glow in their eyes dimmed slightly, and their attacks became less coordinated, more frantic. They shrieked with an almost pained urgency as the sky lightened, their massive bodies recoiling further from the growing light.

"They're weakening!" Sarah gasped, her voice hoarse but laced with a new surge of hope. "The sun... it's hurting them!"

Lilly, her small frame trembling, pushed out one last, colossal wave of power. It wasn't directed at a single creature, but unleashed as a broad, invisible shockwave. A chorus of agonized screeches erupted from the surrounding woods as the remaining creatures were violently propelled backward, smashing into trees with splintering force. Several didn't get up, their grotesque forms lying still amidst the foliage before dissolving into the earth.

Daniel, seeing their weakened state, mustered a final burst of adrenaline. He smashed through a splintered section of wall, stepping out into the pre-dawn gloom. He swung the axe in wide, sweeping arcs, not just at individual beasts, but at the very shadows clinging to the cabin. Rose, tears streaming down her face, directed the last flicker of her flashlight directly into the eyes of a creature lunging for him. It howled, disoriented, giving him the opening he needed to strike a decisive blow.

Silas, with a powerful yell, threw his smoldering torch at a group trying to flank them. The residual heat, combined with the rising light, sent them scattering. The ground was littered with broken branches and the eerie, still forms of the fallen beasts before they too evaporated into thin air.

Then, as the first golden rays of the sun pierced through the dense canopy, a final, deafening shriek tore through the air. The remaining creatures, those still capable of movement, turned and fled, melting back into the deepest, darkest parts of the forest, their forms dissolving like mist as the light strengthened. The sounds of their retreat faded, leaving behind an unsettling silence.

The family stood amidst the wreckage of their haven, panting, bleeding, but alive. The cabin was in shambles, but the nightmare was over. For now.

Catching her breath, Rose clinging to her, Sarah voiced the question that had been gnawing at them all. Her gaze swept from the devastated cabin to the lightening sky. "But why did the light scare them? It didn't bother the ones we fought at the house?"

Lily, her face etched with the same dawning realization, chimed in, "Yeah, it was still daylight when they attacked us." The memory of that first terrifying encounter, vivid and raw, hung heavy in the air. The contrast between the creatures and their behavior then and now was stark, a puzzle piece that didn't quite fit.

Daniel just shook his head, his face a mask of weary confusion, offering no immediate answers. All eyes, therefore, turned to Silas. If anyone could provide a semblance of an explanation, it was him. His mind, usually a labyrinth of complex theories and arcane knowledge, was visibly whirring.

Silas let out a slow, deliberate sigh, the sound a mix of exhaustion and intense concentration. "I can only speculate," he began, his voice raspy from the night's battle, "that these creatures, unlike the others you encountered before, are different. They are... a more advanced form, perhaps. The ones who attacked the house were merely pawns, driven by a primal urge. Sarah, you mentioned issues with the electric grid, and perhaps this is why. They were trying to remove it before they fully invaded our world. These creatures, however, are stronger, scarier than the ones you encountered before, yes." He paused, his gaze sweeping over the family, finding a flicker of hope in their exhausted faces. "But since we now know they have a weakness, this aversion to light, then maybe, just maybe, we have a chance to defeat them for good." His words hung in the air, a fragile promise in the wreckage of their ordeal.

Chapter 17:

They had survived the night, a feat they had doubted would be possible with every bone-jarring impact and terrifying shriek. Their bodies ached with an overwhelming, bone-deep weariness, their minds were weary and haunted by the grotesque images of the creatures, but their spirits, against all odds, remained unbroken as they clung to each other, drawing strength from their shared ordeal.

Lily and Rose, in particular, collapsed on the sofa, their eyes heavy-lidded and distant. The adrenaline that had fueled them through the brutal hours had finally dissipated, leaving them teetering on the verge of unconsciousness. Rose still clutched the flashlight, her knuckles white, even though its beam was long dead. Lily's hands, which had channeled such incredible power, now trembled uncontrollably, her face pale and clammy.

Daniel, equally exhausted, fought fiercely against the urge to succumb to sleep. His own body screamed for rest, every muscle screaming in protest, but his gaze remained fixed on his family. He sat rigid on the edge of a splintered chair, his jaw tight, determined to stand guard. How could he rest when they were so vulnerable, when the nightmare wasn't truly over? His exhaustion was immense, yet his determination to protect them was even stronger.

They assessed their injuries, a grim inventory of the night's battle. Bruises mottled their skin, a testament to the brutal impacts they'd endured, and there were several deep cuts that would clearly require immediate attention. Yet, miraculously, none of the wounds were life-threatening. They had been incredibly lucky, a thought that brought a fresh wave of quiet gratitude.

Silas and Sarah moved among them, their hands gentle and practiced as they examined everyone's wounds. Silas, ever the scholar, applied various herbal remedies he had brought with him, their medicinal properties known to him from his extensive studies. As he worked, he spoke softly, his voice a low, soothing balm to their frayed nerves.

The morning sun, a welcome sight after the endless darkness, cast long shadows through the trees, illuminating the forest floor in a gentle, reassuring light. The world, freshly washed by the dawn, seemed to have transformed. The sheer terror of the night, with its roars and impacts, was replaced by a fragile, almost unbelievable sense of peace. Birds, tentative at first, began to chirp, their songs a blessed contrast to the screeches that had dominated the overnight hours.

They huddled together amidst the splintered wood and scattered debris, the quiet heavy with their exhaustion. The immediate danger had passed, but the question of what came next loomed over them. Staying in the cabin was out of the question. It was a wreck, and its defenses had been shattered. The creatures, they all knew with chilling certainty, would undoubtedly return when darkness fell again, and after all the damage, they were too vulnerable to risk another confrontation. They needed a place to regroup, a place where they could assess their situation, plan their next steps, and perhaps, just perhaps, find some way to fight back more effectively.

"So," Sarah began, her voice hoarse, breaking the silence, "what do we do now? We can't stay here." She gestured around at the ruined interior, the shattered windows and buckling walls.

Daniel, running a weary hand over his face, nodded grimly. "No, we can't. The cars are useless too; they took a beating last night, just like the cabin." He looked to Silas, a silent plea for guidance in his eyes.

Silas, ever the one to weigh options, leaned against a damaged wall, his gaze thoughtful. "We need to move. Somewhere safe, somewhere defensible, and most importantly, somewhere with ample light, or the means to create it."

"But where?" Daniel pressed, a flicker of despair in his tone. "How far can we go on foot, with Lily and Rose exhausted, and all of us injured?"

Sarah, despite her own fatigue, straightened. "There's the old hunting lodge, The Ironwood. It's a few miles north, deeper into the woods, but it's built like a fortress. Stone foundation, thick walls... and it used to have a generator." Her eyes met Daniel's, a spark of determination kindling. "It's a risk, but it might be our best shot at finding some real protection and electricity."

Daniel's eyes widened slightly in recognition. "The Ironwood, I remember it! My dad used to take me fishing up that way. But it's been closed down for years, hasn't it? It's probably just an old hunting shack now."

"Even better," Sarah countered, a sliver of desperate hope in her voice. "Less chance of anyone being there, so we can come up with a plan. And if it has a generator, even a little bit of gas could get it going. We just need light, and a place to stand our ground."

Silas considered this, his gaze drifting towards the path leading north. "A generator could be invaluable. Light, communication... It's a journey, a dangerous one given our condition, but the alternative is to wait here for the next attack. I could find a gas jug in the shed out back, and siphon some fuel out of the cars." He looked at Daniel and Sarah, then to the pale, still-recovering faces of Lily and Rose. "We don't have much time to waste though. So, I say we rest for an hour, gather what supplies we can, and then we move." The decision, though daunting, brought a shared sense of purpose to them.

After a brief, restless hour of forced rest, during which true sleep remained an elusive luxury, the family began the grim task of gathering what little they could salvage. Every movement was an effort, each step a testament to their aching muscles and frayed nerves. Lily and Rose, though still pale and leaning heavily on their mother, helped as best they could, their small hands carefully sorting through scattered items.

Their immediate priorities were clear: food, light, and communication. They scrounged through the damaged kitchen, collecting canned goods, dried fruit, and a few granola bars into a worn backpack. Flashlights were retrieved, along with every spare battery they could find. Daniel also grabbed the radio Silas had used earlier, tucking it safely into his pack. Meanwhile, Silas, ever resourceful, disappeared around the back of the cabin. He returned a few minutes later, triumphantly holding a dusty but intact gas jug and a siphoning hose. With practiced efficiency, he managed to drain the last precious gallons of fuel from the battered vehicles, the scent of gasoline mingling with the lingering metallic odor of the creatures. This fuel, he knew, was their lifeline. It was the key to powering the generator and their best hope for survival. The trek to The Ironwood was a slow, arduous ordeal. What would normally have been a two hour hike stretched into nearly four, each step a struggle against their overwhelming exhaustion. The faint, barely visible trail twisted and turned through the dense woods, the morning sun dappling through the canopy doing little to alleviate the chill in their bones.

Rose and Lily were the most affected. Rose, her small hand clutching Sarah's, stumbled frequently, her eyelids drooping with every third step. Lily, despite her incredible display of power hours earlier, was now a dead weight, her face ghostly pale. Daniel, already operating on pure adrenaline, ended up carrying her for much of the way, his back protesting with every weary footfall. Even Silas and Sarah, though grimly determined, found their movements sluggish, their focus wavering. They moved in strained silence, the only sounds the rustle of leaves underfoot and their own ragged breathing.

Finally, just as the sun began to climb higher, filtering more strongly through the trees, the silhouette of the lodge emerged from the forest. It was exactly as Sarah had described: a sturdy, imposing structure of rough-hewn logs and stone, looking more like a small fortress than a hunting lodge. Its windows were dark, and a thick layer of moss coated the exterior, suggesting years of abandonment.

Relief, sharp and overwhelming, washed over them. They stumbled towards the heavy wooden door, the gas can thumping against Silas's leg. The journey had been agonizing, but they had made it. Now, if the generator still worked, they might finally have a chance to rest, to plan, and to understand the horrifying new world they found themselves in.

The heavy wooden door creaked open, revealing an interior that was both simple and surprisingly inviting. A thick layer of dust coated every surface, and the air hung still and cool, carrying the faint scent of aged wood and disuse. But despite its neglect, the lodge felt solid, a stark contrast to the splintered ruin they'd left behind. A large fireplace, its hearth still filled with unburnt logs, offered a silent promise of warmth and comfort that resonated deeply within their weary souls.

Exhausted and injured, they barely made it past the threshold before collapsing onto the worn wooden floor. Every muscle screamed in protest, every nerve ending hummed with the lingering echo of terror. The events of the past few weeks, culminating in the brutal, sleepless night, had taken an unimaginable toll on them, both physically and emotionally. Their bodies ached with fatigue, and their minds wrestled with the monstrous reality they now faced. Lily and Rose, no longer able to fight the pull of unconsciousness, slumped against each other, their breathing shallow.

After a moment, a groan of effort escaped Daniel's lips as he pushed himself up. Despite his own bone-deep weariness, his parental instincts took over. He began to clear the fireplace, meticulously arranging the dry logs, determined to conjure a comforting blaze. Sarah, meanwhile, rummaged through her pack, her movements slow and deliberate. She found a clean bandana and a precious bottle of water, both meager supplies for the task at hand. With painstaking care, she gently cleaned the grime and dried blood from the girls' faces and hands. She managed a soft, reassuring smile as she handed them each a granola bar, her heart aching as she could see how truly, utterly tired they were, and she desperately wished she could give them proper nourishment, a hot meal, anything more than this meager offering.

Silas, his face etched with a fatigue that seemed to go deeper than skin, pushed off the wall. He needed to find the generator. Before stepping back outside, he turned back to the group, his voice, though weary, filled with unwavering determination. "I know we're all tired," he stated, his gaze sweeping over their battered forms, "but we need to fortify this place. They will find us here." The unspoken threat hung heavy in the air, a chilling reminder that their new haven was only temporary.

Silas pushed open the creaking back door of the lodge and found the generator shed exactly where he'd hoped. Inside, nestled amongst cobweb-draped tools and rusted traps, sat a sturdy, albeit dusty, gasoline generator. He ran a practiced hand over its cold metal, checking the oil, fuel lines, and air filter. It looked old, but surprisingly intact. The engine itself appeared solid, unmarred by rust or rodent damage.

With a grunt of effort, he lifted the gas jug he'd painstakingly siphoned from the cars. He carefully poured the precious fuel into the generator's tank, the liquid glinting in the faint light filtering through the grimy window. He checked the spark plug, gave the pull cord a tentative tug, then a couple more stronger ones. The engine coughed, sputtered, and then with a satisfying growl, roared to life. A wave of clean, mechanical power filled the small shed, a sound that, for the first time in hours, wasn't a snarl or a crash.

A weary smile touched his lips. He let it run for a moment, listening to the healthy hum, before switching it back off. No need to waste their limited fuel during daylight hours. But the fact that it worked, that they had this potential source of light and energy, was a victory in itself. He secured the shed, the knowledge of the generator's readiness a comfort as he walked back inside.

The warmth from the newly built fire was a welcome embrace. Daniel had managed to get a decent blaze going, casting flickering light and shadows across the faces of the exhausted family. Sarah was now tending to his cuts, gently applying pressure and rebinding them with strips of clean cloth.

Seeing the girls finally truly asleep, slumped deeply into the worn cushions of the sofa, a peace settled over the exhausted group. With the immediate threat gone and a temporary sanctuary found, they too allowed themselves to sink into exhaustion. For the next few hours, the only sounds in The Ironwood were the crackle of the fire, the soft, even breaths of the sleeping family, and the occasional creak of the old lodge settling. It was a brief, dreamless respite, a chance to recharge before another meager dinner and the long, uncertain night ahead.

As darkness, thick and oppressive, once more enveloped the forest, the air grew noticeably colder, carrying a damp chill that seeped into the lodge. A strange, almost suffocating stillness descended, a quiet far more unnerving than that of the previous night. The chirping of crickets, and all the other familiar sounds of a summer night were conspicuously absent, replaced by an intense, watchful silence. It was the quiet before a storm, a held breath in the vast wilderness. The creatures, it seemed, were biding their time, no longer announcing their presence with guttural roars but waiting, patiently and malevolently, for the opportune moment to strike. The family could practically feel their unseen eyes, dozens of them, watching from the deeper shadows.

Silas moved with a grim determination, his mind a whirlwind of knowledge and desperate strategy. He began to fortify the cabin, his actions imbued with a sense of urgency. With practiced hands, he boarded up the windows, then proceeded to carve intricate symbols into the wood, a sigil of protection meant to ward off unseen threats. Though, just like before, these wards wouldn't hold them off for long.

Earlier, he had moved around the perimeter of the cabin, where he had drawn elaborate chalk circles, their complex patterns humming with an unseen energy. These were not mere markings but powerful enchantments, designed to disrupt and confuse any demonic entity that dared to approach. As he had worked, he muttered ancient incantations, his voice a low, rhythmic chant that echoed through the cold evening air.

The others, their bodies aching and their spirits weary, helped where they could. Daniel, his strength returning, assisted with the heavier tasks, his broad shoulders and powerful arms a welcome asset. Sarah, her fierce protectiveness undiminished, stood guard, her eyes scanning the woods for any sign of movement. Lily, her powers still recovering, provided a psychic watch, her mind reaching out to sense any disturbance in the surrounding area. Even young Rose, despite her fear, contributed to the effort, handing tools and materials to the others with surprising efficiency.

With the sun fully gone, Silas moved to the generator shed. The pull cord groaned only once, and with a satisfying, rhythmic hum, the generator roared to life, shattering the eerie silence. Inside, the lodge was bathed in the steady, bright light of electric bulbs. The sudden illumination was a sharp contrast to the oppressive gloom outside, pushing back the encroaching darkness and, with it, a sliver of their fear. The hum of the generator was a comforting mechanical heartbeat, a barrier against the unseen horrors lurking just beyond the radius of their light.

Chapter 18:

Daniel, his strength returning though his eyes still heavy, turned the dial on the radio slowly, the faint whirring sound of the tuner accompanying his efforts. Static, loud and unrelenting, filled the small room. He twisted the knob, his brow furrowed in concentration, hoping to latch onto any faint signal, any voice from the outside world. Station after station yielded only the hiss and pop of dead air, a desolate soundtrack to their isolation. A cold knot began to form in his stomach. They were truly alone, cut off from the outside world.

Sarah, watching his futile attempts, felt her own hope dwindle with each empty sweep of the dial. Lily and Rose, huddled close on the sofa, stirred uneasily at the constant white noise. Silas, who had once again settled into studying his scattered books, looked up, his attention drawn by the relentless static. Just as Daniel was about to give up, his fingers brushing against the power switch, a faint, garbled voice broke through the static. He froze, then meticulously adjusted the dial, straining to locate the signal.

Suddenly, with a startling clarity that made them all jump, a voice boomed from the small speaker: "...reports of widespread power outages continue across the tri-state area, coinciding with numerous unconfirmed sightings of large, aggressive creatures. Emergency services are overwhelmed. We don't know why, but it has been confirmed from several sources that these creatures, whatever they may be, do not respond well to light. I repeat, stay in the light! Do not venture into dark, unlit areas under any circumstances. We are receiving reports from multiple sources, from city centers to rural communities, confirming these attacks."

A wave of chilling validation washed over them. It wasn't just them dealing with this nightmare. It was bigger.

The broadcast continued, the urgency in the announcer's voice intense. "While the nature of these creatures remains officially unconfirmed, speculation is rampant. Some are calling them a new invasive species, perhaps a mutated form of existing wildlife, or even a deep-earth phenomenon. Conspiracy theories are running wild, with some suggesting these are extraterrestrial organisms, or perhaps a covert government experiment gone horribly wrong. More rational voices from scientific communities urge calm, theorizing about a sudden, inexplicable shift in animal migratory patterns coupled with an unprecedented surge in geomagnetic activity affecting power grids. Regardless of the cause, the message is clear: our infrastructure is failing, and the dark is no longer safe. Maintain light sources at all costs. We will continue to provide updates as information becomes available. This is Signal News, broadcasting on emergency frequencies..."

The signal then faded back into a wall of static, leaving the family in a stunned silence. The light from the generator hummed in the background. What had begun as their localized nightmare was turning into a global catastrophe.

A heavy silence fell over them once more as they considered their next steps. The sheer magnitude of the threat they faced now, illuminated by the radio's grim broadcast, hung in the air, thick and oppressive. Yet, in the face of such overwhelming odds, their determination burned as a defiant, unyielding flame. They were a family, bound together not just by blood, but by shared terror and an unbreakable will to survive. They would not give up without a fight. Each gaze met the others, a silent pledge of unity in the face of the unknown.

Night was truly upon them now, a vast, inky blackness beyond the illuminated perimeter of The Ironwood. The comforting hum of the generator was their only audible link to a semblance of safety. But soon, that mechanical rhythm was joined by another sound, faint at first, then growing steadily. Distant growls, low and guttural, began to echo through the still night air, rising from the depths of the surrounding forest. They were closer this time, and more numerous than before. The creatures knew they were here.

Every creak of the old lodge, every rustle of the wind outside, sent a jolt of fear through them. They all listened, straining to pinpoint the source of the growing menace. Silas moved to the windows, peering out into the darkness that shimmered just beyond the reach of the electric lights. Daniel gripped the axe, its weight a familiar comfort in his sweating palms. Sarah pulled Lily and Rose closer, her arms a shield against the impending horror.

The growls intensified, morphing into hungry snarls and the unmistakable sounds of massive bodies moving through the underbrush. Was The Ironwood going to hold? Its thick stone foundation and sturdy log walls had felt like an impenetrable fortress just hours ago. But after witnessing the raw, destructive power of these creatures firsthand, doubt began gnawing away piece by piece at their willpower. Would it protect them from what would undoubtedly be another relentless assault? Only time, and their desperate fight, would tell.

The night felt like an eternity, each minute dragging into an hour. Every shadow seemed to shift, every distant snap of a twig sent a jolt of fear through them. They were constantly on edge, their eyes scanning the edges of the illuminated clearing, ready for an attack that never quite came. The creatures remained just outside the bright circle, their glowing eyes like malevolent embers in the inky blackness, a terrifying, silent siege. The sheer presence of these unseen horrors, their patience unnerving, was almost worse than an outright assault. Yet, as the hours crawled by, a sense of gratitude settled over them. The lights were holding. They were keeping the monsters at bay.

Then, just an hour before the first hint of dawn, the steady hum of the generator faltered. It sputtered, coughed, and then died, plunging The Ironwood into immediate, suffocating darkness.

The silence that followed was deafening, swiftly broken by a chorus of triumphant roars and snarls that erupted from the immediate vicinity. The creatures, no longer held back by the light, crashed against the walls of the lodge with sickening thuds.

"Flashlights! Now!" Sarah shrieked, her voice cutting through the chaos. Rose instantly fumbled for hers, clicking it on and sweeping its beam across the nearest window, sending a grotesque face recoiling with a pained hiss. Daniel, axe already in hand, moved to the door as it groaned under the heavy impact.

Simultaneously, Silas, acting on instinct, plunged another broom handle into the dying embers of the fireplace. It caught quickly, flaring into a makeshift torch.

He thrust it forward, its wild flames pushing back the shadows.

But it was Lilly who truly unleashed her power. Seeing the direct threat, her small body tensed, and with a guttural cry, she sent out waves of invisible force. Hulking forms were flung backward, crashing through the undergrowth with sounds of splintering wood and pained howls. She focused her raw energy, creating pockets of violent repulsion around the lodge, forcing the creatures to keep their distance even in the dark.

The next sixty minutes were a frantic, desperate scramble. The family fought as one, a coordinated dance of light, force, and desperate will. Rose and Sarah kept their flashlight beams steady, sweeping it across any area where a creature dared to approach. Daniel met the impacts on the door with his axe, creating a formidable barrier. Silas wielded his flaming torch. And Lilly, though trembling with the effort, continued to push back the onslaught with her astonishing power.

Finally, as the first faint streaky grey began to show through the highest branches of the trees, the growls and impacts began to lessen. The creatures, sensing the approaching dawn, let out a final, frustrated shriek and retreated into the deepest parts of the forest. The Ironwood stood, scarred but unbroken. They had survived, once again, with only minimal damage to the lodge, their exhaustion now compounded by the brutal, final assault.

Chapter 19:

The first light of dawn, tentative and pale, painted the cabin in a soft, ethereal glow. Its gentle illumination revealed the extent of the night's brutal siege: splintered logs, shattered stones, and the lingering scent of sulfur and fear. Exhausted and injured, every movement a protest from their battered bodies, the family slowly stepped outside from their relative safety of The Ironwood. They emerged not into the world they knew, but one that was now transformed. The dense fog that had shrouded the forest was gone, replaced by a clear, crisp morning. The sky overhead was a brilliant blue, grossly tinged with shades of red. And the air around them bit with a harsh blend of clean pine, the metallic tang of dried blood, and decay.

The forest itself was eerily, and unnaturally silent. There was no birdsong, no cheerful chirping that typically heralded a new day. Not a single rustle of leaves, no chittering of squirrels, no distant call of a hawk. Just a heavy stillness that pressed in on them, a vast, echoing void where life should have been. A chilling sense of unease, far deeper than their physical exhaustion, crept over them. Something was terrifyingly wrong.

Driven by a grim curiosity and a desperate need to understand, they ventured cautiously to the perimeter of the woods, their senses on high alert. The undergrowth was brutally trampled, flattened in wide swathes, and the earth was deeply scarred with enormous gouges and strange, burn-like marks; the enduring proof of the previous night's ferocious battle. Every few steps, they found broken branches and uprooted saplings, testament to the creatures' immense power.

As they delved deeper into the forest, a truly disturbing sight greeted them. Animals, both large and small, lay dead amidst the wreckage, their bodies twisted in unnatural, broken positions. A deer, its eyes wide with terror, lay with its neck snapped. A rabbit, its fur matted, was crushed beneath a fallen limb. Birds, their feathers ruffled and still, lay scattered on the forest floor.

Rose gasped, a small, choked sound, and then a sob tore from her throat. Tears streamed down her face as she instinctively covered her mouth. Sarah immediately pulled her close, turning her away from the carnage, while Lily, her own small face pale, wrapped an arm around her sister. They stood there holding her tightly, trying to shield her from the gruesome reality which lay before them.

A wave of horror washed over them all. These creatures were not only attacking humans, they were systematically, and brutally decimating the entire ecosystem. The realization was chilling. This was not just a threat to their lives, but to the very fabric of the world around them.

They returned to the lodge, the disturbing images of the ravaged forest burned into their minds. The cabin, with its warm fire, now felt like a fragile bubble of defiance in a world gone horribly wrong. Their minds raced, each grappling with the terrifying implications of what they had witnessed. If the creatures continued unchecked, if this silent, ecological decimation spread, the entire world could be consumed by darkness, not just literally but figuratively, plunging humanity into an age of unending night and terror.

They were no longer just fighting for their own survival or for their next breath; they were fighting for the very survival of humanity itself, for the future of a world they barely recognized.

Silas, his face grim and etched with a new kind of dread, confirmed their worst fears before he even spoke. He held up a thick, leather-bound journal, its pages brittle with age. "I've been reading something I found in one of those journals from your basement, er, your secret room," he corrected himself, a momentary lapse in the face of the overwhelming reality. "And I kept praying that this was not what was happening, that my theories were wrong, but I fear it may be." His voice, usually so steady, wavered with the weight of the revelation.

"Go on," Daniel urged, his voice low, reflecting the collective tension that gripped them all. Sarah pulled Lily and Rose closer to her, their young faces pale and wide-eyed, hanging on Silas's every word.

Silas took a deep, shuddering breath. "The creatures we fought... they're not ordinary predators. They are something more, something ancient and evil, predating written history. They are harbingers of a coming darkness, a force that threatens to engulf the entire world. This journal refers to their master as Morpheus. He plans to not only invade the earth, but well...take it over completely. He feels apparently as though he was wronged at some point and, anyway, that it is his inherent right to do so. And for whatever reason, now is the time he's chosen to enact this ancient goal of his. This grand, horrific takeover." Silas's gaze hardened, meeting each of their eyes in turn. "He is the one we have to stop. We have to figure out how to close that portal once and for all." His voice was grim, weary, but imbued with a desperate resolve. The fate of the entire world now rested upon their shoulders.

Daniel, his hand trembling slightly, reached for the radio. He desperately needed to know what was happening outside their small, increasingly fragile refuge. How far had the chaos spread? Was anything, anything at all, being done to stop the creatures? He twisted the dial, the static a harsh, unyielding presence, before finally landing on the familiar frequency of a news network they'd listened to earlier. The voice that crackled through the speaker was strained and sounded weary.

"We interrupt this broadcast with an urgent update," the anchor's voice began, tinged with a grim finality. "The situation continues to deteriorate across the nation, and the entire world as well. While initial reports indicated the creatures possessed a distinct aversion to light, the rapidly failing power grid has plunged vast swaths of the country into darkness, leading to a catastrophic increase in casualties. Emergency services are overwhelmed. The National Guard and active-duty military units have been deployed to numerous hot zones, but their efforts are proving largely ineffective against the sheer numbers and relentless aggression of the... anomalies. We've received unconfirmed reports of entire cities falling silent. All citizens are advised to seek immediate shelter and maintain any available light sources. Do not, under any circumstances, venture outside after nightfall. We repeat, do not—" The broadcast dissolved into a cacophony of screams and a final, guttural roar before being abruptly cut off, leaving only the chilling hiss of static in its wake.

Daniel's hand, still resting on the radio, felt icy cold. He stared down at the static, his mind reeling from the chilling abruptness of the broadcast's end. Sarah, her face ashen, clutched Rose to her chest, her eyes wide with a terror she tried to shield from her daughters. Rose whimpered softly, burying her face in her mother's side. Lily sat frozen, her jaw set, though her eyes darted nervously toward the windows. Silas, who had been pacing minutes before, now stood by the window, staring out at the bright mid-morning light. The creatures, they all desperately hoped, wouldn't be out yet. But the unspoken question hung heavy in the air between them. If the news couldn't even finish its broadcast, then did that mean things were changing?

With a knot of dread tightening in her stomach, Sarah pulled out her phone, her desperate need to check on her mother overriding everything else. The cabin's remote location usually meant spotty service, if any, and today was no exception. She had to move around, walking further and further, before a single, precious bar of signal flickered to life. Her heart hammered against her ribs as she finally managed to dial the hospital. The ringing felt endless, each second a stretched agony of uncertainty.

When the operator's voice finally crackled through, he was terse, and sounded as though he were about to pass out from exhaustion . "Lakeside Community Hospital. Please state the nature of your emergency."

"My mother, Martha Taylor, she's a patient there," Sarah blurted, her voice thick with anxiety. "I need to know if she's okay."

The line clicked, and then, after what felt like an eternity, another voice came on. A nurse who sounded exhausted, her tone strained and hushed. "How can I help you?"

"Yes. My mother, Martha Taylor, she's a patient there. Is she okay?" Sarah asked, the words rushed as her anxiety was growing.

"Mrs. Taylor is stable, for now," the nurse replied. "We'll do our best to notify you if anything changes." she said, attempting to end the call.

But Sarah blurted out, "Your generators, are they still running. Is she safe?"

"We've been running on backup generators," the nurse explained, her voice barely above a whisper. "The main grid went down, just like the news is reporting everywhere else. And I've been told that some of the troops will soon be setting up around the building, so that should give us another layer of security."

Suddenly, the nurse's voice dropped even lower, as though she were sensing some immediate danger. "Hold on. I hear something." There was a rustling, a sharp, metallic clang, and then a hurried whisper. "Oh, thank god! The National Guard just rolled into the parking lot. I see them setting up a perimeter, establishing some kind of secure zone around the hospital. I'm sorry, but I have to go."

Before Sarah could respond, the line went dead, leaving her clutching a phone that now offered only silence. Yet despite the pit of fear gnawing at her insides, she at least knew the hospital seemed, at the moment, to be a secure zone, a place where the immediate threat of the creatures might be held at bay. And her mother, though no change, was still holding on. That was at least a bit of hope to cling to.

She stumbled back into the cabin, the short distance she had walked feeling like miles, her legs heavy, her face pale and drawn from the emotional whiplash. The mid-morning sun, usually a source of comfort, now seemed to mock the growing dread inside her.

Daniel met her at the door, his arms open, his expression etched with worry. She collapsed into his embrace, the last traces of her composure crumbling as silent tears began to stream down her face. He held her tightly, the familiar scent of him a small anchor in the swirling chaos which threatened to consume them all.

"It's going to be okay," he whispered into her hair, his voice a comforting warmth to her fragile state of mind. "We'll figure this out. We always do." He wasn't even sure he believed the words which poured from his mouth, but he knew he had to offer them.

Sarah shook her head, her sobs muffled against his chest. "I don't know what to do, Daniel. I feel so helpless," she choked out, the weight of the world pressing down on her. The image of the National Guard setting up a perimeter around the hospital should provide a peace of mind, but instead it painted a grim picture of how dire things truly had become.

He stroked her hair gently, offering silent comfort where his words failed. "We'll find a way to keep our entire family safe," he promised, his voice firm, a silent vow to himself as much as to her. She glanced over his shoulder at Rose, still whimpering softly in her sister's arms.

The immense weight of their situation seemed to rest squarely on Sarah's shoulders. Her mother's precarious condition, confined within a hospital that was rapidly transforming into a fortified stronghold, coupled with the unyielding chaos spreading across the outside world, was a burden she carried with a heavy, aching heart. She wanted to suggest they make their way to the hospital, towards safety. But she knew, as exhausted as they all were, they'd never make it in one day. And spending the night out there…unshelted , was not an option. Plus, she knew that whether they liked it or not, they were the only ones with knowledge of what was really happening. And she wasn't quite sure how that news would be perceived by strangers, especially in a world full of chaos. Daniel's words to her were simple, yet they carried a profound weight of reassurance for her, a lifeline in this ever darkening tunnel. "We'll get through this, Sarah. We have to. For our girls and for each other."

Chapter 20:

The afternoon light filtered through the cabin windows, casting long, distorted shadows that danced on the dust-covered floor. One by one, the family emerged from the depths of a fitful, shallow sleep, their bodies aching from the previous night's terror, but their spirits, against all odds, seemed remarkably unbroken. The shared ordeal, and the collective will to survive had forged an unbreakable bond between them all.

Silas, with his knowledge and insatiable thirst for answers, retreated into the quiet corners, spending countless hours poring over the old, leather-bound books he'd brought with him. His brow was constantly furrowed in concentration as he sought patterns, elusive clues, anything that could offer even a fleeting glimpse into the true nature of the insidious darkness that had so swiftly enveloped their world. More importantly, he searched for how it could possibly be stopped. They all had a chilling suspicion that no one else outside their small circle would ever suspect, or even dare to consider, that this siege was demonic in origin, as opposed to some unexplainable biological event or environmental catastrophe. The more he delved into the often cryptic texts, deciphering faded Latin and archaic symbols, the more terrifying the truth became. He ate little, and slept less than everyone else, driven by a relentless urgency to find the answer.

That evening, as a thunderstorm raged outside, the wind howling like a hungry beast and rain drumming a relentless rhythm against the cabin walls, Silas finally emerged from his solitary study. His face was etched with a grave expression, his eyes holding a haunted, distant look. He moved with a seriousness they had not seen before, gathering the family around the flickering fire, its light battling against the encroaching gloom.

"I've found something," he began, his voice low and raspy, filled with a chilling sense of foreboding that instantly silenced the crackling fire and the storm outside. "A prophecy."

The family listened closely, their hearts pounding in their chests, a drumbeat of dread. Rose instinctively moved closer to her mother, while Lily's gaze remained fixed on Silas, her usual composure replaced by a fierce intensity. Silas spoke of a cataclysmic event, detailed in forgotten scrolls, a chilling convergence of darkness that was prophesied to engulf the entire world. The monstrous creatures they had faced, the ones that recoiled from light and swarmed in the shadows, were not the true enemy, he explained. "As we know, the mastermind behind it all was Morpheus, the god of dreams. This entity's malevolent plan was not merely destruction, but to overtake Earth and rule it as his own domain, transforming it into a realm of eternal night. One final battle is coming," Silas concluded, his voice heavy with the weight of this revelation. A battle that would determine not just their survival, but the very fate of humanity itself.

"This must be the prophecy that my father was talking about," Daniel said, shaking his head slowly, the weight of the revelation settling heavily upon him. He had told him that his great, great grandfather, a man of strange hobbies, often muttered about doorways and hidden knowledge, but

Daniel had always dismissed it as eccentric rambling. Now, it was terrifyingly real. "I can't believe it. How did my great, great grandfather unearth it? And why would he hide such a terrifying truth?"

"I don't know," Silas answered, his gaze distant as he stared into the dancing flames. "The texts don't elaborate on how it was found, only that it was recorded by a witness to the first stirrings, or at least what was believed to be the first. But according to this," he gestured vaguely to the pile of scrolls and leather-bound books beside him, "if we lose, it's game over. Not just for us, but for everyone on earth." The finality in his voice was chilling.

A puzzled frown creased Daniel's brow as Silas uttered the name again. "Morpheus?" he interjected, the name striking a familiar chord from dimly remembered tales of childhood. "Wait, isn't that… in Greek mythology? The one who delivers messages through dreams? He wasn't considered evil, was he?" He looked at Sarah, then back at Silas, trying to reconcile the benevolent figure he recalled with the horrifying scenario Silas was painting. It seemed too bizarre to be true.

Sarah, her eyes widening in a sudden flash of recognition, stiffened beside him. A forgotten detail, a half-remembered warning from an old mythology class she'd taken in college, surfaced in her mind like a cold shard of ice, a chilling addendum to Daniel's innocent query. "Yes, Daniel, he is," she said, her voice barely a whisper, a newfound tremor running through it. "But I remember something else. The myths also said that while he could bring visions and messages, Morpheus could also give terrifying nightmares to mortals who disturbed him, or if he was angered. He could twist dreams into pure torment, trapping people in their darkest fears." She looked at Silas, a fresh wave of horror washing over her. "So, if this... Morpheus... is truly behind all of this, then the creatures, the chaos, the power outages... it's not just an invasion. It's a waking nightmare. And it's designed not just to kill us, but to break us, to drive us mad before we even fall." The implication hung heavy in the air, transforming the physical threat into something far more insidious and psychological.

Another morning dawned, not with the usual gentle rise of the sun, but with a bleak, overcast sky that mirrored the heavy mood within the cabin. It signaled the end of another night, a grueling vigil filled with battles and near-misses against the encroaching darkness. Their exhaustion was heavy in the air, a dull ache in every muscle, but sleep was a luxury none of them could afford, nor dared to seek. The memory of the previous night's horrors, the guttural screeches and the chilling silence that followed, was too fresh.

So, it was with a grim determination that the family began to gather their meager supplies. Daniel meticulously checked the few weapons they possessed including a fireplace poker, and a few sturdy axes; anything that could offer a sliver of defense. Sarah, her face drawn but resolute, organized the dwindling food rations and refilled their water containers. Lily, despite her young age, efficiently packed the first aid kits, her small hands surprisingly steady as she inventoried what remained of the bandages and antiseptics. Rose, still clutching a worn blanket, watched them with wide eyes, a silent testament to the fear that still clung to them all.

Silas, however, moved with a different kind of urgency. His night had been spent not just in defense, but in a frantic search through his collection of books, even as the cabin trembled under the creatures' assaults. He had found something, a fleeting reference, a cryptic hint, in the chaotic hours before the most recent attack. It was a lead, a fragile thread of hope that he believed might hold the key to not just surviving, but to defeating Morpheus once and for all.

"I need to get over to the college," Silas announced, his voice firm despite the tremor of fatigue beneath it. He unfolded a crudely drawn map, highlighting a section of the nearby town. "I'm certain there's a specific professor there, Dr. Anthony Finch. He was rumored to have studied the occult, ancient religions, and obscure mythologies. The kind of knowledge no mainstream academic would touch. If anyone would have specialized textbooks or forgotten lore about beings like Morpheus, it would be him." His gaze swept over their weary faces, a desperate plea in his eyes. "We need to find his collection, his research. Let's just hope the college library, or his office, is still standing, and that the books in it are the ones I'm looking for." The unspoken fear was clear. The creatures, and the chaos, could have destroyed their only chance at obtaining the key to their survival.

It would be a long, grueling hike to the campus, and a journey of uncertainty. They knew with chilling clarity that reaching their destination before nightfall was far from guaranteed, and the thought of being caught unsheltered in the darkness was a cold dread that settled deep in their bones. Yet, despite the immense risks, they also knew these books, these ancient texts Silas believed lay within the college's forgotten halls, might be their only hope of understanding, and ultimately stopping, these monstrous entities.

The forest, once a familiar landscape of peaceful solitude and childhood memories, now seemed alien and overwhelmingly hostile. Every rustle in the undergrowth, every snap of a twig, sent a jolt of adrenaline through their veins. The sudden caw of a distant crow, the unseen scuttling of a small animal in the dry leaves, or even the drip of dew from an overhead branch had them all flinching, eyes darting, muscles tensing. The creatures, though thankfully less visible during the day, still cast an ominous, unseen shadow over the land. Their presence was a constant, suffocating pressure that kept their senses on high alert. Daniel led the way, his hand never far from the ax strapped to his side, his eyes constantly scanning the tree line. Sarah walked close behind him, shielding Rose. Lily, remaining vigilant, watched their flanks as Silas brought up the rear.

As they delved deeper into the woods, the terrain grew increasingly challenging. Dense, thorny undergrowth snagged at their clothes, and steep, rocky inclines slowed their progress to a laborious crawl. The weight of their backpacks, filled with precious supplies added to their already crushing fatigue. Each step was an effort, confirmation of their dwindling stamina. Rose, who had recently been full of boundless energy, began to falter, her small legs growing heavy with exhaustion. Her whimpers grew more frequent, and her pace slowed to a shuffle. Finally, Daniel, seeing the sheer weariness in her small frame, gently lifted her, carrying her for a stretch, her head resting against his shoulder as he pressed onward. Even Lily, the more resilient of the two, showed signs of strain, her usual spirited defiance replaced by a quiet, determined grimace. Yet, the knowledge of what lay ahead, the desperate hope that a solution might be within reach, fueled their determination, pushing them forward through the exhaustion and fear.

Hours later, as the sun began its slow descent, painting the western sky in hues of orange and purple, the outline of the college finally came into view. A once-proud institution, a place of learning and intellectual pursuit, it now stood as a decaying monument to a world that was rapidly fading. Some of the buildings were scarred and broken, skeletal structures against the darkening sky. Countless windows were shattered, gaping like vacant eyes. The thick ivy that clambered relentlessly up the crumbling brickwork, appeared to be reclaiming the campus piece by piece. A sense of foreboding washed over them as they approached, the silence of the abandoned grounds more unsettling than any noise. What was once a place of learning, now seemed like a tomb holding secrets they desperately needed to unearth.

With cautious, measured steps, their shoes crunching on scattered debris, they entered the main building of the college, Abernathy Hall. The interior was a scene of utter desolation, a testament to the speed and ferocity with which the world had unraveled. Dust motes danced in the sparse beams of fading daylight that pierced through shattered windows, illuminating overturned desks, splintered chairs, and a chaotic blizzard of scattered papers. Despite the eerie, oppressive atmosphere, a chilling silence broken only by the occasional groan of the old building, they pressed on, their collective gaze fixed on their destination.

Navigating the corridors of the deserted academic hall felt like an eternity. Each echoing step was a reminder of their vulnerability, the slightest creak of the old building or distant rumble of thunder outside sending shivers down their spines. But then, after what felt like an eternity of searching through abandoned classrooms and silent lecture halls, they found what they were looking for. Dr. Finch's office.

Their relief, however, was short-lived. The door was not merely closed, but rather it was locked. Daniel and Silas exchanged a quick glance.

"Don't suppose you have a key, do you?" Daniel asked, trying to make light of the bad situation. Meanwhile, his gaze was busy assessing the sturdy wooden frame.

Silas peered at the lock, then ran a hand over the heavy wood. "Picking it would take too long, and we don't have the tools. A forced entry is our only real option, but..." He trailed off, gesturing to the silence around them. Any loud noise would echo through the building, alerting anything lurking in the shadows that they were there.

Daniel's jaw tightened. He held up his ax, its sharp blade glinting dully in the fading light. "We don't have time for subtlety, Silas. Sunset's coming." Before Silas could protest further, Daniel swung the ax, the heavy head smashing through the glass panel in the upper half of the door with a sharp, echoing crack. Shards rained down on the dusty floor, the sound impossibly loud in the silence. He quickly reached through the jagged opening, fumbling for the lock, and with a metallic click, the door swung inward.

Inside, the office was a bibliophile's dream and a hoarder's nightmare. The walls were entirely consumed by towering, floor-to-ceiling bookshelves, groaning under the immense weight of countless volumes of knowledge. Silas, his eyes gleaming with a renewed sense of purpose that cut through his exhaustion, moved immediately to the shelves. His fingers traced the spines of books, his mind racing, searching for specific titles that he hoped would hold the answers they so desperately needed.

As Silas delved into his frantic search, Daniel moved to the office doorway, taking up a defensive stance. His ax remained firmly in his grip, his eyes scanning the now darkened corridor outside, listening for any sound beyond the distant rumble of the storm. Meanwhile, the sheer exhaustion of the day, combined with the stillness of the room, began to claim its toll on Rose. She curled up into the desk chair, where she tried to fight against her drooping eyelids for a few moments, but finally drifted off into a much needed sleep.

Sarah and Lily, however, remained wide awake. Despite the pervading sense of danger and the grim reality of their situation, they couldn't help but be drawn into the allure of the thousands of books surrounding them. With cautious steps, they looked through the shelves, their gazes sweeping over the titles, some familiar, many utterly foreign. There was a strange, almost comforting hum in the air, a silent promise of forgotten worlds and ancient knowledge. Even as their hands instinctively reached for their flashlights, ready to snap them on at the slightest hint of movement, a quiet intrigue began to replace some of their fear.

Then, as a glimmer of hope, a thick, leather-bound book, tucked away on a lower shelf, caught Silas' eye. Its title, embossed in tarnished gold, was almost illegible, but he recognized the ancient language, it was the same language he had found both in the hidden room and in Lily's book. A flicker of excitement ignited in his weary mind. With trembling hands, he carefully pulled it from the shelf, dislodging a small cloud of dust. As he opened its brittle, yellowed pages, a rush of excitement and anticipation, potent enough to momentarily push back the despair, filled him. This, he instinctively knew, could be the key they were looking for, the prophecy's missing link.

As the last sliver of natural light began to vanish from the shattered windows, painting the decaying college in hues of purple and deep crimson, Daniel looked at Silas and Sarah. "It's sundown," he stated, his voice low but firm. "We can't risk trying to make it back to the cabin in the dark. We need to spend the night here."

Silas nodded, already assessing their surroundings. "Agreed. The main power grid is out everywhere, so the college lights won't work, probably a blown fuse or worse, but we have the lantern and our flashlights." He held up the bulky, battery-powered lantern. "We should find a defensible classroom or office, perhaps one on an upper floor away from ground-level windows. We can barricade the door and set up a watch." The thought of another night in an unfamiliar, derelict building filled them with dread, but the alternative was far worse. Here, amidst the dusty remnants of knowledge, they would make their stand, desperately hoping the secrets within Dr. Finch's books would hold the answers they had been searching for…before the darkness claimed them all.

Hunkering down for the night, the office space was turned into a temporary, and fragile sanctuary. Rose, deep in the innocent slumber of childhood exhaustion, was now cradled securely in her mother's arms. Sarah lay on the dusty floor behind the large, heavy desk, a makeshift barricade, her body curved around her daughter, offering what little warmth and comfort she could. Nearby, Lily, her youthful energy finally depleted, had slumped over against a towering bookshelf, her head nodding off, the rhythmic patter of rain against the shattered windows a gentle lullaby.

Daniel remained on watch by the doorway, his presence a steadfast anchor in the swirling chaos of the darkness. The thunderstorm raged outside, a relentless drumbeat against the old college building, but within the office, an eerie silence prevailed. The darkness of the night pressed in from all sides, making the shadows within the room feel dense and watchful. Despite the exhaustion that gripped them all,

Silas was a man possessed. With the precious books now within his grasp, he had plunged headfirst into the ancient texts, his brow furrowed in concentration, his eyes rapidly scanning the dense script, desperate to unearth the secrets that might save them all.

As the first faint streaks of dawn bruised the horizon,the family began to stir. With a collective sigh of weariness, they gathered their meager belongings, the familiar weight of their packs a reminder of their newfound, yet nomadic existence. They were a world away from the simple comforts of their own home, let alone the temporary refuge of the lodge, and despite the fitful sleep of the previous night, their bodies were still aching from the relentless exhaustion that had become their constant companion. A peculiar blend of gratitude and gnawing concern settled over them. There had been no direct attacks on them last night, a blessing they had desperately needed, yet the quiet was unsettling. It made them all wonder, with a chilling certainty, what was happening out there? And worse, what was coming.

Silas, with the precious, dust-covered books now clutched securely in his arms, took the lead on the journey back to the lodge. His gaze was fixed on the path ahead, his movements cautious, trying to keep watch for any sign of movement in the re-emerging daylight. Yet, even as his eyes scanned the forest, his mind was miles away, deep in thought. The books he carried held the key to understanding their enemy, to unmasking Morpheus and his monstrous legions. But deciphering them was a daunting, almost insurmountable task, especially with the archaic languages, the cryptic symbols, and the fragmented prophecies. It was a problem that was going to demand absolute focus. He needed solitude, uninterrupted hours to unravel the mysteries hidden within the brittle, yellowed pages, to connect the scattered pieces of the terrifying puzzle. The urgency of his quest weighed heavily on him, a silent burden he carried alone.

Finally, through the weary gaps in the trees, the familiar outline of the lodge emerged at last, a truly welcome sight that pulled a collective sigh of relief from the exhausted family. As soon as they were inside, Daniel quickly tended to the fireplace, until a roaring fire had begun to push back the lingering chill. Sarah, moving with a renewed sense of purpose despite her fatigue, warmed up what was nearly the last of their precious canned soup, its comforting aroma slowly filling the small space. The girls, their hunger overriding their exhaustion, devoured their food in moments before collapsing onto their makeshift beds, seeking a much-needed attempt at genuine rest. Rose was almost instantly asleep, her little body lax with weariness, while Lily, though still alert, seemed to sink deeply into the blankets. Silas, however, his eyes burning with an almost feverish determination, remained utterly engrossed in the pages of the texts he had brought from the college, his fingers tracing lines of forgotten script, relentlessly searching for a glimpse of hope amidst the chilling prophecies.

As the evening wore on, the lodge, usually a place of quiet safety, began to feel different. A strange sensation washed over them, subtly at first, then growing more pronounced. A low, resonant hum began to fill the air, a vibration that seemed to emanate from everywhere and nowhere all at once, growing louder with each passing moment, vibrating deep in their bones. The family exchanged worried glances, their exhaustion momentarily forgotten as a new kind of dread settled in. This wasn't the sound of a storm, nor the movement of creatures outside. This was something else entirely. Something was happening, something huge and undeniably beyond their comprehension, the air crackling with an unseen energy.

"What is that?" Lily whispered, her voice barely audible above the growing hum, her eyes wide with a mixture of fear and awe as the very floorboards beneath them seemed to thrum.

"I don't know," Daniel muttered, his gaze sweeping frantically around the room, searching for the source. "It's... it's not the storm."

Rose, startled awake by the intensifying vibrations and the blinding, ethereal light that suddenly filled the cabin, began to cry out. "Mommy" she wailed, running and clutching onto Sarah.

"What's happening?!" Sarah cried, pulling Rose closer, her own voice trembling as the light pulsed from within the very walls. A surge of raw, untamed energy filled the room, a force so immense it lifted them all off their feet, suspending them weightlessly in the air. They were no longer in the lodge but surrounded by a swirling vortex of vibrant, indescribable color and pure, concentrated light, the familiar world dissolving around them. Fear, mixed with utter confusion, gripped them as they were pulled forward, not into darkness, but into a radiant, terrifying unknown.

Chapter 21:

The blinding light that had consumed the family intensified, morphing into a swirling vortex of color and pure energy. A moment of disorientation overtook them. They became aware of a sensation of complete weightlessness, where up and down ceased to exist. But the thing they were most grateful for was the brief respite from the utter darkness. When their senses, one by one, hesitantly returned, they found themselves in a place unlike anything they had ever seen or even conceived of before.

A vast, ethereal expanse stretched before them, boundless and infinite, bathed in an otherworldly, shimmering light that seemed to emanate from everywhere at once. Floating orbs of various sizes and incandescent colors drifted lazily through the space, illuminating their surroundings with a mesmerizing, dreamlike spectacle. They were no longer anchored by gravity, suspended gently within an invisible force field that held them captive, yet so far unharmed, in the vastness.

Fear mixed with a sense of wonder as they instinctively reached out, their hands grasping for each other, desperate to confirm their collective reality.

"What's going on?" Daniel's voice, usually so steady, was a strained whisper, echoing strangely in the silence.

He floated closer to Sarah, pulling her and a still-dazed Rose near.

"Is this a dream?" Sarah murmured, her eyes wide, staring at the luminous spheres. "But how can it be if we're all here?" She squeezed Rose tightly, as if to prove her daughter's presence.

Lily found herself mesmerized by the silent ballet of light around them. "Where are we?" she breathed, her voice filled with what could only be described as a child's pure astonishment.

Silas pushed aside his terror to try and rationalize the impossible. "This... this defies every law of physics. We were in the lodge. How did we get here?" Questions raced through their minds, a torrent of desperate inquiries, but there were no answers. Only the silent, radiant expanse.

Suddenly, a voice, resonating with an otherworldly power, echoed through the space, seeming to originate from everywhere and nowhere simultaneously, a sound that bypassed their ears and vibrated directly in their very souls. "You have been chosen," it boomed, silencing their frantic whispers.

Fear twisted into utter confusion within them. Daniel, always the one to ground them in reality, was the first to find his voice, though it was little more than a disbelieving whisper. "Chosen for what?" he demanded, his gaze sweeping frantically across the endless expanse.

The ethereal voice continued, weaving a chilling tapestry of their new, terrifying reality. "Your world, once a beacon of harmony and vibrant life, is now teetering on the brink of oblivion. A dark force, ancient and insatiable, seeks to consume it, to harness its very energy for its own nefarious, destructive purposes. And should they succeed, should the balance tip, then it will be the end of humanity forever."

Silas stood rooted to his spot, his mind reeling, struggling to reconcile this cosmic pronouncement with the dusty, academic world he had just inhabited. Beside him, Sarah's protective arms instinctively drew the girls closer, her face a mask of terror and disbelief.

"What?" Daniel interjected, his voice rising, his mind whirling from this new, impossible information. "But why us? Surely, there must be others who could do this. Soldiers, scientists, priests, I don't know... people prepared for something like this!"

The voice, patient yet undeniably potent, continued, its words weaving a deeper layer into the tapestry of cosmic significance. "You are the guardians, the protectors of the delicate balance between light and darkness. While this is not a choice you have made, you are integral to a greater design. You are the chosen protectors of the two sisters, and through them, the prophecy will be revealed."

"We're not protectors," Daniel finally managed, shaking his head, a look of despair etching lines onto his face. His voice was barely a whisper, swallowed by the cosmic hum. "We're just ordinary people, trying to make sense of a terrifying world. We can't even protect our own children from this... this horror." His gaze fell upon Rose, still clutching Sarah, and the raw impotence in his words was heartbreaking.

The ethereal voice echoed in his mind, its tone a strange blend of commanding power and gentle reassurance, cutting through his despair. "You are mistaken," it boomed softly. "You were chosen to be a protector, as were your loved ones. Your residence in that house, your love for your wife, the adoption of the two sisters...your daughters. It was a destiny woven before time, and even Silas's unexpected arrival. All of it was part of a grand design, threads spun into the fabric of your fate."

A stunned silence followed, punctuated only by the distant, celestial hum. Daniel's eyes darted from Silas to Sarah, then finally landed on Lily and Rose, who were being held tightly by their mother. A dawning, horrifying realization slowly began to settle upon him. Sarah's breath hitched, a sharp gasp escaping her lips as her own gaze fell upon their daughters, then snapped back to Silas, a shared, incredulous horror in her eyes. Silas, usually so composed, looked utterly bewildered, his head tilting slightly as if trying to grasp a concept just beyond his reach. Even Lily, despite her fear, seemed to sense the shift, her eyes widening as she looked from her sister to her parents.

Then, with a jolt that felt physical even in their weightless state, the connection was made. The "two sisters." It was undeniably clear. Lily and Rose. Their daughters. They were the ones. The sheer, overwhelming astonishment and the terrifying weight of what that meant crashed down upon them. "You are bound together by destiny, each of you possessing a unique gift," the voice continued, reinforcing their dawning realization. "You are the prophesied protectors, and only you can fulfill this sacred duty." The final words hung in the air, a cosmic decree that left them breathless, their identities irrevocably reshaped in the face of the impossible.

Sarah, still clutching both girls tightly to her, her face etched with a desperate, maternal ferocity, finally found her voice again. "But they are just children!" she cried out, her voice trembling, echoing in the vast, luminous space. "You can't ask them to fight in such a battle. It's not right! They're too young, too innocent!"

"I understand your apprehension, Sarah," the omnipresent voice responded, its tone softer now, almost empathetic, yet still undeniably powerful. "But look again. Truly look, for they are not ordinary children. Surely you have witnessed their gifts, have you not? The subtle shifts, the improbable occurrences, the whispers of what lies beyond the veil? These are not mere coincidences."

Sarah gazed down at the girls, her heart aching with a conflicting mix of fear and undeniable truth. In the quiet moments of their terrifying new reality, she had indeed witnessed glimmers of something extraordinary in both Lily and Rose. A heightened intuition in one, an unexpected strength in the other. But both attributes she had assumed were due to the harsh environment of the foster care system they had endured. She knew, deep in her heart, that the voice spoke truly of their emerging magical abilities. But that knowledge only fueled her fierce resolve. She had to protect them, no matter what. No matter the prophecy, no matter the cosmic stakes, her children came first.

The voice continued, its words weaving around them, resonating with a warmth. "And it is precisely that love for them which I can feel, Sarah, the unwavering love you all have for each other. It is a bond forged in adversity and unbreakable hope, and that will see this prophecy come to pass. It is not their strength in battle, but the strength of your collective heart that will be the true weapon when the time comes."

Each of them stood in bewilderment, reeling from this new, overwhelming revelation. The concept of their ordinary family and one stranger who happened to show up at the right time, and who had since become family, being the linchpin of cosmic salvation. And their precious daughters the central figures, was a truth too vast to fully comprehend, yet impossibly real.

The voice, as if sensing their silent struggle, offered one final, resonating pronouncement, its words echoing not just in the expanse but in the very core of their beings. "The journey ahead will be fraught with peril. There will be trials that will test your courage and your faith. But remember the strength that binds you, and the sacred purpose entrusted to the two sisters. Their awakening is tied to the prophecy, and your role as protectors is paramount. Seek the truth within the knowledge, prepare for the coming conflict, and embrace your destiny."

As the last word faded, the boundless, shimmering expanse around them began to subtly shift. The myriad of floating orbs brightened, their colors intensifying, and the gentle hum that had filled the air swelled into a powerful crescendo. The light, which had been so mesmerizing, now intensified into a brilliant, almost painful white. The sensation of weightlessness returned with an even greater force, pulling and twisting them within the swirling vortex of pure energy. Disorientation washed over them once more, a dizzying rush of sensation and light, before a sudden, familiar jolt brought them crashing back. They lay sprawled on the wooden floor, with the scent of burning embers filling their nostrils, and the distant sound of a fading thunderstorm in their ears. They were back in the lodge, shaken and disoriented, but undeniably back on earth. The only difference was that now, their world, and their understanding of their place within it, had irrevocably changed.

Chapter 22:

An overwhelming sense of disorientation washed over them, a cognitive dissonance that made their heads spin. Where had they truly been? What had genuinely transpired? The vivid, overwhelming memories of the ethereal realm with its booming, disembodied voice, the revelation of their cosmic purpose, and the impossible notion of training for a war with some ancient force. It all felt like a fever dream, too grand and fantastical to be real. Yet, the lingering echoes of the voice in their minds, the undeniable chill that still clung to their skin, spoke of a truth far stranger than any dream.

They looked at each other, their eyes reflecting a complex mixture of awe, bone-deep fear, and a terrifying understanding. They were guardians, protectors of a world teetering on the brink of annihilation. How could that possibly be true? They were just an ordinary family, a scholar, and two little girls, thrust into an impossible war. The weight of this newfound, unimaginable responsibility was immense, crushing them with its sheer magnitude. The battle against the pervasive darkness was not a distant threat, but an imminent reality, and they, the most unlikely of heroes, were supposedly the last, and only, line of defense.

Then there were Lily and Rose. Children. Their innocent daughters. The voice had declared that they would somehow play a vital, central part in this cosmic conflict.

But how could they? Wouldn't that mean putting them in unimaginable danger, exposing them to horrors beyond their comprehension? Every primal instinct within both Daniel and Sarah warred fiercely against that concept, the unyielding, driving need to keep their daughters safe, shielded from the world's harshness, let alone an interdimensional war. The mere thought of them facing such perils twisted their hearts with agonizing dread.

And Silas. How had he, an outsider, become so intricately woven into this impossible tapestry? Was it unknowingly, simply a case of being in the wrong place at the right, catastrophic time? Or was it always destiny, a predetermined path that had brought him to their door? But then, if destiny truly guided all, he couldn't reconcile that with Emma's death, the tragic event that had led him here. She was so young, so full of life, and they had been so deeply in love, preparing to start a family of their own. How could her untimely demise be part of a grand, benevolent design? The questions swirled, unanswered, leaving them adrift in a sea of cosmic uncertainty, the weight of their impossible future pressing down upon them.

Daniel finally pushed himself up, his eyes scanning the faces of his family. "Did... did that just happen?" he asked, his voice rough with disbelief. "Are we... are we really back?"

Sarah, still cradling Rose who was slowly stirring, nodded, her gaze fixed on the dust motes dancing in the sunbeams. "We are," she whispered, a shudder running through her. "But... what *was* that? A dream? Some kind of shared hallucination from exhaustion?"

Silas, ever the rationalist, was already on his feet, pacing the room. "A shared hallucination of such vivid detail and universal sensory input? Highly improbable. Impossible, I'd argue. We all heard the voice. We all saw the... the expanse." He gestured vaguely at the cabin walls, as if still seeing beyond them. His brow furrowed in deep thought. "And the very specific information... the prophecy, the roles we each have to play."

Lily, who had silently watched them all, piped up, her voice small but firm. "I saw it too. And I heard it. Everything." She looked from Silas to her parents, a desperate plea in her eyes. "It was real, wasn't it?"

Daniel ran a hand through his hair, his mind racing, trying to find a logical explanation for the utterly illogical. "If it was a dream, how could we all have the exact same one? Every single detail? And how would we all end up back here at the same time, in the exact same spots we were in when... when we left?" He looked at Sarah, then at Silas. "It had to be real. Right?" The unspoken weight of that realization hung heavy in the air, transforming their fear into a chilling certainty. Their lives had been marked by something far beyond their understanding.

"I have to say, I look forward to speaking with each of you when this whole ordeal is over," Silas said excitedly. "It would make for a great book. But for now, I think we all need to prepare for what is to come," he continued, his voice turning somber, cutting through the stunned silence. He retreated to his small table laden with his journals, textbooks, and the books he had so recently acquired from the college. With a renewed, almost desperate eagerness, he picked up where he had left off, his fingers already tracing the cryptic symbols. He had to find something, anything, within those crumbling pages that would help decipher the bewildering revelations they had just been given, to understand the "grand design," and, most crucially, to find a way to defeat Morpheus and stop the encroaching darkness.

As Silas plunged back into his scholarly pursuit, Sarah's own anxieties took precedence. "I need to call and check on my mom," she murmured, her eyes willing the tears not to fall, the thought of her mother's safety in a world teetering on the brink of oblivion a fresh stab of fear. The phone was her lifeline, her only fragile connection to the life they had known before. Daniel, understanding her unspoken need, simply nodded, his own face etched with a mixture of dread and growing resolve. Sarah grabbed her phone and headed for the door, needing a moment of privacy, and perhaps, a breath of the fresh air outside.

Noticing the bright sun streaming through the doorway, a stark contrast to the cosmic chaos they'd just experienced, Daniel decided to ground his daughters in something familiar. "Lily, Rose," he called softly, trying to inject a sense of normalcy into his voice, "can you two help me gather some more firewood before lunch?" The mundane task was a small, defiant act of normalcy in a world turned upside down, a way to keep their hands busy while their minds reeled from the impossible truth.

Sarah stepped out of the cabin, the sun's deceptive warmth doing little to soothe the chill gnawing at her. She raised her phone, the screen stubbornly displaying *No Service*. She walked a few paces, then a few more, desperation mounting with each step. She tried again, and again, holding the phone aloft, waving it around, cursing softly under her breath. The bars remained stubbornly empty, a mocking symbol of her helplessness. Frustration, hot and raw, began to bubble up. She needed to hear about her mother, to know she was safe in a world that felt like it was breaking. The silence of the forest pressed in around her, broken only by her own ragged breathing.

Finally, with a choked sob, she slumped onto a nearby tree stump, burying her face in her hands. The tears she had been willing away for days, for weeks, now came in a torrent, silent and fierce. She cried for the life they had lost, for the terrifying uncertainty of their future, for the impossible burden placed upon her daughters, and for her mother. She cried until her body shook with the force of it, until her eyes burned and her throat ached, release she hadn't dared to afford herself until now. Alone in the quiet woods, she allowed herself to be utterly broken.

Minutes later, she was unsure of how many, when the storm of emotion finally passed. It had left her spent, but strangely clearer, She took a shaky breath, before wiping her face with the back of her hand, and pulling herself together. She tried the phone one last time, and miraculously, two bars flickered to life. Her heart leaped as she quickly dialed the hospital.

"Lakeside Community Hospital, Nurse Jenkins speaking," a harried voice answered when she finally managed to get through.

"Nurse Jenkins, hello. I'm calling to check on my mother, Martha Taylor," Sarah managed, her voice still a little hoarse.

"Ah, Mrs. Taylor," Nurse Jenkins said, her tone softening slightly. "We've been missing you around here Ms. Monroe. I do hope that you and your family are somewhere safe."

"Yes, we are," Sarah replied, looking around her wondering from which direction the creatures would come next.

"Your mother... she's been much the same. She's woken up a few times, which is good, but it's not long before she drifts back off. We still don't know exactly what's wrong, but the doctors are running tests when they're able. Unfortunately, we're short staffed on this floor, as most doctors have been called to help in the ER."

A wave of relief and dread washed over Sarah simultaneously. "I understand. When she's awake, what is she like? Is she lucid?"

"Well," Nurse Jenkins hesitated, "she talks a lot about a playground. Like she's remembering her childhood, playing with other children. Which is normal in older people. But then sometimes, she shifts, and she'll say *'it's the devil's playground now.'* It's... a bit disorienting. We're thinking it might be a touch of dementia, given her age. Please don't worry too much, Sarah. She's safe here." The nurse's voice sped up slightly. "The National Guard is still outside, the lights are still on, and they're keeping watch. We're well-protected."

Before Sarah could process the strange details about the playground or ask what else her mother had said, Nurse Jenkins' voice turned urgent. "Oh, I'm terribly sorry, I have to go! We have an emergency at the far end of the ward. I'll call you if anything changes!" And with a click, the line went dead, leaving Sarah clutching her phone, the unsettling words about her mother's strange ramblings hanging in the air.

Sarah walked back into the lodge, her steps heavy, her eyes still a little red, though she tried to hide it. Daniel met her at the door, pulling her into a tight, comforting hug. Unbeknownst to her, he had seen her slumped on the tree stump, her shoulders shaking, while he and the girls gathered firewood. His heart had ached for her, but he knew she needed that moment to herself. When he finally released her, he gestured towards the table. "Lily and I got lunch ready," he said, indicating the bowls of warmed, canned stew.

Lily beamed proudly from her seat. "Are you okay, Mom?" she asked, her young eyes full of concern.

Sarah managed a weak smile. "I'm fine, sweetie. Just a little tired. And grandma is still hanging in there, plus the hospital is still safely surrounded by lights and the National Guard."

As they sat down to eat, a semblance of normalcy settled over them, though it was fleeting. Silas, however, was oblivious to the food and the quiet conversation, despite Daniel having told him lunch was ready. He remained hunched over his makeshift desk, surrounded by books, his brow furrowed in intense concentration. He seemed frantic, almost desperate, his fingers flying across the brittle pages as though he was on the cusp of finding something monumental, something that might change everything.

The clatter of their lunch dishes was the loudest sound in there, a brief, domestic rhythm in their otherwise extraordinary new reality. Rose was helping Sarah stack the bowls while Daniel wiped down the small table, and Lily swept up the floor. Suddenly, a deafening crash erupted from Silas's corner, followed by a triumphant roar. They all jumped, their nerves frayed, their heads snapping toward him. Silas stood amidst a chaotic sprawl of books and scattered papers, his eyes wide and burning with a feverish intensity.

"I think I've figured it out!" he shouted, his voice hoarse with excitement and exhaustion. He didn't wait for a response, already diving into a rapid explanation. "The central core is believed to be a nexus of immense power," he explained, pointing frantically to an intricate diagram in one of the texts. "It's said to be a portal that allows these creatures to enter our world. No one knows its true age, but it's thought to be centuries old. Legend has it that when the five points come together, the portal will open, and a cataclysmic battle will ensue. It's not just a conflict between good and evil, but a fight for the very survival of humanity. And... and it's the symbol from the house! The one in the attic, or maybe the basement. But it's definitely one of them, possibly even both."

He pushed a brittle page towards them, his finger tracing lines of elegant script. "Plus, I found this, which may explain why the prophecy is coming to light now, why everything is happening right now: '*When shadows dance, and truth takes flight, and eager eyes pierce through the night. Not mere of flesh, nor bound by time, two sisters walk a whispered rhyme. The guardians join them, by their side, a steadfast force, where destinies collide. When place and moment coalesce, what hidden power will then possess?*'"

Daniel, Sarah, and even the girls stared at the poem, their brows furrowed in confusion. "A whispered rhyme?" Sarah echoed, bewildered. "What does that even mean?"

"And 'eager eyes pierce through the night'?" Daniel added, looking at Silas. "Are those... their eyes? The creatures?"

Silas nodded vigorously, barely containing his excitement. "Precisely! The creatures, watching, waiting for the alignment. And the two sisters can only be Lily and Rose!" His gaze swept over their daughters, who looked back with wide, uncertain eyes. "And the guardians join them by their side... it has to be us. But in particular, I think it means you, Daniel! The house belonged to your family, your lineage connects to this place. You're the one. And the hidden power that will then possess... it must be Morpheus, or whatever power he unleashes. Or possibly it refers to the girl's powers. I'm not sure which."

He slammed his hand on the table, rattling the dishes they'd just cleared. "That vortex! That blinding light that swept us away! It wasn't just a trip; it was a confirmation!

Lily and Rose are the key to stopping Morpheus for good!" He paused, his rapid breathing filling the small room. "Now how, I'm not entirely sure just yet. I don't know how their hidden power works, or how to fully wield it, but we have to trust that when the time comes, when *place and moment coalesce*, we will figure it out. We have to."

Chapter 23:

Sleep became a luxury the family could no longer afford, only snatching brief, fitful periods of rest throughout the long, anxious day. Even then, slumber was shallow, haunted by fragmented images of shimmering voids and booming voices. While Sarah held the girls close, trying to soothe them with hushed words and gentle touches, Silas and Daniel huddled over the scattered texts and hastily drawn diagrams, their voices low but taut with frustration, desperately trying to work out a plan for their return home and, more terrifyingly, how to close the newly identified nexus.

"It all points to the house," Silas muttered, tracing a complex symbol on a grimy page. "The central core, the five points... it has to be connected."

"But how do we close it?" Daniel countered, running a hand through his hair. "We know it's a portal, we know it's unleashing these things, but there's nothing here about a kill switch or a reverse spell. We're just supposed to... what, stand there and yell at it?" His voice was laced with an edge of panic. "And what about the creatures? We can't just waltz in. We need a way to protect the girls, protect ourselves, if we're going to try and do this." Frustration mounted with each unanswered question, each dead end in the cryptic pages. The weight of their impossible task pressed down on them, heavy and suffocating.

Silas slammed a fist lightly on the table, stirring up dust. "No, we can't just yell," he retorted, his voice tight with his own mounting frustration. "There has to be a counter-ritual, a method of sealing it. These texts speak of ancient wards, of closing pathways. It's not about brute force; it's about understanding the source of the power. The portal opened because the five points came together, and that poem implies it was a culmination of events, of people. So, logically, reversing that might be possible. We need to find the specific rituals, the specific energies that contain or negate it. As for the creatures, we can't avoid them entirely, but we can strategize. We use the knowledge we gain here to create a diversion, a temporary barrier, something to buy us time to perform whatever is necessary at that nexus point. It's the only way."

Frustration gnawed at them, a constant, dull ache beneath the surface of their desperate determination. Pages blurred before Silas's eyes, his fingers smudging dust on the pages as he flipped through diagram after diagram, cryptic inscription after cryptic inscription. Daniel, meanwhile, ran a hand through his hair, his gaze sweeping over the same texts Silas had just dismissed, then back to his friend, a silent plea for a breakthrough. The cabin was alive with their restless energy, each man consumed by the urgency of their task.

"There has to be something!" Daniel muttered, shoving a book aside. "A specific sign, a keyword, anything to tell us how to counter this. It's too abstract!"

Silas, mid-sentence in a latin tongue, suddenly froze. His eyes widened, a flicker of something similar to desperate hope replacing the frantic concentration. He looked up, not at Daniel, but towards the corner where Lily and Rose were gazing out the window.

"Lily," he breathed, the name a revelation. "The book Lily found at that abandoned house. The one with the strange symbols and diagrams." He scrambled through a pile of discarded volumes, pulling out a plain, leather-bound book that looked innocuous amidst the more ornate texts. "She... she reacted to this book. She saw something, felt something. She was able to read it."

Daniel's face hardened instantly. "No," he stated, his voice flat and resolute. "Absolutely not, Silas. You saw how she reacted last time. You felt the energy. I will not subject her to that book ever again. She's a child, not some kind of mystical translator. Besides, for all we know, that's what started this damn thing!" His protective instincts flared, pushing back against even the faintest suggestion of exposing Lily to that chilling presence again.

Silas's shoulders slumped, but his gaze remained fixed on the book, a desperate yearning in his eyes. "Daniel, please. We are out of time. How much longer can we continue like this? Fighting creatures at night, always on guard, eating little, and sleeping even less? We are grasping at straws here. This might be it. The missing piece. The central core, the five points, the portal... the answer has to be in here. We don't have another option. We have to try. Just... just ask her to look at it one more time. We'll be right here with her."

Daniel's jaw tightened, his gaze sweeping from Silas's pleading face to the innocent figures of his daughters. The conflict raged within him: the overwhelming need to protect them against the terrifying, impossible odds of their survival. With a heavy sigh, a silent acknowledgment of the desperate situation they were in, he finally relented. "Alright," he conceded, his voice low, "but if she shows any sign of distress, any at all, we stop. Understood?"

Silas nodded, already turning towards Lily, the ancient book held carefully in his trembling hands. "Lily," he began, his voice soft, almost pleading. "I know this is a big ask, and I know what happened the last time you touched this book. But we... we think this might hold the answer to closing the portal, to stopping all of this." He extended the book towards her. "Would you be willing to look at it once more? To see if you can understand anything?"

Lily looked at the book, then at her parents, her small face etched with a mixture of apprehension and a budding sense of importance. She remembered the strange energy that had pulsed from it, the unsettling hum that had driven her curiosity. But she also remembered the distinct feeling that it was important, that it held secrets meant for her eyes. She hesitated for a long moment, the cabin silent around them, every eye fixed on her. Finally, with a determined nod, she reached out and took the book.

Settling down on the rug, the book open on her lap, her small fingers tracing the bizarre symbols and intricate diagrams. Her brow furrowed in concentration, her bright eyes moving slowly across the page, seemingly absorbing the archaic script that was utterly foreign to the rest of them. Minutes stretched into what felt like an eternity, the adults watching with bated breath, hardly daring to breathe. Rose watched her with curiosity. Then an hour later, a subtle change came over Lily's face. Her brow smoothed, and a faint, knowing smile began to spread across her lips. She looked up, her gaze bright and clear, first at Silas, then at her parents.

"I know what to do," she announced, her voice quiet but firm, a ripple of astonishment and relief washing over the small group.

With her revelation, a plan began to form, piece by agonizing piece. They would head back to their house, the place where this nightmare had begun, the following day. Since nightfall was already upon them, casting long, hungry shadows across the room, it made any immediate journey impossible and far too dangerous. The last of their precious gasoline had been carefully poured into the generator, its low thrum now a vital, comforting sound in the enveloping darkness. They could only hope it would hold through the long, anxious hours of the night.

The night crawled by in a torturous rhythm of thundering roars from the creatures, desperate to break through the perimeter. Their guttural snarls and unearthly shrieks tore through the walls of the lodge, making any semblance of rest useless. Sleep was impossible amidst the cacophony outside, and the worry about what tomorrow would bring. They took turns standing guard, their eyes burning with exhaustion. Each shadow seemed to lengthen, each terrifying sound sending a jolt of adrenaline through their weary bodies.

Through the grimy windowpanes, they could glimpse the grotesque silhouettes of the creatures moving on the perimeter, their forms indistinct but undeniably present. Each passing hour felt like an eternity, the minutes ticking by with agonizing slowness. It was only a few more hours until dawn, a sliver of hope on the horizon, but the immediate concern was whether the generator, their lifeline to a semblance of safety, would hold. They listened to its steady thrum, silently praying it would endure just a little longer, just until the sun brought with it the light they so desperately needed to begin their perilous journey home.

As Daniel took watch with only two hours to go, the generator coughed once. Not the stuttering gasp of a machine out of fuel, but a sharp, final choke, followed by an ominous silence. The lodge plunged into darkness, the sudden absence of the thrumming engine deafening in its void. Before any of them could even register the catastrophic failure, the thundering roars outside intensified, becoming closer.

Hundreds of them. They were everywhere. The perimeter they'd relied on vanished as the creatures, no longer held back by the light and noise, surged forward. Glass shattered as grotesque limbs tore through windows, and splintering wood groaned under the force of their assault. Panic threatened to overwhelm them, but then, a blinding flash of light erupted from Lily, radiating outward in a powerful pulse. The wave of energy slammed into the creatures, not destroying them, but momentarily staggering them, pushing them back from the cabin walls with an unseen force.

"Flashlights! Weapons! Now!" Daniel yelled, his voice raw with urgency. Sarah and Rose scrambled for the flashlights, their beams cutting frantic arcs through the chaotic darkness, momentarily disorienting the advancing horde. Silas grabbed the axe they'd used for firewood, its dull gleam reflecting the flickering light coming off of Lily. Daniel snatched up the fireplace poker, its weight a cold comfort in his hands.

But Lily's power, while helpful, was clearly a strain. Her small body trembled with the effort, the light flickering precariously around her. She wasn't sure it would last. Rose, wide-eyed, clung to her mother's leg, both of them aiming their flashlights at the shadowy forms clawing at the windows, their narrow beams doing little to deter the sheer numbers. Silas, axe swinging wildly, was quickly becoming overwhelmed, a snarl of grotesque faces pressing in on him from all sides. Just as a monstrous claw reached for his throat, Lily, with a guttural cry of effort, shot another blinding flash of light directly at his attackers, forcing them back just enough for Silas to gasp for air and recover his stance.

Daniel swung the poker in a desperate arc at the creatures surrounding him, but there were too many. He stumbled, falling to one knee as a creature lunged for him with its snapping teeth and razor sharp claws. Sarah, seeing her husband's imminent danger, didn't hesitate. With a scream, she abandoned her position, thrusting Rose behind Lily. She plunged into the mix, swinging her heavy flashlight like a club. She slammed it into the head of the creature attacking Daniel, forcing it back, but instantly putting herself at terrifying risk as new horrors turned their attention to her. It was a fight for every inch, a desperate struggle against an unrelenting, monstrous wave. Each second stretched into an eternity, the chilling certainty of their impending doom hanging heavy in the air. Dawn was still hours away, and the terrifying truth was stark: they could all perish at any moment.

The battle raged on, a chaotic symphony of snarls, desperate shouts, and the sickening thud of impacts. Daniel, his breath ragged, managed to regain his footing, swinging the fireplace poker at the neverending sea of creatures. Sarah, bruised but unyielding, moved with grim determination, her flashlight a crude but effective weapon. They fought back-to-back, a desperate defense against the tide of creatures. Rose remained pressed against Lily, her small hand clutching the flashlight, its beam a meager shield against the overwhelming darkness. Lilly continued to radiate her light, her face a mask of intense concentration, but the effort was visibly draining her. Each flicker of her power, each desperate swing of a weapon, was a stark reminder of their grim reality. They were holding out, but they weren't sure how much longer any of them could last. The thought of dawn, once a distant promise, now felt like an impossible dream.

With their hope waning, the group was dealt another blow. Rose's flashlight beam burnt out, plunging her immediate vicinity into terrifying darkness. With a piercing scream, she instinctively grabbed Lily's hand, her small fingers clutching desperately to her sister's. A gasp escaped Lily's lips as a surge of energy, far beyond her individual capacity, erupted from their joined hands. An immense, blinding wall of pure, vibrant light burst forth from the two girls, sweeping through the room and out into the terrifying night. The creatures, caught in its overwhelming brilliance, didn't just recoil; they disintegrated, dissolving into clouds of fine dust that vanished as quickly as they appeared.

Silence descended upon the cabin. The only sounds remaining were their own ragged, desperate breaths, echoing in the sudden void. Daniel, Sarah, and Silas stood amidst the dust-filled air, their bodies a tapestry of cuts, bruises, and exhaustion. Lily and Rose sagged against each other, utterly drained, their earlier vibrant glow faded, leaving them pale and trembling. But they had all survived. For now.

Chapter 24:

With heavy hearts, they prepared for their departure. Every clang of steel as they secured their weapons, every rustle of their packs as they gathered supplies, echoed the finality of their decision. The ancient, whispered knowledge from their ethereal mentors, once a comforting presence, now felt like a crushing weight, a burden of impossible expectations. "Time to go," Silas murmured, his heart beating frantically.

Sarah adjusted the worn strap of her pack. Her eyes flickered to her daughters. Lily was meticulously checking the laces of her younger sister's shoes, while Rose clutched to the straps of her own backpack, her eyes wide. "Are you sure we can win?" Sarah's question hung in the air, thick with desperation, yet tinged with a raw eagerness to just be done with it all.

"We have to," Daniel responded, his voice hoarse, "for our daughters." He didn't wait for an answer before moving towards the door. What remained of the cabin, their sanctuary that had barely survived last night's brutal battle, fell into an unsettling silence as they stepped out.

The world outside was a stark contrast to the fleeting calm they'd found within The Ironwood's battered walls. The sky, once a canvas of blue, now bled an unnatural, pulsating red, casting an apocalyptic glow over everything. The air, heavy and stagnant, hummed with an eerie stillness that spoke of impending doom. The familiar forest, a place of solace and life, had been twisted into a desolate wasteland. Uprooted trees lay strewn about the ground, their roots clawing at the air, while others were snapped cleanly in half. It was a testament to the brutal passage of the creatures. Animal carcasses, or what was left of them, also lay scattered on the ground. Any animals that remained were surely hiding, having run away from the carnage.

Fear gnawed at their resolve, yet it was matched by a burning, almost desperate determination. They moved with agonizing caution, every shadow a potential threat, their senses screaming on high alert. Sarah and Lily both had to constantly keep a hold of Rose, pulling her gaze away from the gruesome sights. Despite this, her eyes, wide and glistening, were always on the verge of tears. The silence of the wasteland was punctuated only by the crunch of their shoes on debris and the ragged sound of their breathing. The battle for the very soul of the world had not merely begun; it was already consuming everything they knew, and now, it demanded one last, desperate stand.

As they ventured closer to the town, the true horror of the creatures' reign became sickeningly apparent. Homes were not merely damaged; they were pulverized, reduced to skeletal remains. The remnants of human civilization were scattered like macabre confetti across the barren landscape. The pervasive stench of decay and death, a cloying, putrid scent, clung to the air, assaulting their senses with every labored breath.

They had been walking for what felt like an eternity, barely talking to earth other at all, the desolate landscape offering no solace. Their destination, their home, was now only about a two-hour walk away. They could make it before sundown. This was it. Their final stand. They would either win and save all of humanity, or they would perish trying. There was no other option, no other future.

Sarah knelt, gathering her daughters into a tight embrace. "I'm so sorry for putting you through this," she whispered, her voice trembling slightly, the words catching in her throat.

Lily squeezed her mother's hand. "It's not your fault, Mom." Rose, still clinging to her, looked up into her eyes, and a silent, knowing glance passed between them.

Daniel knelt beside Sarah, pulling all three of them into his arms. "I'm so sorry, girls," he murmured, his voice thick with emotion. "I'm so sorry we couldn't keep you safe from this." He looked at Sarah, his eyes filled with a desperate tenderness. "I love you, more than anything. I just wanted you to know that"

Sarah leaned into him, her voice barely audible. "I love you too, Daniel. Always."

Daniel stood up, his face grim, as he kicked at a loose piece of rubble. "God, I wish we never moved into that house," he muttered, more to himself than to anyone else. He remembered the excitement, the new beginnings, the dreams they'd had for that place. Now, it was just another memory twisted by the nightmare.

Sarah rose, her arm still around Rose, and walked over to him. She placed a hand on his cheek, her touch gentle, a small comfort in the vast desolation. "I know," she said softly, her thumb tracing the line of his jaw. "But we're still alive, and we're together." He leaned into her touch, finding a flicker of strength in her unwavering presence. In this broken world, their bond was one of the few things that remained whole.

From a little ways off, Silas, who had been silently watching their exchange, his face unreadable, finally spoke. His voice, usually a low rumble, was strained. "I don't wish to break up this lovesfest, but…I'm glad I got to know each of you." He cleared his throat, before anyone could reply, "But I think we best get moving." The words hung in the air, an unwelcome reminder of the grim reality that awaited them. The battle for existence, terrifying and absolute, pulsed just beyond the horizon.

Before they could leave, Rose tugged on her mother's shirt. "Mama," she whispered, "I need to go to the bathroom."

Sarah exchanged a glance with Daniel. They were already pushing for time, but Rose's needs couldn't be ignored. "Alright, sweetie. Lily, can you take her behind that big oak? Stay where you can see us, but make sure Rose gets some privacy. I'll get us something to snack on out of my pack for while we walk"

Lily nodded, taking Rose's hand. "Come on." They moved off into the sparse, broken woods, Lily scanning their surroundings nervously as Rose crouched behind the gnarled trunk.

Just as Rose finished, and Lily was about to call out that they were done, a shimmering distortion appeared in the air directly in front of Rose. From it, Elias stepped forth, his usual charming demeanor unsettling amidst the devastation. A faint, knowing smile played on his lips, though his eyes seemed to hold a flicker of genuine concern as they landed on the small girl.

"My dear Rose," Elias purred, his voice like silk, "it seems your family is in quite a bit of danger. But fear not, for I do know how to save them." He spread his hands in a grand, inviting gesture, as if offering a tempting gift.

Rose stared at him, her small heart pounding. He was so real, yet Lily, just a few feet away, hadn't flinched. She glanced at her sister, then back at Elias, uncertainty clouding her tear-filled eyes. A part of her, the logical part, screamed that he was dangerous, a trick. But another part, the desperate part, yearned for his promise. She wanted to save her parents, and her sister, more than anything.

Just then, Sarah's voice, laced with impatience, echoed from their position. "Lily? Rose? What's taking so long? We need to get moving."

At the sound of Sarah's call, the charming smile on Elias's face flickered. He cast a brief look at Rose. "Remember what I said," Then with a final, almost imperceptible shake of his head, he shimmered and vanished, leaving only the unsettling silence of the ruined world in his wake. Rose blinked, wondering if she'd imagined him. She quickly grabbed Lily's hand, her own trembling, and pulled her back towards their parents, a secret weighing heavy in her small mind.

With Rose still clutching Lily's hand, the group set off once more, munching at the granola bars Sarah had handed out. "We'll need to keep our strength up," she had told them. Every step crunched on the desolate ground, the silence of the ruined world broken only by their breathing. The air grew colder, thick with a sense of foreboding that tightened around their chests. Their home, and the nexus located within, loomed closer with every weary stride.

Suddenly, a sharp rustling in a nearby bush tore through the eerie quiet. Every head snapped towards the sound, their hands instinctively flying to their weapons. Adrenaline, a constant companion, surged through their veins. Another creature? Another battle? They braced themselves, their stances tight with desperate readiness.

But it wasn't a creature.

A figure emerged from the foliage, stepping into the blood-red light. An older woman, her hair streaked with silver, her face etched with a familiar weariness, yet her eyes held an undeniable spark of determination.

"Mom?" Sarah gasped, her voice a strangled whisper. Tears welled instantly, blurring the devastated landscape, as the impossible reality of it settled like a stone in the pit of her stomach. She thought back to those long hours spent inside the hospital, waiting for her to wake up and be okay. "How are you here?"

Her mother, Martha, stepped closer, her gaze sweeping over them, lingering on the girls. "Sarah, you must turn back. You're in danger. You're all in danger." Her voice was urgent, filled with a desperate plea.

"Mom, we can't," Sarah insisted, shaking her head, the tears now flowing freely. "We have to do this. There's no one else." She hesitated a moment, "Mom, please forgive me for leaving you at the hospital," she begged, her eyes falling to her daughters, their innocent faces a mirror of the world they fought for.

Martha reached out, her hand hovering for a moment before dropping. "Of course, dear," she said, her voice softening, though the urgency in her eyes remained. "You had your own family to watch out for. But now it's my turn to watch out for my family. You have to turn back, Sarah. If you go through with this, you will all die. We will all die."

"No," Daniel stated firmly, his arm wrapping around Sarah, pulling her into his side. "Hold on a moment," he said, his voice laced with skepticism. "Martha, how are you even *here* right now? You were in the hospital, clinging to life only days ago. Forgive me, but how do we know you're real, and not some figment Morpheus has sent to stop us?"

"It doesn't matter how, Daniel. Not now. There are things you wouldn't understand, not yet. I just... I knew I had to be here. What matters is that you must turn back. Sarah, please listen," her mother pressed, her gaze fixed solely on her daughter, ignoring Daniel completely. "There are others on their way who can close the portal. Please, let them do it. Don't risk yourselves," she said, her gaze moving to Lily and Rose. "Please, don't risk my family, your family."

"Others?" Sarah asked, her mind reeling, trying to reconcile her mother's words with what they'd been told. "What others?"

"There are no others," Daniel countered, his voice sharp with conviction. "We would have been told that. They, God, the universe, whatever it was, didn't hesitate to tell us everything. Every single detail of the risks, the power. Why hold back on that one detail?"

Silas stepped forward then, his eyes narrowed, scrutinizing Martha with an intensity that seemed to pierce the very air around her. He said nothing, but his posture was that of a man poised to strike. Lily, sensing the shift in the adults' mood, pulled Rose even closer.

Ignoring the question, she looked once more into her daughter's eyes. "Sarah, please, you've always trusted me, so I'm asking you to trust me now." Her voice was softer, pleading, but Sarah's resolve seemed to harden with each word.

Martha, growing visibly frustrated by Sarah's silence, grabbed her by the arms, her grip surprisingly strong. "Now, Sarah, I want you to stop this now," she said angrily, her voice rising. "Don't you dare put those girls in danger. Do you hear me?" Her eyes, usually so loving, now burned with a chilling intensity.

Sarah stood there, frozen, tears rolling freely down her cheeks, unable to utter a single word in response. The accusations, the raw anger from a face she loved so dearly, paralyzed her.

Daniel quickly stepped in, his arm coming between Sarah and her mother, pulling Sarah gently but firmly away. "Stop this!" he shouted, his own anger flaring, directed at his mother-in-law. "I would not put my family in danger if there was any other way, and you know that. Or at least you should know that." His voice cracked with a desperate sincerity.

"Huh," Martha scoffed, a sneer twisting her lips. "I was right about you. Remember, Sarah, when I told you not to marry him? That he would ruin your life? Well, look around you now," she said, gesturing broadly at the devastated landscape, a cruel satisfaction in her tone.

Daniel's eyes widened, a dangerous glint entering them. "What?" he demanded, his voice low and dangerous. "You said that?"

"No! No, you didn't!" Sarah cried, finally finding her voice, regaining a sliver of her composure. She stepped forward, shaking her head vehemently. "My mother never said that! She loved Daniel. She thought he was the best thing that ever happened to me!"

"Who are you?" Daniel asked suspiciously, his stance shifting into a protective crouch. Silas, who had been watching with an unnerving stillness, subtly moved to position himself between the children and the figure claiming to be their grandmother. Lily, too, instinctively positioned Rose behind her. Their small group, all but a wide-eyed Rose, quickly reforming into a defensive fighting position.

Suddenly, the figure shifted, its form rippling like smoke. The familiar features of Sarah's mother melted away, replaced by a swirling, inky darkness that coalesced into a towering, shadowy figure. Its voice, no longer Martha's, boomed with malicious glee. "I thought you would listen to reason from someone you trusted, but you refuse!" it shouted, its form radiating malevolence. "You will fail today, and you will all die!" The shadowy entity erupted into a chilling, guttural laugh that echoed through the desolate landscape before it abruptly dissipated, vanishing into thin air as if it had never been there at all.

A heavy silence descended, broken only by the ragged breaths of the family. The stench of decay seemed to intensify in the void left by the creature.

"Are you okay?" Daniel asked, turning to Sarah, his voice thick with concern, his hands gently framing her face.

"Yeah, I think so," Sarah whispered, her eyes still wide, the shock slowly receding. "For a moment, I truly thought my mom..." Her voice trailed off, the horrifying deception still vivid in her mind.

"I know," he said softly, pulling her into a comforting embrace, holding her tight as if to ward off the lingering fear.

Silas, ever practical, his gaze already sweeping over their surroundings, broke the fragile moment. "I fear these visits will be more often, more intense, as we get closer to the nexus," he said, his voice grave. "We all need to be prepared for what else it might throw at us."

They all just stood there, the nexus a dark, irresistible pull. But each of them silently granted Sarah the time she needed to recover, knowing her mind was swirling with a frantic cascade of thoughts about her real mother. Was she truly okay in that hospital bed? Was she safe? Was she being taken care of? Was she still with them in this ravaged world, or had she crossed over into that eternal slumber, spared from this waking nightmare? The question hung heavy in the air, a silent burden carried by them all.

Chapter 25:

"Almost there," Daniel declared, his voice tight with a mixture of grim determination and frayed hope. He scanned the desolate horizon, his eyes sharp, searching for any lurking threats that might emerge from the twisted remnants of the forest. "Just over that hill," he pointed, his arm a rigid line against the unnaturally red sky. The air, thick with the stench of decay and the unsettling stillness, seemed to hum with anticipation. Every crunch of debris under their shoes, every ragged breath, amplified the dreadful suspense of their final approach.

They reached the hilltop, the wind whipping at their clothes, and collectively, they gasped. Below them, nestled in the valley, lay their home. Or rather, what remained of it. The house, once a haven of warmth and safety, now looked more like a skeletal ruin. The roof had a gaping hole in it. The porch railings, once sturdy and inviting, were torn away like brittle twigs. Nearly every window was shattered, leaving behind dark, empty eyes staring out at the ravaged world. The once vibrant garden was now just a patch of withered, unrecognizable flora, choked with debris.

Sarah's eyes immediately filled with tears, reflecting the shattered glass of her former life. "Daniel," she whispered, her voice cracking, "Our home." The words were a lament, a cry for all that was lost.

Daniel wrapped his arm around her, pulling her close, trying to offer comfort even as his own heart ached. This house wasn't just a building; it was generations of memories, of laughter, of life. It had been his family's anchor, their history etched into every beam. "It'll be okay," he said, the words feeling hollow even to his own ears. "It's just a house. We can rebuild. The important thing is that we're together." He squeezed her, desperately trying to reassure both her and himself.

Lily and Rose, sensing their mother's anguish, pressed against her, their small arms wrapping around her waist. They buried their faces into her side, a silent, powerful declaration that their home was wherever they were, as long as they were a family. It was a simple truth, a fragile light amidst the growing darkness.

Daniel then turned, his gaze sweeping over Silas. His voice, though weary, held a renewed edge of focus. "Alright," he began, his eyes fixed on the ruined structure below. "We're here. We made it. Now, tell me, what's the plan to close the nexus once we get inside?" The question hung in the air, cold and stark, reminding them that the emotional toll of their journey was secondary to the terrifying, urgent task that lay ahead.

The question, blunt and urgent, hung heavy in the air. "Lily," Silas pressed, turning to the girl, "You said you knew how to close it, didn't you?"

"I... I think I do," she replied, her voice barely a whisper. "But I can't be certain. If it's changed, if it's different somehow, then I won't know." The immense weight of their predicament, the sheer impossibility of success, seemed to crush every soul present.

It was Rose, small and seemingly fragile, who broke the tense silence. "I believe I know how to close it," she said, her voice surprisingly clear, though still a little small. Her declaration cut through the heavy atmosphere like a sharp stone.

Sarah's eyes, still glistening with unshed tears from seeing their ruined home, widened in surprise. She knelt down, bringing herself to her daughter's level. "How?" she asked, her voice barely a whisper, a desperate flicker of hope igniting in her chest.

"There's a key hidden in the basement," Rose replied, her gaze fixed on the shattered house. "It locks the portal, preventing anything from entering our world." She spoke with a certainty that belied her years, as if reciting something she had learned by heart.

A wave of unease washed over the group. Silas's eyes, usually so stoic, narrowed with suspicion. He had seen the nexus, felt its oppressive power, but had never perceived anything beyond the raw, chaotic energy. "How do you know all of this?" he asked, his voice low, tinged with a deep skepticism. "I saw the nexus, and I never saw any key."

"It's hidden," Rose explained patiently, as if it were obvious. "There's a secret tunnel going beneath the house, and inside is a chamber which can access the portal. It's not in the main part of the nexus."

"But how do you know about it?" Daniel pressed, his concern growing. His eyes darted to Sarah, then back to Rose. He desperately wanted to believe his daughter, but the information seemed too convenient, too specific, too... out of place. He worried that she might be leading them astray, or worse, that something had planted these ideas in her mind.

Rose hesitated, her gaze dropping to the ground. "Someone told me," she admitted, her voice barely audible.

"Who?" Sarah demanded, her own fear beginning to mix with a growing alarm.

Rose hesitated again, her small body tensing. She squeezed her eyes shut for a moment before forcing the words out. "It was Elias," she finally confessed, her voice a strained whisper.

Daniel's face instantly hardened, all traces of comfort vanishing. His jaw clenched. "When did you see Elias?" he asked, the question sharp, almost an accusation, the unsettling implications of her answer settling heavily on them all.

"When we stopped and I had to go to the bathroom," Rose began, her voice barely a whisper, her eyes fixed on the ground at her feet. She twisted her fingers together, a nervous habit. "And on my way back, he stopped me. He said he wanted to help, that he knows how to save us all." Her gaze flickered up to her parents, their faces a mixture of fear and desperation.

"How could you keep this from us?" Daniel demanded, his voice thick with a sudden anger. He took a step forward, his fists clenching at his sides. "Rose, you know how important it is to be honest, especially in times like these! We're fighting for everything, and you withhold crucial information?" His frustration was on edge, born from the immense pressure they were under and the lingering betrayal of the illusionary Martha.

Sarah, however, opted for a more gentle approach, placing herself between Daniel and Rose. "Rose, honey, it's okay," she said, her voice soft but firm. She reached out, gently cupping her daughter's tear-streaked cheek. "But we really want you to be able to trust us. We're a family now. And that means telling us things like this. We're not mad," she clarified, looking up at Daniel, who was still bristling. "It's just that we don't know anything about Elias.

He lied about Silas recommending him, remember? And now he's appearing to you, alone, whispering promises." Her eyes searched Rose's, trying to understand the depth of Elias's influence.

Lily, who had been listening quietly, her brow furrowed with concern, spoke up. "I have a bad feeling about Elias, Rose. I told you I didn't trust him when we were back at the hospital with Grandma. He just feels... wrong." Her older sister's words carried weight, echoing the unspoken anxieties of the adults.

Rose felt a fresh pang of guilt, a hot flush spreading across her cheeks. Her secret, so heavy just moments ago, now felt like a crushing burden. She knew she had made a mistake by keeping it to herself, by letting Elias's smooth words take root. "I'm sorry," she choked out, tears finally overflowing and streaming down her face. "I just didn't want to worry you. And he said it would keep us all safe. That's all I wanted," she replied, her voice dissolving into quiet sobs, her small shoulders shaking. All she had ever truly wished for was to have a family. And now that she had one, she wanted them to be safe and sound. That was what Elias had offered.

Daniel's anger was quickly extinguished by the sight of his daughter's genuine distress. His rigid posture softened, and he knelt down next to Sarah, pulling Rose gently into his arms. "Hey, hey, it's okay, Rose," he murmured, his voice now thick with tenderness. He held her close, stroking her hair, the warmth of his embrace a contrast to the cold fear that had gripped her. "It's okay. I'm sorry that I got so upset. We know you just want to keep us safe. We're not mad at you, sweetie. But we also want to keep you safe. So we just... we need to know everything. Okay?" He pressed a kiss to her tear-soaked hair.

Rose nodded, as she wiped the tears away with the back of her hand, trying to compose herself.

Sarah and Lily joined the embrace. Sarah wrapped her arms around both Rose and Daniel, and Lily squeezed in beside her sister. For a precious few moments, the family huddled together, a small island of comfort and shared love in the desolate landscape. The ruins of their home, the ever-present threat of the creatures, even the grim task ahead, faded into the background. All that mattered was this fragile circle of warmth, this unspoken promise to face whatever came, together.

The silence was eventually broken by Silas, who had patiently observed their reunion. His voice, though still grave, held a practical edge that cut through the lingering emotion. "I hate to break up this moment," he said, his gaze sweeping over the family, then towards the unnaturally red sky where the light, though distorted, was beginning to wane. "But we should get moving. We still have some daylight on our side, and we'll need every bit of it."

Daniel sighed dramatically, throwing his hands up. "Again, Silas? This is twice in one day now that you've ruined a perfectly good moment. Do you just have a radar that goes off whenever things get too sappy?"

Silas caught the slight upturn of Daniel's lips, a mischievous glint in his eyes, and a low chuckle rumbled in his chest. "Something like that. Now move it." Sarah and Lily, who had been trying to stifle their amusement, let out full-bodied laughs, while Rose, who had stopped crying, released a series of giggles.

As they all composed themselves and were preparing to start the trek down the hill, a low, guttural growl rumbled through the air, sending a shiver down their spines. It wasn't a lone sound; it was a chorus, growing louder with each passing second, accompanied by a tremor that intensified with alarming speed. The very ground beneath their feet began to shake, a violent thrumming that threatened to steal their balance. From the distorted, red-hued horizon, dark, monstrous forms emerged, their numbers horrifyingly plentiful. They were a grotesque tide, limbs twisting unnaturally, faces contorted into masks of pure malevolence. A deafening cacophony of roars, snarls, and unearthly cries ripped through the air, a chilling prelude to the desperate battle about to erupt.

The family, their faces now stark with alarm, instinctively stood their ground. The warmth of the shared joy and laughter they had just enjoyed, was instantly scattered, replaced by a dread that gripped their hearts. Every beat echoed like a drum in their ears, a frantic rhythm against the rising tide of danger.

"How is this happening?" Sarah's voice was a strained whisper, her gaze darting between the approaching horde and the still-light, albeit distorted, sky. "It's still daylight."

Silas, his eyes scanning the chaotic scene unfolding around them, offered the only explanation he had. "They're getting more brazen the closer we get to the nexus. That's the only thing I can figure."

The ground bucked and roared as the monstrous forms surged forward, their distorted shapes eclipsing the last vestiges of the unnaturally red daylight. Silas and Daniel didn't hesitate. With practiced efficiency, they moved as one, their axes a blur of glinting steel. Silas, a whirlwind of calculated strikes, met the charging beasts head-on, his broad-bladed weapon cleaving through corrupted flesh with brutal force. Daniel, lighter on his feet, danced around the edges of the horde, his axe a swift arc that targeted exposed joints and vulnerable throats, each swing precise and deadly. Grunts of effort mingled with the wet thuds of impact as the first of the creatures fell.

Sarah, surprisingly agile, brandished the heavy fireplace poker she'd snatched from the lodge. It wasn't an axe, but in her hands, it became an extension of her will. She swung it with desperate ferocity, a scream tearing from her throat as she sidestepped a lunging claw and slammed the blunt end into a creature's grotesque face. Though not designed for combat, the poker's solid weight and her raw determination sent several of the creatures stumbling back, buying precious seconds.

Behind them, Rose and Lily stood side-by-side, their hands clasped tightly between them. Their faces were etched with fierce concentration, eyes closed against the terrifying onslaught. A low hum began to emanate from their entwined figures, a vibration that grew steadily, vibrating through the very air. Then, with a gasp, they unleashed it. A blinding, pristine white light erupted from them, not as a beam, but as an expanding, shimmering wave. It pulsed outward, pushing back the darkness and the creatures within it. The monsters shrieked, their roars turning to agonized howls as the light touched them.

It was more than just light; it was a pure, cleansing force. Where it washed over the distorted forms, their unnatural bulk began to unravel. Their shadowy skin smoked and peeled, their twisted limbs spasmed, and their menacing roars dissolved into gurgling whimpers. The very air filled with the scent of ozone and decay. The ground, still shaking, vibrated with their dying throes. The waves of light continued, a relentless sea of destruction that consumed the horde. One by one, the creatures dissolved, melting into nothing more than wisps of black smoke that dissipated into the air.

When the last of the forms had vanished, leaving behind only the lingering smell and the thrum of the settling earth, the blinding light receded, pulling back into Rose and Lily. They swayed, pale and breathless, but their eyes, when they opened, held a new, quiet power. The field before them was eerily clear, save for the churned earth. The cacophony of snarls and roars was replaced by a ringing silence, broken only by the heavy breathing of the family, still gripping their makeshift weapons, staring at the empty space where terror had just stood.

As Sarah moved among them all, her hands deft and gentle as she checked for wounds, a sense of profound awe settled over the group. The sight of Rose and Lily, so young yet capable of such immense destruction and salvation, was still almost incomprehensible. Their earlier relief at surviving the creature onslaught was now tinged with a deeper, more complex gratitude for the girls' extraordinary abilities. They were invaluable, and would help them fight against the darkness.

While Sarah ministered to their scrapes and bruises, Silas, ever the pragmatist, brought them back to the grim reality of their mission. He once again went over the plan, his voice cutting through the lingering astonishment. "We have to shut the nexus down. And since we don't know if it's the portal in the basement, or the attic, or both, then we have to close them both. I say we divide up and the four of you head to the basement while I go to the attic." His gaze was firm, already picturing the swift, decisive action.

"No," Daniel's voice was unyielding, a rare sternness in his tone. He met Silas's gaze directly. "We are safer together. We are not dividing up. We will proceed as planned. We will close up the one in the basement and then we will all go to the attic."

"I have to agree with Daniel," Sarah interjected, her voice calmer but equally resolute. She gave Silas a look of understanding. "While I admire your tenacity to get this done quickly, I don't think it's going to be easy. And I'm afraid we would be setting ourselves up by trying to divide and conquer. There's safety in numbers after all. Besides, isn't Lily the one who knows how to close it?" Her gaze flickered to Rose and Lily, a silent reinforcement of her point; keeping their most powerful asset protected and together was paramount.

"Yea, you're right," Silas conceded, a flicker of something almost like exasperation crossing his face, quickly replaced by resignation. "After all, the girls are the chosen ones," he said, making exaggerated finger quotes that earned a small giggle from Rose. "We'll do it your way. We better get going."

"Agreed," Sarah replied, the awe of the girls' power still resonating within her, yet focused on the task ahead. "The sooner we get this done, the sooner we can get back to normal. If there is such a thing as normal anymore." Her voice held a note of weary hope, a wish for a return to the simplicity they had lost.

"Yes," Daniel echoed, his gaze finding Sarah's, a silent promise passing between them. "Let's go home." The words hung in the air, a powerful motivation that propelled them forward, away from the ravaged earth and towards the daunting task that lay ahead.

Chapter 26:

The group moved with a cautious determination, their steps steady and deliberate as they began their descent down the hill. Every rustle in the trees, every shifting shadow, drew their immediate attention. Each of them remained hyper-vigilant, their senses acutely tuned to the possibility of more creatures intent on stopping them from reaching their destination. The silence around them, punctuated only by their footsteps, was a stark contrast to the chaos they had just escaped. Slowly, carefully, they rounded the final bend, revealing the familiar silhouette of their home. They walked around to the front, their pace slowing to an almost imperceptible crawl as the full extent of the devastation became apparent.

One by one, their steps faltered until they all stood still, a collective gasp catching in their throats. They simply stared.

The house was an unsightly parody of their memories, a monument to the chaos that had erupted in their absence. The sturdy front door, once a welcoming barrier, had been ripped from its hinges and flung wide, revealing a gaping maw of darkness. Windows, which had once offered glimpses of the cozy interior, were now shattered shards, glittering like malevolent eyes in the fading, blood-red light. The porch railings, meticulously crafted years ago, lay splintered and twisted. Through the gaping openings, they could discern their belongings scattered about. The overturned furniture and personal mementos, all tossed and mangled as though a miniature tornado had ripped through the very heart of their home. They each felt a pang of sorrow for the lost comforts, a deep ache for the normalcy that had been so violently stripped away, though they all knew, deep down, that material items were ultimately replaceable. It was family that mattered.

They stood there steeling themselves, preparing to take that first, daunting step up onto the ravaged porch, when a sharp, piercing scream tore through the air. It was a sound that transcended mere noise; it was pure, unadulterated terror, laced with an agony that clawed at their very souls. Reflexively, they clapped their hands over their ears, the sound resonating not just in their eardrums but deep within their bones.

The chilling scream echoed through the shattered windows, bouncing off the ravaged walls, creating a haunting, layered melody of despair that sent icy shivers down their spines. Despite the paralyzing fear that threatened to grip them, a cold resolve settled over them. They understood, with a clarity that stung, that they had no choice. This was their mission, their undeniable destiny. With hands that trembled only slightly, they made their way onto the porch. Every footfall crunching on broken glass, as they stepped into the ruined house.

The interior was a scene of utter, senseless devastation. Lamps had been shattered, and picture frames lay smashed on the floor. Broken glass crunched beneath their feet with every tentative step, each sound a jarring reminder of the violence that had transpired. A thick, unsettling layer of dust coated everything, a shroud over what was once a vibrant home. The air itself felt heavy, oppressive, laden with a sickly sweet, metallic scent that made their stomachs churn and their throats tighten with revulsion. It was worse than the smell of decay, something utterly unnatural. As they ventured deeper into the house, their footsteps echoing in the oppressive silence, the screams that had drawn them in grew louder, more frantic, a terrifying beacon guiding them further into their nightmare.

Finally, they reached the true heart of the terror, the undeniable source of the screams. In what had once been the spacious dining room, directly over the scorched remains of their family hearth, a dark, swirling vortex pulsed with sinister, malevolent energy. It writhed and heaved like a living wound, a gaping maw of nothingness that tore at the fabric of reality. The screams didn't just emanate from it; they *were* it, the agonizing cries of countless souls, twisted and tormented, trapped within its horrifying grasp, their despair echoing through the very air.

Daniel, his jaw set with grim resolve, stepped forward, his eyes fixed on the abominable gateway. The fear was still there, a knot in his stomach, but it was overshadowed by a fierce, protective fury. "This ends now," he declared, his voice cutting through the demonic wails with his words of defiance. With a practiced motion, he drew his axe, the familiar weight of the hilt a small comfort in the overwhelming chaos.

With a battle cry that echoed his internal resolve, he charged towards the vortex, his blade raised high, a silver arc against the swirling darkness. From within the maelstrom, shadowy, skeletal demons lashed out with fiery tendrils, their desperate attempts to escape hindered by the collapsing reality around them. But Daniel was a blur of motion, his axe a swift, unyielding shield, dodging their attacks with surprising skill and unwavering determination. He ducked under a fiery whip, spun, and plunged his blade into the insubstantial form of a demon, watching it dissipate with a hiss of dark energy.

Hot on his heels, Sarah and Silas joined the fray, their weapons clashing against the encroaching demonic forces with a desperate ferocity. Silas used his axe to carve a path through the lesser demons attempting to flank Daniel, each swing a testament to his strength and unyielding hope. Sarah, with her fireplace poker, became a whirlwind of furious strikes, her smaller frame belying the power behind her blows as she dodged, thrust, and batted away the ethereal threats, protecting both their flanks.

Meanwhile, behind them, Lily and Rose stood side-by-side once more, their hands clasped tight, their faces a mask of intense concentration. The air around them began to crackle and hum with raw power as they channeled their combined energies. A pulsating barrier of pure, shimmering light erupted from them, not only repelling the spectral attackers but also containing the vortex itself, keeping the demons from escaping the volatile, self-destructing portal. The light pulsed, pushing the encroaching darkness back, sealing the abominations within their own dying dimension.

The house shuddered violently, groaning as if in agony, with the sheer force of their clash. Plaster rained down, timbers groaned, and the screams from the vortex grew even louder, more desperate, a final, terrifying crescendo of dying agony. But the group refused to give up. They fought with every ounce of strength they possessed, their determination fueled by the chilling knowledge that the fate of humanity, of their very world, hung in the delicate balance of this desperate moment.

It took only mere minutes, though it felt like an eternity, before the last of the demons, trapped and consumed by the girls' radiating power, were utterly defeated. With a final, agonizing shriek that ripped through the air, the vortex began to fade, its sinister, churning energy dissipating into wisps of dark, foul-smelling smoke that vanished as quickly as they appeared. The terrifying screams slowly subsided, replaced by an eerie sense of peace that settled over the ruined house like a blessing.

The group stood amidst the devastation, their bodies utterly exhausted, muscles screaming with protest, and lungs burning from the exertion. Yet, despite the physical toll, their spirits were undeniably triumphant. They had won another harrowing battle, secured a temporary reprieve, but the heavy silence that now filled the house was a constant reminder that it was far from over. They still had to navigate their way through the house to reach the nexus in the basement, and a chilling uncertainty lingered: they had no idea what more dangers, what other abominations, awaited them in the shadows below.

Their heavy breathing filled the stillness, punctuated by the faint creak of the ruined house settling around them. The air, though no longer thick with the stench of demonic energy, still carried the faint, sickly sweet scent of decay, a grim reminder of their immediate past. The portal in the living room might have been quelled, but they knew the true source, the heart of the incursion, lay elsewhere. With grim determination etched on their faces, they turned towards the basement stairs.

As they descended downwards, each step a conscious effort, their footsteps echoed ominously through the damp, musty air. The narrow wooden stairs, groaning under their combined weight, seemed to stretch endlessly into the gloom below. A pervasive, cold draft swept up from the depths, an unnatural chill that bit through their clothes and sent shivers down their spines, a warning of the malevolence that awaited them.

The descent felt like an eternity, each step bringing them deeper into the earth's embrace and closer to the source of their torment. Finally, their feet met the cold tiles of the basement floor. The oppressive atmosphere intensified, pressing in on them from all sides. Without a word, their eyes met, a shared understanding passing between them. They made their way directly towards the secret room which Silas had earlier discovered. The hidden chamber he'd stumbled upon during his initial exploration of the home.

As they stepped through the doorway, the air within immediately became thick and tangible, crackling with an almost eerie electric intensity. The room was not merely adorned; it was filled, from floor to ceiling, with strange, demonic symbols, painted in what looked disturbingly like dried blood, pulsing with a dark, almost hypnotic rhythm. The very air around them was pulsating with a sinister energy, a low thrum that vibrated through their bones, making their teeth ache. And in the very center of the room, suspended above a swirling pool of black liquid, lay the nexus. It was unmistakably similar to the one Lily had glimpsed in the attic—a churning, kaleidoscopic tear in reality, bleeding dark energy into their world. This was it. This was the true, malevolent source of the demonic invasion, the open wound through which the horrors poured. And the future of humanity, a fragile, desperate hope, now rested entirely on their ability to close it up, to sever this corrupted connection once and for all.

As they drew closer, the raw power emanating from it grew stronger, a dizzying surge that made the hairs on their arms stand on end and sent a strange resonance through their teeth. It felt like standing too close to a raging fire, but instead of heat, it radiated pure, unadulterated dread. A wave of apprehension washed over them, a chilling premonition of the unknown dangers that still lay ahead, but they pressed on, their determination an unyielding anchor in the face of such overwhelming odds.

"How do we do this?" Sarah's voice was barely a whisper, strained against the ominous hum of the nexus. Her gaze was fixed, not on the churning vortex itself, but on a peculiar, intricate symbol etched into the stone directly beneath it. Her mind reeling as to how she never knew this room existed in her own house, especially given the number of trips she's made to the basement. It seemed to pulse with a faint, internal light, distinct from the malevolent glow of the other carvings. When no one immediately responded, the silence amplifying her uncertainty, she glanced around at the group, her eyes meeting theirs. Each face reflected the same question, the same stark realization of their predicament.

Lily spoke first, her voice barely a whisper, her eyes wide with dawning dread. "It's changed. It doesn't look the way I remember it. I mean, the one from the attic. I'm sorry...but...I don't know how to close it."

"Oh boy," Silas admitted, a nervous laugh escaping him as he scratched the back of his neck, his usual pragmatic certainty faltering as he stared at the symbol before him. "She's right. It has changed." He paused for a moment before continuing, "You know, we were so focused on just getting here, on just *sealing* the portal, that... well, now here we are, and we have absolutely no idea how to actually do it. I have no idea how to do it." His confession hung in the air, a blunt admission of their shared, terrifying ignorance. The fate of their world hinged on closing this portal, and they stood before it, utterly without a plan.

The heavy silence stretched, thick with the weight of their uncertainty and the pulsing hum of the nexus. Then, a small, clear voice cut through the oppressive atmosphere.

"I know how," Rose declared, her finger, surprisingly steady, pointing not at the symbol, but at a loose stone nestled within the demonic carvings on the wall directly opposite the portal. Her small face was alight with sudden revelation, illuminating her features. "The tunnel Elias told me about," she explained, her gaze flicking between the stone and the bewildered faces of her family, clearly thrilled to finally have the answer they so desperately needed.

Before anyone else could react, Lily interjected, her voice a sharp, uncharacteristic snap that was a bit louder than she'd intended, echoing in the confined space. She instantly softened her tone, recognizing the hurt in her sister's sudden deflated expression. "Rose, no," she urged, her voice now a gentle plea, "We can't trust Elias. He's probably trying to lead us astray so we get into even more trouble and can't close the portal at all." Her logic was cold, sharp, and entirely based on their past, harrowing experiences with the often deceptive figure.

"Your sister is right," Daniel agreed, his voice firm, leaving no room for argument. He moved closer to Rose, placing a reassuring but resolute hand on her shoulder. "We're not going in there. None of us are. Is that understood?" His gaze swept across the faces of his daughters, then to Sarah and Silas, ensuring complete consensus. The last thing they needed was for someone to descend into a possibly booby-trapped tunnel at Elias's dubious suggestion.

Rose's excited expression crumbled instantly, her pride replaced by a sadness she couldn't quite explain, a mixture of disappointment and a deeper, unspoken fear. She looked around at the others, her hope dimming as she saw they all nodded in agreement with her father, their faces reflecting a shared concern for her impulsive suggestion. "But I don't want any of us to die," she whispered, her voice trembling, the raw vulnerability of her fear echoing in the damp confines of the basement. The thought of losing anyone, especially after they had just found each other, was unbearable.

Sarah knelt down in front of her, ignoring the discomfort of the cold, damp floor. Her eyes, filled with a deep, maternal love and a desperate hope, met Rose's tear-filled gaze. "Rose," she said gently as she pulled her daughter into a comforting hug. "We're not going to die today. You and your sister are going to grow up and live happy, beautiful lives. I promise." Sarah held her close for a moment longer, drawing strength from the small, trembling body, then pulled back just enough to look her directly in the eyes, praying with every fiber of her being that her own terror wouldn't betray the confidence she was desperately trying to project. "But your father is right," she continued, her voice softening further. "None of us are going in there. Okay?" It wasn't a question so much as a gentle, yet firm, demand.

Rose nodded, a small, shaky movement, understanding the gravity of their decision even if it stung her hopeful pride. She sniffled and wiped away her tears with the back of her hand, the movement quick and almost involuntary. But despite her agreement, her gaze was drawn, as if by an invisible thread, to the wall, her eyes lingering for just one more glance at the loose stone and the tantalizing, forbidden tunnel Elias had spoken of. The unshakeable conviction of his words still resonated in her young mind. *I know how to save your family*, he had said.

Silas had already shifted his focus back to the immediate problem which was the nexus. He leaned closer, his brow furrowed in concentration as he traced the intricate patterns etched into the stone around the shimmering tear in reality. "There's a groove here," he pointed out, his finger tracing a thin, almost imperceptible line that seemed to follow the curve of the nexus's energy. He pressed against a section of the stone, testing it. "Maybe if we slide it this way..." he mused aloud, the words hanging heavy in the charged air, suggesting a mechanism, a potential solution.

Daniel, however, remained rooted in caution, his natural inclination towards protection overriding any impulsive urge to act. He hesitated, his eyes narrowed as he considered Silas's suggestion, his gaze flicking from the groove to the terrifying, swirling vortex. "I don't know," he replied, his voice laced with apprehension. "That seems risky. We can't be sure it will close. And what if it..." His voice trailed off, the unspoken consequences too dire to voice fully, his imagination conjuring up the worst possible outcome.

Silas, catching Daniel's unspoken fear, finished the terrifying thought with a grim, knowing shake of his head. "Opens it up all the way and unleashes all of hell in here with us?" The question, though rhetorical, hung in the air, a chilling echo of the danger they faced. The basement, already oppressive, seemed to grow even colder, the hum of the nexus vibrating with renewed menace, as they stood at the cliff of a decision that could either save their world or condemn it.

As they stood transfixed, caught in the agonizing loop of their debate, the pulsating hum of the nexus filling the silence with its sinister rhythm, their hearts pounded with a frantic anticipation, each beat echoing the unspoken question of what to do next. The air in the cramped basement room grew impossibly thick, the oppressive energy of the rift pressing in on them, amplifying their anxiety. Just as the tension became almost unbearable, a blinding, searing light erupted, consuming the entire room in an instant.

Instinctively, they threw their arms up, shielding their eyes against the sudden, overwhelming brilliance, their vision momentarily obliterated.

Chapter 27

"What's happening?" Rose's voice, small and thin, was barely a whisper, trembling with a fear that echoed their collective dread. Her small body pressed against Lily's, seeking comfort in the unexpected terror.

"What is this?" Sarah shouted, her voice laced with confusion, a stark contrast to the sheer panic that tightened her throat. Her eyes, squeezed shut, still registered the painful afterimage of the light. The unexpected shift, the sudden, unknown variable, ripped through their fragile composure.

"I don't know," Daniel replied, his voice strained, filled with an uncharacteristic uncertainty that only deepened the fear in the small, illuminated space. His hand instinctively went to his axe, even though there was nothing tangible to fight, only blinding light and overwhelming energy.

Desperate to ensure her family was safe in the midst of the chaos, Sarah reached out with her free arm, her hand blindly sweeping through the light, searching frantically for her daughters. "Oh thank God," she breathed, a choked sob of relief escaping her lips as her fingers brushed against two small forms huddled together. She immediately pulled them closer, wrapping her arms protectively around them both, burying her face in their hair as if to shield them from the unknown.

Then, through the ringing in their ears and the disorienting glow, Silas's voice, a sudden spark of recognition, cut through the clamor. "We've seen this before," he remembered, the words carrying a strange mix of dread and dawning comprehension. Their memory, though hazy, was beginning to solidify.

When the blinding, overwhelming light finally began to recede, leaving behind shimmering afterimages on their retinas, the group slowly, tentatively, opened their eyes. The horrific, oppressive gloom of the basement was gone, replaced by the expansive, shimmering void. They found themselves standing not on cold, damp stones, but suspended once more within the very heart of the ethereal realm, bathed in a soft, ambient glow that emanated from no discernible source. All around them, myriad glowing beings, their forms shifting like nebulae, drifted silently, observing them with an ancient, knowing patience. A collective gasp of relief escaped them, a shared exhalation of breath that spoke of escaping terror and finding an unexpected, if not still bewildering, sanctuary.

A voice, as vast and ubiquitous as a whisper carried on an endless wind, yet clear and distinct, echoed through the boundless expanse of the ethereal realm. "Welcome back, guardians," it said, the words seemingly forming within their minds rather than reaching their ears, breaking the hushed, awe-struck silence that had fallen over them.

Silas, still reeling from the sudden displacement and the sight of the shimmering beings, had been about to voice his confusion, but the voice preempted him, speaking directly to his unspoken question. "Silas, you alone possess an extraordinary ability to decipher symbols and numbers," the voice replied, its tone imbued with a quiet authority. "Harness your intuition, and trust yourself. The fate of the world depends on it." As if on cue, a shimmering orb of pure light detached itself from the swirling mass of ethereal energy and drifted slowly, deliberately, towards him. It pulsed gently, then settled directly into his outstretched hand. As the light infused him, a complex array of symbols, equations, and arcane diagrams bloomed in his mind, arranging themselves into a coherent solution. His eyes widened, a look of profound understanding dawning on his face.

"I know how to close the portal!" he announced, his voice ringing with a newfound certainty and exhilaration, the weariness of the past hours momentarily forgotten. He gripped the orb, its light pulsing in sync with his revelation. "We must return."

The ethereal voice echoed once more, its intonation shifting, breaking their hopeful anticipation with a note of solemnity. "There's one final piece of information you must learn before you face the coming battle." The light around them seemed to dim slightly, the ethereal beings drawing closer, their collective gaze fixed upon the family, as if preparing to impart a truth that would change everything.

A new, heavy wave of dread washed over the group, eclipsing the fleeting hope and certainty that Silas's revelation had brought. The ethereal light around them, which had seemed so benign moments before, now felt oppressive, the silent, watchful beings suddenly less comforting and more ominous. "What else could there be?" Silas asked, his voice raw with disbelief and the rising tide of confusion. His earlier excitement at deciphering the portal's secret slightly evaporated, replaced by a weariness. Hadn't they faced enough already?

"You must hear the story of Morpheus," the voice declared, its tone deepening, resonating with a gravity that seemed to ripple through the very fabric of the ethereal realm. The name itself felt ancient, heavy with dark power. "To understand his motives and capabilities, you must be prepared." The words hung in the air, a chilling prophecy of an enemy far greater than they could have imagined.

The dread deepened, swiftly transforming back into a biting fear that clawed at their throats. Sarah instinctively pulled Rose and Lily even closer, pressing their small bodies against hers as if to shield them from the unspoken horrors the name *Morpheus* implied. Her eyes darted around the shimmering realm, searching for an answer, a glimpse of this new, unknown adversary. Daniel, his jaw tight, moved immediately to her side, his hand resting protectively on her back, his presence a silent comfort against the overwhelming wave of terror. The knowledge that there was yet more than they already knew, something they needed to be *prepared* for, was a crushing weight. They had faced demons and fought for their lives, but this...this new tale of Morpheus, suggested a deeper, more insidious evil which they were ill-equipped to confront.

The ethereal voice, now imbued with a chilling resonance, continued its narrative, painting a grim picture that only aided in deepening the family's dread. "Morpheus, a name synonymous with dreams and sleep, was anything but serene. He was a god who behaved more like a demon, a creature of darkness. And he had one singular, twisted goal: the complete and utter annihilation of humanity. His plan was meticulously crafted, a symphony of chaos and destruction spanning centuries, a testament to his ancient malice. He began not with overt force, but by subtly infiltrating the dreams of the most influential people across the globe. There, within the vulnerable landscapes of their subconscious minds, he sowed insidious seeds of doubt, rampant fear, and insatiable greed. He twisted their minds, warping their perceptions and corrupting their ambitions until they became his unwitting, and eventually his willing, pawns in a global game of destruction."

"With these powerful individuals—leaders, financiers, innovators—under his unseen control, he meticulously orchestrated a series of devastating events that plunged the world into an unprecedented era of turmoil. Wars erupted across continents, fueled by manufactured grievances and manipulated desires. Economies collapsed into ruin, sending billions into despair and starvation. And as if the world itself mourned, natural disasters struck with unprecedented ferocity, each catastrophe seemingly timed to maximize suffering and despair. The world was teetering on the very brink of absolute chaos, a broken, fractured husk of its former self, and Morpheus watched from the shadows with grim satisfaction, a twisted smile on his unseen face. His meticulously laid plan was unfolding perfectly, the unraveling of civilization a morbid masterpiece."

"Yet, even in the deepest despair, a glimmer of hope persisted. From the ashes of a broken world, a group of unlikely heroes, guided by their unwavering courage and unyielding determination, would inevitably emerge. They were the only ones who could possibly stand against Morpheus and his growing dark army, the last sentinels of light against his encroaching shadow. The fragile fate of humanity, poised precariously on the edge of oblivion, would ultimately rest entirely in their hands."

The final words hung in the shimmering air of the ethereal realm, a chilling echo of a dire prophecy. "Wait a moment," Daniel intervened, his voice cutting through the heavy atmosphere, a sudden jolt of realization flashing in his eyes. "Are you saying this has happened before?"

The ethereal voice resonated with a deep, ancient wisdom, answering Daniel's stunned question directly. "Yes. Just once, but he came perilously close to breaching the portals and unleashing utter devastation upon humanity. In the centuries since, he has been dormant, observing, learning. He has studied the weaknesses in his initial strategies, analyzed the moments of his defeat, and, most critically, he has identified the lineage of the guardians—those destined to oppose him. Thus, he has no doubt devised his plan with ruthless precision, accounting for every variable."

"When?" Silas asked, his voice a mix of academic intrigue and a deepening sense of dread. As a scholar of ancient lore and forgotten histories, the idea that such a monumental event had transpired without leaving a trace in any of his texts was deeply unsettling. "I've never read anything about something like this."

"It was many years ago," the voice answered, a subtle shift in its tone suggesting vast temporal distances. "A band of unlikely heroes uncovered the plot and managed to thwart it before widespread chaos could truly take hold. Back then, the human population was far more dispersed across the globe, living in smaller, more isolated communities. Unusual occurrences, like a blood-red sky or inexplicable shifts in weather, were often attributed to divine intervention, a warning from gods, or simply strange natural phenomena. The isolated nature of settlements also made it less likely that strange, otherworldly noises or localized outbreaks of demonic activity would attract undue attention from the wider world. The pieces of the puzzle were too scattered for humanity to grasp the full extent of the threat."

A sudden realization dawned on Daniel, his eyes widening as a fragmented family legend clicked into place. "My great- grandfather," he murmured, more a knowing statement of great understanding than a question. He had only heard the story his father told him recently, but the true significance had been lost to time and skepticism.

The voice confirmed, its presence affirming his thought. "Actually, a little farther back than even that, but yes. He was truly a hero in his time. It was thanks to his unwavering courage and the sacrifice of his loyal companions that the nexus was sealed and kept hidden from the eyes of both creatures and unsuspecting mortals for all these years. For many generations, the nexus was watched from afar by his descendants, a sacred trust passed down through the bloodline. Your bloodline. But as human civilizations grew and expanded, the world became smaller, less isolated. To better safeguard this crucial secret, your great-grandfather, a man of incredible foresight, built your very home around it. He ensured that his bloodline, your family, would forever keep it hidden away, protecting humanity from the horrors that lay beneath."

"But why such secrecy?" Silas asked, curiously.

The voice replied, "Humanity is already burdened with fear. Imagine the panic that would erupt if this secret were revealed. And then there's the inevitable wave of skeptics and thrill-seekers who would attempt to find and open the portal, oblivious to the grave danger they would pose to themselves and the entire world.'"

"But why is it opening *now*?" Daniel's voice was raw, laced with a mix of both frustration and despair. The revelation that their home was not merely a sanctuary but a centuries-old prison for an apocalyptic threat weighed heavily on him. "All I ever wanted was to keep my family safe, healthy, and happy." His gaze flickered towards Sarah, a silent, heartfelt apology in his eyes for having unwittingly dragged both her and their daughters into this unimaginable nightmare. The responsibility, the sheer, crushing weight of this inherited burden, threatened to overwhelm him.

Sarah gazed back at him, her heart aching with a fierce tenderness for the turmoil she saw wrestling in his eyes. She understood the depth of his desire to protect them, a desire she shared with every fiber of her being. There was no blame, only a shared fear and an unshakeable resolve that they would face this together.

"Man cannot escape his destiny, no matter how hard he tries," the ethereal voice replied, its tone resonating with the somber finality of an ancient truth. The profound words hung in the shimmering expanse of the realm, a stark reminder that some paths are predetermined, woven into the very fabric of existence like immutable threads in a cosmic tapestry. Even the most devout desires for a normal life, for peace and quiet, cannot always deflect the hand of fate.

The ethereal voice continued, its tone now tinged with a sharp urgency that pierced through the shimmering calm of the realm. "Morpheus is a master of deception. He will not confront you head-on in a way you expect. Instead, he will seek to sow discord among you, to unravel the very bonds that tie your family together. He will exploit your deepest fears, twisting your anxieties into paralyzing doubts, and he will relentlessly work to undermine your collective resolve. Do not let him succeed. He will tempt you with alluring visions of a future where humanity is saved, where peace reigns, but it will always come at a terrible, hidden cost. A cost you will only realize when it is too late. He will offer you power beyond measure, unimaginable wealth, and even the seductive promise of immortality. But remember, his promises are nothing more than shimmering lies, meticulously designed to lead you astray, to corrupt your hearts, and to divert you from your true purpose."

"Be vigilant at every moment. Trust your instincts. And most importantly, trust each other, for your unity is your greatest strength against his insidious schemes. Together, and only together, can you defeat Morpheus and save the world from utter annihilation."

The weight of the voice's warning settled heavily upon the group. They exchanged uneasy glances, their minds racing, replaying fragments of past encounters, conversations, and even their own fleeting thoughts. Had they already fallen prey to his influence? Daniel hesitantly broke the heavy silence, his voice barely above a whisper. "I think we've already heard some of these promises before." The admission hung in the air, a chilling confirmation of Morpheus' pervasive reach.

The voice replied, its presence affirming Daniel's suspicion, "Yes, we've been keeping a close eye on you, observing the subtle ways Morpheus has already begun his game. He is, as we warned, a master of disguise, appearing in many forms, whispering in many voices. And despite his cunning, you've done remarkably well to resist his influence thus far, often unknowingly. But understand the greatest challenges, the truest tests of your resolve and unity, still lie ahead."

Then, as the implication of Daniel's words and the voice's confirmation clicked into place, Sarah gasped, her eyes wide with a horrifying realization. "Elias," she breathed, the name a strangled exhalation of shock and betrayal. "Is that him?"

The voice confirmed, its tone laced with a solemn understanding, "No. Elias is not Morpheus himself, but he is more of a soldier for him, a loyal servant. He's been causing trouble from the start, a pawn in a much larger game, subtly working to undermine your efforts and lead you astray." After a brief pause, the voice continued, its tone softening with a discernible pride. "Lily, I'm so proud of you for seeing through his deception. Your abilities are truly extraordinary, and your intuition is a powerful shield. And Rose, I know you want to believe him, to trust in his words because he seemed to offer an answer, but it's crucial to resist that temptation. His guidance would lead you into greater peril, not salvation. Do you understand?"

Rose's small frame trembled slightly, her head bowed in a mixture of shame and disappointment. Her voice was barely audible as she replied,"Yes," the single word a fragile admission of her misguided trust.

"Listen to your family," the voice continued, its resonance deepening with emphasis. "Do not allow Morpheus, or anyone else, to separate you from your family. Your bond is your greatest defense, a fortress against his insidious influence. To break that bond is to leave yourselves vulnerable, exposed to his darkest manipulations. Do you understand?" The question hung in the shimmering air, a test of her comprehension.

Rose nodded, her head still bowed, but this time with a firm resolve that transcended her lingering sadness. Her eyes, brimming with unshed tears, reflected a newfound understanding of the stakes involved, of the true meaning of family in the face of such overwhelming evil.

The voice continued, its tone now directed equally at Daniel and Sarah, a clear mandate of their parental duty. "And Daniel and Sarah, remember what I said. Your children are central to this struggle. Keep them both safe, physically and spiritually, and whatever you do, always keep them in the light. It's now more important than ever."

"We understand," Daniel answered, his voice firm and unwavering, a renewed sense of purpose hardening his resolve. He looked at Sarah, then at his daughters, a silent promise passing between them all to face whatever lay ahead, together.

The revelation about Elias, and Morpheus's insidious nature, hung heavy in the ethereal air. Sarah, still reeling from the knowledge that she, too, had been a target of his manipulation, felt a cold dread trickle down her spine. The memory of the comforting, familiar voice, the loving gaze – all a cruel trick. Her own deep-seated longing for her mother had been turned against her. Her voice trembled, a fragile thread in the vast silence. "My mother..." she began, the words catching in her throat. "He came to me as my mother. Can you tell me if she...?" Her voice trailed off, unable to articulate the terrifying possibility that Morpheus had truly harmed or possessed one of the people she loved most.

The ethereal voice, understanding the unspoken fear, offered immediate reassurance. "Morpheus knew precisely how to exploit your vulnerabilities, Sarah. He seeks to break the spirit, to sow doubt where love resides. But do not worry, your mother is strong and resilient. Her spirit remains untainted, and she's waiting patiently for your return." The gentle certainty in its tone was a comfort to Sarah's tormented heart.

Tears streamed down her face, a wave of relief and gratitude, as she finally managed to choke out, "thank you." The words were barely audible, yet they carried the weight of a thousand unspoken prayers. Daniel and the girls immediately enveloped her in a collective embrace, offering both comfort for the fear she had just endured and a silent celebration of the hope restored. Lily and Rose held onto her tightly, their small hands conveying their own relief.

The voice, its presence now seeming to expand, filled the realm with its final, urgent pronouncements. "It is time. The moments for preparation are over; the hour for action has arrived. Silas, you now possess the knowledge and the power. You must close the nexus, severing this cancerous tie to the demonic realm. The others will aid you in keeping the creatures at bay. They will undoubtedly launch a furious, desperate assault to prevent the portal's closure. This is the day of the final battle, the culmination of generations of prophecy and protection. Do not fear, for you all have already shown your extraordinary strength and unwavering courage. Watch over each other, stand as one, and keep each other safe, for your unity is your ultimate weapon."

A blinding, all-encompassing light engulfed the group once more, and they felt a momentary, disorienting sensation of weightlessness, as if they were being drawn through a cosmic tunnel. When their vision finally cleared, the ethereal realm had vanished. They found themselves back in the damp, musty confines of the basement, the chilling cold draft a stark contrast to the warmth of the realm. The pulsating hum of the nexus filled the air, a physical presence just inches before them, its energy more menacing than ever.

Silas turned to them all, his gaze firm and resolute. The fear was gone, replaced by a fierce determination. "Let's do this," he declared, his voice ringing with conviction, ready to face their destiny.

He wasted no time, dropping to one knee before the ancient stone pedestal that cradled the swirling nexus. His hands, guided by the ethereal wisdom now flowing through him, hovered over its intricate, deeply carved patterns. The air around his fingertips crackled with latent energy.

Around him, a protective circle formed instinctively: Daniel and Sarah stood shoulder-to-shoulder, their stances wide, weapons gripped tightly. Daniel with his sturdy axe, and Sarah with her fireplace poker, were both ready for the inevitable onslaught. Behind them, Rose and Lily joined hands, their small figures a fragile, yet determined, line of defense, their combined magical potential simmering just beneath the surface.

Silas's mind raced, a whirlwind of arcane symbols, precise measurements, and intuitive leaps. The knowledge imparted by the ethereal beings had solidified into a clear, actionable plan. "Turn it clockwise," he muttered to himself, his voice barely audible over the growing cacophony of snarls, growls, and guttural howls that now echoed from beyond the room's entrance, signaling the imminent arrival of demonic forces. His eyes, intensely focused, scanned the complex carvings, identifying the specific mechanism. "Then, when I hear a click," he continued, a thread of concentration in his low tone, "then I slide it backwards into this groove."

He pressed down, his muscles straining against the immense, seemingly immovable weight of the ancient stone mechanism. The task was monumental, the stone resisting his efforts as if imbued with its own malevolent will. Daniel, seeing Silas's struggle, immediately moved to his side, placing his powerful hands next to Silas's. Their combined strength, a surge of raw human will against ancient magic, slowly began to yield results. With a groan of stone against stone, the mechanism began to turn, inch by agonizing inch. A moment later, a deep, resonant click reverberated through the basement. The first phase was complete. Now, all that was left was the final, critical step: to slide it into the designated groove.

As the nexus itself began to hum, its energy vibrating louder, the growls and howls from outside intensified into a frenzied chorus of bloodlust. The very air around them grew colder, rank with the stench of brimstone. "Get ready!" Daniel bellowed, his voice cutting through the rising commotion, his axe already raised defensively. "They're coming!" The thudding of heavy footsteps, the scrabble of claws on stone, and the guttural roars grew deafening, announcing the arrival of Morpheus's army. The door to the secret room would not hold for long.

They watched as the door splintered inward, creating a deafening crack. The creatures burst into the basement, a tide of monstrous forms, their twisted limbs and gnashing teeth filling the limited space. Their eyes, glowing with malevolent intent, immediately fixed on Silas, the one attempting to seal their gateway. The air filled with their guttural roars and the thunder of their heavy bodies hitting the floor.

They fought with a ferocious determination, their individual skills and abilities complementing each other perfectly in a desperate dance of survival. Lily and Rose, their small hands clasped tight, formed a shimmering shield of mystical energy, a pulsating barrier of light that pulsed and pushed back against the incoming horde. Their combined powers, a raw, untamed force, sizzled in the air, creating shimmering concussive blasts that held the creatures off just long enough for Daniel and Sarah to stay on their feet, as they took aim with their weapons.

Daniel was a whirlwind of motion, his axe deflecting claws and cleaving through shadowy forms with practiced precision. He moved with a primal ferocity, placing himself between the most aggressive demons and his family. Sarah wielded her poker with ruthless efficiency, hitting the creatures in their most vulnerable points. She covered Daniel's flanks, her movements fluid and deadly, ensuring neither of them was overwhelmed despite the sheer number of monstrous forms pouring into the room. The basement became a maelstrom of clashing steel, crackling magic, and the guttural cries of demons.

In the midst of the deafening chaos, with growls and roars echoing off the stone walls and the scent of ozone and brimstone stinging their nostrils, Silas bellowed over them, his voice strained with effort and triumph. "It's closed!" He slumped slightly, the massive stone mechanism having finally ground into its final resting place with a soft, final thud.

But the creatures, driven by primal rage and Morpheus's relentless will, didn't falter. Their red eyes still burned with hatred, their relentless assault showing no signs of surrendering, even with their portal severed. They were trapped, and they intended to take as many of their tormentors with them as possible. Seeing his vital task completed, Silas didn't hesitate. He scrambled to his feet, pulling an axe from his backpack. He immediately joined the fray, his own weapon now creating wide, sweeping arcs across the room, adding another layer of defense to the family's desperate stand.

The battle raged for what felt like an eternity, but slowly, inexorably, the tide began to turn. With the nexus sealed, the creatures seemed to lose some of their malevolent vitality, their attacks growing less coordinated, their movements more sluggish. Finally, with a collective, frustrated roar, the creatures began to retreat, their monstrous forms dissolving and fading into the deepest shadows of the basement, melting away like smoke until only the lingering stench of their presence remained.

Exhausted, battered, and bruised, the family collapsed to the ground, their bodies aching from the brutal ordeal. Every muscle screamed in protest, every breath was a conscious effort. Daniel and Sarah slumped against the wall, and Lily and Rose, their magic spent, lay huddled together. And Silas simply sat down, in the middle of the floor, where he had stood. They weren't sure if the battle was over, but for now, in the eerie silence of the basement, they had survived.

Chapter 28:

"I closed it, so they shouldn't have continued coming after us. This wasn't the right one," Silas muttered, his voice laced with a fresh wave of frustration and exhaustion as he stood over the now-sealed nexus in the basement. He ran a hand through his hair, shaking his head. "Or maybe we need to close both portals." The chilling implication hung in the air, that the valiant battle they just faced might have only been half the solution.

Exhausted, but with determination still burning in his eyes, Daniel pushed himself off the wall. "Well then," he replied, his voice a little hoarse but firm, "let's head to the attic." The attic. Another whispered family legend, more secrets that had been hidden in their home. The second portal, it would be there.

With a collective groan of aching muscles, the group began their slow ascent. Their footsteps, usually heavy and hurried, now echoed with a weary drag in the quiet house, each stair a small challenge. The stale, musty air of the basement slowly gave way to the scent of rotten flesh on the first floor. As they reached the hall leading to the second floor, a chilling, almost otherworldly sound caught their attention. It was a faint, harmonious hum, like a distant choir.

The hallway ahead was plunged into an unnatural darkness, deeper than any shadow. The only light emanated from the faint, ethereal glow of a figure emerging from the oppressive gloom. Its form was shifting and morphing before their startled eyes, a fluid dance of light and shadow, until it coalesced into a being of breathtaking beauty. It was an angel, clad in a flowing, pristine white dress that seemed woven from moonlight. Her hair, a cascade of pure gold, framed a face of serene perfection, and from her back unfurled magnificent, feathered wings that softly beat the air, stirring invisible currents.

"Welcome, my friends," she said, her voice a soothing melody that resonated with an impossible beauty, echoing in the confined space. "I've been waiting for you."

The group exchanged wary glances. Every instinct screamed caution. They had just fought demons; now, an angel? The voice was calming, almost hypnotic, but after Morpheus's previous deceptions, trust was a luxury they could not afford.

"What do you want?" Daniel asked, his voice steady despite the growing unease tightening in his gut. His hand instinctively grabbed ahold of his axe, a silent promise of protection for his family.

The angel's smile broadened, an elated expression that seemed to illuminate the dark hallway. Her eyes, pools of liquid gold, twinkled with a captivating, almost hypnotic light. "You have fulfilled your request as the guardians. The portal in the basement is sealed, and Morpheus has been contained. You may stop now, and return to your lives. The fight is over. For your heroism, for the courage you have shown in the face of such darkness, I have been granted permission to give each of you one thing, anything your heart desires." Her voice was a silken caress, each word a perfectly pitched note designed to soothe and entice.

She held out her delicate hands, and from their outstretched palms, shimmering visions began to manifest in the air before them, tailored precisely to their deepest, most private longings. Sarah saw a world utterly free from suffering, a vibrant tapestry of peace where no child cried from hunger and no soul knew despair. Daniel envisioned a relaxed, comfortable life, a tranquil existence where the greatest challenges were choosing what book to read or which movie to watch, with his family safe and utterly oblivious to the supernatural dangers that had just consumed their lives. Lily gasped as she saw herself exploring ancient ruins, discovering lost civilizations, her life a grand, unending adventure filled with wonder and discovery. And Rose, her small face alight with innocent longing, saw herself enveloped in the warm, loyal companionship of a gentle creature, a shaggy-haired dog with kind eyes, a friend who would never leave her side.

Then, the angel turned her golden gaze, fixing it solely on Silas, her eyes boring seemingly into his very soul, peeling back layers of ambition and unspoken dreams. "And you, Silas," she murmured, her voice now a conspiratorial whisper, woven with the irresistible promise of ultimate recognition. "Imagine the power you could wield, the ancient knowledge you could unlock, the secrets of the cosmos laid bare before you. You would be written about for generations to come, your name echoing through the records of history, remembered as the scholar who truly understood the universe. The notoriety, the accolades, the undeniable mark you could leave on the world... Didn't you always wish to be a best-selling author, to share your profound insights with all of humanity, to have your words shape the minds of millions?"

Silas' mind hesitated, racing with the dazzling possibilities the angel presented. The visions of fame, knowledge, and recognition shimmered enticingly, momentarily eclipsing the grim reality of their current predicament. For a fleeting second, the deepest, most secret desires of his heart warred with his newfound resolve. But then, as if an icy splash of water hit him, he remembered the ethereal voice's solemn warning: *Morpheus is a master of deception. He will tempt you with visions... his promises are lies.* He shook his head, the momentary weakness banished, his resolve firming like concrete. "No!" he declared, his voice ringing with renewed conviction. "We must close the nexus. Both of them. No matter what you offer."

The angel's smile, rather than faltering, widened, revealing a chilling edge that had been absent moments before. Her golden eyes, no longer twinkling kindly, held an unnerving intensity. "Oh, but you will," she purred, her voice losing some of its melodic sweetness, replaced by a subtle, almost imperceptible undertone of something ancient and predatory. "I know your weaknesses, your fears. I can offer you everything you've ever wanted, everything you truly crave, the deepest desires buried within your heart." Her gaze swept over each of them, as if cataloging their vulnerabilities.

"We won't fall for your tricks," Silas countered, his voice gaining strength, now filled with unwavering determination. He wouldn't be swayed.

"He's right," Daniel agreed, his initial awe and confusion finally giving way to a chilling clarity. The angel's perfect facade had cracked, and the underlying malevolence was now undeniable. He took a protective step forward, his hand still on his axe, and gave the angel a stern, accusatory look. "We know it's you, Morpheus."

The angel's golden eyes, however, did not even flicker toward Daniel. Her gaze remained fixed solely on Silas, completely ignoring Daniel's accusation as if he were a mere gnat buzzing in the air. Her expression softened once more, morphing into one of sympathetic understanding, a look designed to pierce through all defenses. "Silas," she whispered, her voice once again a gentle, compassionate melody, imbued with an irresistible sorrow. "Not even if you could be reunited with your wife, Emma?"

The name struck Silas like a physical blow. The air rushed from his lungs, and for a painful moment, the entire world seemed to shrink to that single, impossible question. Emma. His lost love, taken too soon. His breath hitched, and a raw, guttural sound escaped his lips. "Emma," he gasped, his feet moving before his mind could process, taking an involuntary step forward, drawn by the agonizing pull of a love he thought forever lost.

Daniel reacted instantly, his hand shooting out to grab Silas firmly by the arm, pulling him back from the ethereal figure. "No, you know this isn't true. It's another trick, Silas! Don't fall for it!" His voice was sharp, urgent, cutting through the angel's insidious whispers. He could see the yearning, the flicker of desperate hope in his friend's eyes, and he knew that look of pain could lead to their undoing.

Silas looked at Daniel, his eyes wide and watery, clouded with deep sorrow. "But my wife, Emma," he choked out, his voice a whisper of pure agony. "She's all I've ever wanted. Just to see her again, to hold her, to kiss her, to tell her… everything." The vision the angel had conjured, the mere mention of her name, had momentarily shattered his resolve, transporting him back to a grief he had long tried to bury.

Sarah, now fully snapped out of her own brief enchantment by the angel's temptations, stepped in to assist Daniel, placing a hand on Silas's shoulder. "Silas, no!" she almost screamed, her voice piercing the air with a desperate plea, trying to break him from the trance. "You know your wife is gone. Remember how he used my mother against me. He's twisting your pain, preying on your deepest sorrow! He's doing this because he knows that you are the one with the knowledge, the one who can help us stop him. We *need* you, Silas." Her words were a lifeline, anchoring him to the present, and back to their desperate fight.

Slowly, and begrudgingly, he broke through the fog of grief. Shaking his head, as if clearing cobwebs from his mind, Silas looked up at the radiant, yet now menacing, angel. The pain was still there, but clarity was returning. "No," he said, his voice gaining strength, stern and resolute. "It's not possible. Emma… she wouldn't want this. She wouldn't be part of *your* lies."

Amidst the swirling tension and the sharp exchange of words, Lily and Rose stood close, their small hands clasped even tighter. While the adults engaged in the verbal battle, the sisters remained acutely aware of the shifting energies in the hallway. Lily instinctively tightened her grip on Rose's hand as the angel's soothing facade cracked and her true malice began to show. Rose, though younger and perhaps less understanding of the nuanced deception, felt the distinct chill that accompanied the angel's darkening expression, her innocent eyes widening slightly as the beautiful features warped into something far more menacing. Their silence was not born of inaction, but of a quiet readiness, their combined magical power a shimmering, dormant force, waiting for the inevitable moment when they would be called upon again to defend their family.

The angel's beautiful face twisted, its features darkening instantly, the golden light in her eyes replaced by a cold, furious glint. Her voice lost its melodic quality, becoming sharper, colder, edged with pure contempt. "You're all foolish," she hissed, her wings flaring slightly, stirring the dust in the hallway. "You're throwing away your chance at a better life, at everything you truly desire. You choose suffering and destruction over paradise. Very well then. You have chosen your fate."

The angel's face, now fully contorted with malevolent fury, lost all semblance of beauty. Her eyes blazed with a terrifying, golden inferno as she raised a delicate hand. From her outstretched palm, a wave of suffocating darkness swept over them, not merely dimming the light but consuming it. The hallway, moments ago a familiar part of their home, was suddenly plunged into an oppressive void, filled with the disorienting, terrifying sound of howling winds, as if a storm of cosmic proportions raged within the confines of their house. The air grew heavy, thick with an almost physical dread that squeezed their lungs and stole their breath. The group struggled to resist the overwhelming, crushing force, their bodies trembling uncontrollably, their knees threatening to buckle under the unseen pressure. Fear, cold and insidious, snaked its way into their hearts.

Just as it seemed they were about to succumb, their spirits on the verge of breaking, a blinding, pure light erupted seemingly from nowhere, a beacon of defiant hope in the oppressive gloom. It pulsed with an almost divine warmth, pushing back against the encroaching darkness. The angel recoiled, hissing as if burned. The angelic disguise momentarily flickering to reveal glimpses of something far more grotesque beneath. Forced to step back, its form shimmering with frustration and pain.

"You've made your choice," she hissed, her voice no longer melodic but filled with unbridled rage and a chilling promise of retribution. "But you won't escape my wrath. This is only the beginning. You will mourn this day."

With a final, menacing glare that promised unimaginable suffering, her form dissolved into the deepest shadows of the hallway, vanishing as completely as she had appeared, leaving the group alone in the sudden silence. The oppressive darkness lifted, though the air still crackled with residual malevolence. They knew, with a certainty that chilled them to the bone, that this was merely a skirmish in a much larger war. The real battle would probably take place upstairs, in the attic. Morpheus would no doubt make it difficult for them. But for now, they had managed to resist Morpheus's insidious temptations, a small but vital victory.

From above, seemingly echoing from the very structure of the house, the ethereal voice could be heard, clear and resonant, its words a final, crucial instruction. "Remember, stay in the light. Avoid the dark at all costs."

As they huddled together in the dimly lit hallway, their flashlights casting eerie, dancing shadows that stretched and twisted with their every breath, the weight of the impending, final battle settled upon them. A collective gasp, sharp and sudden, escaped their lips as their flashlights, one by one, began to flicker erratically, their beams weakening, then dying completely with a soft, final click. The hallway was plunged into near-total darkness, a chilling realization compounded by the fading light filtering in from the few windows. The sun was setting, its last golden rays rapidly receding, and it would be utterly dark in only minutes.

"We have to stay in the light!" Lily cried out, her small voice trembling, a stark echo of the ethereal voice's recent warning. Rose let out a small, terrified whimper, her tiny body shaking uncontrollably against her mother's side. Sarah pulled both girls closer, enveloping them in a tight embrace, her own voice barely a whisper as she tried to soothe them. "It'll be okay. We'll be okay." But even as she spoke the comforting words, her eyes met Daniel's across the darkness, and a shared, unspoken truth passed between them. Fear was creeping into their hearts, threatening to extinguish their flickering hope. They were all battered and exhausted from the relentless assault in the basement, their muscles screaming, their minds weary, and the worst, they knew with grim certainty, was obviously yet to come.

Silas, fueled by a surge of frustration and adrenaline, let out a sharp grunt. His fist, still clutching his now-dead flashlight, slammed against the plaster wall beside him. The sudden, unexpected impact sent a jolt of fear through them all, a collective jump in the deepening gloom. But then, a wave of relief washed over them as, miraculously, the impact caused his flashlight to flicker back to life, its beam piercing the overwhelming darkness. "We're back in business," he announced, his voice gruff but laced with a renewed, if tired, determination, the words echoing through the sudden silence.

With a determined nod, Silas took the lead, illuminating the path ahead as he began to ascend the creaking staircase. Each step was a haunting reminder of the unknown dangers that undoubtedly awaited them on the upper floors. The silence of the old home, once comforting, was now punctuated only by the eerie creaks and groans of settling wood, the faint whisper of unseen currents, and the thumping of their own anxious hearts, all adding to the growing, almost unbearable tension.

A collective, shaky sigh of relief escaped their lips as they finally reached the second floor landing, a momentary respite from the oppressive gloom of the staircase. "Come on, let's go!" Daniel urged Silas, his voice barely above a whisper, recognizing the urgency of their mission. The stairs leading to the attic, and their ultimate destination, were at the very end of the long, shadowy hall, hidden behind a simple, unassuming white door. Its antique brass doorknob seemed to gleam faintly in the dim light filtering from Silas's flickering flashlight, almost as if calling out to them, beckoning them towards their destiny. Or was it, a chilling thought whispered in the back of Daniel's mind, beckoning them to their demise?

Shadows, distorted and grotesque, danced around them like malevolent spirits stirred by an unseen force, their unease amplified tenfold by the unnatural silence that had settled over the upper floor. Every familiar creak and groan of the old house seemed to have ceased, leaving only an ominous stillness that pressed in on their ears. The only sound that broke this eerie quiet was the ragged, panicked symphony of their own breathing.

Silas, his gaze fixed on the white door, slowly extended his hand. His fingers hovered just inches from the doorknob, the gateway to the next, crucial step of their fight. It was in that precise moment, just as his fingertips were about to make contact, that a chilling, high-pitched whirring noise echoed behind them, growing rapidly in intensity. It was a sound both alien and terrifying, like a thousand unseen gears grinding into motion, accompanied by a growing chill in the air. Turning as one to face the encroaching darkness behind them, they were instantly engulfed by a fresh wave of shadows. These were not mere absence of light, but tangible, terrifying forms twisting and writhing, coalescing into monstrous shapes from the periphery of their vision. With no other option, the attic, and the second nexus, would have to wait.

They immediately snapped into fighting stances, their hearts pounding a frantic rhythm against their ribs. This wasn't the brute force of the basement, but something more insidious. Silas and Daniel instinctively raced to the front, their bodies tense, braced for the onslaught of the swirling, formless demonic creatures that now filled the hallway. Daniel unleashed his raw strength, his axe a brutal extension of his will, its blows sending the shadowy monsters reeling, momentarily breaking their cohesion. Silas, his eyes narrowed with focused intensity, did his best to keep pace, his own axe flashing to shield Daniel's flanks, preventing any creature from getting behind their combined guard.

Sarah, no less formidable, wielded her fire poker. Her movements a blur of fierce determination. Every swing was a testament to her courage, and her maternal urge to protect her children. Her strikes were surprisingly effective against the ethereal forms, forcing them back with unexpected force. Behind the front line, Lily and Rose, their powers surging in the face of danger, erected a pulsating, protective barrier around them all. It shimmered with a soft, internal light, absorbing the attempts of the creatures to claw and bite their way through, their combined will holding the defense firm.

The confined space of the hallway made the battle a desperate, claustrophobic struggle. The air grew heavy with the stench of ozone and an acrid, burning smell as magic clashed with demonic essence. Just when it seemed the battle was nearly over, the monstrous forms beginning to thin, a sickening flicker preceded the absolute failure of Silas's flashlight beam. The single, crucial source of light died, plunging the group back into darkness. At the same time, the children's protective powers began to falter, the shimmering barrier flickering, then fading entirely. The monsters, sensing their sudden vulnerability, pressed their attack with renewed vigor, their guttural snarls echoing in the blackness, their unseen claws reaching out to tear them apart. Panic, cold and sharp, threatened to overwhelm them.

With one last, desperate surge of strength, fueled by adrenaline and a desperate plea from within, Lily flicked her wrist. A raw, untamed burst of her power, amplified by Rose's fear and sisterly connection, unleashed a devastating wave of blinding energy. The creatures that had pressed so close were instantly engulfed in the searing, purifying light. Their terrifying forms contorted, dissolved, and then disintegrated into nothing more than wisps of acrid dust that quickly vanished, leaving only the lingering smell of burnt ozone in the air. The hallway, though still dark, was clear.

Silas, his hand trembling slightly, reached once more for his unreliable flashlight. With a grunt of frustration, he once more struck it against the wall, a desperate gamble that miraculously paid off. The beam flickered, then caught, pushing back the oppressive darkness that had engulfed them moments before.

As soon as the light sprang back to life, cutting through the shadows like a lifeline, Daniel shouted, his voice raw with urgency. "Go! We have to close the nexus now. Before Morpheus tries something else!" The near-death experience in the hallway had solidified his resolve; delay was no longer an option.

Silas, his heart pounding, wasted no time. He lunged for the doorknob, twisting it with a decisive turn. The attic door, old and heavy, groaned in protest as it slowly creaked open, revealing a narrow, dust-laden staircase that climbed steeply into deeper shadows. It was leading them to their ultimate objective, beckoning them forward. One by one, their movements swift and determined despite their exhaustion, they ascended, their footsteps echoing ominously through the silence of the upper reaches of the old house. Every creak of the wood beneath their feet seemed amplified in the quiet, adding to the tension.

They were halfway up the winding stairs when, "Wait!" Sarah's voice pierced the tense silence with sudden, undeniable panic. Her breath hitched, and her next words were a strangled cry. "Daniel, where's Rose?" The question hung in the air, a chilling pronouncement that sent a fresh wave of terror through them all, colder than any demonic presence. The beam of Silas's flashlight swung wildly, desperately sweeping the empty space behind them, confirming their worst fear. Rose was gone.

Chapter 29:

"Rose!" Lily cried, her voice laced with growing hysteria, as she frantically spun around, her eyes darting through the meager light, searching for her sister. "Oh no, you don't think..." Her voice trailed off, swallowed by a chilling realization that settled over them like a shroud. The unspoken fear, heavy and suffocating, hung in the air between them.

"We have to find her," Sarah insisted, her voice trembling as she clutched Daniel's arm, her grip tight and desperate.

"Okay, let's search the bedrooms. She's probably just hiding in one of them," Daniel said, his voice a strained attempt at reassurance, though a tremor betrayed his inner turmoil. His eyes, wide and darting, told a different story, reflecting a terror he tried in vain to conceal.

Silas, his jaw clenched, grabbed Daniel's arm, his gaze intense, pinning him in place. "It won't be long before we're under attack again. We have to close it now," he insisted, his voice low and guttural, the weight of their impossible choice pressing down on him.

Daniel sighed, a heavy, frustrated sound that echoed in the stifling silence of the old house. "I understand, Silas," he began, his voice strained but firm, "but I am not leaving my daughter behind. We have to find her." His gaze, though filled with a desperate fear, held an unwavering resolve.

"Rose, please answer me!" Sarah's voice, though tinged with panic, resonated with a fierce determination as she began to move. Without a moment's hesitation, she turned towards the first bedroom door, her hand reaching for the doorknob. Lily, now trembling, clung tightly to her mother's arm, her wide eyes darting into the darkness. Daniel, his own fear momentarily eclipsed by his fatherly instinct, led the way, pushing open the bedroom door and stepping into the inky blackness beyond.

Silas watched them go, his mind a battlefield of warring thoughts. He knew, deep down, that finding the little girl was undeniably the right thing to do, a moral imperative that screamed louder than any danger. Yet, a chilling, logical voice whispered of the terrifying stakes. The thought of the encroaching darkness, the grotesque creatures that had already breached their world, sent a shiver down his spine. In a desperate, split-second gamble, a decision born of grim necessity, he turned and raced further up the creaking stairs. His mind, in a twisted form of hope, clung to the desperate belief that wherever Rose was, once the final portal was closed, she would be safe from the monstrous invasion that threatened to consume them all. He ran, not towards the immediate danger, but towards the desperate hope of ending it.

Panic, cold and insidious, began to coil in his gut, tightening with each passing second. He tore through the attic with a frantic energy, tossing aside every forgotten box, every musty trunk, and checking every shadowy crevice. The air grew thick with the scent of dust and desperation. Yet, the nexus, the key to their very survival, remained maddeningly elusive. A cold sweat beaded on his brow as the terrifying truth solidified in his mind. He didn't forget where the nexus was, but rather it is in fact gone. They were alone, utterly unprepared, and at the mercy of an unknown, impending doom that clawed at the edges of his sanity.

His heart hammered against his ribs, a frantic drumbeat against the suffocating silence of the attic. His gaze, wild with desperation, darted across the room, each dusty corner a potential hiding place. The once-familiar space, now a maze of shadows and forgotten relics, seemed to mock his dwindling hope. "It can't be gone," he muttered, his voice barely a breath, a fragile whisper against the encroaching dread. His trembling hand swept over the rough, worn wood of an old chest, searching, pleading for any tangible sign of the nexus, the ethereal gateway that held their fate in its unseen balance. *It has to be here, I know it was here.* But there was nothing. The empty space where it should have been was nothing but a hollow void.

"It's not here!" Silas's voice, a raw cry of fear and disbelief, ripped through the oppressive silence of the dusty attic, the sound echoing hollowly. His face, already pale, drained of all color as the full gravity of the situation crashed down upon him. He had to warn the others, but the crushing weight of lost time pressed in on him, a relentless countdown to an unimaginable horror.

With a surge of renewed urgency, fueled by a primal need to protect not only those he cared for, but all of humanity, he lunged for the attic door, racing down the creaking stairs. He was only halfway down, his feet thudding against the aged wood, when a sudden, violent gust of wind, seemingly from nowhere, tore through the darkness. It ripped his flashlight from his grasp, sending it clattering down the steps before it extinguished with a final, feeble flicker, plunging him into an absolute, suffocating darkness. A moment of pure, unadulterated panic seized him, his heart pounding a frantic, desperate rhythm in his chest. The darkness was disorienting, pressing in on him from all sides.

As his eyes struggled to adjust to the sudden void, a sound, faint at first, then growing louder with each agonizing second, pierced the silence. A low, guttural growl, a predatory rumble that vibrated through the floorboards and directly into his bones. Fear, sharp and electrifying, propelled him forward, his hands outstretched blindly, desperately searching for the cold, unyielding security of the handrail. He stumbled down the remaining steps, his fingers brushing against the cold, smooth wood of the banister. The growl was closer now, a chilling promise of what lurked in the darkness behind him.

Finally, his hand connected with the cold, reassuring brass of the doorknob. With a trembling grip, he twisted it. The heavy door groaned on its ancient hinges, a drawn-out protest as it creaked open, revealing a sliver of the dimly lit hallway beyond. His axe, a familiar weight in his hand, was raised, ready. Just as he was about to step through the threshold, a formless, shadowy figure, a blur of malevolent intent, lunged from the oppressive darkness behind him, its presence a chilling void. With a surge of adrenaline, Silas stepped through and slammed the door shut with a force that rattled the very foundations of the house, the sickening thud echoing through the silence. But he knew more would come, and that the door would not hold them.

Meanwhile, in the suffocating darkness of the bedroom, Sarah's voice, a fragile thread woven with a mixture of desperate hope and mounting fear, echoed through the silence. "Rose," she called out, her gaze sweeping frantically across the room, willing her daughter to materialize from the shadows. "Rose, where are you?"

Lily stood rigidly beside her mother, her wide eyes scanning every shifting shadow, every obscured corner. A profound sense of dread, cold and pervasive, washed over her as she imagined the worst. Her little sister, lost somewhere in the oppressive darkness that had so swiftly enveloped their home. Or, a far more terrifying thought, taken by Morpheus, the ancient entity who sought to unravel their reality and destroy them all. The thought alone felt like a cold hand clutching at her heart.

Daniel, hunched low, his head almost touching the dusty floor, peered intently under the bed, his face etched with a deepening worry that bordered on despair. "No," he muttered, his voice barely audible, the single word a crushing weight of disappointment.

Sarah, her movements quick and desperate, moved towards the large, built-in closet, her fingers fumbling for the sliding doors. They grated open with a dry, rasping sound. Dust motes, disturbed by the sudden air current, danced like ghostly sprites in the feeble beam of her flashlight as she peered inside the cavernous space. "Rose?" she called out again, her voice barely a whisper this time, choked with rising anxiety. Her arm swept through the hanging clothes, pushing aside forgotten fabrics, desperate to ensure her daughter wasn't hiding, perhaps playing a terrifying game of hide-and-seek behind them.

Disappointment, sharp and bitter, etched itself deeper across her face as the closet yielded no answers. With a heavy sigh, she turned towards the ensuite bathroom door. It creaked open, revealing a small, dimly lit, and empty room. Sarah and Lily exchanged a worried, silent glance as Daniel emerged from the small space. He had diligently searched every possible hiding spot – under the sink, behind the toilet, and even in the cold, porcelain bathtub – but there was no sign, no trace, of Rose. The silence in the room felt heavier now, charged with their collective fear.

They moved quickly across the dimly lit hallway and into Rose's bedroom. It was a small, cozy space, a sanctuary painted in soft pastels, now feeling eerily quiet. A toy horse, tipped on its side, lay abandoned on the braided rug, a poignant and stark reminder of the child who was tragically missing. The playful innocence of the room clashed violently with the escalating terror gripping their hearts.

They each fanned out, frantically searching. Daniel dropped to his knees, peering under the dust-ruffled bed, his flashlight beam cutting through the shadows. Sarah methodically pulled back the floral curtains, revealing only the darkened windowpane, or what was left of it. Lily, her small hands trembling, flung open the wardrobe doors, revealing neatly hung clothes and empty shelves. Every nook and cranny, every potential hiding spot, was meticulously examined, but the answer they so desperately sought remained elusive. There was no sign, no trace, of Rose. A cold, heavy dread, like a shroud, settled over them, a chilling realization of the true extent of the invisible danger they now faced. The house, once their haven, had become a hunting ground.

Lily's eyes, wide with growing panic, darted frantically around the room, taking in the empty spaces. "Where is she?" she whispered, her voice a thin tremble, barely audible above the frantic pounding of her own heart. "We have to find her, now!" Her urgency for her sister's return was a raw, unfiltered cry.

Sarah and Daniel exchanged a worried glance, a silent acknowledgment of the terrifying possibilities. They knew, rationally, that they had to stay calm, to think clearly, but the insidious tendrils of fear were creeping in, tightening their grip with every passing second. The unspoken question hung heavy in the air between them: What if

Morpheus, the malevolent entity they all feared, had already gotten to her? The thought was a chilling, soul-numbing whisper of horror.

Suddenly, a crashing sound from the hallway ripped through the tense silence, followed by a guttural growl that sent shivers down their spines. Hearing the commotion, they burst from the bedroom, stumbling into the shadowy corridor. "Rose!" Lily shrieked, her voice echoing with desperate hope and gnawing fear, convinced the noise might be her sister.

Desperately hoping for the best, yet bracing for the worst, panic surged through them as they saw the raw terror etched on Silas's face, illuminated briefly by the sliver of light from their flashlights. His chest heaved, and his eyes were wide with unspeakable dread. "What's wrong?" Daniel demanded, his voice sharp with a sudden, icy dread.

"The nexus is gone," Silas replied, his voice barely a whisper, a strained, broken sound that carried the weight of their impending doom. The words hung in the air, a death bell in the suffocating silence.

"What?" Sarah whispered, the word barely escaping her lips, her heart racing in her chest. The raw flicker of fear she saw mirrored in Lily's wide, innocent eyes sent a sharp chill down her spine, colder than any draft in the old house.

Daniel, his own face a mask of escalating dread, didn't wait for a reply about the nexus. "Did you find Rose?" he asked, his voice trembling, betraying the desperate hope clinging to his words.

Silas, his gaze heavy with the weight of his discovery, could only offer a slow, painful shake of his head. A wave of exhaustion washed over Daniel, not just physical, but soul-deep. The stress of the past few moments, the terror of their situation, was evident in the deeply worried lines etched on his family's faces. He pushed down the rising panic, focusing on the immediate, bewildering problem. "How can a nexus just disappear?" he finally asked, his gaze fixed on Silas, searching for answers in the older man's haunted eyes. "Are you absolutely sure it was there?"

"Yes," Silas replied, his voice firm despite the underlying tremor of his own disbelief. "It was."

"It was!" Lily insisted, her small voice rising in urgency, affirming Silas's claim. "I saw it too!" Her confirmation, meant to bolster their belief, only deepened the mystery and the gnawing fear.

"What do we do now?" Sarah asked Daniel, her voice edged with rising panic, the edge of hysteria creeping in. Her hands wrung together, a silent testament to her inner turmoil. "Rose is still out here somewhere, and now we don't even know where the nexus is." Her voice trailed off, a choked whisper as her eyes began to well up with tears, reflecting the crushing despair that threatened to overwhelm them.

Daniel, seeing the despair settle over his wife and daughter, fought to regain a semblance of control. He scanned the hallway, his mind racing for any remaining possibility, any flicker of hope. "We still have Lily's room to search up here," he said, his voice trying to project a confidence he didn't feel, silently praying, desperately hoping, that was where Rose would be. *We need a win here*, he kept thinking to himself, a silent mantra against the darkness. *Just one win.*

"Right, okay," Sarah replied, her voice still thin, but with a flicker of renewed purpose, as she turned sharply towards Lily's room.

As the group made their way into the remains of Lily's room, which now felt less like a child's sanctuary and more like another battleground, their hearts sank. Rose was nowhere in sight. They went through the motions, checking under the bed, peering into the wardrobe, but with each empty space, each untouched toy, all hope was rapidly disappearing. The silence of the room was punctuated only by their ragged breaths and the frantic beat of their hearts, each thud a countdown to an unknown horror.

Silas scanned their faces, each etched with a mixture of terror and fading hope. "She could be downstairs," he suggested, the words a hollow offering. But his gut, a cold, knotted coil in his stomach, told him a different, more chilling story. He knew, with a certainty that made his blood run cold, that Morpheus hadn't just taken Rose; he had lured her away, into the pervasive, suffocating darkness that was steadily consuming their home. The entity was playing a cruel game, toying with them, drawing them deeper into its sinister web.

The group, propelled by a desperate, shared urgency, tumbled down the staircase, their footsteps thudding heavily against the worn wood, reaching the first-floor landing with a collective gasp of breath. The air here felt colder, heavier. "Which way?" Sarah asked, her voice sharp with panic as she glanced wildly down the diverging hallway.

"Let's split up one more time," Silas suggested, the words tasting bitter even as he spoke them. It was a risky move, but time was a luxury they no longer possessed. "Daniel, you three check that way," he said, pointing towards the kitchen and the back of the house, "and I will go this way," he finished, gesturing towards the shadowy entrance of the living room, where the light seemed to die completely.

As much as they hated the thought of separating, of diluting their strength in such a perilous moment, they knew time was an accelerating enemy. Nodding in grim agreement, each group dispersed, their forms quickly swallowed by the deepening gloom as they resumed their frantic, desperate search for little Rose. Night was fully upon them now, a heavy blanket that smothered any lingering natural light, casting long, shifting shadows that danced like unseen predators. From outside, from the very edges of their invaded world, low, guttural growls echoed in the distance, closer now, a chilling reminder of the horrors that lurked just beyond the fragile walls of their home.

Silas froze, a sudden, horrifying clarity washing over him. His face, already pale, was etched with a grim realization. He remembered the hole in the wall, the key that Elias had told Rose about, the one hidden deep within the basement. *I need to find the others*, he thought, his mind racing, the urgency building into an unbearable pressure. "The basement!" he shouted, his voice a raw, desperate cry that echoed with terrifying resonance through the silent, suffocating house. "We have to get back to the basement!" The words were a lifeline, a desperate plea to turn back from the path of inevitable doom.

Daniel, Sarah, and Lily, their own search of the kitchen and Daniel's office proving fruitless and only deepening their despair, heard Silas's frantic shout. A new surge of terror, cold and absolute, propelled them forward. They raced towards the basement door, their hearts pounding in unison. To their horror, it was already ajar, a gaping maw of blackness. Silas, without waiting, was already descending the steps, his determined figure shrinking, then completely disappearing, into the impenetrable darkness below. The growls from deeper within the house seemed to intensify, drawn by their very presence, a terrifying promise of what awaited them.

Silas reached the bottom of the creaking steps, his feet landing on the damp, cold tiles of the basement floor. The dim, wavering beam of his flashlight barely managed to pierce the oppressive, inky darkness that seemed to swallow all light. A low, guttural growl, a sound that vibrated deep in his chest, rumbled from the depths of the shadows. Then, a grotesque, shadowy figure emerged, its form flickering and indistinct in the meager illumination. It was taller, more menacing than anything they had encountered before, its outline shifting as if struggling to fully materialize in their reality. Its eyes, two pinpricks of eerie, malevolent red, fixed on him, burning with an unholy intelligence.

Before he could even fully react, before his mind could formulate a plan, the creature lunged. It moved with unnatural speed, its long, clawed hands, tipped with razor-sharp talons, reaching out to ensnare him. Silas, relying on pure instinct and the quickness that had saved him countless times, dodged the attack. He swung his heavy-duty flashlight in a desperate, wild arc, connecting with the creature's shifting face. It roared, a sound of raw fury that tore through the silence of the basement, its form rippling and contorting as if the very impact of the light was an abomination to its shadowy existence.

Just as the creature, its red eyes blazing with renewed malice, was about to strike again, a frantic scramble of footsteps echoed around him. Daniel, Sarah, and Lily had burst into the basement, their faces illuminated by the bobbing beams of their own flashlights, casting dancing shadows around the monstrous entity.

"What is that thing?" Sarah gasped, her voice choked with a mixture of terror and disbelief. Her eyes darted from the flickering creature to Silas lying on the ground, then to Daniel. It didn't quite look like the same, relatively more defined, monsters they had fought before. This one was different, more ethereal, more terrifying. Its very presence felt like a tear in the fabric of reality.

Together, a desperate, united front, the group fought the creature, their combined efforts barely holding the shadowy entity at bay. Silas swung his axe, the blade whistling through the air, while Daniel aimed frantic, desperate blows with his own weapon. Sarah, armed with her flashlight, tried to disorient it with beams of light, but the creature seemed to absorb the illumination, its form flickering and regaining its malevolent shape. Lily, in a desperate attempt to demolish the creature, flicked her wrist, unleashing bursts of her power. Its attacks were relentless, a whirlwind of shadowy claws that raked across their clothes, tearing fabric and leaving stinging welts on exposed skin. Its roars vibrated through the very foundation of the house, a sound that promised unimaginable pain. But they refused to give up, fueled by the desperate hope of finding Rose and the instinctive need for survival.

With a final, desperate surge of adrenaline, Lily, seeing her family falter, instinctively unleashed all the power she could. A blinding burst of pure, raw light shot from her outstretched hands, striking the creature full force. The entity shrieked, a high-pitched, agonizing sound that seemed to tear at the very fabric of the air, a sound of pure agony. Its shadowy form writhed and convulsed, then collapsed to the ground, dissolving into wisps of black smoke that quickly dissipated into nothingness. The basement was suddenly silent, save for their ragged breaths.

Without a moment to spare, they rushed deeper into the basement, propelled by a renewed, frantic urgency. Walking through the door of the secret room, their hearts were busy pounding a relentless rhythm of fear and adrenaline in their chests. They had to find Rose; every second felt like an eternity, ticking down to an unknown, terrible fate.

As they burst into the hidden chamber, their flashlights sweeping wildly, a collective gasp escaped their lips. There, shimmering in the center of the room, was not the familiar, closed portal they had just left, but something far more unsettling. "The nexus," Sarah gasped, her voice barely audible, choked with dread. It was larger, more volatile, pulsing with an unstable, sickly green light.

The others froze, their faces etched with a dawning, terrifying realization. "This isn't the one we closed," Silas muttered, his voice hoarse with disbelief, his gaze fixed on the menacing, swirling vortex before them. This was something new, something far more dangerous, and it hummed with an undeniable, malevolent power.

"No, it's not," Daniel agreed, his gaze fixed on Silas, a silent question passing between them. The new nexus pulsed with an ominous, sickly light, utterly different from the one they had known. "Do you think..." he trailed off, his hand lifting to point towards the ceiling, where the other portal should have been, "it was moved down here after you closed the first one?" The idea was horrifying, suggesting a level of malicious intelligence they hadn't anticipated from Morpheus.

Silas shook his head slowly, his frustration evident in the tight line of his mouth. "But how?" he murmured, the question hanging heavy in the air. *How could a gateway between dimensions simply relocate itself? It defied everything they understood about these creatures. Then again,* he thought, *how much could they really know for sure.*

"Can you close it?" Daniel shouted, his voice strained, barely audible over the low, guttural growls that were now unmistakably heading their way, growing louder with terrifying speed. The sound echoed through the basement, vibrating through the very floor.

Silas hesitated, his gaze locked on the swirling, unstable nexus. He felt the immense power radiating from it, and a chilling premonition settled deep in his bones.

"Can you close it!" Daniel repeated, his voice rising, sharper this time, a desperate plea for action.

"Maybe," Silas replied, the word a reluctant admission. His eyes met Daniel's, grave and filled with a deep sorrow. "But Daniel, if we do, I fear we may lose Rose forever." The implication hung in the air, a devastating blow to their already fractured hope. If Rose was somehow linked to this new nexus, closing it might sever her connection to their world entirely.

Sarah's eyes widened in horror, reflecting the terrifying weight of Silas's words. "What?" she shrieked, the sound raw with agony, clutching Lily so tightly that the child winced. A sudden, dizzying wave of nausea roiled in her stomach, making the room tilt, threatening to overwhelm her. The thought of losing her daughter permanently, banished to some unfathomable void, was unbearable.

Lily, however, was fueled by a fierce, childlike determination that cut through the despair. Breaking free from her mother's desperate grip, she dashed towards the gaping hole in the wall. "I have to find Rose!" she declared, her small voice ringing with conviction, utterly fearless in her resolve, despite the tears welling in her eyes.

Daniel, his heart sinking with a heavy, leaden weight, moved instantly, grabbing Lily and pulling her back from the threshold of the unknown. "No, you can't go in there. You have to stay in the light." His voice was firm, but his eyes, filled with anguish, darted to his wife. "But one of us has to go," he said, the terrible truth dawning on them all. Someone had to venture into that dark, shifting reality.

"I'm going in," Sarah declared, her voice firm, filled with the undeniable power of a mother's love. "I'm her mother." Her conviction was absolute.

Daniel, his face etched with worry and the agonizing weight of the decision, shook his head vehemently. "No, Sarah. You're too valuable to risk. The girls, they need a mother." He glanced at Lily, then back at his wife, his determination hardening. "I'll go."

Silas, his eyes suddenly filled with a strange, almost serene sense of peace, stepped forward, his gaze fixed on the shimmering nexus. "Let me go. I'm old. I've lived a full life." He looked at Daniel, a wry, knowing smile touching his lips. "Besides, I've dealt with strange occurrences before. My knowledge might be more useful."

"No, you're the only one who knows how to close the nexus," Daniel protested.

A heated argument erupted, their voices echoing in the low-ceilinged room as the growls from outside grew ever closer, more menacing. Sarah insisted on going, citing her maternal instinct, an unbreakable bond that compelled her. Daniel argued for his strength and experience, his role as the protector of his family. Silas, meanwhile, offered his wisdom, his long years of confronting the bizarre, and his quiet willingness to make the ultimate sacrifice. Lily interjected her own opinion, as being the protector of her little sister, when she could get a word in. The fate of Rose, and perhaps their world, hinged on this agonizing choice.

As the heated argument raged, their voices mixing with the ominous growls from outside, a small, dusty figure emerged from a different, previously unnoticed hole in the wall. The arguing voices instantly ceased, replaced by a collective, stunned silence.

"Rose!" Sarah exclaimed, the sound a choked cry of overwhelming relief. She pulled the child into a fierce, tight embrace, crushing her against her chest as if to reassure herself Rose was truly real. "What happened? Where have you been?" Her voice was muffled, thick with emotion.

"Why did you come down here alone?" Daniel asked, his voice a bit sharper than he intended, the residual fear and frustration momentarily overriding his relief. He knelt, his hands gently gripping Rose's shoulders, searching her face for answers, as well as for any injuries.

"Are you okay?" Sarah asked again, pulling back slightly but still clutching onto her, her eyes frantically scanning every inch of her daughter for any sign of injury, dirt, or anything amiss. While Lily, a sobbing bundle of relief, clung desperately to her sister, refusing to let go.

"I'm fine," Rose replied, her voice trembling, small and fragile. Her eyes, wide and glistening, were fixed on her parents. "I'm sorry," she whispered, the apology a tiny, broken sound. "But I wanted to save everyone. Elias said..." Her voice trailed off, the words catching in her throat as tears welled up in her eyes, blurring her vision. "He said I could save everyone, but I couldn't. I couldn't do it." The last words were a heartbroken whisper, and the tears, no longer held back, spilled over her eyelids, rolling down her dusty cheeks as she dissolved into quiet sobs, burying her face in Sarah's shoulder. The weight of an impossible burden had been placed on such small shoulders.

"Oh, Rose," Sarah murmured, her own voice thick with unshed tears, as she hugged both her daughters close, rocking them gently, the relief profound but tinged with the frightening revelation of Elias's manipulation. Silas and

Daniel exchanged a grim look, the mystery of Elias's true intentions deepening with Rose's tearful confession. The true fight, it seemed, was far from over.

Chapter 30:

"We have to close the nexus now," Daniel shouted, his voice filled with urgency as he instinctively prepared himself for another fight, his axe gripped tightly in his hand. The low growls from beyond the wall were no longer distant echoes; they were becoming more menacing, drawing closer with each passing minute, a chilling promise of imminent attack.

Silas, however, was transfixed by the swirling vortex. "This one looks different," he stammered, his brow furrowed in desperate concentration as he studied the intricate, shifting symbols that pulsed within its sickly green light. He ran a trembling hand over the rough stone of the wall beside it, as if trying to decipher a secret language. "It's not like the one before. There's something... wrong." An unease settled over him, a sense of deep, cosmic incorrectness emanating from the portal.

"What? What's wrong?" Daniel shouted, raising his voice to be heard over the rising crescendo of snarls and scuffles that would soon engulf them, the air growing heavy with the scent of dust and unseen decay.

"I'm not sure," Silas replied, his eyes still fixed on the nexus, his mind racing to comprehend the anomaly. "I just... I don't think this is it. This isn't the one."

"It has to be!" Daniel shouted back, his patience worn thin by exhaustion and the relentless pressure. "It's the only one we've found down here! What else could it be?"

"It looks like the one I saw in the attic," Silas replied, taking a step back, his head tilted as he examined it more closely, a dawning realization slowly forming in his mind. The patterns, the energy signature, were uncannily similar to the portal he had initially found upstairs, the one that had vanished. "Well," he said, his voice trailing off, a new, terrifying possibility solidifying in his thoughts.

"Well what?!" Daniel and Sarah both shouted at him in unison, their voices laced with a desperate mixture of frustration, fear, and impatience. They needed answers, and they needed them now, before whatever horrors lurked just beyond the threshold burst through to claim them.

"I really don't think this is the one I saw," Silas insisted, his voice laced with growing alarm as he moved closer, his flashlight beam tracing the intricate, glowing patterns on the nexus's surface. He pointed with a trembling finger. "See, this symbol here should be over there, and I don't recall this one at all," he added, his finger now hovering over a peculiar, unfamiliar symbol etched near what appeared to be a rudimentary handle or lever. The feeling of wrongness, of a deliberate misdirection, was overwhelming.

"What do you mean?" Sarah asked, point blank, her voice sharp with impatience and fear. "Is this not the nexus?" Her eyes darted from the shifting portal to Silas's troubled face, desperately seeking a clear answer amidst the escalating chaos.

"No, I think this is definitely the nexus," Silas replied, his voice firming with conviction. The raw, humming power radiating from it was undeniable. "I can feel the energy emanating from it. But I think, perhaps, it's been changed to throw us off our game. A trap, or a diversion." He looked at Daniel, a chilling realization dawning on him. "It's like Morpheus is toying with us"

"Well, can you close it?" Daniel asked, his voice strained, the worry in his eyes now entirely forsaking him as he stared at his family. His wife, his daughters, all of them vulnerable. The growls from outside were now right at the basement door, accompanied by sickening scraping sounds. They were out of time for debate.

"All I can do is try," Silas responded, his gaze fixed on the malevolent glow of the portal. His eyes, however, betrayed the fear he was too afraid to speak out loud. The fear that this altered nexus might not respond to his knowledge, or that messing with it could have unforeseen, catastrophic consequences for all of them. He knew this attempt might be their only chance, and it was a gamble of terrifying proportions.

With his brow furrowed in intense concentration, he was still studying the perplexing, altered nexus, desperately attempting to work out a plan, when the doors of the basement suddenly flung wide open with a deafening crash. The sound reverberated through the very foundation of the house, a terrifying herald of what was to come.

"They're here," Sarah said, her voice barely a whisper, a stark statement of their impending doom as she released Lily and Rose, resuming her fighting stance.

"Get it closed now!" Daniel roared, his voice raw with a desperate urgency, as he instinctively took his fighting stance, the axe clutched like a lifeline in his hands.

The creatures that surged through the opening were unlike anything they had ever encountered. These were not the shadowy, indistinct figures from before; these were twisted, truly demonic forms, their bodies rippling with dark, visible energy that seemed to distort the very air around them. Their eyes, glowing an unnatural, searing red, seemed to pierce the very soul, stripping away courage and hope with a single glance. Their numbers were overwhelming, an endless tide of nightmares.

"Get it closed!" Daniel shouted again, his voice strained with effort as he and Sarah, fueled by sheer, desperate will, began landing blows on the creatures that swarmed at them. The sounds of impact, of snarling and hissing, filled the confined space.

Lily and Rose, their small faces etched with a grim determination, rallied together. Their hands clasped, a faint, shimmering light began to emanate from between them, growing steadily into a pulsating, protective barrier of pure magic. The barrier pulsed, holding back the monstrous tide, creating a desperate, shimmering shield between them and the ravenous creatures, allowing Silas precious, agonizing moments to continue his work on the puzzling nexus. The fate of their world, and their very lives, now rested solely on the strength of two small girls and the desperate gamble of an old man.

Daniel and Sarah fought desperately, a whirlwind of motion against the darkness, their weapons flashing in the dim, chaotic light of the basement. They moved with a grim determination, striking out at the monstrous forms that swarmed them. But the creatures were relentless, their movements swift and brutal, their shadowy claws and snapping jaws forcing the couple further and further back. The sheer number of them was overwhelming, a tide of pure malevolence.

With a sickening snarl, one of the larger, more distorted creatures lunged, catching Sarah off guard. She cried out, stumbling backward and falling to the cold, damp floor. Even as she hit the ground, she twisted, desperately trying to land another blow with the fire poker, her body already surrounded, the monsters encasing her in a living, squirming cage of shadow and teeth. Her struggles grew weaker, muffled by the press of their grotesque forms.

Lily and Rose, their small faces strained with immense effort, despite their best efforts, struggled to hold the line. The shimmering barrier of light they had created pulsed erratically, flickering at the edges as the monstrous horde pressed against it with increasing force. Cracks, like spiderwebs, began to appear in its ethereal surface, threatening to collapse and expose them all to the overwhelming tide of nightmares. The energy draining from their small bodies, their hands trembling with the effort.

Suddenly, Silas's voice, raw and strained, but laced with a surge of desperate hope, cut through the din of snarls and struggles. "I think I've got it!" he shouted, his words barely audible over the terrifying chaos that enveloped them. His eyes, fixed on the shimmering, unstable nexus, glowed with a fierce concentration.

His face etched with intense focus, reached out and touched the pulsating surface of the nexus. His fingers, guided by instinct, moved with surprising speed and precision, manipulating the interwoven locks that were in the middle of the glowing circle. Each twist and turn of the ancient mechanism seemed to resonate with a deep, cosmic hum. As he completed the final adjustment, the intricate symbols on the device began to shift and change, rearranging themselves with a blinding flash of light.

A massive surge of raw, unbridled energy pulsed through the entire room, emanating from the nexus like a silent scream. The demonic creatures, caught in the otherworldly blast, let out a collective, agonizing shriek, a sound of pure torment and unnatural pain that echoed off the basement walls. Their forms began to wither and decay with horrifying speed, like ancient parchment burning from within. Their shadowy bodies distorted and fragmented, dissolving into clouds of fine, black dust that swirled briefly before vanishing entirely.

The oppressive darkness, which had moments before seemed like a living entity, retreated with astonishing swiftness, pulled back into the nexus. As it vanished, the room was filled with a soft, ethereal glow emanating from the now-stabilized portal, bathing everything in a gentle, otherworldly light.

"We did it," Silas breathed, the words a ragged whisper of relief. The tension that had held him rigid for what felt like an eternity finally released, and he slumped to the floor, a weary smile spreading across his face as he looked at the others, his eyes filled with a quiet triumph. The battle was over.

Weary and bone-tired, but with an immense, surging joy, Daniel quickly helped Sarah to her feet, his hands gently checking her for injuries. "Are you alright? You took quite a hit."

She nodded, a shaky breath escaping her lips, before they both enveloped their daughters in a fierce, protective embrace. "Are you both okay?" Sarah asked, her voice thick with emotion, her eyes scanning Rose and Lily's exhausted faces.

Before either girl could answer, before they could even fully register the relief of their parents' embrace, another figure began to coalesce from the deepest shadows of the basement. It wasn't a growling beast, but something far more ancient and terrifying. A towering, impossibly lean figure, its body cloaked in an inky darkness that seemed to drink the very light. Its eyes, burning with an intense, cold hatred, fixed with unnerving precision on the small, huddled group.

They watched in transfixed horror as the towering figure slowly, deliberately, stepped into the soft, ethereal glow of the now-closed nexus. Its form shimmered and shifted, coalescing from pure shadow into something more defined, more terrifyingly real. It was a face they had never seen before, yet its presence radiated an ancient, undeniable power. This was Morpheus, the god of dreams, but his features were twisted into a mask of pure malice, his eyes burning with a malevolent, unquenchable fire. This was clearly the undisputed King of Nightmares, his very form a testament to the darkness he commanded.

"You thought you had defeated me?" Morpheus sneered, his voice a chilling whisper that slithered into their minds, colder than the basement air. "You thought you could control the dreamscape? You are but mere mortals, destined to be consumed by the darkness, by *my* endless night." A dark, cruel laugh escaped him, a sound that promised eternal torment.

The relief that had just begun to settle over Daniel's features vanished, replaced by a fresh wave of despair and confusion. He spun on Silas, his voice raw with disbelief. "How can this be? I thought you closed the nexus! You said it was shut!"

Silas, his triumphant smile fading into a mask of dawning horror, could only stare at the nightmare god before them. His eyes, wide and filled with the terrifying realization of his failure, flickered between Morpheus and the now inert, closed nexus. "I did," he replied, his voice barely a whisper, filled with a crushing uncertainty. "Didn't I?" The question hung in the air, a desperate plea for reassurance that would not come.

Daniel's eyes, sharp and calculating despite the raw terror, scanned the room, searching for any weakness in the towering form of Morpheus, any vulnerability in the newly revealed nightmare god. Sarah, meanwhile, had instinctively pulled Lily and Rose even tighter behind her, pressing them against her back, her body a trembling shield against the monstrous presence. "We need to find a way to stop him," Daniel said, his voice surprisingly resolute, cutting through the heavy silence.

"But how?" Sarah whispered, the fear thick in her voice.

The group exchanged worried glances, a silent confirmation of the impossible odds stacked against them. They had faced countless challenges, battled shadowy creatures, and closed dangerous portals, but none as terrifying, as fundamentally overwhelming, as this. The fate of their family, and indeed, the entire world, hung precariously in the balance, and they, a handful of exhausted, fearful mortals, were supposedly the only ones who stood a chance of saving it.

Morpheus smirked, the cruel twist of his lips revealing sharpened, almost predatory teeth, his eyes gleaming with malicious intent. The air around him seemed to grow heavier, colder. "You think you can defeat me, mere mortals?" he scoffed, his voice laced with disdainful amusement. "You cannot comprehend the power I wield. I am the very fabric of your unconscious, the architect of your deepest fears."

"We've faced creatures before, and we've overcome them," Daniel retorted, his voice firm, refusing to waver despite the overwhelming dread. He stepped slightly forward, placing himself more directly between Morpheus and his family. "We'll find a way to stop you." His words were a desperate declaration, a defiance born of sheer desperation.

Morpheus simply laughed, a cold, hollow sound that echoed through the basement, resonating disturbingly in their very bones. It was a sound utterly devoid of mirth, filled instead with an ancient, chilling power. "You're blind to the truth," he said, his gaze sweeping over them, lingering on Rose and Lily for a fraction of a second. "I am not the enemy. You are. You cling to a false reality, a fragile construct of light and order that prevents true understanding."

An icy chill ran down their spines as Morpheus's cryptic words hung in the air, dripping with dark meaning. They couldn't fully comprehend what he meant, how *they* could be the enemy. But they knew one thing with absolute certainty. That this being, this King of Nightmares, sought to destroy them, and they had to stop him, no matter the cost, no matter the terrifying secrets he claimed to hold. The air around him thrummed with unspoken threats and unimaginable power.

"We'll see about that," Silas declared, his voice ringing with defiance despite the impossible odds, a final spark of unyielding human spirit. "We won't let you destroy the world, not the way you destroyed my Emma." With a guttural roar, he drew his axe from his belt, the glint of the blade a stark contrast to the shadowy form of Morpheus. Without a moment's hesitation, fueled by a lifetime of hunting down the encroaching darkness, he ran toward Morpheus, throwing himself into the impossible fight with everything he had left.

Sarah screamed, "No!" as she watched him take his suicidal charge. Daniel, too, lunged forward, his hand outstretched, desperate to pull Silas back towards them, but he only managed to grasp empty air. It happened too fast.

Morpheus simply raised a hand, a gesture that was both swift and lethally dismissive, like the strike of a venomous serpent. There was no grand incantation, no visible blast of energy, just a flicker of dark power. And in an instant, Silas had been turned to dust before their horrified eyes, his form dissolving like a wisp of smoke, his axe clattering to the floor, a forlorn symbol of his sacrifice.

"No!" screamed Sarah, the sound ripped from her soul, fresh tears streaming down her face as she instinctively grabbed hold of her girls, pulling them tighter against her, shielding their innocent eyes from the unbearable sight of Silas's obliteration. Her body trembled uncontrollably, a mix of grief, terror, and a simmering rage.

Daniel, his face a mask of shock and searing grief, stepped forward, his axe clenched so tightly his knuckles were white. The dark, dangerous look of revenge flared in his eyes, momentarily eclipsing the fear. He was ready to follow Silas into oblivion.

"Such bravery," Morpheus grinned mockingly, his voice dripping with cruel amusement, unaffected by Silas's sacrifice. He tilted his head, his burning eyes fixed on Daniel. "But unless you wish to meet the same swift and utterly futile fate, then I suggest you reconsider your next step, mortal."

"Daniel, please," Sarah whispered, her voice barely audible, choked with both tears and fear, her whole body shaking violently. She knew, with chilling certainty, that they couldn't lose him too. They had to find another way.

Daniel took a shuddering step back, the axe, once a symbol of his defiance, now feeling like a useless weight in his hand. He slowly lowered it, his gaze drawn to Sarah's face. Her eyes, wide and glistening with unshed tears, mirrored his own, reflecting a crushing mixture of fear, of utter failure, and the undeniable, chilling certainty that this was it. This was their last day. The realization settled over them like a cold, heavy shroud, muffling the chaos of Morpheus's mocking laughter and the lingering scent of ash from their friend's demise.

He didn't need words to understand her. Every unspoken fear, every shared dream for their daughters, flickered between them in that silent, agonizing moment. Sarah, still shielding Lily and Rose behind her, her body trembling, met his gaze with a look that spoke volumes: *We tried. We failed. But at least we're together.* It was a look that pleaded for peace in their final moments, for connection amidst the crushing despair. His chest ached with a love so fierce it was almost unbearable, knowing that soon, it would all be gone. He reached out a trembling hand, not for a weapon, but for his wife, for his family.

Chapter 31:

Daniel, shaken from his shared moment of silent despair with Sarah, not by Morpheus's sneering voice or another demonic growl, but by the unexpected sound of laughter. It wasn't the cruel, hollow sound of the nightmare god. No, this was a bright, clear, innocent sound that cut through the oppressive dread like a beam of sunlight. It was his daughter's laughter, Rose's laughter.

He blinked, tearing his gaze from his wife's face, and looked at his daughters. Both Rose and Lily were smiling, their faces, moments ago streaked with tears and fear, now lit with a genuine, infectious joy. Rose was giggling, a soft, bubbling sound, her eyes twinkling. Daniel felt a confused, yet undeniable, warmth spread through his chest. He didn't understand why they were laughing, why they were smiling in the face of such overwhelming odds, but watching them, a small, genuine smile touched his own lips, a fragile flicker of hope in the deepening gloom.

A sudden, electrifying realization jolted within him, hitting him like a physical blow, cutting through the haze of despair and confusion. The ethereal voices he'd heard before, the whispers that had guided them through impossible odds, echoed in his mind with newfound clarity. They hadn't just spoken of the nexus; they had spoken of *them,* the two sisters. The girls were the key.

"Rose, Lily," he breathed, his voice thick with a sudden, overwhelming hope, his eyes widening as he looked from his giggling daughter to the terrifying creature behind him and then back to their bright, innocent faces. "Your powers. You can defeat him." The words, though simple, carried the weight of a desperate prophecy, a last, desperate gamble against the King of Nightmares.

"Daniel," Sarah finally spoke, her voice laced with a raw mix of disbelief and anguish. "Why would you ask them to do such a thing?"

"Don't you see, Sarah?" Daniel pleaded, his gaze locking onto hers, desperate for her to understand. "The voice we heard, the whispers that guided us... it's them. They are the key to defeating Morpheus for good. I hate it more than anything to ask this of them, but it's the only way. The only way to save humanity." He searched her eyes, a desperate plea for confirmation about this terrible, but necessary choice.

Morpheus's laughter echoed through the basement, a sound like grinding ice that sent fresh shivers down Daniel's already trembling spine. "I am immortal," he scoffed, his voice dripping with power and contempt. "You cannot kill me, you fool."

"Girls," Daniel pleaded, his voice laced with a desperate urgency, his eyes fixed on their small faces. "Lily, Rose, you have to trust me. You have to do this now." His words were heavy with the weight of the world, urging them to unleash their extraordinary powers one last, final time. Not just to save themselves, not just to save their family, but to save everyone on the planet, to put an end to this suffocating nightmare once and for all. Every fiber of his being screamed against asking this of his children, yet he knew, with chilling certainty, that it was the only path that remained.

Rose giggled once more, a soft, otherworldly sound that sent a confusing warmth through him, a strange twinkle of light dancing in her eyes. For a fleeting moment, he thought she would concede, that she and Lily were about to unleash their incredible power and take this nightmare monster down, ending their terror forever. But instead, Rose looked directly into his eyes, her gaze unnervingly calm and far too wise for a child. "Don't be afraid," she whispered. "This is the way it was always meant to be."

Lily, her smile equally unsettling, reached out and gently grabbed her sister's hand, their small fingers intertwining. "You just have to do as our father asks," she said, her voice clear and untroubled, as she stared directly at Morpheus, the King of Nightmares, with a look of chilling admiration that tore at Daniel's very soul. Her words, spoken with a serene certainty, chilled him to the bone, leaving him numb with a terrifying realization.

"What?" Daniel stammered, his voice barely audible, a strangled sound of utter disbelief. The words Rose and Lily had uttered, the way Lily had looked at Morpheus, twisted in his gut. "What are you saying, Lily?" he asked, his voice cracking, terrified that the answer would confirm his worst, most unspeakable thoughts. That his daughters, the two girls he and his wife had adopted, nurtured, and loved with every fiber of their being, were actually the offspring of Morpheus, the King of Nightmares himself. That this whole terrifying ordeal, every battle, every sacrifice, every agonizing choice, Silas' life, had been nothing more than an elaborate, cruel set-up. A twisted game orchestrated by Morpheus so that he could take over their world and reign freely, plunging it into an eternal abyss of darkness and annihilating all of humanity.

His mind raced, a whirlwind of horrifying implications and crushing betrayal. He thought of his wife, the woman he loved, standing silently between the girls, her presence a heavy weight. She had been so quiet since Rose's strange utterance, since Lily's unsettling gaze. She must be in shock, her world crumbling just as his was. But he was too afraid to look into her face, too afraid to see the reflection of his own dawning horror, the inevitable pain of this monstrous revelation. He knew that seeing her shattered, seeing her realize the same terrible truth, would rip him apart, a final, unbearable agony in this nightmare.

Before either Lily or Rose could offer another unsettling word, Morpheus interjected, a slow, chilling smile spreading across his face, a truly monstrous spectacle in the soft glow of the nexus. "Girls," he beckoned, his voice a silken, resonant purr that seemed to draw them in. Without a moment's hesitation, they walked past Daniel, who remained utterly frozen, his mind reeling from the betrayal. They moved as if drawn by an invisible string, their steps light and unburdened by the terror that gripped their adoptive parents, walking directly into the open arms of their true father, Morpheus, the King of Nightmares.

Morpheus enveloped them in a shadowy embrace, his dark form softening slightly as he looked down at them. "You did well, my daughters," he said, his voice now laced with what could only be described as beaming fatherly pride. It was a sight that twisted Daniel's stomach, sickening in its perversion. "You will both be rewarded well here in our new home." His gaze swept around the basement, implying a dominion far beyond these shattered walls.

"Thank you, Father," they both chimed, their voices sweet and innocent, their faces upturned, smiling at him with an adoration that was utterly heartbreaking. Their eyes, once filled with childlike wonder for Daniel and Sarah, now shone with a cold, almost regal admiration for the very entity that sought to destroy everything Daniel held dear. The realization solidified in his mind. Lily and

Rose had not been rescued by Sarah and himself; they had been delivered.

No, no, this can't be happening, Daniel thought to himself, a desperate, silent plea echoing in the back of his mind. He shook his head, a futile attempt to dislodge the horrifying images and the crushing weight of betrayal that now threatened to consume him. His gaze, wild and searching, finally landed on Sarah, the only anchor in a world that had suddenly, violently, turned upside down. She was the one constant, the one undeniable truth in a reality now overrun by nightmares.

He stumbled towards her, his hands instinctively reaching for her shoulders, gripping them tightly as if to ground himself, to assure himself she was still real, still *his*. He looked into her eyes, searching for a shared understanding, a familiar reflection of their life together. He wanted to say something, anything, to mend this shattered moment, to somehow make this impossible situation better, or to make it simply vanish, plunging them back into the comforting normalcy of what they had before the nexus ever opened. He wanted to tell her he loved her, that he was sorry, that he would fix it.

But a deep, bewildering confusion overtook him, an icy tendril coiling around his heart as he stared into the very eyes of the woman he loved. Her expression, previously a mirror of his own despair, now held something utterly alien, something that didn't align with the shared horror of their current reality. The truth, in that moment, became even more distorted, more terrifying than any nightmare Morpheus could conjure.

Sarah's face was bathed in a soft glow, a beautiful smile gracing her lips. Her gaze, filled with an unshakeable adoration, drifted between the terrifying figure of Morpheus and the two shadowy forms that now stood beside him, which she clearly saw as her daughters. "I have such a beautiful family, don't you think?" she murmured, her voice a soft, melodic whisper, laced with an almost childlike wonder.

Daniel, his heart a frantic drum against his ribs, could only stare, his mind reeling in a desperate attempt to reconcile the woman he loved with the delusion before him. "What, Sarah?" he choked out, his voice hoarse with disbelief, "Sarah, those are not our daughters. They're that... monsters!" His shout ripped through the fragile peace of the moment, a desperate plea for her to see the terrifying reality.

The serene mask on Sarah's face shattered instantly. Her head snapped towards him, her eyes, once soft and loving, now blazed with a chilling, incandescent rage. "How dare you," she hissed, each word a venomous dart, "how dare you call my daughters the children of a monster? They have the best father in the world!" Her voice rose with each word, absolute conviction ringing in her tone as she once again turned her gaze, brimming with admiration, even a disturbing, fervent love, towards Morpheus.

"What?" Daniel stammered, his voice laced with a desperate plea. He reached for Sarah, his hands finding purchase on her upper arms, stroking them in a frantic attempt to impart some warmth, some sense of reality. "Sarah, you can't believe that, can you? You're just in shock, that's all. The trauma of... everything, it's making you see things." He spoke quickly, his eyes searching hers for any flicker of recognition, any sign that the woman he knew was still in there.

Sarah's gaze, however, remained unsettlingly serene. A faint, almost imperceptible smile touched her lips, a smile utterly devoid of warmth or a hint of her usual playful nature. She didn't flinch from his touch, nor did she acknowledge the frantic energy in his voice. Her eyes, wide and unnervingly placid, simply held his.

"Shock?" she murmured, her voice a soft, steady current, each word perfectly articulated, carrying an unshakable conviction that sent a chill down his spine. "No, Daniel, there's no shock here. Only clarity. I have never been more in control of my mind, never felt more present, more *alive*." She paused, her gaze drifting back towards her daughters and Morpheus. "And it's all because my family is finally back together," she continued, her voice swelling with a joy that was horrifying in its context, "exactly where we should be." She turned her eyes back to Daniel, and for a fleeting moment, he saw a glimmer of the Sarah he loved, but it was quickly overshadowed by the tranquil delusion that had consumed her. "My beautiful daughters, Lily and Rose," she announced, her voice filled with a mother's pride, "and the love of my life, Morpheus, the King of Dreams, the King of my Heart, my King." Her words hung in the air, a chilling testament to a love utterly twisted and tragically misplaced.

The air grew heavy with the weight of her words, a chasm opening between them that Daniel knew, with a sickening certainty, he might never be able to bridge. The last vestiges of hope, of understanding, drained from him. His grip on her arm, which he hadn't even realized he was still holding, went slack. His knees buckled, the strength utterly abandoning him, and he crumpled to the cold floor. He lay there, utterly broken, the shattered fragments of his life and his love scattered around him, illuminated by the horrifying delusion that had consumed his family.

Daniel lay there in his despair. His eyes, wide with a horrifying clarity, were fixed on the scene unfolding before him. He watched, utterly powerless, as his daughters clung to this creature of nightmares. Then, his stomach lurched, a wave of nausea washing over him, as Sarah, the woman he had loved with every fiber of his being for so many years, walked over to join them. She didn't hesitate. She bowed, a gesture of submission that twisted Daniel's gut, and then, slowly, deliberately, she leaned in and kissed him. The kiss was not a chaste peck; it was a long, passionate, horrifying display of misplaced affection that shattered the last remnants of his sanity.

A vengeful scream tore through his mind, unheard. He couldn't let this stand. He couldn't. His fingers, numb moments before, now scrabbled for purchase on the cold floor, his hand reaching, one last time, for the familiar, comforting weight of his axe. It lay there, a forgotten sentinel of a life that was rapidly unraveling. With a grunt, he dragged himself upwards, every muscle protesting, every joint screaming in agony. The world swam before his eyes, but his grip on the axe was steady.

His gaze, narrowed and fierce, locked onto Morpheus. The creature, still holding his wife in a horrifying embrace, seemed to mock him with its very presence. A surge of desperate, bone-deep rage fueled him. He would put an end to this. He would expel this nightmare from his life, from Sarah's life, once and for all. This dark charade had gone on long enough.

With a roar that was more animalistic than human, Daniel lunged forward, the axe a gleaming arc through the dim light of the room. He swung with every ounce of his remaining strength, aiming for the creature's chest, for its very heart, if it even possessed one. But before the cold steel could connect, a blinding burst of light erupted, a silent explosion of raw power. Daniel felt an invisible force slam into him, lifting him off his feet and sending him flying across the room. He hit the far wall with a sickening thud, his vision spiraling into a kaleidoscope of pain and blackness.

Chapter 32:

A dull, rhythmic throb echoed behind Daniel's eyes, a persistent drumbeat against the inside of his skull. He groaned, a raw sound that scratched at his throat, and tried to shift, but a wave of nausea rolled over him, pinning him to the cold, unforgiving surface beneath him. The air was stale, thick with the scent of stagnant air and a faint, metallic tang he couldn't quite place. His eyelids felt impossibly heavy, glued shut by an unseen force, and when he finally managed to pry them open, the world swam into a blurry, indistinct mess.

He was on the basement floor. The concrete pressed hard against his back, and the familiar chill of the damp air seeped into his bones. What had happened? Fragments of memory, sharp and jagged, pricked at the edges of his consciousness, but they refused to coalesce into a coherent narrative. There was a fight, he thought. An axe. A blinding light. But it all dissolved into a frustrating fog, leaving him with only the lingering ache and a sense of disorientation.

A shape loomed over him, blocking out the meager light. His eyes struggled to focus, the blurry outline slowly resolving into a familiar face. Sarah. She was leaning over him, her beautiful, brunette hair falling around her like a dark curtain. A soft, gentle smile played on her lips, a look of contentment that eased something tense within him, even as a tiny, unidentifiable part of him screamed in warning.

"Daniel?" Her voice was a melody, clear and warm, devoid of any of the chilling detachment he vaguely recalled. "Are you awake?"

The world spun for a moment, then settled. He blinked, trying to clear the lingering haze from his vision. Sarah. Here. Smiling. A wave of relief, potent and disarming, washed over him, momentarily eclipsing the confusion and the throbbing pain in his head.

His hand, still trembling slightly, reached out for her. The touch of her skin, warm and solid, was an anchor in the swirling chaos of his mind. An intense sense of certainty settled over him, pushing back the lingering tendrils of confusion. They had won. The fractured, terrifying images that still flickered at the edge of his memory – the monstrous forms, the chilling calm, the unholy kiss – they had to be nothing more than the dying echoes of a nightmare. A truly terrible, vivid nightmare from which he had just mercifully woken up.

A surge of relief, so powerful it almost brought tears to his eyes, washed through him. They were alive. They were here, together, in their home, in their basement. That was all that mattered. The details of the dream, however disturbing, faded into insignificance compared to the tangible reality of his wife's presence, her soft smile, her hand in his. He squeezed her fingers, a silent testament to his profound gratitude. He felt a deep, abiding peace settle over him, a sense that the world, despite everything, was finally right again.

He leaned his forehead against hers, the cool touch of her skin soothing against his throbbing head. Tears, hot and insistent, pricked at the corners of his eyes, not of sorrow, but of overwhelming relief. "Lily, Rose," he murmured, his voice thick with emotion, the names of his daughters a sweet refrain on his tongue. "Our daughters, where are they?"

He pulled back just enough to scan the dimly lit basement. And there they were. Standing just beyond Sarah's shoulder, bathed in a faint glow, were his girls. They were smiling, their faces bright and innocent, their eyes sparkling with joy. Another wave of peace washed over him, chasing away the last remains of the nightmare. He grinned back at them, a wide, unrestrained smile of pure happiness. They were safe. They were here. Everything was truly alright.

But just as quickly his smile faltered, a cold dread seeping into his bones. His gaze drifted just beyond his daughters, to the deeper shadows that clung to the far wall of the basement. A figure emerged from the gloom, its form coalescing with an impossible grace. Morpheus. The King of Nightmares, not a figment of a dream, but horrifyingly real. He moved with an unsettling fluidity, stepping up behind Rose and Lily, his long, dark arms snaking out to rest casually over their shoulders, a possessive gesture that made Daniel's blood run cold. And then, slowly, chillingly, that terrifying, horrible smile spread across Morpheus's face, a silent, triumphant sneer that confirmed Daniel's deepest fears. The nightmare had not ended, but rather for him, it had just begun.

Daniel's breath hitched, the sudden, icy grip of terror a stark contrast to the warmth of Sarah's hand still clasped in his. His eyes, wide with horror, darted from Morpheus's chilling smile to Sarah's face, searching for a flicker of the woman he knew, a sign that she saw the monster looming behind their daughters. But her expression remained serenely tranquil, her smile unwavering as she followed his gaze to the King of Nightmares.

"Oh, Daniel," Sarah purred, her voice soft and imbued with a frightening sense of peace, "there's no need to look so worried." Her thumb stroked the back of his hand, a gesture of reassurance that only deepened his dread. "The girls are perfectly fine."

She shifted slightly, pulling her hand gently from his, and her gaze, now alight with a strange, possessive adoration, settled on Morpheus. A slow smile spread across her face, mirroring, in a horrifying way, the one on the creature's lips. "After all," she continued, her voice gaining a quiet, unwavering strength, "they're with their father. Their real father."

"Sarah, this can't be happening," Daniel pleaded, his voice ragged with disbelief. He reached out, desperate to grasp her arm, to shake her out of this horrifying trance. "We adopted them, remember? Lily and Rose. They are our daughters. Yours and mine. We're their parents, their mom and dad." He tried to infuse his voice with all the shared memories, all the love, all the undeniable truth of their life together.

For a fleeting moment, a flicker of something resembling confusion crossed Sarah's face, a slight furrowing of her brow that ignited a desperate spark of hope in Daniel's chest. He pressed on, seizing the opportunity, his eyes darting to the shadowy figure of Morpheus.

"It's him," he choked out, his finger trembling as he pointed towards the creature. "He's doing this to you. He's twisting your mind, making you think that they're his daughters, that you..." The words caught in his throat, a vile taste blooming on his tongue. He could barely force them past his lips, the very idea was like acid in his gut. "That you love him," he finally managed, the last two words laced with a deep, visceral disgust that caused his stomach to churn. Every fiber of his being recoiled from the horrific implication, the desecration of their life, their love, their family.

"Right," Sarah said, a soft, almost pitying laugh escaping her lips. It wasn't a cruel sound, but it held a chilling detachment that grated against his nerves. "Daniel, you're not making sense. You're confused. Just think about it, truly." Her eyes, so recently filled with a flicker of confusion, now held a disturbing clarity. "We did adopt them, yes, that's true in a way, in *your* way of thinking. But that means, doesn't it, that they have a real biological mother and father."

She paused, her gaze drifting over to Lily and Rose. A tender, impossibly loving smile blossomed on her face, a look Daniel had once cherished, now utterly corrupted. It was the smile of a mother gazing at her beloved children, a smile that solidified the horrifying delusion.

Then, her eyes, filled with an unsettling serenity, returned to Daniel. "So you see," she continued, her voice gentle, as if explaining a simple truth to a bewildered child, "Morpheus is their real father, their biological father." Her hand gestured vaguely towards the King of Nightmares, a gesture of acceptance. "And I," she declared, her voice gaining an unshakeable certainty that sent a fresh wave of nausea through him, "I am their real biological mother. Daniel," she finished, her eyes fixed on his, shimmering with an ancient, terrifying knowledge, "I gave birth to them centuries ago."

The words struck him like a physical blow, each syllable a shard of ice shattering the last remnants of his reality. Centuries ago? It was impossible. Madness. Yet, the conviction in her eyes, the horrifying calm in her voice, left no room for doubt about her belief. He shook his head slowly, a desperate, futile gesture. The words failed him, stuck in his throat, choked by the sheer, overwhelming horror of her delusion. There was no argument against such an absolute, unshakable conviction. Whatever Morpheus had done to her, she truly believed it.

"Daniel," Sarah continued, her voice softening, a hint of something resembling patience in her tone, "I understand your confusion. This is a lot for you to process, I know. But if you'll just let me explain, truly explain, it will all make sense."

She turned her head, her gaze drifting, almost magnetically, to Morpheus. Her eyes locked with his for a long, silent moment, a connection so deep it seemed to hum in the air. A private understanding passed between them before she slowly turned back to Daniel, her expression serene once more.

"I fell in love with Morpheus a very, very long time ago," she explained, her voice dropping to a near whisper, laden with the weight of centuries. "Times were different then, obviously. The worlds were less separated, more fluid. But there was so much chaos, so much upheaval, and he… he was to be sent away. To another world, another realm, for reasons that now seem so distant."

A shadow, a flicker of profound despair, crossed her face, dimming the light in her eyes. It was a fleeting glimpse of an ancient pain that twisted Daniel's stomach. "I couldn't lose him, Daniel," she confessed, her voice thick with raw emotion, "I couldn't. The thought of a life without him, a world without his presence, was simply unbearable." Her gaze found Morpheus again, a deep, unwavering devotion etched into her features. "So, we set a plan in motion and were wed immediately. Our plan worked, and I became the Queen of Dreams. By his side, together we ruled over the Dream World."

A smile spread across her face, radiating a chilling contentment. "We were so happy, Daniel," she recounted, her voice light with reminiscence, "being together, forging our path, creating... havoc for those who were deserving." A soft, almost childlike laugh escaped her, a sound that given the current situation, was more disturbing than comforting.

"With me by his side, our combined power, the ancient forces that wished to send him away, to another plane, to a barren existence, knew they had to devise a different strategy. They had not been prepared to face our united front. I had brought many formidable allies to our side, beings of immense power and cunning, and they had underestimated the depth of our bond, the strength of our growing court."

Sarah's gaze softened, growing wistful as it drifted towards Lily and Rose. "In the meantime," she continued, her voice filled with a tender warmth, "along came Lily. Then Rose." She looked at her daughters, her beautiful daughters, her eyes brimming with a mother's pride and adoration. "We became so wrapped up in our growing family, our beautiful, perfect family," she said, her voice a dreamy sigh, "that we... we momentarily forgot about our enemies. We let down our guard, basking in the pure, unadulterated bliss of the life we had created."

Her expression darkened then, the wistfulness giving way to a raw, burning anger that seemed to ignite the air around them. "It was then," she hissed, her voice trembling with suppressed fury, "that they fell upon us. They ambushed us, stealing our joy, ripping our family apart." Her eyes, once soft, now blazed with the memory of that horrible violation. "They sent Morpheus away, to some desolate, unreachable place," she cried, tears, real tears, finally spilling from her eyes, tracing paths down her serene face. "Somewhere I could not reach him, no matter how hard I tried, no matter how much I searched." Her voice cracked, utterly broken by the weight of centuries of separation as her gaze, wet with sorrow, found Morpheus's eyes, mourning their lost time, a silent lament for an eternity stolen.

"We are together now, my love. And I promise, nothing will ever separate us again," Morpheus declared, his voice a deep, resonant rumble that seemed to fill the basement. Lily and Rose still clung to his sides, their small forms dwarfed by his imposing presence, seemingly content in his chilling embrace.

Sarah wiped the last tears from her face, her features settling back into that unnerving calm, a radiant smile gracing her lips as she gazed at her reunited family. Then, with a slow, deliberate turn, she faced Daniel once more, resuming her fantastical narrative.

"Thankfully, they did not take my children from me," she continued, her voice gaining a newfound strength, tinged with a quiet triumph. "But those who had followed our reign, our loyal subjects in the Dream World... some ran out of cowardice, fearful of meeting the same fate as their King. But there were a few, Daniel. A precious handful of dedicated soldiers, unwavering in their loyalty to me, their Queen. They remained by my side through the long, desolate centuries."

Her eyes, now distant, seemed to see beyond the confines of the basement, recalling the arduous passage of time. "It took so many years," she murmured, a profound weariness briefly shadowing her features, "so many countless cycles of time, to find out how to break the curse that bound Morpheus, how to unravel the threads of his banishment and be reunited again as a family. And that,

Daniel," she said, her gaze fixing on him with an intense, unsettling clarity, "that is where you came in."

Daniel sat there, rooted to the cold tiled floor, his head spinning as if caught in a violent whirlpool. Every word Sarah uttered spun a web of impossible fiction, a tale so utterly removed from their shared reality that it could only be one thing: an elaborate, cruel nightmare Morpheus was playing on him. And Sarah… his beloved wife… she had to be caught in some cursed dream, a powerful illusion where she honestly, completely believed every insane word she was uttering. There was no other explanation, no other way to comprehend the chasm that had opened between them. His mind swirled, a frantic storm of thoughts, desperately trying to conjure an idea, anything, any way to shatter this dark illusion and get them all—his real wife, his real daughters, and himself—out of this waking nightmare. "What do you mean?" he managed, his voice thin, laced with a heavy dose of skepticism he hoped would betray none of the sheer terror bubbling beneath the surface.

Sarah's lips curved into a soft, familiar smile, the one Daniel had fallen in love with, the one that used to melt his anxieties away. Now, it only sent a shiver of dread down his spine. "It took a lot of research, Daniel," she began, her voice light, almost playful, as if discussing some trivial pursuit. "Your family wasn't exactly easy to find, you know." A soft, airy laugh escaped her, a sound that in any other context would have been charming, but here, it was chillingly out of place.

"But we finally tracked down your lineage, deep into your ancestral lines," she continued, her gaze momentarily distant, as if sifting through centuries of forgotten history. "Of course, we had already uncovered the prophecy. The one that spoke of a chosen protector who would come together with the two sisters. The one who held the key to

Morpheus's return." Her eyes brightened, a proud glint in their depths as she turned to Lily. "Thanks to Lily, my cunning daughter," she said, bestowing a warm, loving smile upon the spectral child. Lily, in turn, beamed back, a strange, ethereal light emanating from her as if truly basking in her mother's praise, visibly proud of having played such a crucial part in mending their fractured family.

"She is brilliant, isn't she?" Sarah asked, turning back to Daniel, her gaze expectant. "Why, you've seen it yourself, haven't you? Her ingenuity, her knack for puzzles, for finding what's hidden?" When he offered no response, his mind reeling too much to formulate a coherent thought, she simply continued, unfazed by his silence.

"It was then that we devised a plan. A rather intricate one, if I do say so myself." A faint, amused chuckle bubbled up from her throat. "It took a couple of attempts, of course. Mortals can be surprisingly resilient and, at times, infuriatingly unpredictable." Her smile thinned, replaced by a flicker of ancient annoyance. "We had almost succeeded once, you know, when your own great-grandfather, a stubborn old man, managed to close the portal on us. Not only that, but he then found a way to hide it away, to obscure its very existence from even our most powerful spies." A wave of fury once more surged into her voice, a chilling echo of the anger she'd displayed earlier, reminding Daniel that beneath the serene surface lay a formidable and vengeful power.

The flash of anger vanished as quickly as it had appeared, melting away into Sarah's unnerving calm. A soft, almost delighted laugh bubbled from her lips once more, a sound that grated against Daniel's frayed nerves. "Oh, but then, Daniel," she began, her eyes sparkling with amusement, as if sharing a delightful secret, "you'll never guess what happened next?"

Even Lily and Rose, still clinging to Morpheus's side, mirrored her amusement, soft giggles escaping them as they seemed to recall the very memory their mother was about to share, their ethereal forms shimmering with shared delight.

"I came up with the most brilliant plan," Sarah continued, her voice filled with self-admiration. "The only way to truly secure Morpheus's return, to break the final seal, was to infiltrate the humans. To become one of them." A faint wrinkle of distaste creased her brow. "Though they are truly wretched creatures, and these bodies," she paused, gesturing dismissively at her own form, "are so… breakable. So fragile and fleeting." She shuddered delicately. "But nevertheless, it was a means to an end, a necessary step."

Her eyes, wide and unnervingly bright, fixed on Daniel. "Oh, but here's the truly good part," she said, leaning forward slightly, as if sharing the climax of a thrilling tale. "I almost married your father! Can you believe it?" Her laughter returned, a light, tinkling sound that echoed eerily in the basement. "Of course, you never would have been born then, which would have been a shame, I suppose. A minor inconvenience in the grand scheme of things, but still." She waved a dismissive hand. "But don't look so sad, my dear. He would have adopted two beautiful girls, just as you had." Her gaze drifted to Lily and Rose, a possessive warmth in her eyes.

Daniel felt the nausea surge, a cold, bitter wave rolling in his gut. His mind, already reeling, suddenly latched onto a long-buried memory. His father, years ago, during an awkward, fumbling "sex talk," had spoken of a woman. A woman so incredibly beautiful, so captivating, that he had almost married her. But then, he'd said, along came Daniel's mother, and for some inexplicable reason, he just liked her more. The pieces, terrifying and grotesque, slammed together in Daniel's mind with a sickening click.

The basement air suddenly felt impossibly thick, suffocating him. The tiled floor tilted beneath him. His stomach gave one final, violent lurch, and he leaned over, emptying the contents of his stomach onto the cold, hard concrete. The acidic bile burned his throat, but the taste of it was nothing compared to the bitter horror that had just consumed his soul. The world swam, then spun violently, the last remnants of light dimming to nothing. A crushing blackness enveloped him, mercifully pulling him into unconsciousness.

Chapter 33:

A cool, damp cloth pressed against Daniel's forehead, jolting him back to a hazy awareness. The metallic tang of bile still lingered in his mouth, but the overwhelming nausea had subsided, replaced by a dull, persistent ache in his head. He blinked, despite the minimal amount of light in the basement , it was a cruel assault on his eyes. Sarah's face, now devoid of the chilling amusement, hovered above him, her expression a mask of gentle concern. A small, clear glass of water appeared in front of him. "Here," she murmured, her voice soft and gentle. "Drink this. Your body is probably dehydrated, not to mention you've been... agitated. It will help."

Despite the terror gripping his mind, and the lingering nausea, his body responded instinctively to the offer. His hand, trembling, reached for the cool glass. He brought it to his lips, intending a small sip, but the water was so incredibly refreshing, so desperately needed, that he found himself gulping it down, draining half the glass before he even consciously registered it. Only then did the realization hit him: he was parched, his throat scratchy and dry. When was the last time he had drank something? Or eaten, for that matter? His mind, a chaotic mess of fractured memories and terrifying revelations, struggled to grasp the answer. He couldn't remember. The past, once a solid foundation, had become a shifting, unreliable landscape.

He tried to speak, to form a question, a protest, anything to pierce the surreal calm that had settled over Sarah. A guttural sound escaped him, but before he could articulate a single word, her cool fingers pressed gently against his lips.

"Shhh, you need to rest," she murmured, her voice a soft, almost hypnotic lullaby. "Just finish your water, and listen. There's more to tell, and it's so important that you understand everything."

But the idea of understanding, of accepting this twisted reality, was utterly abhorrent. "No," Daniel rasped, pulling his head away from her touch. "No, I can't. I can't hear any more of this." The basement felt like a suffocating tomb, filled with echoes of a truth he couldn't bear.

His gaze tore away from Sarah, sweeping wildly around the room, up towards the low ceiling, as if seeking an invisible presence. His voice rose, raw and strained, escalating into a desperate scream that seemed to bounce off the concrete walls. "Where are you?" he bellowed, his plea directed at the unseen, the heavenly. "Where is the voice that helped us before? The one that guided us, that told us we were the protectors? The one that showed Silas how to close the nexus, how to end all of this?" His voice cracked, laced with betrayal and agonizing confusion. "How could you abandon us now? How could you leave us to…to this?" His words hung in the air, a desperate, unanswered cry into the silent, indifferent world beyond.

"Daniel," Sarah said gently, her voice cutting through his desperate cries like a soft, sharp blade. "I'm sorry, but whoever you're speaking to, they aren't there. They were never there."

She allowed a moment of silence to hang in the air, giving him space for her words to sink in. But when she saw the desperate hope still flickering in his eyes, the frantic search for a hidden presence, she continued, her voice devoid of regret. "The voice was never real, Daniel. The vast ethereal place in the sky, it was all an illusion."

"No," Daniel gasped, shaking his head vehemently. "No, you saw it too! We all did. Silas, me, you… how can it be an illusion if we all…?" The words trailed off as a horrifying realization dawned on him. His face, contorted with confusion a moment before, twisted into a sickening mixture of disgust and anger. His gaze snapped to Morpheus, his finger jabbing accusingly towards the shadowy figure. "It was him, wasn't it?!" he spat, the accusation dripping with venom. "You did this! You played us!"

Morpheus let out a low, guttural growl, a sound of growing impatience, but Sarah interceded before he could speak. "No, Daniel." Her voice was firm, unwavering, laced with a chilling pride. "It was not Morpheus. It was me. I did it. All of it. It's always been me and the girls. All the illusions, the guidance, the… orchestration of events." Her eyes met his, unblinking, utterly devoid of remorse. "Even when you thought our lives were in danger, Daniel, when you fought so bravely to protect us… we were… we were acting. Playing a part." A faint, almost imperceptible sigh escaped her lips. "Please understand. It was the only way. The only path I had in order to put my family back together."

"Are you crazy?!" Daniel roared, his rage boiling over, snatching away the last remnants of his composure. He lurched forward, straining against the invisible bonds of his exhaustion. "All this time, you played me?! Our life, our love, our memories… Was *any* of it real? Was *any* of it true?!"

Sarah looked down, her gaze fixed on the cold tiles beneath her feet, seemingly composing herself, or perhaps simply savoring the moment. When she finally looked back into his eyes, her expression was serene, almost compassionate. "The voice, yes, that was an illusion. The angel we saw earlier, the one you believed was Morpheus in some altered form… that was me, my own power manifesting. But the shadow creatures you fought, the ones that guarded the portal, those were real. Though the fights I guess you could say, for the most part anyway, were orchestrated by us. But everything that has happened around you, around the world, the red sky, the collapsing reality… all of that, Daniel, that was real. Can't you see?" she pleaded, a desperate, almost childlike sincerity in her voice. "I had to get my family back. I had to."

"And what about me?" Daniel's voice was barely a whisper, the last fragile tendril of hope clinging to a desperate question. "Did you ever… did you ever love me?"

Sarah looked down again, her gaze dropping to the tiled floor, utterly unable to meet his shattered eyes. The serene mask she wore cracked just enough to reveal a fleeting, almost imperceptible struggle within her. But then, it hardened, settling back into that chilling composure. "No," she stated, the word delivered without malice, yet with a devastating finality that struck him harder than any blow. "I could never betray my one true love." She turned to Morpheus, her gaze lingering before she looked back at Daniel. "You were always a means to an end, just like poor, pitiful Silas. I needed someone with his knowledge to find the prophecy and then unwittingly help me bring it to pass. You were both nothing more than tools in a very long, very complicated plan."

A scream tore from his throat, a gut-wrenching cry that ripped through the stale air of the basement and echoed off the concrete walls, a testament to a soul which had just been utterly annihilated. The sound was not just pain, but the sound of every shared laugh, every quiet moment, every whispered promise being incinerated in an instant. His legs gave out beneath him, and he crumpled to the cold floor, landing with a jarring thud, truly broken.

His body shook with silent sobs, his face buried in his hands, the bitter taste of betrayal overwhelming every other sensation. After a long, agonizing moment, his voice emerged, muffled and defeated, barely a whisper against the cold tile. "Just get it over with then," he mumbled, his body limp with despair. "Kill me." The words were an invitation to oblivion, a plea for an end to the unbearable torment of a life revealed as an elaborate, cruel deception.

"No, Daniel." Sarah's voice, though still gentle, held an undercurrent of steel. "I won't kill you. That would be... inefficient. And frankly, a waste." She knelt, moving with an unsettling grace, bringing herself closer to his broken form. "But I can make the pain go away. All of it. The confusion, the heartache, the betrayal you feel right now. I can erase it, replace it with something beautiful." Her hand reached out, hovering inches from his face, her touch radiating a warmth. "I can give you everything you ever wanted, Daniel. A life of perfect bliss, where every dream is realized, every desire fulfilled. Just say yes."

"No," Daniel rasped, trying to push himself away, to inject conviction into his voice, but his ravaged spirit and physically weakened state betrayed him. The word emerged as a barely audible whisper, a fragile thread of defiance against the overwhelming despair. "Kill me. I don't want anything from you. Nothing."

Just then, two small, ethereal figures detached themselves from Morpheus's side. Rose and Lily, his daughters, his *real* daughters, if only in memory, glided over and knelt beside their mother. Their faces, so innocent, so beautiful, were etched with a strange, compelling earnestness.

"Just say yes, Daddy," Rose whispered, her small, cool hand gently caressing his cheek. Her touch, usually a source of comfort, now felt chillingly alien.

"Then we can all be together," Lily added, her voice a soft, alluring echo, her eyes wide and pleading. "As a family, forever."

Daniel's head snapped up, the throbbing pain in his skull momentarily forgotten in a surge of pure, bewildering confusion. His gaze darted from Rose to Lily, then to Sarah, and finally back to the two little girls who called him daddy. What was happening? He knew, with an instinct that screamed in his soul, he should scream *no*. He knew, with a certainty that clawed at his gut, that whatever *yes* entailed, it could be nothing good, nothing pure. But the insidious allure of their words, the impossible sweetness of *together* and *family*, warred with the stark, brutal reality Sarah had just laid bare. His mind, still reeling from the dizzying torrent of revelations, latched onto the only question he could form. "What?" he managed, his voice hoarse, a look of total and utter confusion etched onto his face. "Say yes to what?"

"To being with us," Sarah replied, her smile radiant, so beautiful, as she gazed down at him. It was the expression of a woman offering the world, offering salvation, rather than eternal damnation.

Daniel looked again into Sarah's face. She was so incredibly beautiful, even now, even after everything. He could almost glimpse the woman he had fallen in love with there, just behind her eyes, a shadow of the wife he thought he knew. And then he turned to Rose and Lily, both of them still smiling at him, their faces innocent, their eyes bright with an unnatural, yet captivating, light. They were his girls, even if the truth of their history was a monstrous lie. The yearning to protect them, to keep them safe, was a reflex deeply ingrained in his very being.

A bone-deep weariness settled over him. The fight had left him feeling drained, the revelations had broken him, and the promise of an end to the pain, a return to *family*, however twisted, was a siren song he found himself tragically weak to resist. Looking back at Sarah, a defeated sigh escaped him. "I could never say no to you," he whispered, the words heavy with resignation, a final surrender to a love that had become his undoing.

"Then say yes," Sarah urged, her voice a soft, seductive caress, the final push over the cliff's edge. Her smile widened, a triumphant gleam entering her eyes, as if she knew, with absolute certainty, that he was going to do as asked.

"Yes," Daniel breathed, the word a mere whisper, a final surrender exhaled into the stale basement air.

In that very instant, an impossible sensation washed over him. His very essence, his consciousness, his soul, seemed to detach from his physical form. He was hovering, a luminous, ethereal specter, gazing down at his own body slumped on the cold tiled floor. He watched, with a horrifying detachment, as Morpheus, King of Nightmares, a being of shadow and ancient power, began to coalesce, to solidify, to enter into its new vessel. His own vessel. The sight should have driven him to madness, should have compelled another guttural scream, but an overwhelming, unearthly peace settled over him instead, muffling the terror, and silencing the rage.

A bright, glowing light bloomed in the periphery of his vision, soft and inviting, pulsating with a warmth that promised release. Without conscious thought, drawn by an irresistible pull, he turned and drifted towards it. He passed through the shimmering veil of light, and in the next moment, he stood before his farmhouse.

Not the dilapidated, haunted structure he had just been inside of, but the one from his happiest memories. It stood bathed in the golden light of a perfect afternoon, familiar and comforting. And he knew, with an absolute certainty that resonated deep within his newly untethered soul, that inside, beyond that welcoming door, he would find Sarah and their two beautiful daughters, Lily and Rose. His true Sarah. His true daughters. He didn't know what would happen on Earth, whether reality would unravel, or if this tranquil scene was simply another layer of illusion, or even if he still existed in any tangible sense. But he didn't care. The bitter ache of betrayal, the crushing weight of deceit, all of it had vanished, replaced by an overwhelming, serene happiness.

He stood there for a moment, basking in the warmth of the perfect day, watching as the farmhouse door swung open with a soft creak. And then, running toward him, a cascade of joyous giggles, came little Rose, her arms outstretched, her face alight with unadulterated joy. Beside her bounded a happy, barking labrador, its tail wagging furiously, a blur of golden fur. In the doorway, framed by the warm light of the home, stood Sarah and Lily, both laughing, their faces beaming with genuine happiness, welcoming him.

He was home.

Epilogue:

It's been six months since the day I got my true love back. Six months since that final, exquisite moment of Daniel's foolish, human sacrifice, a willing offering so that Morpheus, my magnificent King, could walk among this realm, free and unbound. I knew that Daniel would do anything for love. For the illusion of family that we dangled before him, for the pleading faces of his daughters. And I was right. Humans are so deliciously, tragically gullible. Their hearts, so easily swayed by sentiment, are their ultimate weakness. A weakness we exploited with chilling precision.

The sky, once a tiresome canvas of insipid blue, is now a lovely, perpetual black, streaked with the hues of deep purple and blood-red. It's a masterpiece of our making, a constant reminder of our dominion. The air is an icy caress for the dwindling humans who remain, those stubborn, desperate pockets who have, so far, evaded our grasp. Their breath mists in the frigid air, a fleeting testament to lives that will soon be extinguished. Within our first week of true freedom, of Morpheus fully manifesting, roughly fifty percent of the global population was simply… erased. Dissolved into the ether, swallowed by the nightmares we unleashed, or simply ceased to exist as their fragile minds buckled under the weight of waking terror. By six weeks, we had eliminated another ten percent, creating a symphony of despair across every continent. The groups that remain are slowly, agonizingly, being hunted down. But that's quite alright. Because unlike them, unlike these fleeting, mortal playthings, we have all the time in the world. Eternity stretches before us, and the earth is a playground for our desires.

We have taken our rightful place, not merely as rulers of the Dream World, but as the unchallenged sovereigns of this material realm. The King and Queen of Dreams…and of Nightmares. To the humans, perhaps, it is torment. To us, it is merely the natural order restored. Lily and Rose, our beautiful, cunning daughters, have never been happier. Their eyes, once veiled by mundane existence, now gleam with ancient power, reflecting the twilight of this dying world. They bask in the presence of their reunited family, their true family, thriving on the currents of fear and despair we have woven into the fabric of reality. With the assistance of Elias, our most loyal soldier and second in command, they are advancing rapidly. Not only in their knowledge, but also in their still growing powers. Perhaps they are even destined to surpass Morpheus's own terrible greatness one day. But the best thing is their laughter. No longer constrained by the quaint comforts of a human home, it rings with the joyous, unfettered freedom of true nightmare beings.

The cities, once monuments to human arrogance, are now silent mausoleums of glass and steel, occasionally punctuated by the screams of the unwary. The few remaining humans huddle in their pathetic enclaves, clinging to remnants of a hope we delight in crushing. We allow them just enough leash to feel a flicker of defiance, only to snatch it away when their optimism becomes too bold. It is a slow, methodical process, the extinguishing of a species. Some perish from the relentless cold, others from starvation as their fragile systems collapse. Many more simply succumb to the terrors we weave directly into their minds, their waking hours becoming indistinguishable from the most hideous dreams. We twist their perceptions, turn their loved ones into monsters, infest their thoughts with inescapable dread until they simply give up, their spirits shattering like glass.

The Earth itself is transforming, reflecting our will. Lush forests wither and die, replaced by skeletal, twisted groves that whisper secrets of fear in the perpetual dark. Rivers run black with despair, and the mountains, once grand and stoic, now loom like jagged teeth against the bruised sky, casting long, menacing shadows. We have claimed the very essence of this world, reshaping it in our image. The air, once filled with the cacophony of human industry, now carries only the low hum of our power, the faint, distant whimpers of the last mortals, and the delighted whispers of our growing legions.

Daniel's sacrifice was the key, the final piece in a puzzle centuries in the making. His desperate, loving "yes" unlocked the deepest prison, and shattered the most ancient wards. He truly believed he was saving his family, ushering them into a new era of happiness. And in a way, he did. Just not in the way he had envisioned. His consciousness, what remains of it, drifts now within Morpheus's expanded being, a faint, familiar echo that sometimes surfaces, a whisper of human weakness that only serves to amuse us. He chose love, and his perceived family, over the world. A perfectly human choice of course, perfectly exploitable.

This is not the end of times for us. It is merely the beginning. The glorious dawn of our true reign. The realms are opening, slowly, subtly, as our power expands, intertwining this physical world with the limitless expanse of the Dream World. Soon, there will be no distinction. Only our will. And our family, whole and unbroken, will preside over an eternity of beautifully orchestrated nightmares. The old gods, the ancient protectors, whatever feeble forces once held us back, they are silent now. This is our realm. This is our victory. And it is more beautiful, more absolute, than any dream.

This is our playground now.